WHISPERING
DEATH

WHISPERING

DEATH

Garry Disher

Published by
Soho Press, Inc.
853 Broadway
New York, NY 10003

Library of Congress Cataloging-in-Publication Data

Disher, Garry.
Whispering death / Garry Disher.
p. cm.
ISBN 978-1-61695-174-0
eISBN 978-1-61695-175-7
1. Challis, Hal (Fictitious character)—Fiction. 2. Destry, Ellen
(Fictitious character)—Fiction. 3. Police—Victoria—Melbourne—
Fiction. I. Title.
PR9619.3.D56W48 2012
823'.914—dc23
2012023876

Interior design by Janine Agro, Soho Press, Inc.

Printed in the United States of America

10 9 8 7 6 5 4 3 2 1

For Jo Tapper

WHISPERING
DEATH

Chapter 1

Grace was as good a name as any, and this morning Grace was in Hobart, strolling through a well-heeled corner of Sandy Bay, casing the secluded houses. A Friday morning in spring, a sea fret receding to Storm Bay and the Tasman Sea, it was good to be alive, and she attracted no attention in her tennis whites worn over tracksuit pants, sunglasses, Nike trainers, and perky billed cap. A racquet handle poked out of her gym bag, telling you she was an idle young wife, maybe a young professional on her day off, even—if you were the suspicious type—an adulterer wearing a cover story.

But no warning bells. No cause for a stop-and-search. She belonged there.

In fact, it was hide in plain sight, Grace hiding behind the cap and shades, hiding the fact that the tennis skirt was Velcroed to the bodice and the gym bag held burglary tools, gloves, and heavy-duty vinyl sacks. One shouted accusation, one query, and she'd be gone. Rip away the skirt, ditch it together with the cap, bag and shades, and she'd be transformed into a jogger, and who looks twice at a jogger?

'Always expect the worst,' Galt had drummed into her, 'and you'll never be caught off guard.'

Another thing Galt told her was to avoid apartment buildings. Well, there were none here. There's always someone at home in an apartment block, Galt said, always a sad soul sitting at a window all day long, hoping for a diversion to brighten the unvarying hours.

Next, Grace checked for children: toys, bikes, skateboards, even a little pink gumboot, discarded in a front yard. Yes, kids go to school, Galt would say, but not if they're a toddler or they've got the chickenpox, not if it's a curriculum day for their teachers. And a kid at home means an adult at home.

Vehicles were on Galt's checklist, too. Grace knew she was in a land of two-car households, two adults working 9 to 5 in highly paid jobs. No shift workers here. Play it safe, Galt always said. If there's a vehicle in the driveway, the carport, move on. Or a closed garage door. Doesn't mean the garage is empty.

Finally, choose your targets to minimise the nosy-neighbour problem. The people worth stealing from paid top dollar to block an outsider's line of sight, Galt said. She should look for high hedges, sloping land, tree density, and curved streets.

The rest Galt hadn't taught her. 'I can show you how to stay under the radar,' he'd said. 'I can keep my people off your back, but you were the break-in queen long before I found you.'

Grace made a rapid pass through the little neighbourhood. Trees and bushes crowded most of the houses. No one about, only a workman bolting a gate to a picket fence, another rolling a lawnmower off a ute. The houses ranged from weatherboard bungalows to sharply modern glass and concrete structures, with Tudor houses, Tuscan villas, and small, tiled, steeply-gabled 1930s mansions in between. She mentally selected four targets and went to work.

The first was a nightmarish arrangement of interconnected concrete cubes, set well back from the street behind a high fieldstone wall. She entered the grounds briskly, as she always did, as if her best friend lived there and they'd arranged to play tennis. When she was halfway to the front door she blew a high-frequency whistle, the kind audible only to dogs. She was answered at once by frenzied barking, one deep-chested, the other a high yap.

She retreated.

In the next street was a low 1970s ranch house set among gumtrees. No dogs. She made a quick circuit of the building, testing knobs and handles and peering through windows. Occasionally she found unlocked doors and windows, fake alarm boxes or no security at all, but often those places had nothing worth stealing. Grace went around the house again, this time running a small camping compass around the door and window frames. The compass needle dipped to indicate a live current at all but the front door. People had a misplaced faith in the security of their front doors, perhaps because most front doors face the street. Grace tested it again. A slight deflection of the needle near the latch.

It was a glass door, comprising a single pane secured around the edges by narrow wooden beadings. Grace fished a metal bar from the gym bag and prised away the beadings, stacking the strips neatly beside her, until the whole pane was revealed. Then she removed it using a pair of glazier's suction caps and propped it against the wall beside the entryway.

She slipped into the house, and into the smell of money. The building itself was ugly, a throwback, but the interior was starkly modern, with polished floorboards, minimalist glass and leather, a pair of Brett Whiteley bird drawings on one wall. The Whiteleys might bring a few grand, but their size ruled them out. She photographed them in case she wanted to come back for them, in a year or so, when the owners had recovered from their shock and dismay. Meanwhile she'd show the images to Finch, see if he knew a potential buyer. She also snapped a pair of Fuzan Satsuma vases. Turn of the past century, she thought. Worth about $5,000. A few hundred bucks from Finch, but they were too big to go in the gym bag without risk of damage.

After a quick assessment of the house, Grace settled on the main bedroom and the study. The starkness was modified here by everyday clutter: in the bedroom a cracked-spine paperback, a foil strip of painkillers, an errant sock; in the study a couple of chewed ballpoint pens, an in-tray stacked with invoices and letters, a set of golf clubs, and a water pistol. It all said something about home life, family life, neither of which interested Grace. She began to tug open the drawers.

She was out of the house within five minutes. In the bag were a pair of emerald earrings, a Bulova watch, an iPod Classic, a Toshiba laptop, and some unused AutoCAD software, still in the box. The software alone was $6,000 new, the computer $3,000.

In the next street was a plain weatherboard cottage with a modern extension at the rear, vast and airy. No dogs, another easy front door, but at the last moment she saw a cornice-mounted red light blinking through a gap in the sitting-room curtain. She checked another room: another red light. She had no intention of going in against motion detectors. She moved on to the fourth and last target on her list, a pretty loft house with a steeply pitched roof and cathedral ceilings. Again, dog-free. No motion detectors that she could see, and a front door that was alarmed only at the latch. Every part of the door was wooden: an outer frame, a cross member, and plywood panel inserts secured by thin beadings. She decided to remove the bottom panel and crawl through.

But first, a diversion. She took a pair of shoes, size eleven, from her bag, slipped them over her runners and went over to crouch in the loamy soil against the side wall. Something to occupy the detectives who would be called to investigate.

Then she went to work. Prise away the beadings, fasten two

eyehooks to the panel, wiped clean and sprayed with bleach to screw with her DNA. When the fumes cleared she jerked the panel out of its seating and put it aside.

She crawled in. Her hip caught in the narrow opening, snagging a tiny white thread. She always incinerated her outfits after a job—clothing, gloves, footwear—but she paused to remove it anyway. Why give the cops a chance to add 'possibly wears tennis whites' to her profile?

This house was fussy and careworn. The carpeting was expensive but the pattern varied from room to room and never quite matched the walls or curtains. There were too many knickknacks: porcelain shepherd girls, nests of wooden bowls, glass paperweights threaded with colour, family photographs in heavy silver frames (plate, she noticed), and someone liked elephants. Herds of them—wood, glass, papier-mâché—trampled and trumpeted along window ledges and corner tables.

But there was a little Sydney Long aquatint on one wall, possibly a family heirloom. Grace removed it from its ugly frame, rolled it into a narrow tube and slid it into a hollowed-out racquet handle.

She checked all of the rooms and settled on some easy-to-move electronics—a portable hard drive, a video camera, and the prize, a top-flight Canon digital SLR worth over ten grand.

Grace strolled back to the pub on the corner and then down the hill to her rental car, parked outside a gym beside the water. No one stopped her, and if they looked, it was at the arrogant way she loped along. All the young women loped here. They felt entitled. Grace liked messing with that.

Chapter 2

Grace used a restroom at Hobart airport to reinvent herself as an executive in a hurry: pantyhose, heels, black jacket, narrow skirt, and briefcase. If you were an airport official, you wouldn't tangle with her.

By late morning she was on the mainland, changing clothes again, dressing down this time: loose jeans, grubby trainers, stretched cotton hoodie. Then she collected her Golf from the long-term car park and headed along the Tullamarine Freeway toward the centre of Melbourne, knowing it would be hours yet before her break-ins were noticed.

The Golf hummed. She'd thought long and hard about her choice of car. All of her rules were simple. 'Don't get caught,' obviously, 'know when to walk away from a job,' and 'have a fallback position.' But a central one was 'never work close to home.' She always operated outside of the state. Perth, Brisbane, Adelaide, the Gold Coast, Noosa, Launceston, Hobart . . . wherever the money was. Never in New South Wales. The wrong people knew her there. Galt people. Interstate then, and sometimes she drove to and from a job. Long distances, so comfort was important. If she ever had to run, she wanted plenty of torque and power. Plenty of safety features, in case she rolled or pranged. Good handling on hairy corners and switchback roads.

Hence the Golf. A Porsche, Audi, BMW, or Alfa would have been nice, but noticeable. No one would look twice at a Falcon, Holden, or Camry, but they were salesmen's cars, they handled like boats, and Grace needed a convincing cover story ready to explain what she was doing on a major interstate in the middle of the night. And so she drove a two-litre diesel Golf, a young woman's car, perfect for a cute young contracts lawyer with a fear of flying. No self-respecting drug courier or jewel thief would drive one; no highway cop would get an itch to chase one.

Of course, it made sense to fly sometimes. Imagine being subjected to a spot search on a car ferry with a boot-load of gear. . . .

Today she had a clear run on the toll road between Melbourne airport and the city, and again when she headed south over the West Gate Bridge, high winds buffeting the little car, and down into Williamstown, where the mean grind of old Melbourne coexisted with bright young mortgages. Factories and workshops sat next to pastel little townhouses with cute, candy-coloured cars in the driveways. Grace wound down her window. The air, dense and still, was faintly salted from the Bay. The trees, branches barely moving, seemed dazed from the years-long drought.

She parked in a cramped yard behind a corner pub. She'd dressed down at the airport, and now her demeanour was down, too, a little defeated-looking as she trudged with a plastic shopping bag down the block to Steve Finch's second-hand shop. Leaning on his display window as if to remove a stone from her shoe, she scanned the area for stakeout vans, cameras behind curtains, or cops inside the shop. Nothing. She went in. If the cops came now, she was just a punter with a few bits of rubbish to pawn.

Nothing ever changed in Finch's shop. Open seven days a week, dusty TV sets and VCRs in the window, boxy computer monitors on card tables, cartons of vinyl records, cassette tapes and paperback books. Islands of unloved and unlovely furniture to negotiate before she found Steve at an ink-stained counter, working the keyboard of a sleek new Mac. He reeked of after-shave. It fought the mustiness and won.

'Be with you in a minute.'

He hadn't looked up, wouldn't have heard her above the radio, set to a thrash station and marked down to $15. But he would have seen her on the security monitors. Cameras covered all the corners and overlooked the street, side paths, and back yard. In fact, Grace had advised him what to install where.

Hadn't looked up, and hadn't used body language to warn her either, meaning there were no cops behind a wardrobe or lurking in his office.

She studied him. Finch's face was crammed with large features slapped onto a narrow skull, nose and chin hooking forward, ears like sails. He wore his hair long as if to bulk up the narrow-ness. He was about forty, tall, well-dressed in a cotton shirt and trousers. His fingers were grimy, probably from tinkering inside the guts of the turntable lying in pieces beside the computer.

'Needs a new motor and rollers,' he said, reading her mind. Still not looking at her.

He tapped a few more keys and peered at the screen. 'Place in California can ship them to me.'

'Worth it?'

Now he looked at her. 'Is it worth it? Collector's item, Suze.'

Susan was as good a name as Grace, or any of the others she used. She also had passports, credit cards, and driver's licences in names she hadn't used yet, names of babies that had died around the time she was born. And there was an old name, Nina, lurking in her dreams that seemed real where the others didn't. But just now, with Steve Finch, she was Suze, short for Susan.

He grinned at her as a thought entered his head and raised one finger. 'Something to show you.'

A photograph of his baby son, the child clutching a chair and looking outraged. 'Took his first steps about ten seconds later,' Finch said.

'How gorgeous,' Grace said.

The new young wife, the pregnancy, the maternity ward, and now the first footsteps, recorded in photographs that Steve insisted on showing her whenever she came to do business.

'How's your little one?' he said now. 'Any new photos?'

'Steven Finch, dealer in stolen property and sentimental family man,' said Grace, opening her wallet to a series of small photographs in clear plastic sleeves, the first a toothy, blonde three-year-old.

Finch grabbed the wallet and peered. 'Cute,' he said, then flipping through. 'Awww, look at her in her tutu.' He peered again, read aloud—'Hurstbridge Community Childcare Centre'—and glanced worriedly at Grace. 'Your sister's out there, right?'

Grace let pain show fleetingly, evidence of an old heartache, a heroin habit to feed, trying to get back on track, but you know how it is. She swallowed, coughed, and managed to say, 'I see her whenever I can.'

Steve nodded, still doubtful. 'Who's this? Your parents?'

Grace leaned over the counter, cocked her head at the opened wallet. 'Yes.'

'Autumn Years . . . where's that?'

'Out in Lakes Entrance.'

He frowned. 'Not exactly close to your sister.'

'Can we get on with it?'

Finch was still looking at the image of Grace and an elderly couple posed before a home unit in a series of home units. 'You look too young to have parents in a retirement village.'

Grace shrugged.

'Sorry, none of my business,' said Finch, who liked to make her well-being his business. 'What have you got for me?'

She described the morning's takings.

'Let's have a look-see.'

She left the shop first and drove the Golf to a car park behind an abandoned factory. When Finch arrived in his van, she opened the boot. His face emotionless, he drew on cotton gloves and sifted through the items. 'No coins, stamps? Those I can always handle.'

'Not this time.'

He ran an ultraviolet light over laptop, iPod, and cameras. When a name and a phone number showed on the Canon, he thrust it away as if scorched. 'Get rid of this.'

She would. Several grands' worth, into the sea.

He was frowning at the ground, working out costs and disbursements. 'I can go two grand,' he said.

His tone was always apologetic, but, in Grace's mind, $2,000 was pretty good for an hour's work, and sometimes he paid a lot more, depending on what she had. The apology also said that he knew how soon she'd run through the money, feeding her habit, but what could he do? He had a business to run.

She showed him her photographs of the vases and the Whiteleys. 'I might go back for them one day.'

Finch gave her a half nod as if to say, yeah maybe, if she lasted that long, then counted out her cut in crisp $100 notes. 'Stay in touch, okay?'

'Sure.'

Grace had a landline, an iPhone, and several cheap pre-paid mobiles, but no one ever called her. She called them. If someone wanted her, they used the Hotmail account.

Then Finch glanced around at the cracked concrete wastes and said, 'Can't stay, can you?'

She never had stayed. She didn't want to have sex with him or listen to his crap. Clean yourself up, spend time with your daughter, family's important. . . .

'What's the time?' she asked, as if she wasn't rejecting him out of hand.

'Noon.'

'I'd better go,' she said. 'I'm having a new fridge delivered.'

'Fair enough.'

She pointed the Golf at the city, up and over the West Gate Bridge, but wasn't going home. Home was in another direction, and she didn't need a new fridge. She was on her way to the Peninsula town of Waterloo. Out of habit and instinct, she would avoid the toll-roads and drive sedately for the speed and intersection cameras.

Chapter 3

The best place for lunch in Waterloo was Café Laconic. Detective Constable Pam Murphy fronted up to the counter and ordered her usual, focaccia and take-away green tea. Grab a napkin, she told herself, you're wearing a white T-shirt.

She was walking back to the car when her mobile phone rang. 'Murphy.'

It was the duty sergeant, something about a naked woman seen in bushland along a back road north east of Waterloo. 'Sorry to do this to you Murph, but I don't have any uniforms available.'

'All right, I'll deal with it.'

Her Subaru was parked outside the camping shop. She got behind the wheel, demolished her lunch with some nifty finger-and-napkin work, then crawled up High Street, mindful of the new speed bumps and the 50 km/h signs, mentally plotting her route to the back road where someone had seen a naked woman. It wasn't her job, first response. In a perfect world, the duty sergeant would have sent a patrol car to investigate. Then, if they'd found a crime, a victim, the machine would kick into gear: crime scene examiners, more CIU detectives, a police surgeon, a pathologist, an ambulance. . .

But this was life in the age of budget cuts. She was often

obliged to use her own car on police business. Coming to the roundabout at the top end of High Street, she turned right and found herself stuck behind a muddy Land Rover, which was stuck behind the Frankston bus. The little cavalcade lumbered north past tyre outlets, paint shops, furniture barns, and car dealers, the small-town commerce soon giving way to modest factories, storage depots, and rural suppliers.

At the outer edge of the town, the Land Rover pulled into a timber yard, and now she was directly behind the bus, which was behind a shire mower, the blade-head at the end of its yellow articulating arm buried in the high grass and bracken that lined the road. Sparks flew; pebbles, shredded plastic, glass, and aluminium were kicked up. Pam flinched, thinking of the hassle if she had to claim for a new windscreen. She still owed her parents $5,000 on the Subaru. She was due to visit for Sunday lunch soon, and her father would grill her about the car, and was she taking good care of it. . . ?

She planted her foot and swung out. The road ahead was clear as she overtook bus and mower, and at the next roundabout, she took a side road into an unlovely region north-east of Waterloo. The municipal tip was out here, among the unexplained shed complexes and failed yacht builders, their blighted yards crammed with rusted hulls. Dead gumtrees stood in untended paddocks on both sides of the road, etching the sky like pencil strokes. Weeds choked the wire fences; flags of smoke flew from the distant smokestacks on Western Port Bay. It was a corner of the world that always seemed damp to Pam: mould crept, trees dripped, and small animals died in ceiling cavities. It was a dumping ground, a good place to die.

She came to a small brick house in a weedy stretch of farmland. Crouching close to the road, it was crowded with rose bushes and lavender, a couple of gumtrees overhanging the roof tiles. Otherwise there was nothing, only untended paddocks and a ragged stand of pittosporum, wattles, bracken, blackberry thickets, and mostly dead gumtrees a hundred metres behind the house.

She got out, watched by two women. The one standing in the driveway next to a grimy Daihatsu van was middle-aged, wearing a monocular on a strap around her neck, faded brown overalls, a woollen cap, and work boots. The other, much older, watched from the veranda, her legs frail in baggy stockings, her lips working, her hands trembling on a walking frame.

Pam smiled, raised her hand hello, locked her car, and entered the driveway. 'Police,' she announced, giving her name, observing the scratches on the overalled woman's arms and across one cheek, the licheny bark and twigs snagged in her cap. 'You reported a—'

'Body. Over in the reserve.'

The woman turned to point, and Pam saw that something odd was attached to the crown of her cap: a pair of cloth eyes, staring heavenward, large white ovoids with creepy black pupils.

She dragged her attention away. 'A body?'

'Didn't they tell you?'

As Pam glanced around uneasily, she saw the van was stencilled with the words ANIMAL RESCUE, meaning the woman spent time outdoors. At this time of year, the magpies were nesting and would swoop if you got too close. Pam had been pecked as a child. A swooping magpie would still freak her out. Did a pair of cloth eyes on your head really repel magpie attacks?

'Someone reported seeing a naked woman, not a body. Perhaps you could give me your name?'

'Jan Overton.' The woman shook hands briskly.

'So, you found a body?'

'Young woman, naked, very dead,' Overton said. 'Come on, I'll take you.'

Even standing she was restless, an outdoors woman who hated stasis, and now she strode with pumping arms to the side gate.

Pam called out to stop her. 'Perhaps you could give me the details first.'

'As you wish.' Overton swung back to rejoin Murphy, the mon-ocular bouncing on her chest. She halted, plucking a twig from her hair, the action oddly domestic and intimate, as though she'd found a split end. 'So here's the story. Mrs. McIntosh—that's her on the veranda—called me about a sick koala.' She paused with a hint of challenge. 'That's what I do, rescue and nurse sick and injured wildlife.'

Pam nodded.

'She'd had a young koala in her garden for a few days,' Over-ton said. 'This morning she noticed it had mange. That's a sure sign of low immunity, maybe chlamydia. The poor things are starving half the time, what with the drought. Not to mention their habitat being bulldozed for all the ugly great McMansions going up everywhere.'

Overton was younger than Pam had first thought, about thirty-five, but baked by the sun, and she carried an air of griev-ance. Maybe she thought no one appreciated her years of toil on behalf of the animal kingdom.

'The koala had gone by the time I got here,' Overton went on, 'but it was no mystery where.' She pointed to the tattered tree reserve behind the old woman's house. 'So I headed over into the fray. Mosquitoes and blackberries . . . you get the picture.'

Pam nodded, indicating the woman's arms. 'So those aren't koala scratches?'

Overton shook her head. 'The poor thing's still in there some-where. To get to the point, I came to a clearing, and you know the rest.'

She waited until Murphy obliged: 'A naked body?'

'Yes.'

'What did you do?'

'Phoned the police.'

Tense, inquisitive, Pam said, 'Did you touch the body?'

'No.' Overton squared her shoulders. 'I didn't want to contaminate the crime scene.'

Pam left it at that. She gazed across at the knot of trees. 'I'd like you to take me there, but not into the clearing itself.'

Overton nodded. Their route was not fully a walking track but a path of least resistance where the undergrowth was thinnest. Blackberry canes snatched at their clothing and ground moisture seeped into their shoes. Twigs snapped; the air was heavy with drowsy mosquitoes and rotting vegetation. Overton stopped and froze. 'I don't believe it.'

The clearing was empty.

Chapter 4

It was a patch of dank grasses and bracken no bigger than a back-yard swimming pool, the undergrowth partly flattened near the centre where it abutted a stone reef. Pam remained standing on the rim of the clearing and glanced around. Clearly the body wasn't dead but had got to its feet and wandered off. Or someone had retrieved it.

Or the story was bullshit. She turned mildly to Overton. 'The light's tricky. You're sure you saw a body?'

'I swear, lying by that rock,' Overton said, hands on belligerent hips.

It was unfortunate, but Pam loathed her. The reaction had begun more or less on sight and was growing as they stood there. She didn't try to fight or understand it. It happened to her once or twice a year, an instantaneous reaction to face, voice, body and manner, the whole package. She used to tell herself she must be a bad person or perhaps was sensing inherent badness in someone, even that it was chemical. Now she accepted there was no logic to it.

And it didn't necessarily mean Overton was lying. The dismay struck Pam as genuine. She glanced around the clearing again, reluctant to enter. 'Perhaps if I could use your telescope thingy.'

'Monocular,' said Overton, lifting the strap over her head.

The device was warm from her body. Pam put it to her eye, and the clearing swam, and then the rock sharpened and filled her vision, the surface a pattern of fissures and lichen. There was staining, but if it was vegetable, animal, or mineral, she couldn't tell. She scoped out the surrounding dirt and grass, and still nothing. If there was blood and, more to the point, a blood trail between the clearing and the back road on the other side of the little reserve, then only Luminol spraying at night would map it. Without a body she wasn't about to authorise that.

'I need to hunt around for a while, so perhaps you could go back and keep Mrs. McIntosh company?'

Overton scowled and retreated, stumping through the gloomy trees.

When she was gone, Murphy made a notebook sketch of the clearing and the rock. If a crime had been committed here, a stills photographer and a videographer would make a more accurate and permanent record. Then she circled the clearing, keeping to the far edge of it, looking for drag marks, blood, anything at all. It was pointless. She couldn't tell. Overton had probably seen something, though.

The clearing lurched as she was hit by a wave of dizziness. Another one: The attacks had started a week earlier and occurred a few times a day. Sudden movements seemed to cause them, but so did no movements at all. She lost a second of her life. It left her opening and closing her mouth and blinking her eyes for a few seconds. A side effect of coming off citalopram? Lisa, her GP, hadn't warned her it might happen—had wanted her to go on to a higher dose, if anything, not stop.

Pam took her time walking back to the house and followed the voices to the kitchen. A chilly place, the domain of an old woman who has little money and failing eyesight. Dust, crumbs, crusty forks, low-wattage light bulbs, greasy smears across the table and benches. Jan Overton and Mrs. McIntosh sitting amid it, waiting as tea steeped in a dented aluminium pot and biscuits staled on a chipped plate.

The old woman was astounded to see her. 'Are you the meals-on-wheels?'

Pam smiled. 'Police, Mrs. McIntosh.'

'Never. Where's your whatchamacallit?'

'My uniform? I left it home today.'

Jan Overton sniffed. The old woman worked her mouth. 'I didn't do anything.'

'Of course not,' Pam said. 'I was wondering if you'd seen anyone wandering around in the trees behind your house.'

Mrs. McIntosh stared wonderingly. 'Who?'

Overton took a frail hand and stroked it. 'A young woman, perhaps? Or anyone at all?'

Distress showed in the old woman's eyes. 'Are you from the council?'

'The council? No. You had a koala in your garden, remember?'

'I use tank water,' the old woman said, turning her attention to Pam Murphy. 'I'm not on mains water. So you can put that in your pipe and smoke it.'

Pam had been told that her smile didn't always reassure, but she tried it now, pulling up a chair. 'It's okay. We know you're not wasting water. But you do have a lovely garden, must take a lot of upkeep. Does anyone help you with it, Mrs. McIntosh? Granddaughter, niece?'

'Where?' Mrs. McIntosh said, staring about.

Pam tried a new tack. 'Perhaps you can help me. I'm not that familiar with this area. There's a dirt road over there, beyond the trees, Waterloo's in that direction, the council rubbish tip is over there. . . . Do you have any close neighbours, Mrs. McIntosh?'

'Eric and I owned a thousand acres here, once upon a time. All gone now.'

'I'm sorry to hear that.'

'I won't sell. You can tell them that.'

'Quite right,' Pam said. 'It's lovely and quiet out here. You most probably know all your neighbours, what kinds of cars they drive?'

She bristled. 'Where?'

'Mrs. McIntosh, did you hear or see anything suspicious last night or this morning? Someone in the trees, strange lights or sounds or cars?'

'We had a little .22 rifle. We gave it up in the amnesty.'

'Very wise. What about your neighbours? Do you think they might have seen or heard anything?'

The old woman was scarifying. 'Them? All they're good for is uprooting good apple trees and putting in grape vines. They live up in the city, and I never see them.'

Overton was glaring at Pam now, so she eased out of the conversation and the house and sat in her car for a while. The next step was Missing Persons, local hospitals, and if that came to nothing, a background check on Jan Overton. Meanwhile, she'd take the long route back to Waterloo—skirt around the nature reserve and back along Waterloo-Dandenong Road.

Mrs. McIntosh's road deteriorated, after a few hundred metres, into powdery drifts and bone-shaking corrugations. Pam eased along, listening to pebbles ping inside the wheel arches. At the T-intersection she turned left, another chopped-about farmers' road leading her around the far side of the reserve. Here she found a gate in a falling-down fence hung with fox pelts and a bare patch of ground where anyone mad enough to stroll through the reserve could park. She got out and made a skirting examination of the dirt. A faint suggestion of tyre tracks— but why wouldn't there be? No drag marks. No blood that she could see.

Maybe lovers had come here last night; something went wrong, and the girl ran off. Or they had drunken sex in the clearing, and she was left behind to sleep it off. Or nothing happened at all.

Pam returned to the Subaru and followed the track to the end, relieved to turn left onto bitumen for the fast run back to Waterloo. That's when she saw the fancy gateway, and there was her CIU colleague, Scobie Sutton, gloomily scribbling in his notebook. She pulled over, got out. 'Scobie.'

Sutton was tall, morose, and thin, his black suit gaping and flapping around his fleshless limbs. 'Pam.'

'Breaking the back of local crime, I see?'

Sutton seemed to think about taking the question seriously, but then a smile transformed his face. 'Something like that.'

'Where's your car?'

'I came with Tankard. He's up at the house.'

'You sent Tank to question a citizen?'

Scobie scowled. This time he'd failed to read her. 'John's all right,' he said loyally.

They stood side by side and contemplated the gateway. One of its pillars dripped with the words: I'M COMPENSATING FOR A SMALL DICK. Pam grinned. The spraycan vigilante had been active for two months now, always targeting ostentatious driveway entrances, a recent fashion trend on the Peninsula, a sign of brash money. She ran her gaze over the cream-coloured pillars, the irregular fieldstone blocks, the curving, baronial wings rising from the dying spring grasses, the oiled hardwood gates. The house itself was out of sight, at the end of a long driveway that wound through trees to a hillside overlooking Western Port Bay.

The graffiti was a variation on the others she'd seen in the past few weeks: A CASHED-UP BOGAN LIVES HERE and JUST BECAUSE I'M RICH DOESN'T MEAN I HAVE TASTE and, simply, WANKER. Pam thought the vigilante deserved a medal, but he—or she—had become a headache for CIU. A victim with money and clout had put the hard word on the local member of Parliament,

who had put the hard word on Inspector Challis's superintendent, who had put the hard word on Challis, who had tried to
put the hard word on the rank-and-file. Pam had told him he
must be joking if he thought these people were victims and if
he thought already-overstretched police resources should be
wasted investigating a bit of graffiti.

So Challis handed the investigation to Scobie Sutton, who
never complained.

Pam lingered a while, yarning with Scobie. He hadn't seen
anyone—certainly not a naked woman, he told her, blushing a
little.

Then, almost immediately, they heard a voice, 'Help me,
please help me.'

Startled, they glanced across the road.

Jan Overton's victim, thought Pam, beginning to move. Young,
naked, filthy, she must have stumbled through bushland to get
here.

Sutton followed her across. The woman was clasping the top
fence wire with both hands, rocking and keening like an abandoned child. As though the notional obstruction of the fence
was a kind of last straw.

'It's okay, it's okay, you're safe now,' Pam crooned, helping
her bend between the wires.

'I was raped, someone raped me,' the young woman said.

Scobie draped his suit coat around the thin shoulders and
Pam noted the scratches automatically, the blood, the bruises,
looking for drifts of dry semen. Then they were at the car. 'Scobie, could you get my first-aid kit from the Subaru?' She gave the
woman a drink from a bottle of water.

'My name is Pam, and that's Scobie,' she said. 'We're police
officers.'

The woman stiffened as if she might bolt. 'Chloe,' she whispered.

'Do you know who did this to you, Chloe?'

At that moment, a police car came down the driveway from the house, the engine decelerating, tyres growling on the gravel as the car nosed through the gate posts. John Tankard got out, a man with a barrelly torso and vast thighs barely contained inside his constable's uniform. 'What's up?'

The response was instantaneous. Bucking violently in Pam's arms, Chloe screamed, 'Keep him away from me, keep him away from me.'

Chapter 5

Hal Challis was stroking Ellen Destry's bare feet, thinking how shapely they were and how much he was going to miss them over the next eight weeks.

Noon, an early lunch on the deck of her house before the taxi came to collect her. Five P.M. flight to London with a stopover in Singapore, so she needed to be at Melbourne Airport by 3 P.M. Allowing ninety minutes for the taxi ride—covered by her study grant—she'd need to leave by 1:30 P.M. Plenty of time for lunch in the sun.

They'd already had the quickie.

Challis kneaded an instep absently. Ellen's feet seemed light in his lap. He admired the fine down on her legs, the taut length of her calves. She was watching him with a drowsy smile, so he halted his gaze at the hem of her shorts and admired the view beyond her side veranda.

Ellen had bought this house in Dromana, on the southern slope of Arthurs Seat, two months ago. He could see why she liked living here. Small, shaded houses on narrow, sleepy streets, some sealed, others no more than potholed dirt tracks marked NO THROUGH ROAD. The bay visible between the houses and trees farther down the slope. A village atmosphere, with shops at the bottom of the hill and the beach close by for her morning walk. And the freeway only a quick couple of blocks away.

But it wasn't a place he could live in—not that either of them wanted that. But they did want each other, so it was all right. A modern arrangement, some nights spent together at his place or at hers, others spent apart.

'You could fly to Europe with me,' she said.

'I could.'

No he couldn't. Spend eight weeks as a tagalong boyfriend while she studied regional sex crimes policing in the UK, Ireland, and parts of Germany, France, and Holland? Ellen busy with her European colleagues during the day and writing up her notes at night, while he trudged over the hard flagstones of one cathedral after another?

It was only for two months. He had ongoing criminal investigations and junior detectives to oversee, and anyway he'd rather travel with Ellen when they both had time off.

'But I know you won't,' she said.

He gave her a sweet, tired smile. They would talk often, as close to face-to-face as you could get with a webcam.

A seed pod dropped from one of her garden trees and bounced off the bonnet of his Triumph, which was parked in her driveway. Watching his gaze shift to it, Ellen said, 'Why don't you use my car for the duration?'

His TR4 was uncomfortable and frequently unreliable, and she said so now, again.

'Or,' she added, 'surprise me while I'm away, and buy yourself a new car.'

He'd already thought he might do that, in fact. 'Am I someone who doesn't surprise you?'

She jumped from her chair and onto his lap. 'God, Hal, constant surprises, most of them welcome.'

'I thought a BMW.'

'Another surprise.' She paused. 'Though I'm not sure I could be with someone who drives a BMW.'

They kissed, and the weather-rotted fabric of his deck chair began to tear under their weight. They stood and surveyed the damage. 'I'll fix it while you're away. New canvas, upholstery tacks. . . .'

Not only that: her lawn was no better than a patch of dirt and dry grass, the decking needed a couple of coats of stain, several windows were stuck, the TV antenna resembled a kite caught in a tree, and weeds grew in the gutters. He gazed at the outside walls: new paint job.

She gave him a complicated look. 'I don't want . . . you'll have plenty. . . .' she said, trying to find her meaning.

He knew. She didn't want him to be her knight in shining armour, didn't want to be beholden. By the same token, he didn't want to throw himself into doing everything for her. It was complicated. The relationship was new, and they were still drawing lines in the sand, in an amiable kind of way.

As if to dispel any hint of tension, she came to him, wrapped him close so that he felt the beat of her heart. 'I'm going to miss you.'

'Me, too.' He paused. 'I could come to the airport.'

She shook her head under his chin. 'Please don't. I couldn't bear it, all that hanging around. Besides, Larrayne will be there.'

Ellen's daughter was at university now but still a little hostile around Challis. 'Okay.'

'Sighs of relief all around.'

They fetched two kitchen chairs, and Ellen lowered her feet back into his lap. 'How will you spend the weekend?' She sounded as if she needed to know he wouldn't be miserable with her gone.

'I thought I'd make tentative steps to sell the Dragon.'

'Good.'

'Really?'

In her practical way she said, 'Look, I thought it was great you were restoring an old aeroplane. Totally un-cop like. But I can see your heart isn't in it any more.'

Challis was relieved. 'My interest seemed to evaporate the moment I tightened the last screw.'

She nodded. 'How do you sell an aeroplane?'

'I thought maybe a broker. There's a man called Warren Niekirk, deals in vintage planes.'

'A local?'

'Yes.'

'That's handy.' She looked at her watch. 'I'd better change.'

But she didn't move. An explosive racket drove the birds from the trees, and Challis glanced across at the neighbouring house. Two women lived there, gardeners at the maze on Arthurs Seat, each with a biker boyfriend, and one of the boyfriends was firing up his Harley Davidson.

'The music of the suburbs,' Challis said. 'Do they know you're police?'

'Don't think so.'

His phone rang. He stared at it, sitting there on Ellen's warped veranda table, and willed it to stop.

'I hate your ring tone.'

'What's wrong with it?'

'It's the same as that woman's in *Love Actually*.'

'What woman?'

'The one with the mad brother.'

Challis couldn't remember the film or the ring tone. He wasn't someone who had favourite films. Ellen was. On her reckoning, she'd seen *Love Actually* a million times.

He pressed the talk button. 'Challis.'

'Boss, we've got a rape,' Pam Murphy said.

And Ellen Destry, about to jet off and learn how to deal with rape cases, read his face and swung her graceful feet to the floor.

Chapter 6

Early afternoon, a room in the Waterloo hospital, Pam Murphy briefly clasping Chloe Holst's forearm. 'Do you mind Inspector Challis being here, Chloe?'

Challis was propping up a wall, trying to be unobtrusive. He smiled but remained silent where he was. 'I don't mind,' Holst said, her voice damp, cracking a little.

'We spoke to your parents and the doctor, and they said if you're up to it we could ask you a few questions. Meanwhile, no one's going to carry out any more forensic indignities on you, okay? But we do need to ask you what happened.'

Chloe Holst collapsed against her pillows, stared at the ceiling, and said, in a rapid monotone, 'I was on my way home when he flashed his lights at me from behind. Then he—'

'Could we go back a bit?' Pam said, her voice low and warm in the chair beside the bed. 'Home from where?'

'The Chicory Kiln.'

'Don't know it.'

Challis murmured from the wall, 'It's a winery-bistro place on Myers Road.'

'Okay.'

Challis said, 'Had you been drinking? We have to ask these kinds of—'

The young woman in the bed tossed in anger, then winced. 'Why doesn't anyone listen? I work there. I hardly ever drink, and I don't drink at work. I was simply going home.'

'I'm sorry,' Challis said. 'By the time information gets to me sometimes it's wrong or inadequate.'

'I've told this story so many times.'

Once, thought Challis, to Pam—and a million times to yourself. And when the sex crimes squad gets involved, you'll have to go through it all again. 'When we have all the details we won't need to bother you again,' he said lamely.

Chloe Holst shot him a look from her right eye. The left looked pulpy and black, swollen shut, three stitches bisecting the eyebrow. Angry finger-bruising around the neck, bruises to the upper arms, and, hidden beneath the bedclothes, bruising to the thighs and tears to the vagina and anus. 'What about in court?' she asked, almost inaudibly.

Pam Murphy mustered a smile. 'You didn't see his face, so it may not come to that.'

Holst touched her hand to her split lip and grew teary. She was about to speak but sank again into the pillows heaped behind her.

The little room, like the corridor outside it, smelt of life and death and blood and cleansers and chemical intervention. Murphy knew the smell all right. She'd visited enough suspects and victims in emergency rooms over the years, been treated for cuts and bruises. She glanced around at Challis and then out of the window and saw nothing to guide her through this. Sergeant Destry would know what to do, but she was on her way to Europe.

She turned to Holst again. 'What happened after he flashed his lights?'

'It happened near the intersection with Balnarring Road, so I was slowing down anyway. I hate that corner.'

A high-speed blind corner, a fatal corner over the years, with no clear view of traffic belting down the hill until you were half-way across the intersection. 'Me too,' Pam said.

'He flashed his lights at me from behind, then cut across in front of me as I was stopping. Then he got out and started waving ID at me.'

Challis said, in his low voice, 'Can you describe the car?'

'A newish white Falcon.'

'Sure?'

'My dad has one. I actually thought it was him for a moment.'

'What time was this?'

'About midnight.'

'No other traffic?'

'No.'

'Go on.'

'I thought maybe my rear lights weren't working, or I'd hit something, you know. I thought something serious was wrong, so I wound down my window.'

Pam Murphy said, referring to her notes, 'You told the ambulance officers that you were raped by someone wearing a ski mask. Was he wearing a ski mask when he stopped you?'

'I know what you're asking,' the young woman said, with some wobbly heat. 'How come I didn't just drive off, right? But he wasn't wearing the mask when he stopped me, plus it was dark, plus he had his hand up to his eyes like my headlights were blinding him. Plus he was wearing a police uniform, and he shouted at me, sounding really urgent, said for my own safety I had to pull in under the trees.'

Pam pictured the small parking area on the southeast corner, abutting Buckley's Reserve, a school bus stop five mornings a week but otherwise used only by drivers taking a mobile phone call, blackberry pickers, road-repair gangs on a tea break from patching potholes. She pictured it at night, full of tricky shapes and shadows. 'Just to be clear, the man who abducted you wasn't Constable Tankard, the policeman who frightened you this afternoon?'

Chloe Holst shook her head. 'Too fat. It was . . . I just saw the uniform and freaked out.'

'I understand. Then what happened?'

'I was scared. I didn't know what I'd done wrong. I hadn't been drinking or speeding, but I thought I must have done something wrong, or something bad had happened to my mum and dad or something. Anyway, I did what he asked, and before I could get out or anything, he climbed into the back seat and put a knife to my neck. He pricked me with it, look.'

A small, scratched hand pulled down the neckline, the delicate jaw craned upwards, revealing flesh that looked shockingly naked to Challis just then. A short, clean nick.

'After that I just about lost it.'

'You didn't see his face?'

'He was behind me, and by then he had the mask on. Plus gloves, you know, latex ones.'

'Let's stay with him for a bit. He was wearing a police uniform?'

'Yes.'

'Jacket over a shirt and trousers, or just the shirt and trousers?'

'Shirt and trousers.'

'Short sleeves? Long?'

'Long.'

Less chance of being scratched, Challis thought. 'Footwear?'

Chloe frowned, looking from him to Pam Murphy to the ceiling. Then her face cleared. 'Black lace-ups. He kicked me in the stomach later on.'

Plain black shoes with a featureless flat sole, thought Challis. 'Uniform cap?'

'Yes.'

'What kind of voice did he have?' Challis didn't want to suggest that the rapist spoke with an accent. Some victims were conditioned to believe that only an outsider, a foreigner, could have hurt them so badly. 'I'm assuming he did speak?'

'Kind of a hoarse whisper. It was put on. I wouldn't say he had an accent or anything.'

Pam Murphy asked: 'Any smells that you could identify?'

'What, like BO?'

'Anything.'

'I didn't smell anything, but he got all sweaty, you know, as he was. . . .'

They nodded.

'Wait. Bad breath.'

Since starting in the job, Challis had come to believe that rottenness of character often manifested itself physically. He doubted there was any science to support the notion but believed it all the same. 'From alcohol, drugs, bad teeth?'

Holst shook her head miserably. 'I don't know.'

'Doesn't matter. You're doing brilliantly. This won't take much longer. I'm sure you want to see your parents.'

Holst tossed in distress. 'This will ruin them, my dad.'

'I'm sure it won't,' said Pam.

'What would you know?'

Pam patted the skinny forearm. 'You're doing so well, Chloe. Let's get all the details out of the way so you can rest. After the man overpowered you, I assume he took you to his car and—'

'You assume wrong. He told me to drive.'

Challis shifted from the wall. 'His car, or yours?'

'Mine.'

'He left his car there?'

'Yes.'

Challis hadn't been told this. He'd assumed—and so had the

others, apparently—that Holst had been abducted and raped in the culprit's car. He smiled, held up a finger, and said, 'Murph?'

'Boss.'

'Give me a moment.'

Challis stepped into the corridor, flipped open his phone, and called John Tankard, who was with Scobie Sutton and a forensics team, searching the bushland clearing where Chloe Holst had first been seen. 'Anything?'

'We found the clearing, big rock in the centre, blood and tissue,' Tankard said.

'Got another job for you,' Challis said and told them about the cars. 'Our guy probably dumped her, then drove back and swapped cars again, but can you get over there and check? If her car's there, have it trucked to the lab.'

'Will do,' Tankard said. He paused. 'This is not going to follow me, is it?'

'No, John, you're in the clear. The man who took her claimed to be police. She was just reacting to your uniform.'

'Thanks, boss.'

Challis returned to the room. Nothing had changed: The space was sterile despite the air of distress, Pam Murphy was sitting in the chair beside the bed, holding Holst's hand. 'Sorry, Chloe, please go on,' he said. 'He told you to drive. Do you remember where?'

'I don't know. It was dark.'

Pam asked, 'Are you from the Peninsula?'

Holst shook her head. 'Not really. Moved down here with my mum and dad last year. Safety Beach. I don't know the Western Port side very well.'

'Did he take you to a beach, a park, a house? What can you remember?'

'Just along some dirt roads. Kind of farm smells.'

'Was he alone? You didn't meet up with anyone else?'

'No.'

'Did he phone anyone?'

'He hardly talked at all. Kind of grunted what he wanted me to do. Except he got really angry when I started crying, like he hated it, told me to shut up and punched me in the side of the head.'

'Edgy? Unstable?'

'Like he was on drugs,' Holst said, then shrugged. 'I don't know,' she wailed, 'how would I know?'

Pam clasped her hand, waiting, and asked gently, 'He made you take your clothes off?'

'Yes.'

'Where are they?'

'I don't know.'

Burnt, thought Challis, dumped. Unless he was a souvenir hunter. 'Where did he rape you?'

'Where do you think? My mouth, my vagina, my—'

'I mean, in the car? On the ground?'

'Both.'

'What did you do or say?'

'I begged him at first, then when I tried to bite him, he hit me really hard. It really, really hurt.'

Pam said gently, 'I was called to an incident earlier this afternoon, someone reported seeing a body in a clearing a couple of kilometres from where we rescued you.'

'We were on this dirt road. He told me to get out, and I saw these trees, and I just ran,' Holst said. 'It was dark, and I fell over a stump or something and hit my head.'

Pam clasped Chloe's forearm. There was a school of thought that you shouldn't get close to a victim, shouldn't try to share the burden, because you couldn't. Pam worked best when she didn't take that notion too far. 'We've tested for fluids. If he's in the database we'll—'

'He used a condom.'

'Oh.'

'This guy's like really organised. You know what he did when he was finished? Washed me all over with this wet cloth, then combed my hair and pubes, then ran this kind of sticky roller thing all over me. Like some kind of super CSI freak or something.'

A part of Hal Challis calculated the odds of finding any forensic evidence. Another began to measure the mind of the man responsible. 'How did he carry all these items?'

'Backpack.'

'Colour? Brand?'

She shrugged. 'A daypack. Really organised.'

'Have you been aware of any unwanted attention lately?' Challis asked. 'At work or where you live? Anyone following you, accosting you in the supermarket, that kind of thing? Phone hang-ups, heavy breathing, stuff left on your doorstep?'

A miserable head shake. 'No.'

'Boyfriend trouble?'

She stared at her hands. 'Don't have a boyfriend.'

'Any unwanted advances? Friend or work colleague who won't take no for an answer?'

'Nothing like that.'

Pam squeezed her forearm again, then turned to Challis with a question on her face. Challis stepped away from the wall. 'Chloe, we'll leave you in peace now. You've been a great help, very observant.'

She was weeping. 'For what good it'll do. I don't know what he looks like, and the way he cleaned up afterward. . . .'

Pam Murphy stood, gave the forearm a last pat. 'There's always something a guy like this overlooks. We'll get him.'

That's how Challis and Murphy were going to leave it, rote parting words, said thousands of times over the years by thousands of police officers. But Chloe Holst said, 'Do you think it was my fault?'

Pam sat again, clasped the limp hand, and said feelingly, 'Never in a million years, Chloe. Don't ever let yourself think that. It was his fault entirely.'

The young woman looked away as if she didn't believe it. 'He said I made it easy for him, if I'd been more security conscious it wouldn't have happened.'

Chapter 7

And so Challis was not feeling receptive to the newspaper reporter who ambushed him in the hospital car park.

'I can't comment on that.'

'Oh, come on, Inspector. If I write that a senior officer refused to confirm or deny that the suspect in an alleged abduction and rape is a policeman, everyone's going to know it's a cop.'

'Not an alleged abduction and rape,' snarled Challis. 'The real deal.'

The reporter had given his name as Jack Porteous, of the *News-Pictorial*. A small weekly newspaper—local Waterloo, Mornington, Cranbourne, and Frankston editions—owned by a national media outfit. Challis had never spoken to the man before. All he wanted to do was get in his car—parked beside Pam Murphy's Subaru—and return to the police station. He'd already made a mental checklist: request assistance from the sex crimes unit at police headquarters; obtain a list of local offenders, another of stolen police uniforms and ID; ask for preliminary forensics from the nature reserve and the victim herself; find the rapist's car. . . .

'Okay,' Porteous said, 'I'll drop the "alleged." Can you at least tell me anything about the victim? The state of her injuries, her mental state, her—'

'You're not serious,' Challis said.

In the act of unlocking the Triumph, he turned to reassess the man. Jack Porteous was about sixty, with a grizzled face, limp grey hair, a tight little drinker's belly, deep parenthetical lines on either side of a truculent mouth. A time-worn man, dignified by his clothing: pressed trousers, crisp shirt, fashionable jacket, glossy black shoes. An old hand, Challis thought. If Porteous had been pensioned off or sought a sea-change after years of toil at one of the big dailies, he was unlikely to be satisfied with covering the Under 15s Netball final. He tried a more diplomatic tack.

'All I can say is a young woman was brutally abducted and sexually assaulted. We've only just come on board. We have no clear suspect at this stage. Meanwhile, the investigation will be rigorous, without fear or favour.'

'So, it was a cop.'

'If you're relying on hospital porters and ambulance officers for your information, you might want to rethink your methods.'

Porteous held up a warding-off palm. 'Whoa. That's why I'm asking you.'

Challis unlocked his car, strapped himself in, lowered the window. 'We'll issue a statement when we know more.'

The reporter shrugged, defeated. 'Suit yourself.'

Challis ground the starter. The engine turned sluggishly. He tried again.

'Sounds like your battery's on the way out.'

Challis wasn't interested in the reporter's diagnosis. He wanted Porteous to leave. He wanted Pam Murphy to materialise: Murph would have a set of jumper leads in her car.

He sat there.

Porteous wasn't finished. 'I'd have thought, inspector level, you'd be provided with an official car and your own driver.'

It was not said to bait Challis, but it was a last straw. Challis got out, leaned his rump on the Triumph.

'I'm going to take your remark seriously.'

'Okay,' said Porteous, wary but game for anything.

'You wonder why I'm using my old bomb for police work? I'll tell you. We're under-resourced. You look at my unit, CIU: there's only one serviceable unmarked car available to us at present, and if we didn't use our own cars a lot of the time, we'd never get to a crime scene at all. It's just as bad for uniformed police. Some nights there's only one marked patrol car or divisional van on the road. Lack of vehicles and manpower. Police resources are pathetic, no matter what kind of spin the government or force hierarchy put on it.'

'Uh-huh.'

'So far this month I've spent more than eighty dollars of my own money on police gear—camera batteries, paper for the photocopier, you name it.'

Porteous was scribbling, Challis too electric to care.

'Waterloo has the lowest ratio of police per population in Victoria, so if you're burgled or assaulted, you'd better come and talk to us about it—because we haven't the manpower or resources to come to you. Proactive policing is a thing of the past. Front-line hours have fallen by eighteen percent; violent crimes have risen by nearly fifty. There's a population explosion on the Peninsula, for Christ's sake, complicated by the financial crisis, and they want to strip us of money and manpower?'

'There's talk of part-time hours for certain police stations,' said Porteous.

Challis knew he was being prompted and gave a sharkish grin. 'The cutting edge of police work. It's ten o'clock at night, you're hurt, frightened, running for your life, too poor to own a mobile phone, there's no public phone, and outside the darkened doors of the police station is a button to press that plays a recorded message to dial triple zero.'

He had a steam up now. 'Sick leave is at an all-time high,

morale is at an all-time low, too many of us are on stress leave. Our computer systems are from the past century. We don't fight or investigate crime; we file paperwork.'

'Makes it hard.'

'Meanwhile, every March, the state government spends fifty million to stage a car race that no one watches.'

They stared at each other. 'I don't know what it's like in the newspaper game,' Challis said, 'but I can see police officers of the future signing on as sub-contractors, providing their own handguns, cuffs, vehicles, and radios, responsible for their own superannuation, health plans, and holiday pay. Words like "mission statement" will be used a lot.'

'And crime?'

'Crime prospers,' Challis said.

He got his car started and returned to the CIU office on the first floor of the police station, wondering what he'd just done.

Headlines next Tuesday, irate calls from Superintendent McQuarrie, disciplinary action?

Or would Porteous count the rape as the juicier story?

He reached for the phone. The head of sex crimes said, 'We're pretty stretched, Inspector. I can give you one officer, Monday morning.'

Challis had to be content with that. The Peninsula would have its own sex crimes unit when Ellen returned from her study tour, and in the meantime, CIU would have to muddle along. He entered the open plan CIU office and left a note on Scobie Sutton's desk, asking him to compile lists of local sex offenders and police who'd reported the loss or theft of their ID or uniforms.

He returned to his office, swivelled in his chair. The clutter was comforting around him: files and folders on the floor and cabinets and his shelves leaning this way and that with bound regulations, trial transcripts, a book called *Written on the Skin* by Liz Porter, and a greasy repair manual for the Triumph.

He tried to picture the rapist cop. It wasn't unknown for policemen to 'rescue' intoxicated women from pubs and parties and rape them in their homes, or coerce sexual favours in return for tearing up a speeding ticket. But abduction?

He grimaced: Blame it on the job? Staff shortages, doubling up of duties, no public appreciation, and finally someone cracked?

That reminded him: Murph had said she'd emailed him a list of her vehicle expenses. He nudged his computer mouse. The monitor blinked into life, showing several new emails. Most he deleted, but printed Pam's and one from Force Command, advising all districts to be on the lookout for a holdup man. Caucasian, aged in his forties, suspected of robbing banks and credit unions along a coastal stretch of southeastern New South Wales and now believed to be operating across the border in northeastern Victoria and, more recently, Gippsland.

He swung in his chair, looked at his watch. Murphy should be back from the hospital soon. He pondered her a little. She seemed off her game lately, a little vague and flat, given to brief, strange gestures, a kind of stiffening and staring into space.

She was turning into a good detective, Murphy. Unlike Sutton. Scobie was too credulous to be a good detective, without capacity to understand wickedness. He could read bank records and CCTV footage, but not people.

A voice leaning against his doorjamb said, 'Miles away, boss.'

Challis swung his feet off the desk, his chair protesting. 'Always thinking, Murph, you know that.'

'My mentor,' Pam Murphy said drily.

'How's Chloe?'

'Her parents are with her, and they've brought in a counsellor.'

Challis nodded. 'Check this out.' He handed her the bank-robber email and watched her face as she read it.

'Are we worried, boss?'

'Us? The Waterloo CIU?'

'Well, when you put it like that. . . .'

Challis gave her a tired smile. 'Meanwhile we'd better warn the local banks, so if you could take a wander down the street. . . .'

'Sure.'

'Then we'll take a drive out to the Chicory Kiln.'

Chapter 8

Grace had taken her time driving to Waterloo. Lunch first, at a bistro in the bayside suburb of St Kilda. Some window-shopping and then a stroll along the beach, letting the sun seep into her bones. Bright sunlight today, feathered by scudding clouds, a brisk wind that had her wrapping her arms around her breasts.

And so it was mid-afternoon before she was on the road again, glimpsing choppy waters whenever she glanced along the little side streets that laddered the Nepean Highway. Reaching Frankston, she turned left at a beer barn and made her way southeast in stages to the outskirts of Baxter and down into Somerville.

This was a semi-rural world of boutique horticulture, native and indigenous plant nurseries, New Age healers, and tradesmen who preferred life on a couple of hectares to life in a town. Vigorous spring grasses and fruit trees, flowering wattle and scabby pines. Dams, post-and-rail fences, and horse yards. Signs advertising eggs, horse manure, and garage sales. Delivery vans, family station wagons, a Gribbles pathology car, farm dogs braced on the trays of Holden utes. Grace drove sedately. She'd never been booked for any offence in all of her years of driving and didn't want to come to the attention of the unmarked highway patrol car—a high-speed blue Holden—that she'd seen lurking around this part of the Peninsula during the past year.

Rather than head down through Tyabb, she took Eramosa Road to the Waterloo road, the long way around, but this was habit and instinct, too. She didn't see the unmarked pursuit car, but along a stretch of farmland, she did see a police car parked inside an elaborate new gateway, a beefy-looking uniformed cop and a scarecrow in plain clothes standing in contemplation of the words I'M COMPENSATING FOR A SMALL DICK that were spray painted across the face of a concrete column. Grace slowed the car and gawked, as anyone would, and pulled away again.

As she neared Waterloo, the landscape grew a little untidier: lower incomes, some light industry, gorse and blackberry jungles on vacant lots, a couple of abandoned businesses. Waterloo's Cheapest Cars, nylon flags snapping on a line that stretched from an unpainted shed to a power pole. But, closer in, the town was more prosperous, boasting five banks.

One bank in particular. Grace had come to Waterloo for her safe-deposit box. She had other banks and bank accounts throughout the country, escape funds of a few thousand dollars in each, but only one safe-deposit box. She knew there was usually no call for rural banks to supply these boxes. Local businesses were small, individuals' tastes modest. The idea of spending $50,000 on a necklace, let alone wearing it to the Football Club Annual Ball, was absurd. If a farmer here, or a shopkeeper there, did own a $100,000 bearer bond or a handful of Krugerrands, it was considered a canny investment and stored in a city bank or a lawyer's office safe.

But the Peninsula was different from many rural areas. Grace had smelt money as soon as she'd driven through the area one weekend two years ago. Some of the money was old, discreet and family-based, bound up in land and sweeping sea views, but most of it was new, and often on vulgar display locally, at garden parties, vintage wine launches, twenty-firsts, and charity balls. Hence the VineTrust Bank and its little back room full of safe-deposit boxes.

Perfect for Grace. A safe-deposit box in a town where she wasn't known but wouldn't stand out, in a region that was nowhere near where she lived, and in a state where she was not active. Where Galt wouldn't think to look for her. And so, on that October day two years ago, she'd walked into the VineTrust on the main street of Waterloo and rented one of their biggest boxes. 'I sometimes need to store folios,' she explained and paid for five years in advance.

They understood. They were very discreet. They didn't know what a folio was or what it might contain, but from time to time they did see Grace with a large, flat folder or binder. They thought she might have been an artist or an architect. They didn't think 'thief,' stowing a stolen painting. She was known as 'Mrs. Grace' to the young and middle-aged women who took her to the windowless back room furnished only with a plain chair and a table.

Today Grace parked in a street parallel to High Street and slipped into the women's room at the Coolart Arms hotel, where she dressed up and a little out: black tights under a short purple skirt, dark glasses with purple frames, a narrow purple hair band, oversized scarlet hoops in her ears. All of it intended to shift attention away from her face. Then she left the pub through a side door and cut through a narrow lane, the Sydney Long aquatint and the cash from Steve Finch in her briefcase.

'Mrs. Grace,' said Rowan Ely, who happened to be passing the help desk, wearing a smile that Grace read as genuine, a smile she'd earned over the past two years.

She gave the manager a dazzling smile and said, in her low voice, 'Hello, Rowan.'

'What can we do for you today?'

Grace murmured that she was thinking of setting up an Advance Saver account.

'We can do that for you,' Rowan Ely said, asking a teller for the forms and a brochure.

Grace had no intention of opening any such account, but it was the kind of business a client might want to transact. 'Let me take the paperwork home with me,' she said, glancing at her watch. It was cool inside the main room of the bank, a little grave and hushed, as if the people at VineTrust dealt exclusively with old money.

Still looking at her watch, she said, 'If I could have access to my safe-deposit box briefly?'

'Of course.'

Ely picked up his phone and murmured into it. Brisk seconds later, a slight, middle-aged woman appeared. Joy, senior teller, said her nametag, and she beamed in recognition. 'Mrs. Grace.'

'Please call me Susan.'

They conducted the preliminaries—register consulted, signature, both keys produced, the box located and removed to the little back room—and when she was alone, Grace drew on cotton gloves and lifted the lid. In a corner of her mind was the usual nagging fear that the treasures she'd acquired—with Galt and without him—might have vanished since her previous visit. But everything was intact: bundles of cash, a gold ingot, coins, and stamps. There were also three sets of false ID and two digital holdings: a photographic record of her burglaries on a memory card and her house deeds and other personal documents on a flash drive. Finally, there was an old photograph, dated 1938, that she believed was a link to her past. She added Steve Finch's $2,000 and the Sydney Long, closed the lid, and got out of there.

She hesitated for a moment on the footpath, thinking that she'd forgotten something. Unease flooded in, followed by the thousand calming distractions of ordinary life. She was low on tampons: maybe that's what it was.

But as she emerged from the pharmacy next to the VineTrust Bank and turned toward her car, a voice said, 'Anita?' and a current shot through her.

She hoped it didn't show, hoped she didn't falter. Her heels snapped past the little shops as she continued walking to the laneway that led to her Golf.

'Oi! Anita!'

She walked on, the laneway about five metres away now.

She heard him come in hard behind her but knew it would be a mistake to run or respond. She was innocent. This was an innocent mistake. Her name was Grace, and she had no reason to stop or flee just because someone had hurled the name Anita at her back. A tourist bus belched past, WINERY EXPRESS scrolled along its flank. Cars trailed it. Two women emerged from a hair salon; a man tested a telescopic lens outside a camera shop; a pair of schoolboys emerged from a bakery, sausage rolls in their fists.

Grace felt fingers clamp her shoulder and spin her around.

She let astonishment, then alarm, flood her face. Consternation, a touch of irritation. Her eyes behind the dark lenses assessed the man, then flashed to where he'd been standing when he first called her name. A bug-smeared campervan, a woman stowing bags of groceries at the open side door, and two small children licking ice cream cones. A long camping holiday, guessed Grace.

Back to the man, his hand now manacling her forearm, his knocked-about boxer's face fixed intently on her. 'Please, I am knowing you?' she said.

He hesitated. He'd known Anita in Sydney, three, four years ago. Anita had been on the fringe of things. So had he. Still was, but he was also a family man, presently touring the country with his wife and kids. Since last seeing Anita, he'd idly wondered if she was in jail or on the bottom of Sydney Harbour, given the people she moved with. No, she was here, in Victoria, a little coastal town southeast of Melbourne. With a foreign accent.

'Anita?'

'Please, you are hurt me, my arm,' Grace said.

'Come off it, Anita.'

Grace tugged and attempted to attract the attention of the people going about their business in Waterloo. She stumbled, seemed to hang from the man's hand, which was broad and scarred. His name came to her, from her old life: Corso.

'Leave her alone,' an old woman said.

'Mind your business,' snarled Corso.

People seemed to melt away. Grace was alone. 'Please, you hurt me very badly,' she said.

A woman said, 'Excuse me.'

'None of your business lady, okay?'

'I'm afraid it is. Let the woman go, or I'll arrest you.'

Grace felt the fingers unlock. Corso stepped away from her. 'Look, mistaken identity, that's all. No harm done.'

'Ma'am?'

Plain clothes and a Crime Investigation Unit ID. About thirty, quizzical but tense, with the compact grace of an athlete. 'Ma'am?' said the cop again.

'Is nothing.'

'Was this man hurting you?' persisted the cop. 'Do you wish to press charges?'

'Look, I got the wrong person, okay?' said Corso, backing away.

'Stop right there, please, sir,' the cop said. She turned to Grace. 'Are you all right? Are you hurt?'

'Is nothing. This man, he is mistake me.'

'Is this true, sir?'

By now Corso's wife and children were hovering. 'Corse, for god's sake,' the wife said.

'Misunderstanding,' Corso said, holding up both palms to the detective, eyes sliding away.

She nodded at the campervan. 'Is that your vehicle, sir?'

'Er, yep.'

'Passing through?'

'That's right.'

'Heading for. . . ?'

'Across to Perth, then up the coast to Darwin and across the Top End,' said Corso, swelling a little at his own intrepidity.

'Where in New South Wales are you from?'

The question let Corso know that his registration plate had been noted. He toed a crack in the footpath and said, 'Sydney.'

The cop said nothing for a while but watched him. 'Have a safe trip, sir.'

Corso sauntered to the campervan, his family buzzing around him, the cop still watching, Grace watching the cop, who seemed alert, restless, unimpressed by the things that came her way. And before Grace was quite ready, the cop had swung around and subjected her to the same scrutiny. 'Are you sure you don't know that man?'

'Yes, of course,' Grace said, with the dismissive shrug and hand gestures of a foreigner.

The cop watched Corso drive away. 'Do you need a doctor? A glass of water? Somewhere to sit?'

'Like old woman?' scoffed Grace.

The cop gave her a nice half grin, nodded, and headed toward the bank.

Chapter 9

Pam Murphy had noticed these things about the woman: a slight, ill-defined foreign accent, as though she spoke English at work but another language at home or had lived for long periods in different English-speaking countries; a beautiful face, once you looked past the dark glasses and showy purple; a trace of fear under the bewilderment and indignation.

Now, in the VineTrust foyer, she jotted time, date, location, and Corso's name, description and New South Wales registration number in her notebook, together with a short narrative of the incident. Then she pocketed the notebook, showed her ID to a teller, and was taken to a partitioned office. The sign on the door said ROWAN ELY: MANAGER.

'Take a seat,' Ely said with an amused frown, shutting the flimsy door on them. In fact, all of the fittings looked cheap to Pam, prefabricated out of artificial materials of a pastel nothing-colour, possibly grey.

'Now,' said Ely, 'what can I do for the police?' He paused, winked roguishly. 'I can assure you I paid that parking fine.'

Pam smiled. Ely was the kind of town politician who knew whose hands to shake. When Waterloo had become more popular as an end-of-school-year party destination, he'd cajoled her into addressing the town council on safety and security measures, and had even invited her to a Christmas barbecue last year. 'It's not the speeding fine,' she said, 'it's the embezzlement.'

At the expression on Ely's face, Pam grinned and held up a placating hand. 'Joke, sorry. I've come about this.'

She handed Ely the Force Command email, explaining about the bank robber's inexorable move south and west.

The manager listened, frowning. He was about fifty, soft-looking, face and forehead smooth and gleaming. Crisp white cuffs, a thin gold watch strapped around one narrow wrist by a strip of black calfskin. His clean fingers played a tune on the pristine desk blotter.

'Naturally we're always advised of recent holdups,' he said, when Pam finished, 'but never in terms of—' he rolled one wrist, searching for the words '—of mapping one fellow's movements. I can see why you think he's headed this way.'

'We're advising local banks to take extra precautions,' Pam said. She glanced about her as if taking the measure of the Vine-Trust's corner location, on High Street's main roundabout. Too exposed to tempt a hard man with a sawn-off shotgun?

'I'll certainly warn my staff to be on the lookout,' Ely said.

Pam nodded, staring past Ely's shoulder to the louvered window and High Street beyond the darkened glass, traffic and pedestrians passing by, unconcerned. 'We'll see if we can provide extra uniformed patrols. Meanwhile you could empty the tills more regularly during working hours, or whatever it is you do.'

'Well,' said Ely, the jokester, 'that would be in the order of secret banker business.'

Pam gave him an empty smile, shook his hand goodbye, and stepped out on to High Street. A late afternoon in September, a warm wind and cloud wisps above, shoppers parting around her, some even saying hello. She began her walk back to the police station, passing the Thai restaurant, the women's fitness centre, the new bookshop. As she drew alongside the father-and-daughter barbershop, Janis spotted her through the glass and clacked her scissors inquisitively. Pam pantomimed maybe next time and continued past the welfare office and over the railway line, her thoughts returning to the attack on Chloe Holst. She recited an old police mantra: What do I know? What don't I know yet? How can I find out?

Chapter 10

As she steered the Golf down the other side of the Peninsula, Grace thought hard about the incident with Robert Corso, weighing it up, consciously resisting paranoia. Paranoia could undo you just as certainly as a pointing finger, a hand clamping your shoulder, a voice saying, 'Got you.'

First, what would the detective recall of the incident? A faintly exotic-looking foreign woman was being accosted by a tough-looking man, but so what? Plenty of strangers passed through Waterloo, tourists attracted by the Peninsula's coast and hinterland, wineries and bed-and-breakfast cottages. She'd be more inclined to remember the man who posed the threat, not the victim.

So, Corso.

Grace thought there was a good chance that she'd fooled Corso: the wig, the accent, the unlikely location. Plus, it seemed he hadn't been in Waterloo looking for her but passing through, a driving holiday with his family. He might say nothing. But the incident would be imprinted on his mind—he'd accosted her, she'd denied her old name, and a cop had intervened—and one day he might fall into conversation with someone who'd known her in Sydney, a bouncer or a barman or someone connected to Galt. Or he'd make the kind of phone call that begins, 'This might be nothing, but today I thought I saw . . .' and the people around Galt would send in some goons or ask Corso to stick around and investigate.

Had he seen her come out of the bank? Even if the tellers or the manager did talk to Corso, or to Galt's goons, they wouldn't connect a mysterious woman with a foreign accent to the woman they knew as Mrs. Grace. And for the past two years Grace had altered her appearance each time she visited the bank: mini-skirt one day, scruffy jeans or business suit the next. Cropped black hair, blonde wig, tennis hat. Flashy cheap earrings, tiny diamond studs. To the tellers and the manager, she was a woman with the means and the time to dress as she liked. Beholden to no boss. A lucky woman, warm, artsy, a little extroverted. Nothing like the woman Galt had spent two years looking for.

Besides, Grace didn't live in or near Waterloo. Nowhere near. She rarely visited the place.

But. . . .

But she had been spotted there. Grace chewed that over as she drove. She'd be well advised to clean out the box and find another bank like the VineTrust, in another town like Waterloo. And she did need such a box, a secure place for her valuables and her keepsakes. A place she could visit and daydream about, a place for her secrets as much as her treasures. The box represented who she was. If the police ever searched her home, they wouldn't find a thing to tell them anything about her.

This was Grace's reasoning as she neared Sorrento, the lowering sun flashing in the waters of Port Phillip Bay. Only 60 km/h here, almost a crawl, and she felt a little panicky at that speed. Then 50 km/h, then 70, 60 again, and finally she was at the ferry terminal, too early for the 6 P.M. sailing. She parked outside the pay station and stretched her back. Mild air, the water barely lapping the coarse sand, and the awed feet of a toddler and his

crouching mother. A dog racing to catch a Frisbee, gulls wheeling. Stretching behind her were the Sorrento cliffs and the cliff
top houses. Who knew what riches they held? And she'd told
herself she'd forbidden herself to touch a penny of it.

Grace needed coffee for the final stage. And something to read
on the ferry. She walked back along the short branch road that
led from the Nepean Highway to the ferry station and climbed
the hill to the main street, which was busy with the kids or cars
driven by the kinds of young women who married doctors and
real estate agents. Cliché, Grace. Yeah, but clichés were useful
in Grace's line of business. They helped her to analyse a place,
helped her to decide if it was worth her while. Sorrento was—but
the rules were clear: Never operate in your own back yard.

She asked for a double-shot latté and sat at a table beneath a
plane tree. 5:35 P.M. The 6 P.M. ferry to Queenscliff would dock
at about 5:45 P.M. And as she sipped and allowed the late sunlight to warm her bones, she gazed at the passersby, trying to
place them. Retirees, tourists, local business people. And vaguely
artsy twenty-somethings, who ran the bistros, made jewellery, sold
boutique wines and nasty clothing. There were reaches in the
lives of people that Grace had never known or comprehended,
and she swallowed a lump in her throat.

She drained her coffee, crossed the street, and entered a news
agency. Here she browsed the magazine racks until she'd located
the latest *Home Digest.*

THE FERRY CROSSED THE bay, and Grace read her magazine.
She read intently. *Home Digest* was one of her bibles. It helped her
work out who to rob next.

When the ferry docked in Queenscliff, she drove down the
clanging ramp and over the sand drifts on the exit road, curving
past some unlovely light industry before reaching the old part
of the town. The cops were always vigilant here, especially about

this time on a Friday, when the tourists got an early start on the weekend.

Then she was out the other side and heading for Ocean Grove and Barwon Heads. After that, Breamlea, a tiny town off the beaten track, which few people knew existed. Tourists, if they weren't going to Queenscliff or Barwon Heads, headed for the Great Ocean Road, not some slumbering strip of houses tucked into a bank of high dunes and serviced only by a general store in the caravan park. The people from her old life would never think of holidaying there. They liked casinos, resorts, glitzy shops. They liked to fork out on overpriced accommodation, T-shirts, and sunglasses, trawl around like extras in *The Sopranos*. Breamlea wasn't the place to do that.

Grace drove into the carport of an ungainly house on stilts, as pedestrian as any beach house in Australia, retrieved her luggage and climbed the steps to the deck, some of the tension leaking away. She had a four-cornered life: thieving, selling to fences like Steve Finch, banking the proceeds, home. It was a life of movement and corners, and she couldn't see any other way to run it. A shut-away life, ordered, solitary, built on habits that kept her below the radar.

Dusk was deepening. Grace turned on the lights, the radio, tipped leftover stew into a saucepan, and lit the gas under it. There were always leftovers in her fridge, and she always heated them properly, not by microwave. Tomorrow she'd cook.

She showered, stepped out with a towel wrapped around her head, pulled on tracksuit pants and a T-shirt, no underwear. She was home, there were no protocols to follow. Home. Well, it had been for two years; she didn't know if she'd ever find anywhere she could put down deep roots. Home, and fully paid for. But hers was a day-by-day, week-by-week kind of life, and there was a better-than-even chance she'd have to walk away from it one day—away from the warm light on the slate floor, the comfortable sofa, the patchwork bed cover made by a local woman, the local jams and chutneys in her fine dresser. The tiny Hans Heysen watercolour (legitimate) on the wall. The ground-cover plants clinging to the dunes, the windy beaches, and the wheeling gulls.

She'd bought an Elan Shiraz and a Merricks Creek Pinot in Waterloo. Shiraz with the stew, she thought. The Pinot tomorrow with salmon, maybe. She drank half of the bottle and mused, but the itch was upon her. Grace took her wine glass to her study, powered up the computer, and gambled away $7,600 in a little under thirty minutes.

Chapter 11

Grace's Sandy Bay break-ins might have gone unnoticed until early evening, except that the owner of the Sydney Long aquatint happened to slip home at lunchtime. He worked in downtown Hobart, he told the attending police constables, and discovered, late morning, that he'd left his mobile phone on the kitchen bench. 'Still plugged into the charger,' he said. 'Normally I wouldn't have bothered, but I needed a couple of numbers.'

He told the story again when the detectives arrived, taking their sweet time about it. Eventually those detectives arranged a door knock, and so a second break-in was discovered, and then the third, and the owners were notified, and, in halting and not very urgent stages, an investigation was mounted as the day progressed, a detective senior constable named Wilmot in charge.

Wilmot was making a sketch of the loft house grounds late that afternoon, the front door in relation to the driveway, garden beds and street, and noticed a man watching him from the other side of the road. A thin, taut wire of a man. Contained, snidely amused. Charcoal jacket, white shirt, jeans, walking shoes. Casual, but costly, and worn with assurance. Wilmot was thinking Sandy Bay toff, someone idle and pointless, when the stranger headed toward him and came through the gateway, not a care in the world.

'Excuse me, sir,' Wilmot said, 'this is a crime scene. I must ask you to leave.'

'She was wearing a tennis dress,' the man said, 'carrying a gym bag.'

Wilmot's mind scouted around for guidance and direction. 'Er, who was?'

'Your burglar.'

Before he could tell himself not to engage, Wilmot said decisively, 'Sorry to disappoint you, but it was a guy. He trod all over the garden in size elevens.'

The man offered a mild grin but there was a snake in it. 'It's what our girl does.'

'If you know anything about a crime, sir, I must ask you to—'

The newcomer wasn't listening. He turned side-on and gestured toward the end of the street. 'Check the pub on the corner. Their car-park camera. It catches her walking past the entrance at eight thirty-seven this morning, wearing tennis gear and carrying a gym bag. The cute, bouncy type. At nine fifteen A.M. she came by again, heading out.'

'You checked their CCTV? On what authority?'

The guy spun around, shot out his hand. 'Andy Towne. Got in at four-thirty.' He gave Wilmot the kind of grin that means nothing at all. 'Don't fly Virgin Blue, by the way.'

Hostility rose in Wilmot, and he ignored the hand. 'I don't give a rat's arse who you are or how you got here. Why you're here and what I'm going to do about it is another matter.'

Towne creased his face good-naturedly, but the eyes stayed flat. He struck Wilmot as someone on whom everything had an equal impact: small children, chaos, a visit to the dentist, blood letting.

'Mate? You hear me? How about you piss off, and let me do my job.'

Slipping a slender hand into an inside pocket, Towne waved identification at Wilmot, still wearing the smile. Wilmot saw a likeness of Towne and the words NATIONAL CRIME COMMISSION before the ID was secreted again.

Wilmot flushed. 'Whoopy do.' He felt inept and tongue-tangled. Andrew Towne, he sensed, had summed him up at first sight as a time-server. Or the cunt treated everyone with barely concealed contempt.

Wilmot looked away. The Derwent River had been flat and grey under the morning fog, then glinted briefly when the sun banded it. But the afternoon was drawing to a close now, the sun losing the fight to the mountains and a new fog shroud.

He turned to Towne again. 'Mate, all I'm looking at is a handful of simple burglaries. What makes it federal?'

Towne looked bored. 'We've been tracking this bitch for the past two years. She operates all over the country, always where the money is—Noosa, Port Douglas, North Shore, Adelaide Hills.' He nodded. 'Here in Sandy Bay.'

Wilmot absorbed that. 'You got here pretty quick.'

Towne offered one of his arid smiles. 'Our intel is good.'

Any information system could be programmed to raise a red flag, Wilmot knew. Depending on the parameters. 'She work alone?'

'Let's just say she's part of something loose and shadowy,' Towne said. 'ATM skimming, credit cards, identity theft, burglary to order, shoplifting raids.'

'Foreign gang?' said Wilmot.

Towne bared his teeth.

Wilmot snapped. 'So what do I do now?' Irritated. 'Kiss your sweet arse and go home?'

Towne crinkled his eyes again, but they remained as flat and fogged as the river.

Chapter 12

In the Chicory Kiln that evening, seated at a window overlooking vineyards on Myers Road, Pam Murphy read from the boxed paragraph on the front of the menu:

"'The Chicory Kiln—so called because there was once a chicory kiln where the bistro now stands—offers the ultimate in relaxed dining on the Peninsula, and. . .'" She glanced at Challis. 'Boss? Know what a chicory kiln is? Or chicory, for that matter?'

'Edible plant,' said Challis, his face dark and hawkish in the candlelight.

'And?'

'Rarely grown anymore.'

She cocked her head. 'Edible in what way?'

'Salad leaves and coffee.'

'Aha. Coffee. Hence your interest.'

The only coffee that Challis trusted was the coffee that he made. Wouldn't touch the canteen coffee. Always asked for tea if a doorknock witness offered coffee.

He smiled at her blithely. 'They used to roast and grind the roots. During World War II, it was added to coffee or used as a substitute.'

'Fascinating.'

Challis was unmoved. 'Early in my career I was posted to Phillip Island. Chicory kilns everywhere.'

Then she saw his face shut down, as if a shadow from his past had crept in. She'd heard the whispers over the years. He'd met his wife on the island, and she'd gone with him from one rural posting to another as he rose in the ranks. Then, somewhere in central Victoria, she'd started sleeping with one of his colleagues, and she'd conspired with her lover to kill Challis. Something about an anonymous call and a lonely bush track. The wife was dead now. Suicide in jail. The lover was due for parole in a year or so.

Pam thought about these things as she tore off a hunk of coarse bread and dunked it in a small bowl of olive oil. Local olive oil, according to the menu. She chewed the pungent bread, wiped her mouth and fingers.

'Have you ever drunk chicory coffee?'

Challis shuddered. 'God, no.'

Pam grinned, then glanced around the Chicory Kiln's interior, which evoked Tuscan villa, New England barn, and Bedouin fort in roughly equal parts: gnarled posts and beams, terracotta floor tiles, vaulted ceiling, whitewashed earthen walls. The diners sat at heavy wooden tables, cooled by ceiling fans in summer and warmed by an enormous stone fireplace in winter.

The diners, this Friday evening, were a mix of locals and weekender tourists. Young, middle-aged, old. Kids on a first date, a hen's party of shire office workers, the Waterloo postmaster and his wife, a family singing "Happy Birthday" to an ancient crone.

And Murphy and Challis, who'd come to question the staff and stayed for dinner.

Eva—German backpacker, twenty-six years old, charged with washing the Chicory Kiln's dishes, making the salads, sometimes clearing the tables—had talked to them during a cigarette break in the stinking air beside the bins in the rear

courtyard, smoke dribbling from her mouth. 'I am not knowing this girl Chloe so much. I am here three weeks only. I
make the oranges from the trees on the river, I serve the food
in Sydney, I cleaning houses in Byron Bay. That is all who I
am. I know nothing. I hope you catches this man. You see my
visa if you want.'

That was at 5:30 P.M. Over the next hour, as other staff arrived
for work, Murphy and Challis had taken them aside and asked
them the same questions. How well do you know Chloe Holst?
Did anyone ever visit her at the restaurant, take her home, meet
her in the car park after work or during a work break? Are you
aware of any confrontations between Chloe and a stranger, a customer or another member of staff? When did you last see her?
Where? What was she doing at that time?

The other waitresses, Kelly and Gabi, grew frightened and tear-
ful. Kelly was in Year 12 at Westernport Secondary College; Gabi
was on a gap year between school and university. Neither knew
much about the world beyond home, school, the Peninsula, and
the Chicory Kiln. They'd been vaguely aware that something had
happened to Chloe, but snatched? Raped? She was just so nice,
always friendly and cheerful. They looked out over the car park
with dark eyes and wrapped themselves inside their arms. Pam
asked how they were getting home.

'Dad,' said Kelly.

'My boyfriend,' said Gabi.

'Did anyone ever pick Chloe up after work?'

'She's got a car,' they said, forgetting Chloe briefly, thinking
about what a car would mean for them.

The boys who flicked around the kitchen, darting from cutting board to frying pan, freshly washed plate to pinned-up dinner orders, said they barely knew Chloe. 'Take a look around.
We're flat out. We'd divvy up the tips at the end of the night, say
goodbye, and that was that.'

Poor Chloe.

We barely knew her.

She hadn't been working here that long.

She was nice. A fun person.

She kept to herself a bit, but she wasn't, you know, a snob or anything.

It's so dark out there at night. The car park and that.

Myers Road is always a bit creepy at night.

Yeah, you get your perverts. They, like, put their hand on your hip while you're telling them the specials, even when their wife is sitting right there.

Look down your top and that.

Ask what time you get off work.

Complaints? Sure. Sometimes. You know, this fork's dirty, my meal's cold, this hasn't been cooked properly, if you think I'm giving you a tip you've got another thing coming—that kind of thing. No big deal.

Not enough to stalk and abduct and rape a girl over.

The owner-manager lived on the premises. She and her husband—retired accountant, liked to grow the Chicory Kiln's herbs and vegetables and manage the wine cellar—would clean up when everyone had gone, then unwind in front of the television, and last night had been no different. Skype conversation with their daughter in Salzburg. Studying violin.

'Any police officers ever come to the Chicory Kiln?' Challis asked.

'Police? Like, on a raid?'

'As customers.'

'Sure, I guess so, but how would we know? It's not as if this is a McDonald's; we're not handing out free hamburgers and chips to the boys in blue. No offence.'

And so Challis and Murphy stayed on for two more hours, eating dinner, talking, watching, making everyone nervous.

Pam had ordered gnocchi, Challis lasagne. 'How come you get yours straight away, and I have to wait?'

'They make each gnocchi ball lovingly by hand,' said Challis.

'Ha, ha. How come you always order lasagne?'

'I'm trying to replicate a formative experience, when I ate the perfect lasagne.'

'Okay, I'll bite—where and when?'

'Johnny's Green Room, Carlton. Late 1980s.'

'Was I even born then? And are you eating the perfect lasagne this evening?'

'Not even close.'

'What you might call a lost cause.'

It occurred to Pam Murphy that she was happy. She hadn't been happy. Last year she'd gone to bed with a fellow cop who'd posted naked images of her on the Internet. She'd destroyed him, the revenge sweet. Then some kind of reaction had set in, panic attacks, anxiety, jitteriness. And Pam Murphy—athlete, expert pursuit driver, competent detective—was not at ease with the fact that she hadn't been able to pull herself together.

She'd gone to her GP, who'd ascertained that she wasn't suicidal and prescribed citalopram. The anxiety went away, sure enough, but so did a lot of things. Pam Murphy considered her few months on the citalopram as lost months. A low-level dullness had ruled her. She lost her spark. She didn't even give a stuff about whether or not she had sex. And because she still had bad days sometimes, the anxiety returning, the GP had increased her dose from 20 mg to 40 mg per day. If that doesn't work, the GP said, we'll go to sixty, or try a new generation SSRI.

Not try to find out what was wrong, just up the dose.

So Pam had stopped, cold turkey, and right now she was feeling happy. Yeah, she was kind of attracted to Challis, but she didn't want to sleep with him. Besides, he was in love with Ellen Destry. It was the fact of sitting in candlelight with a nice man, a man she knew, a man who wouldn't hurt her or play games with her.

Challis glanced at his watch. 'I'm calling it a night.'

She wanted to say, 'Don't leave.' But it was eleven o'clock, and the dining room was empty. They paid, walked out into the moonlit car park, Challis standing very close to her, and she very aware of him as they watched the last cars leave one by one. No CCTV. She thought it likely the abduction had nothing to do with the Chicory Kiln and found herself saying, 'It was opportunistic.'

Challis said, 'Opportunistic choice of victim, but he stalked her first.'

'Yes.'

A tired-looking man arrived in a station wagon. Kelly hopped in, full of talk. A short time later, Gabi was picked up by a boy in a little Subaru, the car doof-doofing, the speakers almost shaking the car on its springs. When Gabi whispered in his ear, he turned the volume down, shot the detectives a scared look, and drove sedately out onto Myers Road.

Chapter 13

Challis lived on a dirt road inland of Waterloo and woke on Saturday morning to find an SMS from Ellen Destry: Arrvd Spore Yerp 2moro XXX.

Arrived Singapore, Europe tomorrow. Kisses. His spirits galvanised, he walked with vigour in the dawn light and planned his weekend. Doorknock the back roads where Chloe Holst was found this morning, talk to the aircraft broker this afternoon, do some odd jobs on Ellen's house tomorrow.

By 8:30 A.M. he was in his old Triumph, heading for the nature reserve where Chloe Holst had been dumped and thinking about a new car. The Triumph was a rustbucket, rattly and unreliable. Distinctive to look at and almost fun with the top down, but unreliable. He should sell it. Sell it and the plane, he could afford to buy a decent car. He'd miss the Triumph's dampish winds, though, its sensitivity to the Braille of every road surface.

There was a crime scene van at the reserve, two officers picking around the outskirts. There'd be others inside the reserve itself. He drove on until he'd reached the end of the road and turned into the first driveway.

A small kit house hung with potted plants, a handful of goats in a pen behind it. A young woman, vaguely hippie in a long skirt and leather sandals, with grimy ankles, answered his knock. She was sweetly effete, incense hanging in the fibres of her clothing, and she hadn't seen or heard anything.

The next house, half a kilometre along, was a severe arrangement of corrugated iron cubes that advertised itself as 'The Wellness Centre.' No one answered his knock.

No one at home at the next stop, either, a weatherboard house in a yard choked with trail bikes and dogs, the dogs all teeth, ribs, drool, and rusty chains. Then he came to a small brick house set in several hectares of unloved apple trees, where a raw-boned woman said viciously: 'Someone pinched our ride-on mower last month, and it took you lot a week to come out and have a bloody look. So no, I didn't see any bloody thing on Thursday night, all right?'

The last house before the T-intersection with the Dandenong-Waterloo road was announced by a rotting gate. A rotting mailbox, a weedy driveway that disappeared between the trunks of the highest pine trees Challis had ever seen. He opened the gate, drove through, closed it, and bounced the Triumph over ruts to a small fibro farmhouse so deep in the shadows that the walls wore moss. It looked diseased. Weeds spouted in the gutters. Thin hens pecked desultorily, and an old dog lifted and lowered its tail. There must be little houses like this all over the world, he thought. Rural America, rural Norway. It's where the old and the poor and the forgotten go to hide, in the only space they can navigate.

He got out and approached the house. Reaching the front step, he turned to get his bearings. The road was clearly visible: he simply felt like he was buried in the woods. He knocked, and after some time, an old man opened the door a crack, revealing one eye and a whiskery cheek. 'Good afternoon, sir,' Challis said, holding up his ID and saying he was from the police.

He didn't get a chance to say why he was there. The old man

disappeared into the gloom, returning a moment later with a spiral-bound notebook. 'What day?'

'I beg your pardon?'

'Nighttime? Daytime?'

He'd scribbled vehicle make and registration numbers in his notebook, together with times and dates. 'Thursday night,' Challis said.

'Thursday, Thursday. Sorry, I was at me daughter's.'

It didn't matter; Chloe Holst had been driven to the reserve in her own car. But her rapist might have scouted around in the days and weeks before snatching her, so Challis said: 'Your notebook could be very useful to the police. May we borrow it? I'll make a photocopy and return it on Monday.'

He was expecting resistance, but the man stuck out his chest and firmed his chin. 'Happy to help, happy to help.'

Challis took the proffered notebook, flipped through the pages, frowned and looked more closely at the scribbled information. 'These are all trucks and vans, not cars.'

'Well, obviously.'

'I don't follow.'

The old man couldn't believe Challis's ignorance. 'You don't think them people smugglers come into Western Port Bay with just one or two people aboard, do you?'

Chapter 14

Meanwhile, Pam Murphy had awoken feeling jittery, close to panic. That was nothing new. Some deep breathing helped; she avoided coffee.

But the dizziness was starting to bother her. She went online, Googling the withdrawal symptoms of her antidepressant, recalling the advice of her GP: 'I don't think you should quit, but I can see that's what you want, so make sure you phase out slowly, over several days.'

Several days? Hell, according to the Internet, that should have been several weeks, even months. Even then some chat-page respondents reported long periods of dizziness, mild auditory and visual hallucinations, something screwy with their eyes, itchy skin. And the special kind of dizziness she'd been feeling was called a 'brain zap.' Exactly right, she thought.

As for some of the antidepressants recommended by her doctor, some had been associated with suicides and murders in various parts of the world. The things the doctors don't tell you, she thought. The things they don't know.

She switched off and thought about the day. Challis wanted her to interview Chloe Holst again—but not at 6:30 in the morning. Checking the tide times, she strapped her surfboard to the

Subaru and headed to Point Leo, where she pulled on her wet-suit and paddled out to catch a few waves. The brain zap got her a couple of times, making her misjudge, spoiling her run into shore, but the surf, the sand, and the air itself were a tonic. And although she didn't speak to the other surfers, she felt a bond with them, with their boards under their ropy arms, sand on their powerful feet, a crusting of saltwater on their slender jaws.

By late morning she was starving. As she headed back to her rented house in Penzance Beach, she ran her mind around the contents of her fridge and considered the Balnarring supermarket on a Saturday morning. The obvious solution was a smoked salmon baguette from the Merricks General Store, before the car park filled with Melbourne Porsches and Audis.

The food settled her. She drove aimlessly for a while, thinking of her parents, thinking she should drive up to the city tomorrow, spend the afternoon with them. But when the time came, would she have the energy? They were old, querulous, stubborn, didn't know why she'd become a cop, wondered why—unlike her high-achieving brothers—she wasn't married.

Never in a million years would she tell them she'd been on antidepressants.

Then Dido was singing "White Flag" on her CD of illegal downloads, and she felt like crying. The only solutions were work and love. And given that she didn't have any love in her life, she thought it was time she did some work.

By 12:30 P.M. she was at the Waterloo Community Hospital, a small place, low and sleepy under gumtrees. Busy today, for some reason, with individuals, couples, and families walking to and from the car park, grouping in the foyer.

'It's often like this on weekends,' said the admissions clerk, a small, round, slyly humorous woman with frizzy hair, RACHEL on the badge pinned to her breast pocket. 'They get drunk and wake up on Saturday or Sunday morning with a broken arm or a shredded ear and no memory of how it happened.' She snorted with laughter. 'Or they wake thinking, "Look! A sunshiny spring morning, I must do some mowing or slashing or chainsawing. I must climb onto the roof and clean out the gutters."' She shook her head. 'And don't get me started on Father's Day, Christmas Day. . . .'

The woman was a tonic to Pam. They grinned at each other, kindred spirits. They both had jobs helping people in distress, and therefore a full repertoire of stories of stupidity and ingratitude.

Just then a man staggered in. A huge, white, hairy apparition of tiny, bum-crack shorts, a wife-beater singlet, and rolls of porcine flesh, holding a bloodied hand to his chest. His face was petulant and needy. 'Need some help here,' he bellowed. His family pressed in behind him. A cowed wife; hot, avid children.

Rachel and Murphy leaned automatically toward each other. 'Chainsaw,' Pam murmured.

'Pruning shears.'

'Not the bloke's fault.'

'Of course not,' Rachel said. 'His tool's to blame.'

A quick, shared snigger, then Rachel worked a vivid smile onto her face and called across the foyer, 'Yes, sir, let's get someone to take a look at you.'

Pam nodded goodbye and headed down the corridor to Chloe Holst's room. She found a middle-aged woman sitting beside the bed, handing the girl a tissue. 'I'm sorry, I'll come back another time.'

Holst managed an exhausted laugh and sank into her pillow. 'It's not what you think. Wherever I was the other night, it's given me hay fever. Pam, this is my mum.' She was pinkly damp around the nose and eyes.

'Chloe suffers dreadfully from hay fever,' the woman said, 'just like her dad.'

'Mrs. Holst.'

Pam had been in situations that played out like a cheap novel, the anguished parent demanding, 'Have you found the monster who did this to my daughter?' but Chloe's mother was content to prattle on about her daughter's allergies until Chloe said, 'Mum, for God's sake, it's not important.'

Finally, responding to her daughter's cues, Mrs. Holst gathered her bag. 'I'll just be in the cafeteria.'

'Thanks, Mum.'

The younger women watched her go then looked at each other, smiling.

'Sorry, she always talks a lot when she's upset.'

'She has plenty to be upset about, and so do you.'

'I'm okay. I'm alive.'

But looking exhausted and diminished, Pam thought. She pondered the damage she couldn't see.

Chloe was racked with sneezes again. 'Remind me never to get a job outdoors. The tiniest bit of pollen and I—'

Pollen. Pam made a mental note, then they talked for a while. But Chloe added nothing new to her account of the attack, or the man who had done it.

Chapter 15

Challis checked in with the crime scene officers at the reserve, then headed for the little airport a few kilometres north of Waterloo.

He ruminated on the past ten years, all that had been transitory and permanent. He'd been a solitary figure, a little lonely and probably sad, when he'd taken up the position of CIU head at Waterloo. New to the Peninsula and still stunned by the knowledge that his wife and her lover had wanted him dead. A chance visit to the local air show had rekindled an interest from his childhood—a time of balsawood kit planes and spotting for the crop dusters on the hilly paddocks of the South Australian wheat country. Dreams in which he floated above the ground.

Entranced by the vintage aeroplane display, he'd let it be known that he'd like to buy one, preferably unrestored. Six months later, he bought a 1930s Dragon Rapide which was gathering dust and a colony of rats and mice in a hayshed outside Toowoomba.

In the years that followed he spent his spare time, his blessed quiet hours, tracking down missing parts, engineering others. Ten years of snatched afternoons and weekends, ten years of hangar and machine-tool hire, ten years of outlaying all his spare cash. But ten years of mental and physical relief from the dirt he walked in every day. As he'd restored the Dragon, the Dragon restored him. And she was beautiful, an elegant silver dragonfly.

Now he simply saw the Dragon as a phase of his life that had come to an end.

A truck load of timber held him up outside Waterloo. It was turning into a low-lying paddock on the left, a housing estate named Copley Downs, still under construction and at this stage just an open mire of culverts, heavy tyre tracks, concrete slabs, and skeletal house frames on senseless curved streets. Challis thought about what he'd said to the reporter yesterday afternoon. Young, cash-strapped families would move in to Copley Downs and put pressure on the local services, including the police. As for the name, Copley had been a stalwart of the football club, a man who spent his time drinking and bashing his wife. Having played half a season of League football however, he was a local celebrity. The world we live in, Challis thought.

He drove through a stretch of farmland to the outskirts of Tyabb: some straggling pine trees, a weather-beaten girl-guide hall, a sad strip of shops, a solitary traffic light. A bus and half a dozen cars were stopped for the red. Challis braked gently, and the Triumph stalled. He started it, nursed the accelerator. The old car shuddered, and then he was at the intersection, turning left.

Now he was passing a scattering of bungalows, the airfield beyond that, rambling antique shops on his right. Tyabb owed some of its reputation to the airfield and the annual air show but was better known as a mecca for anything old. Most of the dealers operated out of a massive converted railway workshop, others out of houses, sheds and barns situated on the main roads of the town. Challis slowed the car and pulled into the driveway of an old church. A sign on the picket fence said THE DOLL'S HOUSE COLLECTIBLES FINE ART ANTIQUES W. & M. NIEKIRK PROP. Beneath it was another sign: NIEKIRK CLASSICS, with stylised images of an old plane and an old car.

He got out. He could hear a distant aero engine. A young woman appeared in the doorway, slightly plump, cheery, under-dressed, jiggling a three-year-old girl on one hip. 'Can I help you?'

'Are you Mrs. Niekirk?'

The girl got a kick out of that. 'I'm Tayla, the nanny. Mrs. Niekirk's up at the airport.'

She didn't know about Mr. Niekirk, so Challis thanked her and headed to the airfield, entering via a slip road that led to a gate and a collection of admin buildings and hangars. He was tempted to check on his Dragon, but resisted. He steered around the perimeter, passing a dozen parked Cessnas and Pipers, to a couple of hangars on the far side. He pulled up against the side wall of the first hangar. A wooden sign above a small door read NIEKIRK.

He got out, yawned, stretched the kinks out of his spine, con-sciously holding back. He was a tall man, probably underweight, and still wore the tired pallor of a long winter and longer hours. Part of him wondered, as he spotted a Beechcraft make a bank-ing turn above farmland at the far end of the landing strip, if he was about to take a step that he might regret. The plane flat-tened out, came in shallowly over the access road, and touched down neatly. Nothing new, yet Challis watched with a childlike pleasure.

He stepped around to the front of the building and halted in his tracks. Two flatbed trucks were parked there, a front-end loader. Beyond them, in the dim interior, a huddle of overall-clad men were scratching their heads beneath a looming World War II warplane. Bristol Beaufighter, thought Challis automati-cally, admiring the stubby, menacing shape. Long-range fighter-bomber, designed in Britain and built in Australia, deemed 'whispering death' by the Japanese.

The Beaufighter claimed most of the space, both engines thrusting forward of the bulbous snout like a crab's claws. He walked along the left flank, overhearing one of the men say, 'Dismantle the wings first? Tailplane?'

Challis could see an office in the corner. Behind the plane, stacked here and there against the walls, there were old wardrobes, colonial-era sideboards, antique chairs with moth-riddled upholstery. The hangar was a useful space if you were a second-hand dealer with an overflow of stock.

The office door was open, a woman standing at a filing cabinet. Hearing his footsteps on the cold concrete floor, she turned to face him. She was tall, angular, about forty, wearing a loose white shirt over black tights, a little harried-looking as she peered at him over maroon designer frames. 'May I help you?'

'Mrs. Niekirk?' he asked, conscious that he sounded like a policeman.

She seemed to flare up. 'I've had it with you people. We're complying with that order.'

Challis held up both hands. 'I'm sorry, I'm not here about any order.'

She went very still and waited, tense under the surface. 'What can I do for you,' she said flatly.

'My name is Hal Challis, and I own an old aeroplane, and I'm thinking of—'

A narrow hand went to her throat. Challis saw small chips of gold there, gold on her fingers and earlobes, too. And a flicker of dark emotions. 'Sorry to disappoint you,' she said, barely moving her mouth, 'but my husband is going out of the aircraft business.'

'Oh. That's a shame.'

With an effort, the woman shook off whatever had been affecting her. Her voice a low, pleasant rasp leavened with a smile, she offered her hand and said, 'Mara Niekirk. Please forgive me, I sounded harsh.'

'That's okay.'

'The thing is, we had our fingers burnt recently. Do you see that heap of junk out there? The men and the trucks?'

And Challis thought at once: The Beaufighter's being repossessed. 'Yes.'

'My husband has a sideline business, brokerage. He puts people who have a classic car or aeroplane to sell in touch with people who want to buy one. But this time'—she gestured at the plane beyond the office door—'he thought he'd be buyer and seller himself. More profit, you see. He even had a UK client lined up, prepared to pay a hundred thousand pounds sterling. The next thing you know, the federal government steps in and says the deal can't go ahead. Fifty thousand dollars down the drain.'

'Ouch.'

'Needless to say, I'm a little cross.'

Challis didn't ask where the husband was. In the doghouse somewhere. Instead, he asked why the Beaufighter couldn't be exported.

'According to the officious little bureaucrat who slapped the order on us, that damn plane has cultural heritage significance. If Warren tries to ship it overseas, it will be confiscated, and he'll be hit with a heavy fine, even jail time.'

Challis jerked his head at the trucks. 'So you've found a local buyer?'

Mara Niekirk grimaced. 'It doesn't rain but it pours. It seems the man who sold us the plane may not have had rightful ownership of it.'

'It's being confiscated?'

Mara Niekirk held up a finger. 'Repatriated is the word they used. It's going to the War Memorial in Canberra, and when the ownership issues are thrashed out, we'll get a tax break under the cultural gifts program. Did you know such a thing existed? I didn't.'

Challis stored the information, Mara Niekirk watching him steadily over the rims of her glasses. 'Which is not the same thing as getting our money back.'

'Can't you sue?'

'Hah!'

So the man who'd sold it to them can't be found, or he's broke, guessed Challis. He eyed the metal walls, hung with a number of prints and drawings: a Charles Blackman schoolgirl; a Brian Dunlop print of an open, curtained window; a matched trio of Brett Whiteley artist's proofs; an homage to Van Gogh.

Mara Niekirk, watching Challis appraise them, blew a tendril of brown hair away from her nose. 'This room needed a certain something.'

'So, no more dealing in aeroplanes.'

'Or vintage cars, my husband's other side interest.'

Challis gave her a crooked smile. 'Pity. I also have an old Triumph sports car I want to get rid of.'

She returned the smile. 'Can't help you.'

Chapter 16

Until a year or two ago, Sundays had been a sacred day for Scobie Sutton—sacred in the holy-day sense and sacred in a family-spending-the-day-together sense. A bit of a sleep-in, late morning church—Sunday School for Roslyn—and the afternoon for visiting his wife's mother and sister, or an excursion to Healesville animal sanctuary, or catching up on household chores, gardening, and homework—hoping that God didn't mind.

But Beth had lost her job and with it, it seemed, something of herself. Their church being less than helpful, she'd turned to a crackpot sect known as the First Ascensionists. She'd tried to gather Scobie and Roslyn to the fold, and when that failed she'd turned her back on her little family for a while.

She was better—a lot better than she had been—but now she spent her days abjectly saying, 'Can you ever forgive me?' and 'You must hate me.' It was wearisome. She phoned Scobie at work several times a day; she hovered in the doorway whenever Roslyn did her homework or practised on the electric piano in the evenings.

Father and daughter had the patience of saints; and at least they were out of the house during the daytime hours of the working week. Weekends were different. There was absolutely no escaping the heavy weight of Beth's presence. And so it came as a great relief to them when Beth's mother and sister had stepped in, offering to take her off their hands on Sundays.

And this Sunday, alone with his daughter at last, Scobie mopped up the maple syrup with the remains of his Sunday morning pancake and said, 'Thought we'd go to the zoo today, see the new baby elephant.'

Roslyn was thirteen, and her face sometimes—often?—fell into the disobliging lines of young adolescence, but right at that moment she was a little girl. Her eyes lit up. 'Yay!'

She was a light in his murky world. Sutton knew that he wasn't like Challis or Murphy, could never be like them. Yeah, they probably found some crimes upsetting, but they'd long stopped revealing it, and he was certain that many police officers didn't get upset with any of it. Never had, never would. Their attitude was simple: Some humans are scum, and it's our job to put them away, not save, understand, or heal them. Not bleed as the victims have bled. A victim was a statistic, that's all. But Sutton, arresting a Mornington man for inserting a beer bottle and a pool cue into an elderly woman's vagina last week, had wept. Would he be better off not coming face-to-face with murderers and rapists, thugs and bullies? He'd spent Friday afternoon and most of yesterday with the crime scene officers, conducting a line search of the reserve and signing for and transporting the evidence to the forensics lab. He'd enjoyed that. But he was a frontline detective and working the Chloe Holst case was bound to sink him further into the mire.

Driving his daughter around was the cure he needed, and half an hour later they were heading toward the city, Scobie steering his sensible Volvo up through Somerville and Baxter. But you can't control everything. Before he could do a thing about it, they were alongside a gateway freshly defaced with the words AN ERECTION TO MATCH MY IMAGE OF MY DICK.

Too late, he said, 'Don't look,' and his daughter said, 'Da-a-ad,' as if she'd grown up quite suddenly when he wasn't paying attention and left him behind.

CHALLIS HAD SPEND THE night in Ellen's house so that he could get an early start on his list of odd jobs.

Stained the deck first. This time on Friday he'd been sitting out here with Ellen, feeling a kick of desire.

Painted the laundry room.

Aching muscles stopped him at lunchtime. He stepped outside to stretch the kinks in his back, saw the garden hose lying there, and decided to wash the dust off his car. The Triumph's soft top was cracked, the rear Perspex milky, and Challis realised halfway through that he'd find water on the floor and seats when he got behind the wheel.

He stood for a while, his gaze roving from the droplets on his car to the glassy bay. He liked standing here, in the mild sun. He didn't want to leave. There was a ship on the water, sharp and motionless as if snipped from tin.

He went inside, showered, changed, and locked Ellen's doors and windows. Just as he was climbing into his car, he heard the shudder of poorly tuned suspension behind him, the crush of tyres. He got out. A tired, sun-faded green Hyundai was nosing into the driveway, something about it seeming to express indignation with his presence, his car's presence, even before he recognised the driver. Eventually the little car spurted close to the front steps, leaving him barely enough room to back out.

The driver got out and scowled. 'Mum didn't say you'd be here.'

'How are you, Larrayne?'

He'd never quite warmed to Ellen's daughter, perhaps because he seemed always to put her in a bad temper. He didn't know if

she hated him, resented him, wanted her mother to have no
private life, or wanted her parents back together again. The last
was unlikely.

The passengers were piling out of the Hyundai: a young man
from the front seat—Larrayne's boyfriend?—and a young couple
from the rear. All four looked bleary, the men unshaven and the
women streaked and bruised with mascara and lipstick. The men
wore stained jeans and tight shirts over T-shirts, the buttoning
hit-and-miss, and the women wore crumpled, tugged-about little
dresses over holed tights. As they stood, stretched, yawned, and
looked around at the house, the view, Challis caught an eddy of
alcohol, cigarettes, and dope.

'Long night?'

'Any of your business?'

The boyfriend touched Larrayne's forearm as if to calm her.
He was a tall, skinny, sweetly smiling boy, probably good for Larrayne and probably doomed. 'Semester break,' he told Challis.

Challis nodded.

'We were hoping,' Larrayne Destry said, 'to spend a few days
here.'

Meaning what did Challis think he was doing there, and did
he intend to stick around all week, and, generally, what gave him
the fucking right?

Challis gave her a high-wattage smile for the pleasure of it and
said, 'I'll be out of your hair in just a moment.'

'Are you living here now or something?'

Challis shook his head, still with the smile. 'Just doing some
odd jobs around the place. Be careful of wet paint.'

Larrayne frowned over his words as if looking for lies and
loopholes. Finding none, she wheeled around and opened the
boot of the car. Without the scowl, she was simply a twenty-one-
year-old student, ordinary in a fair-haired, fine-boned, Ellen
Destry's-daughter kind of way.

Challis stuck one of his cards under her windscreen wiper. 'If you need anything.'

'We won't.'

SUNDAY WAS NOT A day of rest for Grace. She'd spent the afternoon at an Internet café in Geelong, downloading a few megabytes of Google Earth onto a flash drive. Inconvenient, but untraceable. Now, late afternoon, she was at home in Breamlea, examining the maps on her own laptop. By dusk she knew the exact location of a house in South Australia's Clare Valley owned by a man named Simon Lascar, knew it in relation to his neighbours and the town itself, knew her best escape routes.

As for knowing about Lascar and his house, she thanked her collection of clippings from *Home Digest, Home Beautiful, Décor,* and similar magazines. In her view, these publications existed to allow people with more money than sense to tell the world about how much money they had in the house they'd built, bought, or refurbished—in full colour, over several pages, including close-ups of small, pricey belongings.

What *Home Digest* didn't say—but various websites did—was that Mr. Simon Lascar had built his Clare Valley monstrosity on the site of a colonial-era cottage of historical importance, using two million dollars embezzled from pensioners' savings. The magazine did say that he was an eclectic collector of Australiana: an Adelaide gold pound worth $300,000; a 1930 penny—unfortunately not one of the six proof pennies still in existence but one of the 2,000 that had found their way into circulation—worth $25,000; a 1620 Dutch rijksdaalder from the wreck of the Batavia worth $1,500; a third watermark, two shilling stamps (a kangaroo superimposed upon a map of Australia) worth $4,000; a first edition of J. J. Keneally's 1929 *The Inner History of the Kelly Gang,* worth $2,000; a two-shilling note issued for use in the Hay internment camp during World War

II, worth $5,000; and a $30,000 Holey Dollar struck from a 1794 Spanish dollar.

And his wife liked to collect silver. Sterling, not plate: flatware, teaspoons, demitasse spoons, toddy ladles, fish servers, sugar bowls, napkin rings, and candlesticks. Grace was betting there'd be some crap too—mass-produced plate or pieces with no maker's mark—but she knew how to separate it from the good stuff. In the past two years, since escaping from Galt, she'd spent hours on the Internet and in libraries, studying makers' marks, vintages, hallmarks, and other distinguishing features of antique sterling silver.

Some of Grace's magazine clippings went back months, even years. Some she might never act on; a clipping was rarely enough, in itself, to give her all the information she needed. As for the Lascar story, she'd clipped it out two years ago and was only moving now because she'd spotted another Lascar story: According to the latest *Who Weekly*, the Lascars were in Honolulu for the marriage of their daughter to a minor American actor and would be away for three weeks.

As afternoon faded that Sunday, Grace walked along the beach at Breamlea and planned the hit on Lascar. She was alone, and the waters raced toward her flank, and the wind howled hard against her back. She reversed direction. Now the wind was gritty, stinging her face and hands. The seabirds fought it, wheeling like paper scraps. She altered course to avoid a dead seal, then veered inland, up and down a canyon in the dunes, finally emerging near the general store at the entrance to the caravan park before walking back along the road toward her house. Drive to South Australia on Wednesday, she thought, hire a car in Murray Bridge on Thursday, clean out the Lascars that night, return to Victoria early Friday morning. Fence some of the gear to Steve Finch around lunchtime, stow the best in her safe-deposit box in Waterloo that same afternoon.

And, as she walked, Ian Galt's harsh voice scraped across her mind: 'Always know that you can walk away from a job, even if you've invested a lot of time and money in setting it up.'

Rules, rules. . . .

Chapter 17

Eight A.M. Monday, Challis checking his pigeonhole for mail. A shift was going off duty, another coming on, so the main corridor was hectic, uniformed and plainclothed police and civilian staff shouldering in and out of doors, balancing files, equipment belts, canteen tea and coffee. Since Friday he'd received several memos and a handful of flyers, most of which he tossed into the recycle bin before heading upstairs. An officer from the sex crimes squad was due, but she was coming down from the city, and Challis had no idea when she'd arrive.

As always, he brewed coffee in the tearoom, making enough for Scobie Sutton and Pam Murphy, who were not in yet. After that he sat, thinking, in his corner office.

The Triumph had been difficult to start that morning, and the idea of selling had grown firmer in his mind. There was bound to be a Triumph nut somewhere in Australia, willing to fork out for an elderly TR4—but the car was probably worth very little, and if, like the Niekirks, he wasn't allowed to sell his plane, he'd never be able to afford a new car.

Challis sipped his coffee and swivelled in his chair, using his feet on the open bottom drawer of his desk as leverage. The outer offices were quiet. He checked his watch, idled a while, then jerked forward and typed 'Trading Post' into Google, waited five years for the site to load, and made an Australia-wide search of TR4 prices.

Christ. One car in the whole country, fully restored, low mileage on a new motor, new everything, asking price $35,000. Surely his old bomb would fetch at least twenty?

He continued to idle, listening to voices and footsteps. Pam Murphy arrived, stuck her head around his door, grinned and chatted. They never ran their tongues for long. She disappeared into the tearoom, and then Sutton was knocking, saying, 'Someone from sex crimes at the front desk.'

'Thanks. You and Murph wait in the briefing room.'

Challis headed downstairs, pausing for a moment to gauge the visitor on the other side of the glass before he stepped through to the foyer. He saw a young woman with long black hair and stylish black-rimmed glasses, dressed in a cotton jacket over tight jeans and a T-shirt. She also wore the fatigue of long hours, but that vanished when Challis was buzzed through. She seemed to spark with energy, sticking out her hand, giving her name as Jeannie Schiff, sergeant. And she stared at Challis, a sizing-up.

'Thanks for coming down,' Challis said. 'As I said on the phone, our sexual offences team isn't in place yet, so we could do with some help.'

'Well, yeah,' drawled Schiff. 'Abduction and rape? A bit different from some sad bloke waving his penis at schoolgirls.' Her voice was raspy, low, not unpleasant, but sharp underneath.

Challis shrugged mentally and said, 'My team's upstairs.'

She followed him. He paused outside the briefing room. 'Tea? Coffee? Proper coffee.'

'You wouldn't have green tea?'

Challis wouldn't have had green tea before Pam Murphy joined CIU. Now the teabag jar was crammed with exotic brews. 'No problem.'

The tea made, he introduced her to Sutton and Murphy and stepped back to prop up one of the side walls. The morning sun striped the long briefing room table. On the other side of the window he could see the treetops that marked the rear of the car park.

Schiff took command of the room, standing at the head of the table. All that had been tense, uncertain, or vigilant about her had disappeared, replaced by an air of calm authority, a routine determination. She'd been through this before and knew how it would play out.

'We'll work this on several fronts,' she announced, without preamble. 'Witnesses, if any, local sex offenders, forensics, victimology.'

The morning sun was coming in hard behind her. She was a hazy shape, and seeing his officers wince and shade their eyes, Challis stepped behind her and released the venetian blind. It fell with a clatter.

Schiff ignored him. He leaned his shoulder against the wall again.

'I'm due in court this afternoon,' Schiff said, glancing at her watch, 'so this will be a racing visit, to get you started. I'll be back tomorrow, and then I can give you until the end of the week, okay?' She didn't pause to find out. 'Right. Three main areas to action. First, do we have a list of local sex offenders? We need to start knocking on doors tomorrow.'

She cast an interrogative look at Challis, who said, 'Constable Murphy will do that.'

Schiff flashed Pam a smile. 'Next, the cop angle bothers me. Why would a police member announce himself? Did he hope to intimidate? Well, it did intimidate, but did he think Ms. Holst would be too scared to tell police that she'd been raped by a police officer? I need someone to run a nationwide search of similar cases, cross-referenced against police who have been arrested, charged, jailed, or suspected of sex offences and against police officers whose ID or uniforms have been stolen recently.'

Scobie Sutton raised his hand. 'I'll do that.'

'Good, thank you. Next, Ms. Holst herself. Her movements last Thursday night, workmates, family, friends, old and current and wannabe boyfriends. . . . I want to know who she is, in other words. Look at Facebook and Twitter to see if anyone had it in for her. Any altercations at work, pissed-off workmates and customers.'

Challis uncoiled from the wall. 'Constable Murphy and I have been working on that.'

Schiff gave a vivid smile. 'Terrific. Maybe we'll get a result sooner than expected. Meanwhile, forensics. Early days yet, I imagine.'

Scobie Sutton stirred. 'Preliminary results are in. Plenty of fibres and prints in and on the victim's car, but no way of knowing whose.'

'No hits in Crimtrac?'

'Not yet.'

'Anything at the scene?'

'Ice-cream wrappers, plastic bags, Coke bottles, the usual.'

'Anything on the victim?'

Here Sutton squirmed. 'He cleaned her up, unfortunately. He used a condom, popular brand, according to the spermicide.'

He coughed to clear his throat. His words had conjured images that Sutton, who had been a detective for twelve years, couldn't cope with.

'Thank you, Constable. I wonder about the cleaning up he did. A policeman? Someone who watches CSI on TV?'

They didn't have an answer for her.

Pam Murphy seemed about to add to the discussion but slumped in her seat again. The morning was deepening outside the police station.

Chapter 18

Elsewhere in the police station, John Tankard was changing into his uniform and facing down smirks. The guys had heard what happened last Friday, the naked chick appearing out of the bushes and screaming at the sight of him. Thank Christ it had been cleared up quickly. He hadn't abducted and raped anyone. But, as he gave each of his mates the finger, he couldn't help wondering: Did you do it? Or you?

Then, to cap off this brilliant start to the day, he was told to report to the Traffic Management Unit. 'They want you for an RBT.'

A random breath test campaign. 'Jesus, Sarge, not again.'

Tankard was an old hand in the ranks of uniformed constables at Waterloo. Mostly, he roamed around in the divisional van, answering calls. Throwing drunks out of bars, arresting a wife who'd stuck a knife in her husband or vice versa, handing out on-the-spot fines for jaywalking.

But now and then he was seconded to Traffic. The TMU was always engaged in some blitz against motorists: drink driving, unregistered vehicles, speeding, failure to wear a seatbelt. . . . A unit of ten officers, but there was always someone in court, on holiday or down with the flu, so guys like Tank took up the slack.

'Your local knowledge and sparkling personality, Tank.'

'Yeah, thanks, Sarge.'

John Tankard was pink and sweaty. Short hairs sprouted from the fleshy rolls above his collar, his heavy damp limbs pushed at the seams of his uniform. He didn't welcome too much action on the job, yet his chief impression of his last RBT, earlier in the year, was of incredible boredom. Even shifting location every few hours had only amounted to a few minutes of activity. Mostly an RBT consisted of standing around in the sun or the rain with your finger up your bum, hoping some idiot would try to dodge the breathalyser or pick a fight.

'Now?'

'Right away.'

Tank hauled out leathers, cap, and yellow jacket from the storage locker, balanced his sunglasses on the visor of the cap, and joined the others in the Traffic briefing room on the ground floor. The window caught the morning sun and flashed from the windscreens creeping along the McDonald's drive-through on the other side of High Street. Big mistake, spotting Macca's: now he felt hungry. He moved his gaze to the kerb outside the police station where the Unit's patrol cars and motorbikes stood in full, snarling livery, waiting to terrorise the good citizens of the Peninsula.

Weariness took the place of hunger, and he dragged his eyes away. He glanced around at the other officers: all men, all young, all petrol heads. They loved the storm-trooper gear, the cars and bikes, as Tank himself had once. But he was thirty now, and he felt old here, in this room, with these guys.

The briefing started. It was a pep talk, as if the Unit C.O. had seen too many war movies. He slapped one hand into the palm of the other as he spoke:

'A vital job, gentlemen. Three fatalities on the whole of the Peninsula last year, six so far this year.

'And it's spring—season of love, boozy lunches, winery tours, and eighteen-year-olds finishing their exams. Lovely. But not to be seen as excuses for stupid behaviour on the open road. Zero tolerance, gentlemen. Let's get the dills off the road.

'So we'll set up on hills, we'll set up on corners and bends, and we'll be out every day for the rest of the week. And just when the locals get wind of us in one location, we'll move to another—only to return a couple of days later, same road, different hill or bend.

'Keep them on their toes, guys, okay?'

His words fired the young ones. One of them even whooped. Tank looked out at the street again, the pursuit cars festooned with antennas and stripes, and wondered if he'd be given the chance to drive one. It was usually his job to say, 'Blow into this, please, sir,' not give chase in a fast car. Strangely, sir or madam would always show a moment's hesitation, a flicker of disquiet, as if they had something to hide. Maybe they were scared of germs.

'Another thing,' said the Traffic boss. He passed around a stack of A4-sized photographs. 'Be on the lookout for this guy.'

A grainy shot of a guy carrying a shotgun, face averted, beanie pulled low over his brow. 'Robs banks,' the Traffic boss said. 'Apparently he's headed this way.'

Chapter 19

Tuesday, publication day, and by 8 A.M. Challis was lifting a copy of the *News-Pictorial* from a wire rack outside the news agency on High Street. He read it in the car.

Jack Porteous had been circumspect with the abduction and rape, at one point writing, 'an unconfirmed report that a man wearing a police uniform.' Challis supposed that was better than an outright accusation and turned to the reporter's second story.

Again, fair, accurate reporting. Challis had said all the things Porteous reported him as saying. The thing was the reporter had given more weight to Challis's unimpressed view of the state government and police command than his list of daily operational concerns.

Challis gnawed at the inside of his mouth. With any luck, the story would fizzle out. He was only an inspector, the newspaper only a local weekly. If anything he said was thought to matter, Porteous's mates on the Melbourne dailies would have called him by now.

He started the car, drove to the police station and found a silver Holden slewed crosswise in the senior officers' section. He pulled the Triumph into a space beside the dump bin at the rear.

When he switched off, the motor ran on with asthmatic wheezing, smoke, and a last heaving shudder.

'Ah, the smell of unburnt fuel in the morning,' John Tankard
said, watching him. 'The rattle of misfiring cylinders.'

Challis got out. 'This is a classic of British motoring, John.'

'Classic of something, anyway.'

Tankard was ready to hit the road with the RBT team, but
clearly had something else on his mind. He coughed, toed the
potholed asphalt. 'Read what you said about resources and manpower, sir,' he said shyly. 'You hit the nail on the head.'

Challis thanked him and entered the station through the rear
doors, wondering how others would see the story. Plenty of side-
long looks, a couple of nods and smiles. But no one said anything
as he walked down the main corridor to check his pigeonhole—
the usual crap—and the overnight log. A handful of burglaries,
bar fights, car thefts, but nothing resembling abduction and
rape. He signed out the CIU Falcon, brought it around to the
car park exit, and waited for Scobie Sutton to arrive.

WHEN PAM MURPHY REACHED work that morning, there was
a Post-It note on her desk, asking her to meet the sex crimes
sergeant in the car park at the rear of the police station. She
found Jeannie Schiff fiddling with a mobile phone beside an
unmarked silver Holden, the car at a haphazard angle across the
slots marked SUPERINTENDENT and INSPECTOR.

'Where first?' asked Schiff, barely looking up from the screen
of her phone.

Pam had spent yesterday working on the sex offenders
list. Glancing now at the folder of names, she said, 'Laurance
Matchan in Penzance Beach.'

They got into the car. Schiff said, 'Point the way' and spurted
toward the exit.

And there was Challis, propped patiently against the driver's door of the CSU car. Schiff pulled up alongside him, Pam powered down her window. 'Morning, boss.'

'Constable,' said Challis with a nod. 'Sergeant.'

'Inspector.'

'Off to talk to scumbags?'

Pam nodded. Tiptoeing a little, she said, 'Er, you haven't read the local paper by any chance?'

Challis crossed his arms. 'Completely different Inspector Challis.'

'That's what I thought. See you later, boss.'

'Good luck.'

Schiff accelerated out onto the main road. 'What was he on about?'

Pam shifted in her seat. Choosing her words, she said, 'The weekly paper ran a story quoting him on police under-resourcing.'

Schiff shrugged; she didn't care. 'What do we know about Laurance Matchan?'

Pam opened her folder. Matchan, she said, had managed a group home for four men and one woman with intellectual disabilities in Mornington. 'When he realised the men were fighting each other to have sex with the woman, he drew up a roster, but before long he was having sex with her too. At trial he argued the sex was consensual, and anyway he'd saved the men from having to visit prostitutes. He got out six months ago.'

'What a charming fellow,' said Schiff, speeding through Waterloo. 'Who else?'

Pam leafed through the files, rattling off a series of outlines. Most of the local sex offenders were small fry, their crimes considered minor by the courts—lewd conduct, carnal knowledge of a minor, fondling and groping—and she'd had to decide which of them were capable of graduating to abduction and rape. She'd been able to rule some out—three were aged in their late '70s, a couple were borderline mentally disabled and couldn't drive—but there were still quite a few. In the end, she'd used her instincts. If a man looked like a brute in his mug shot, she prioritised him. She also paid close attention to those who lived near the reserve, owned a car, and might have access to police equipment and forensic knowhow. A Somerville ambulance driver, for example. It wasn't very scientific, but she didn't tell Schiff that.

Soon they were passing through open farmland, some of the paddocks cropped for hay, the unmown grass flexing in long, rolling waves as the wind passed over it. Schiff was silent, unreadable, and Pam found herself saying, 'Sarge, do you think it *will* turn out to be a cop?'

'Entirely possible.'

Pam subsided. The police were often maligned, with or without good reason, and this would make it worse. COP RAPIST? That had been the headline in Saturday's *Herald Sun*. If the rapist was a cop, he deserved to be found, tried, and punished, but Pam would hate to be in the middle of all that. The police boys' club would chew her up and spit her out if she crossed it in any way; yet she could feel as protective of her colleague as the next officer. Us against them, the police against the rabble.

Meanwhile she had to spend the day with a woman who gave every appearance of impatience and boredom, as if a rural investigation were beneath her. They rode in silence until Pam stirred and said, 'Next left.'

Penzance Beach was at the end of a side road that ran off Frankston-Flinders Road, and as they drew near, she wondered whether to tell Schiff that she lived there, in a little house opposite a chicken farm at the poorer edge of the town.

'This is where I live, coincidentally.'

'Yeah? Not friends with Laurence Matchan, are you?'

'No.'

'Nothing to worry about, then,' Schiff said, looking about as they entered the little settlement. 'Pretty place.'

This was the heart of the town: fibro shacks on stilts, log cabins, weatherboard cottages—humble holiday and permanent homes on small blocks, all of it squeezed into a small space between the bay waters and a long ridge. Schiff followed the road as it curved around parallel to the beach, slowing for speed bumps, until Pam said, 'Turn right.'

Now the road climbed up on to the ridge, where the big money lived, in huge houses that clawed for air space giving uninterrupted views of the sea. Behind them were dwellings smaller than the cliff-top mansions but larger than the sea-level cottages, the homes of prosperous family doctors, accountants, teachers, electricians. And that's where Murphy and Schiff found Laurence Matchan, in a plain old farmhouse that faced the grasslands behind the town, set in a weedy garden shaded by a giant palm tree.

Matchan answered the door. He was middle-aged, comfortable rather than fat, thick hair threaded with silver, some acne scarring. A crumpled tan suit over a light blue shirt; dark blue tie knot an enormous wedge under his chins. A grey, fatigued cast to his face, as if life had let him down.

'Going somewhere, Mr. Matchan?'

'Reporting to police, if you must know.'

Schiff looked at Murphy, who asked, 'Parole condition?'

'Yes.'

'Which station?'

'Rosebud.'

'Where were you last Thursday night?'

'Here.'

'Can anyone vouch for that?'

'No.'

'So we have a problem.'

'My wife left me while I was in jail. She took the car, the house. . . . This is my sister's house. She's overseas for a year.'

Pam glanced at the empty carport, at the empty street that ran past the house. 'Do you have access to a car, Mr. Matchan?'

'No.'

A horn tooted. A taxi pulled up.

'My ride,' Matchan said, and he almost smiled.

SCOBIE SUTTON WAS OFTEN late—his wife, getting his kid to school—and Challis made allowances. As he waited, he fiddled idly with his mobile and heard the beep of an incoming text message. Superintendent McQuarrie, and clearly the super had read, or been told about, the *News-Pictorial* story: *My office, 1 P.M. Fri, consider PA rep.*

Bring the Police Association in?

He's not going to sack me? wondered Challis. On his golf day?

Then Sutton was parking his Volvo and hurrying across to the CIU car, agitated, his upper lip beaded with perspiration. Nerves or health, thought Challis, getting behind the wheel, waiting for Sutton to buckle himself into the passenger seat. 'You okay?'

'Sorry I'm late, sir. Roslyn tells me at the last minute she was supposed to be at school at seven forty-five because all the year sevens are taking a chartered bus to the Olympic pool in Frankston, and of course we missed it, and I had to chase it down the road.'

Sutton was a shocking driver. Challis pictured the knuckles clenched on the wheel, the pointless surges and braking, the overtaking on hills and blind corners. 'You're here now,' he said, starting the car and heading north through the town.

Cranbourne was outside their district but fewer than thirty minutes from the Chicory Kiln. After fixing it with the officer in charge, they were given a room and access to a trainee constable named Rick Dixon, who had reported his uniform stolen from a laundromat dryer a few days earlier. Soft, perspiring, very young, Dixon had gelled hair and a sulky, plump lower lip. 'I swear I was only gone five minutes. Slipped out to pay some bills.'

He might not be lying, Challis thought, eyeing him closely, but he is skating a little. 'Where was this?'

'Near where I live.'

'And where is that?'

'Berwick.'

'Name?'

'Er, Richard Dixon, sir.'

'Not you, the laundromat.'

'Not sure, sir.'

Sutton said, 'Can you give us a location?'

Dixon described a strip of shops, a Mobil service station on one corner, a VideoEzy opposite, enough for Challis to locate it using a telephone directory.

With Dixon out of the interview room, he dialled the number.

'Yeah,' scratched a voice in his ear. 'I remember. Officious little prick—no offence.'

'Do you have security cameras?'

'Mate, this isn't exactly the Bank of England.'

'Was any other clothing stolen that day?'

'That's the whole point: None was stolen, then or any other day. The moron used hot water and a hot dryer setting and his lovely new uniform shrank. Tried to blame it on me.'

Challis called Dixon back and said, before the trainee had time to sit, 'You made a false theft report.'

Dixon's colour drained away; perspiration beaded and ran. 'No way.'

There were times, like now, when Challis questioned the training academy's selection procedures. He'd discerned a kind of cravenness in Dixon at the start of the interview; now the trainee contrived to look wounded, distantly accusing and aggrieved, working innocence onto his soft face and puzzlement into his tangled eyebrows.

This enraged Challis. 'You fucked up. You ruined your uniform because you're ignorant, and rather than fork out for a new one you tried blaming another person and made a false report. Were you hoping you'd be issued another uniform, free of charge?'

'You're so wrong about this.'

'You're so wrong about this, *sir*,' barked Challis.

Dixon's eyes scouted for a way out. 'Will this go on my record?'

'What did you do with the old uniform?' Sutton asked.

'Binned it. Look, I'm sorry, okay? Sir? Won't happen again.'

'That's for sure,' Challis said, even as he pictured himself in Dixon's position, being bawled out by a superior officer when Friday came around.

Meanwhile he was stuck in Cranbourne: the paperwork fallout from Dixon's dishonesty, the laundromat story to be checked, the rubbish bin to be located and searched, not to mention the shire tip.

THE DAY PASSED. FOR Pam Murphy it had boiled down to questioning pathetic men with weak alibis who didn't resemble the man described by Chloe Holst and scary men who did resemble him but had cast-iron alibis. Tedious. Unbearable if the sex crimes sergeant had remained standoffish, but Jeannie Schiff had gradually unwound, growing talkative, relating blackly comic stories of some of her victories. And her defeats. At one point, early afternoon, she revealed how she'd been torn apart by the defence barrister in court the previous afternoon, and Pam was astonished to hear a faint catch in her voice.

After that, she found herself stealing looks at Schiff. A finely-shaped nose and cheekbones, a mole at the hinge of her jaw, wisps of hair escaping the knot at the back of her head, long fingers tapping the steering wheel. A strong woman, Pam thought, confident, very beautiful, you wouldn't want to get on the wrong side of her—yet less scary, suddenly. She wondered what it would be like to spend time with Jeannie Shiff away from work and found herself watching the way Schiff's plump bottom lip peeled slowly from the top whenever she began to relate another story, about another deadshit rapist, another deadshit barrister.

'You can understand why there are so many lawyer jokes,' said Pam, after one such story.

Schiff shot her a look. Pam felt the gaze flicker all over her: face, breasts, lap, and face and breasts again. Her chest tightened, she tingled low in her trunk, and although the responses were not unfamiliar or unwelcome, she didn't know what to do with them, not now, not yet, not here. To deflect all that, she related courtroom stories of her own, and so they rode north and south, east and west, crossing the Peninsula in the springtime warmth.

Mid afternoon they knocked at a house in Tyabb. 'Hello, Richard,' Pam said.

Richard Van Der Net blinked at them, his face creased and puffy, his hair this way and that. He hadn't bathed or shaved, and Pam Murphy could imagine the miasmic conditions under which he lived. 'Quick word.'

Van Der Net sniffed. According to his driver's licence, he was twenty-eight years old. He'd lived here, with his parents, for six months. Before that, Somerville. Before that, South Frankston, Chelsea, Pakenham. . . .

'Don't have to talk to no cops.'

Schiff took out her notebook and wrote in it, muttering, 'Time, four thirty-two P.M., suspect refused to cooperate with police.'

'Whoa. What are you writing? What do you mean, suspect? I done nothing.'

Pam opened a folder, revealing a series of grainy mobile phone photographs. 'Remember these, Richard?'

Van Der Net had been arrested after several complaints

during the previous summer. He liked to drive to the Peninsula's beaches and bother women who were walking or sunbathing. He'd begin by admiring their bodies, then ask if they'd watch while he masturbated. Most ran away, some froze, one took photographs.

'I like this one, Richard.'

The sands at Merricks Beach, mild sunshine, Richard plucking at his penis.

'And these.'

Richard walking back through ti-trees, a pack on his back. Richard getting into his Toyota van. A shot of the numberplate.

'What gets me,' Schiff said, 'is how fucking dumb you guys are.'

Van Der Net's mouth was open. He wanted to duck inside the house, but Pam was blocking the doorway. He hovered on a dingy patch of grass between door and front gate, looking desperately at the street beyond Schiff's stylish shoulder. He seemed to sense that freedom beckoned out there on the poky streets, but freedom of a treacherous kind.

Van Der Net rubbed his mucousy eyes and nostrils. Filthy teeth: rotted by amphetamines was Pam's guess. She supposed you could pity him. You'd have overlook the distress he'd left behind him over the years, though.

'You keep moving house, Richard.'

'So?'

'What, asked to leave? Given warnings? Told you weren't welcome?'

'I just, you know. . . .'

'Where were you last Thursday night?'

'I never did nothing.'

'You graduated from waving your willie around to abduction and rape.'

Van Der Net opened and closed his mouth and eventually

fainted. His mother came to the door and said, 'I'll have you for police brutality.' Then his father appeared and threw a punch. Phone calls were made, police cars arrived, the paperwork became a headache, and at the very last moment, a methadone clinic nurse gave Van Der Net an alibi that Murphy and Schiff couldn't shake.

'A big, fat zero.' said Jeannie Schiff when it was all over. 'So how about a drink?'

AT THE END OF his working day, Challis poured himself a scotch. He looked out at the closing-in light of evening and talked to Ellen Destry on Skype.

'He wants me in his office next Friday. I should consider representation.'

'He didn't phone you, just sent a text?'

'It was curt, even for a text. As if he didn't trust himself to speak.'

'To sack you?'

'He probably can't do that,' Challis said, 'but he can make life uncomfortable.'

They were silent. Challis reached out a hand to the webcam as if to touch Ellen's face. 'You've been gone four days already.'

'What, you're saying the time drags when I'm around?'

Challis held up a finger. 'Let me rephrase that.'

Chapter 20

Wednesday started with a briefing in CIU, croissants piled on a plate at the centre of the long table. Scudding clouds today, and without a morning sun beating through the windows, the walls and carpet were grey and sombre. Begging for colour, finding it in Jeannie Schiff's vivid lipstick and glossy black hair.

And Pam Murphy's earrings. That was unusual. Challis peered, realised he was looking at a trickle of tiny feathers in finely spun silver set with chips of turquoise.

She caught him looking and went pink. 'Dream catchers, boss. Navaho.'

'Oh.' He had no idea what dream catchers were. He only knew she was looking happy, a spark in her eyes. Meanwhile Schiff was simultaneously checking her mobile and watching him with a lazy-lidded half smile. So she's read the story about me, too, he thought. But then he sensed another undercurrent, and switched his gaze covertly from one woman to the other, not quite trusting his instincts. Then he shrugged inwardly: nothing to do with him, only the job mattered at this point.

'Our duties for today,' he said, leaning one shoulder against a wall. 'Sergeant Schiff?'

'Pam—Constable Murphy—and I will continue with the

register. Admittedly, we're scraping the bottom of the barrel now. Knicker-sniffers and teenage boys who slept with an under-age girlfriend.'

She stopped to stare at him, and he realised it was his turn to speak. He smiled, the smile there and gone again, unpeeled from the wall, and leaned over the table to break off a corner of almond croissant, dusting the powdered sugar from his fingers. 'Constable Sutton and I will keep going on the stolen uniform and ID reports.'

Schiff turned her gaze onto Sutton, and Scobie's twig-like fingers agitated his set of manila folders as if he'd become unglued a little.

FIRST UP FOR CHALLIS and Sutton was a Waterloo officer named Jeff Greener. Five minutes to 8 A.M. and he was in the canteen, about to go on duty. They took him through to an empty room on the ground floor.

'Am I in trouble?' Greener asked, looking untroubled.

'Not yet,' said Challis, some steel in his voice. 'You reported your uniform stolen last month?'

'That's right.'

'ID, too?'

'Just the uniform.'

'Circumstances?'

Greener gazed at Challis. He was an older man, a senior constable with receding hair and deep creases beside his mouth. He'd been a copper for a long time and was not impressed by a senior officer's impatience. A man with a nerveless quality, oddly appealing.

He glanced away from Challis, taking in Sutton and Sutton's collection of files. 'You have my report, sir,' he said calmly. 'My house was burgled. Three of my neighbours were burgled, then half a dozen in Balnarring one hour later. A regular crime spree.'

Challis decided to drop the harshness. He leaned back, twisted his body around, lay one arm across the back of his chair. 'Do you know who it was?'

Greener smiled crookedly. 'We rounded up and bashed the usual suspects, but you know how it is, the smart ones don't hang onto stolen gear, they shift it straight away. My guess, they shoved my uniform into an incinerator soon as they realised what they'd lifted. Or they sold it to someone who'll use it to hijack a payroll.'

Or go hunting for rape victims, thought Challis.

As they broke from the table, Greener said, 'Sir, for what it's worth, I think you spoke the truth, and I think you've got guts.'

'Thank you,' Challis murmured, oddly touched.

'Don't let the bastards grind you down.'

MEANWHILE PAM, WITH SCHIFF in the passenger seat, was driving the sex crimes Holden to the outskirts of Waterloo, where a collection of cheap housing known as the Seaview Estate nestled in a vast, shallow depression in the landscape. The place evoked complicated feelings of dread and sympathy in her. She knew that the Seaview struggled. The city of Melbourne was seventy-five minutes northwest by road, or one hour by train from Frankston, and some of the estate's working residents made that journey every day. Others worked in Dandenong factories and businesses, or more locally in Waterloo and elsewhere on the Peninsula, awaiting the next round of job cuts.

But living beside them on the estate were the underemployed, the unemployed, the elderly poor, struggling single parents, and Housing Commission, welfare, and Mental Health clients. Uneducated and unhealthy, left stranded by the IT revolution. Most were law abiding, but a handful were responsible for some of the nasty—and plenty of the mundane—crime in Waterloo, a permanent heartache for social services and a headache for the police. And they were largely invisible to the people who treated the Peninsula as a playground: Melbourne's retirees, sea change professionals, cocaine footballers, and casino executives.

Out of nowhere, Jeannie Schiff said, 'Does he like you?'

'What? Who?'

'Challis.'

Pam said quickly, 'I hope so, but not in the way you mean. He's got someone.'

'Have you got someone?'

'We're here,' Pam deflected the question and slowed to enter the estate's little streets. The houses were cramped, almost forlorn, but orderly. Most of the lives here were orderly: Only a handful of the bland façades concealed the kinds of misery and sour ambition that warranted the attention of the police.

Bernie Fahey's house was mildewed red brick, the houses on either side yellow brick. His lawns were parched, clumps of dry grass dotted with outbreaks of bare soil, as if animals scratched there for worms, buried bones, or a place in the sun. The front door showed years of kicks and slams and the scratches of powerful claws, but today it was ajar, and Schiff nodded toward the figure materialising there. 'Pam,' she said warningly.

'I see him,' Murphy said. 'The man himself.'

They got out. Fahey, dressed in greasy overalls, wiping his hands on an oily rag, spat at the ground as they approached. He had the pinched face of a fifty-year smoker and was small and wiry, a useful trait for a mechanic. Or for a man who liked to crawl through windows or into roof cavities, kidding himself he was a burglar when really he was a rapist who targeted women who lived alone.

Giving him a grin guaranteed to rile, Pam said, 'Hello, Bernie. Don't tell me you're servicing the Harley on the sitting-room carpet again?'

'Fuck off.'

'Now, now, let's not get off on the wrong foot.'

'Fuck off's what I say to Jehovah's Witnesses and cops.'

'Just a quick word, Mr. Fahey,' said Jeannie Schiff.

'Who's the girlfriend?' said Fahey, ignoring her.

'That would be Sergeant Schiff of the sex crimes unit,' Pam said, 'and she'd like a quick word, all right?'

'See this?' said Fahey.

He lifted a leg of his baggy overalls, revealing a plaster cast. His eyes gleeful, yet aggrieved, he said, 'Come off me bike six weeks ago. Can't drive, can't work, can't hardly walk.'

Pam gave her grin again. 'Can't hardly walk between the sofa and the fridge?'

'Not funny. So whatever it is you fucken think I did, I didn't.'

Pam ran a flat stare over the cast, the scribblings of friends and family. 'To Grampa get well soon Jemma XXX' and 'Another good man bites the dust' and 'You never washed this leg anyway.'

Another dead end.

CHALLIS AND SUTTON'S NEXT stop was the Mornington police station. Allocated a small room behind the front office, they interviewed a sergeant named Paul Henry, whose wallet and warrant card had been stolen from a gym locker while he was lifting weights one evening after work. Other lockers had also been broken into. There were security cameras but none in the change rooms or locker area.

'That was nine months ago, sir,' Henry said.

His look of curious sympathy told Challis that here was another reader of the local rag. 'Ever get your wallet and ID back?'

Henry looked exhausted, a man who lived on coffee and long hours. 'No, sir.' He yawned and added, 'Nor my uniform.'

Challis glanced sharply at Scobie Sutton, then back at Henry. 'I thought only your wallet was stolen. Did we know about the uniform?'

Henry shrugged. 'I reported it.'

'It was also in your locker?' asked Challis, aware that Scobie Sutton was fumbling through his files.

Henry shook his head with a weary kind of disgust. 'I had a dry-cleaning docket in the wallet. For my uniform. The pricks collected it.'

'Cameras?'

'At the dry-cleaners? No.'

NEXT STOP, FLINDERS. PAM Murphy briefed Jeannie Schiff as they drove. Wired on speed one afternoon six years ago, Ron Varley had stopped for two fifteen-year-old girls who were hitch-hiking home from the Between the Bays music festival. When they refused to get into his car, he got out, grabbed both by the wrist, and manhandled them onto his back seat. One shot across to the other door and escaped, convinced that her friend was with her.

She wasn't.

Varley's wife opened the door, took one look at Murphy and Schiff, and said, 'What's he done now?'

'May we speak to him, Mrs. Varley?'

'If you don't mind driving all the way to Ararat.'

Pam sighed. 'The jail?'

'Locked up six months ago. Don't you people talk to each other?'

'Clearly not enough,' muttered Schiff, and the two women trudged back to their car. Seated, they glanced at each other, Pam a little nervous, expecting a reprimand, but Schiff grinned. Leaning in from the passenger seat, she placed two warm fingers on the back of Pam's hand and said, 'Anything that can go wrong, as they say.'

Pam had heard it before. 'I know, I know, Murphy's Law.'

Then to Mt Martha and the home of Carl Saker. After perfecting the art of taking photographs under women's skirts, Saker had moved on to fondling schoolgirls on the Frankston train, and, finally, raping sexworkers.

According to his mother—and a quick phone call confirmed it—Saker had been in the psych unit of the Frankston Hospital since last Tuesday.

Steven Brough of Rosebud had raped an eighty-five year-old woman in a nursing home in 1998. On his release, he'd gone to live with his parents. Six weeks later, he'd committed suicide.

'So much for up-to-date records,' Pam said.

Schiff grinned. 'We need to redefine your law, Murphy. *Every-thing that can go wrong, will go wrong.*'

By now it was mid-afternoon. They interviewed three more men before evening. All had solid alibis.

MEANWHILE CHALLIS HAD FRITTERED away his afternoon in Mornington, first checking that Sergeant Henry had reported the theft of his uniform from the dry cleaner, then questioning the dry cleaner and the gym staff. Sutton trailed him mutely, cowed by his cold vehemence and focus, know-ing he'd stuffed up.

On their way back to CIU, they were obliged to stop at free-way roadworks. A great scar had been carved across farmland on either side of the road. Makeshift security fences enclosed concrete drainage pipes, heaped soil, and heavy earthmoving equipment. Sutton said, 'I wonder if Frankston will die when the bypass is running.'

Challis ignored him and took out his phone. 'Anything?'

'Nothing, boss,' said Murphy. Challis could hear voices, a hint of music, in the background. The pub? He could do with a drink. 'Maybe our rapist's not a local. We're only a little over an hour from the city.'

'Could be.'

Then Challis noticed that the cars ahead of him were moving, and Scobie Sutton was humming in agitation and checking his watch. 'Sorry, Murph, got to go.'

He pocketed the phone, put the car into gear, and moved on with the traffic. 'You all right?'

'I need to collect Ros from a friend's house.'

'Where does the friend live?'

'I told her between five and six, and it's already five past six.'

Conversations with Sutton were often like this. 'Scobie, where does the friend live?'

'Somerville.'

'We're almost in Somerville.'

'That's what reminded me.'

'Well, give me the address.'

Sutton looked shocked. 'Sir, we can't, this is a CIU car, we're on duty.'

'Give me the address, for God's sake.'

Sutton complied, subsiding into his seat, giving directions to a section of new housing opposite the shopping centre. Challis drove grimly, not trusting himself to speak, and when the feeling passed he said, with some heat, 'Scobie, you might find life easier if you had another line of work.'

'Like what?' Sutton cried. 'I'm forty-three years old, still only a constable; police work's all I know. What else can I do?'

'You could move sideways.'

'Sideways?' Sutton said. But he was thinking now, and said again, 'Sideways. . . .'

MURPHY FINISHED SPEAKING TO Challis and had put the phone away just as Schiff reached across the table to touch the dream catcher earrings. 'The colours suit you, the silver and the turquoise against your neck.'

Pam knew she was blushing. She touched the earrings self-consciously. 'Normally I wear studs. Just felt like a change.'

There were subtexts to that statement: I felt like looking attractive; I felt like looking attractive because *you* are so attractive; I felt like looking attractive for you. Pam looked down at her own hands.

They were in the Hermitage, a converted Edwardian house on the Esplanade in Mornington, with views across the waters of the bay to the sun as it flattened itself on the horizon, the vast yellow glow broken here and there by the blockish shapes of container ships steaming out the Heads. A veranda, a lounge with club chairs, a bistro that specialised in salads and seafood. Soft lighting and barely audible music. The clientele was about right, too. No yuppies to speak of, no one from the bowls club down the road, no blue singlets or pay-day apprentices.

'Nice,' Jeannie had said, on first stepping through the door.

And she'd added, eyes hooded, smiling unreadably, 'A special place to bring people.'

A place to bring *special* people, did she mean? Pam was saved by Challis's phone call.

Now the waiter was there, depositing their drinks. 'Cocktails, my treat,' Jeannie had said, and Pam admired the tall, frosted glass, thinking it would be okay to get a little drunk tonight. Her hands looked lovely in the dim light, she thought, the fingers shapely on the glass. Beautiful, actually. But of course what she was doing, she knew, was avoiding the powerful pull of Jeannie Schiff's gaze from the other side of the table.

'Pam.'

She looked up into a lazy, complicit smile and a pair of blue eyes darkening with the dying light.

Chapter 21

Thursday morning, Grace woke up in the South Australian town of Murray Bridge.

She'd arrived Wednesday afternoon, driving the Golf, and paid for four nights' accommodation in an on-site caravan. Now, showered and dressed, she walked to the main street and rented a white Camry. Three hours later she was in the Clare Valley wine country north of Adelaide, where small, humped hills concealed wineries and tiny historic towns. Vines lay over the hill folds and along the valley floor, presided over by old stone houses with sun-faded corrugated iron roofs and verandas.

The farms gave way to suburban blocks as she entered the town of Clare. Here there were more stone dwellings but a greater number of bland brick veneer houses dating from the 1970s. A Shell station, an irrigation outfitter, a stone hall, a stone church, a K-Mart, some cafes, everyday shops, pedestrian crossings, and a handful of banks. For a largish town, there wasn't much of a main street, but when Grace explored some of the side and parallel streets she found hardware barns, supermarkets, a medical clinic, a high school, a municipal pool, and a mostly-dry creek set with barbecues and benches under massive, silvery gums.

After making a couple of passes through the town, Grace took out her Google Earth maps and made her way along a snaking dirt road that took her above the valley, into a knot of pretty hills, with tall gums, secluded farmhouses and wineries on winding side tracks. And the eyesore built by Simon Lascar.

There were no indications that the Lascars had returned from attending their daughter's wedding in Honolulu. The gates were locked, the curtains drawn. Rolling down her window, Grace scoped the house and grounds with binoculars. Drifts of leaves on the driveway and garden paths. The lawn needed mowing.

She was tracking across the windows and walls when three cars appeared, two heading for the wineries or farms farther along the road, an electrician's van approaching from the other direction, raising dust. Grace needed time to finish her inspection but knew that someone might remember a woman parked on the side of the road in a white Camry, a Hertz sticker on the rear window. That's when she noticed a FOR SALE sign on the property opposite the target house: five acres, with a main house, a self-catering cottage licenced for bed-and-breakfast use, sheds, fencing, tall, pale gums, and a muddy dam.

FORTY MINUTES LATER, SHE was riding around in the passenger seat of a bulky black BMW, with a real estate agent named Brent, who was saying regretfully, 'The recession's hit everyone hard.'

But not Brent. Brent owned four agencies in the mid-north of South Australia, and the BMW was worth over a hundred grand.

She guessed boy wonder also owned a matching sedan for the pretty wife, maybe a boat, a Ducati, jet skis, home theatre, swimming pool, a paddock for the horses. And he wasn't yet forty. Good-looking, in that adolescent way of men who've never been obliged to struggle. He drove his BMW as if he wanted to run small Korean cars off the road. The aftershave was classy but overdone. Grace could scarcely breathe. The aircon ruffled the wispy hem of her skirt and drew his gaze from the road.

'At least interest rates are down,' Grace said.

He ignored her. In his Clare office, thirty minutes earlier, he'd been led to understand that she had money and wanted to buy a secluded rural property, one or two hectares. That had got his juices going: Brent had five such properties on his books.

Now, as they drove, she saw doubts creep in. He wasn't a man skilled at hiding his thoughts. 'A lot of city folk head up this way,' he said carefully, 'and after they've sunk their savings into wineries, bed-and-breakfast joints, alpacas, Christmas tree farms, lavender, roses, back-road bistros, you name it, along comes the recession, and they go belly-up.' He paused. 'Or they can't afford to run two places and offload the country weekender.'

Meaning, *Can this chick afford a winery, a back-road bistro, a weekender?* He shot her a look. She gazed at the unwinding road, rich and bored.

He sighed. 'First on the list,' he said, powering the BMW onto a dirt road, 'is a winery.'

They were at the gates moments later; the sign outside said twenty hectares. 'Not really what I'm looking for,' Grace murmured. She'd clearly said one or two hectares. Had he listened? Did he ever listen?

Unperturbed, he took her to a craft gallery attached to an architect-designed, corrugated-iron house. The house was probably cool inside but looked hot in the sun. The iron flashed blindingly. 'Sorry, no,' she said.

'Terrific views,' he pointed out.

'Not really what I'm after,' she said.

'Right,' he said, wheeling out of there.

They drove on, across the faces of the little hills, the vines orderly on the down slopes and in the valley below, Grace gazing out of her window, Brent—well, Brent was interested in two things, a sale and a better sense of her thighs under the summery cotton.

'This next one's a beauty,' he said, barrelling down a sealed road. 'Just come on the market, too.'

After a short distance he turned off and followed a dirt track through crowding trees above the Hutt River, to where a low-slung house commanded valley views. Rendered hay-bale walls, rainforest timber decks, a clever shutter system to harness sunlight and repel heat. 'And your neighbour across the road,' said Brent, giving her some eyebrow work, 'is a Channel 9 news-reader.'

'Really,' said Grace, as if her life depended upon it.

'No lie,' said Brent.

Grace asked a few questions that had nothing to do with how much the place cost, then asked to see the next place on his list. 'Don't give up on me yet,' she said brightly.

'A bed-and-breakfast,' he said. 'Very solid property, very solid. Lovely location.'

They drove, Grace gazing out, Brent's gaze flicking between the road and her crotch. She didn't care. Scoping out the area with a real estate agent was good cover. Everyone seemed to know old Brent. He'd acknowledged waves from pedestrians and oncoming drivers half a dozen times since they'd set out from his office.

'So, what do you reckon?' he said, pulling into the bed-and-breakfast property opposite the Lascar house. 'Quite something, eh?'

Grace let herself be dragged around for twenty minutes. She met the vendors, even met the retired couple staying in the bed-and-breakfast cottage. She walked, looked, asked questions, casually scoped the views with her binoculars, until she believed she knew exactly how she would rob the house on the other side of the road.

'Look, sorry to hassle you, but I've got another client,' said Brent, looking at his watch.

Grace smiled warmly. 'Thanks, I've seen enough to make a decision.'

Music to Brent's misshapen ears. He wouldn't rush her. He'd take her mobile number and call her, maybe tonight.

They drove out, Grace glancing idly at both sides of the road. A couple of little creeks, dry now, rose in the hills and crossed the road. She noted where the culverts were, their size and accessibility. Meanwhile the verges were typical for a country road, with graded runoffs, tufts of grass, stone reefs, and broken glass, the shards blinking here and there in the dappled light.

BACK AT HIS OFFICE in the main street of Clare, Brent held her dry hand in his damp one for a long beat, putting plenty of meaning into the squeeze and the eye contact. This kind of thing happened often to Grace. As always she was fascinated yet deeply fatigued by it. Promising to give the bed-and-breakfast property her deepest consideration, she slipped through a laneway to the clinic behind the main street, where she'd parked the Camry. The time was 4 P.M.

By 4:30 P.M she was standing under the shower in a motel bathroom, eyes closed, letting the jets pummel her back, neck, and shoulders. It helped her to think about the job. If she didn't think about the job, she'd think about the messiness of life, and that would paralyse her.

Then she stretched out on the bed and slept. She'd told herself to wake at 9:30 A.M and on the dot, she returned to the world fully alert, her heartbeat slow and even.

BY MIDNIGHT GRACE WAS tramping around in the soft dirt between the Lascars' garden shrubs wearing size eleven shoes over her canvas slip-ons, cotton gloves on her hands. As Galt had said, the night he nabbed her, 'We can lift prints from inside latex gloves, you know.'

Completing the forensic misdirection, she removed the shoes and broke into the house. First she hovered at the entrance to every room, assessing the black holes, the areas where the ambient light failed to penetrate—behind doors, partitions, and furniture. When satisfied, she masked her torch and probed farther, now comparing the layout of each room with the *Home Digest* images stored in her camera. Most of the rooms had not been altered in the two years since the article had appeared. Then she photographed the rooms that had not been featured in the magazine. There was a medium-sized John Perceval oil hanging on a wall in the sewing room and an Imari vase on the hallstand. If Steve Finch thought he could offload them, she might come back one day for another go.

Finally she went to work with her prise bar and lockpicks, placing Mary Lascar's silverware into one of the empty duffle bags and Simon Lascar's coins, stamps, and banknotes into the other. No $300,000 Adelaide gold pound, unfortunately: in a safe deposit box, she guessed, or sold to pay for the daughter's wedding. The silverware was easy to locate: bureau, sideboard, and behind glass doors. The collectibles were in a floor safe under a shoe rack in the main closet. Using the same reasoning, she more or less went straight to where Lascar had made a note of the combination: in pencil, on the rear panel of his sock drawer. Not all of Grace's jobs were this easy, but many were.

Then she slipped out of the house, dressed in her dark clothes, carrying her treasures.

SHE SPENT THE REST of the night in the motel, having arranged an early check-out with the manager. By 5 A.M. on Friday she was on the road, heading south along the valley, back through the little towns. At Tarlee, on the Barrier Highway, she cut across country to the Barossa Valley. Here there were more vines, and old wine-making names, and, in the dawn light, a greener, more

Europeanised landscape. The Barossa was her back road to Murray Bridge and her Golf. In this way, she avoided the city. Adelaide was small and efficient, but it was a city. She thought that cities, in their stop-start way, chopped you up; they'd certainly done it to her.

She came to the back end of the Adelaide Hills. Green now from the spring rains, the hills would be bare by midsummer, the grass dead, sparse and brittle, the eucalypts dusty and heat-struck, losing limbs and waiting mutely for a bushfire wind. Yet the hills were also formed of folds and clefts suggesting the slack limbs of entwined lovers, townships, orchards, and hobby farms forming pubic shadows. Grace felt elated, as if floating high above the world, beneath a sky that stretched from treeless horizon to treeless horizon, the river a green scribble below. Then she descended to the river flat and returned the Camry. She drove the Golf east, across the border into Victoria.

Chapter 22

'Are you a team player, Inspector?'

Early Friday afternoon, and Challis was not in McQuarrie's office at regional headquarters but a conference room at Waterloo police station. He'd been about to drive to HQ, as ordered in the superintendent's SMS, but time and location had been altered at the last minute.

To keep me off balance, he thought. He gazed at the three senior officers ranged opposite him, their heads and torsos reflected in the gleaming table top. One man, an Ethical Standards inspector, wore a plain dark suit. Superintendent McQuarrie and the third man, an assistant commissioner named Laughlin, wore full uniform, as though off to a funeral. All three had come striding in attended by a handful of junior officers. The tactic had been clear to Challis: Intimidate my friends and allies at Waterloo, and make my denunciation more public.

'Inspector?' said McQuarrie. 'A team player?'

Feeling that he'd wandered onto the set of a bad film, Challis tried to read the mood of his fastidious, slightly built boss. McQuarrie had reason both to thank and to resent him. Challis's clear-up rate was high, and he'd investigated the murder of the super's daughter-in-law with tact. But he knows I don't respect him, thought Challis, and hates to be reminded that I know his son was active in a sleazy sex-party scene, and that it was Ellen who broke a paedophile ring involving police under his indirect command.

'I'm waiting,' McQuarrie said.

Challis didn't answer but spent a moment watching the man in the suit. The Ethical Standards officer, yet to speak, looked resentful and ill at ease, and Challis relaxed minutely. After all, it wasn't as if he'd been selling drugs from the station safe or drinking with gangsters.

Unless the man was there as backup, for when they needed to press trumped-up charges against him.

He turned to McQuarrie again. 'Depends, sir. Do you mean am I a team player no matter what? Or only when the team's worth playing for?'

The superintendent blinked. He'd expected an automatic 'yes.'

Laughlin could see this going nowhere. Casting McQuarrie a fed-up look, barely disguised, the assistant commissioner leaned solid forearms on the table and said, 'What the superintendent means is, what the hell are you playing at, Inspector? Hmm?'

Laughlin reminded Challis of his first high-school headmaster, a man similarly tall, bespectacled, scowling, similarly prim and outraged, similarly vain about his cap of thick, tightly combed hair.

The headmaster had been an unimaginative desk thumper, loathed and feared, an unimpeachable man of authority who dragged his wife and children from one rural posting to another, leaving behind stressed staff, depleted church congregations, and demoralised football and cricket teams.

'Sir?'

Irritable now, Laughlin said, 'Do we need to give you the benefit of the doubt?'

Challis waited, wondering why the big guns? Why an assistant commissioner? Did anyone really care that he'd complained about shortages and budgetary matters? Everyone did that, in all professions. But government employees are expected to keep their mouths shut, and he'd gone a step further and taken a swipe at the State Government for propping up the Grand Prix every year. The Premier and his ministers were sensitive about it, probably knew the race was wasteful, unpopular, and environmentally unsound, yet were obliged to appease powerful people, and so they played up the tourist dollars that flowed to a handful of cafes and hotels and dismissed the critics as disgruntled residents and greenies. Less easy to dismiss the views of a detective inspector, he supposed.

Christ, thought Challis, maybe I'll become a folk hero.

He gazed evenly at Laughlin, wondering who had put the hard word on him, and how. 'Sir?'

'Don't "sir" me. Are you aware that crime data is only one factor when apportioning resources across a Division?'

This is coming down to statistics? thought Challis incredulously. He said nothing.

'Statistically,' Laughlin said, 'there has been no change in crime rates, no matter what *you* say. Some minor crimes are up, but that is attributable to the current economic climate; namely, the rising price of petrol. Motorists are driving off without paying and stealing number plates to fool the CCTV cameras at service stations.'

'Sir, with respect, we won't get far quoting statistics at each other. My argument is that we are seriously under-resourced, and if the government were able to prioritise—'

'You were quoted as saying crime figures are up, as though we are losing the fight.'

'I was saying that we can't win the fight if we don't have sufficient manpower or resource funding. Waterloo is fourteen officers *fewer* than it should be. If you look at last month's roster, we fell well below the recommended guidelines of one sergeant and four junior officers per shift.'

Challis's mouth was dry; the topic was dry. He didn't feel angry or intimidated or anxious or defensive, just a little bored. He wasn't going to win anything here, not more money or trained officers or even respect. He wanted to go out and do his job, not sit here.

'Hal,' said Superintendent McQuarrie chummily, trying to reassert himself and put Challis on side, 'arguments about resourcing across a Division are irrelevant, given the changing nature of police work and the influence of the new technologies, some of which we are yet to discover.'

Challis tried to see the substance of the man's argument and failed. Given that a question hadn't been posed, he remained silent. It was a tactic he used in interrogations: hold back, use silence.

'Can we trust you, Inspector Challis?' said Laughlin.

Well, that was a clear enough question, but not one that Challis intended to answer.

'After all, you have seriously compromised the Force,' Laughlin said, arms folded, staring like a fierce prophet. 'What is essentially an internal matter was made political when you brought the State Government into it.'

Challis said innocently, 'Sir?'

'That nonsense about the Grand Prix race costing fifty million a year, money that could be spent on supplying police stations with torch batteries, for God's sake.'

'And vehicles, radios, extra staff,' Challis said.

'It must be very stressful, your job,' said Laughlin, trying for an understanding smile and transforming himself into an awful parody of a counsellor or doctor, a man with Challis's best interests at heart. Challis said nothing.

'Many officers of your rank burn out. Nothing to be ashamed of.'

It was clear that Laughlin thought it was shameful. Challis continued to stare.

'Many officers find it beneficial to take stress leave—supported by Work Cover, so they're not out of pocket. They come back refreshed—even find new careers.'

Laughlin waited for a response. When it didn't come he dropped the smarm and leafed through a file. 'I see that three months' long service leave is owed to you.'

And McQuarrie butted in, saying, 'Your girlfriend is on an overseas junket at the moment, I believe? By herself?'

You bastards, leave Ellen out of it, Challis thought, as his phone began to vibrate in his pocket.

'I need to take this,' he said.

As they gaped, he left the room, flipping open his phone. The screen revealed no name, only a number he didn't recognise. And he could scarcely hear the voice, it was so soft and distraught.

Chapter 23

'Larrayne?'

That terrible sobbing whisper again. 'Please, you've got to come.'

'I can barely hear you. Use the landline.'

'I can't, they're in the sitting room.'

'Who is? Where are you?'

If a whisper could be a shriek, that's what Challis heard. '*Mum's.* These awful men came barging in. Please, you've got to help me.'

'Are you hiding?'

'They let me go to the loo.'

'They didn't take your phone away?'

'I'm in Mum's dressing gown. I had the phone in the pocket.'

'Switch to vibrate, and I'll call you back.'

'*No.* Please.'

It was as if she feared losing contact. Challis ducked into the canteen. Spotting Jeff Greener there he beckoned, miming urgency, and led the way down the corridor at a run, the phone pressed to his ear. 'Did you call triple zero?'

She said, in a wobbly, frustrated voice, 'I don't know where I am. I mean, I can find my way here in the car, but I sort of don't know the name of the street or the house number.'

Well, Ellen's move to Dromana was recent. And Larrayne had never struck him as being very organised. 'I'll do that.'

He was in the car park now. Tossing the CIU car keys to Greener, he said, 'Dromana, flat out all the way.'

'You got it.'

When they were streaking out of Waterloo, Challis called the Rosebud police station, reported a home invasion at Ellen's address, asked for a couple of cars to attend. Then he sat back to wait, the line to Larrayne Destry still open, trying to picture the interior of the house. Were the university friends still there? If so, where? In the sitting room with the men? He pictured the corridor between it and the kitchen, the two doors along it, one to the bathroom, the other to the toilet. Plasterboard walls, meaning that sounds carried, whispers, too.

Larrayne's voice crackled in his ear. 'Hal?'

'Still here, Larrayne.'

'Are you coming?'

'On the way, and I've called it in.'

Challis glanced at the instrument panel. Greener was doing 130 km/h, sometimes 140. Even so, they were fifteen minutes out, at least.

'I'm scared.'

Challis pictured Larrayne in Ellen's vast white dressing gown. 'I know you are,' he said gently. 'You've a right to be. But don't let these guys see it.'

There were sniffles, and he thought about her remaining phone credit, his own phone credit and battery life. 'Are your friends still in the house?'

'They're tied up. They've got tape around their arms and legs and across their mouths.'

Challis was puzzled. Overkill, he thought. Students, a modest, slightly run-down house, why a home invasion?

Pretty soon Greener had them barrelling past the glassblower at the Red Hill turn-off and down the hill toward the coast, a pretty drive, a slow, winding drive, but Challis, blind to the charms, was pressing a ghost accelerator with his right foot. 'Larrayne, is it a robbery?'

'No,' she whispered.

Sexual assault? He was looking for a way to ask it when she went on, 'They came bursting in saying we stole their girlfriends' marijuana plants. They're acting crazy.'

'What girlfriends?'

'Next door.'

Challis pictured the house with the two women with biker boyfriends. The timing made sense when you realised that students and junkies—and students who were junkies—tended to sleep until noon. 'Did you steal their plants?'

'*No*. We—'

'*Get your arse out here, bitch.*'

'Oh God.'

'Larrayne, don't let them—'

'*Now, bitch.*'

Challis heard Larrayne Destry call out to the man on the other side of the door, 'You're scaring me. You just made me sick over everything.'

'*Well, make it quick.*'

Challis waited. She'd done well, lodging a word picture in the bikie's head: human waste and odours and messiness.

Then her voice was in his ear again. 'He's gone, but I don't have much time.'

'We'll be there in a few minutes.'

There were crackles in the atmosphere and no reception bars on his phone. 'Fucking black spot,' he muttered.

'Sir?' Greener said, not looking at him, barrelling the CIU car down the long hill to the flat paddocks at the bottom, whisking it right then left onto the road into Dromana. Past the drive-in theatre, Challis pointing Greener toward the freeway entrance, holding the phone close to his face, waiting for reception.

One bar, two, then three, and Larrayne's panicky whisper, 'What happened?'

'I lost reception. Look, hold on, we're almost there.'

'I can hear them yelling at the others. Hitting them. *Give us back the plants, or we'll cut her tits off, cut your dicks and your ears off,* stuff like that. I'm so scared.'

'You're doing really well,' said Challis feelingly. 'You're using your brain, you're strong, and you're going to be OK.' He thought and said, 'Is it possible one of the others stole the plants without your knowledge?'

A pause. Too late, he saw the misstep. 'My life's in danger, and you turn cop on me? That is so typical.'

Probably a good thing, the old Larrayne showing itself. Outrage was better than panic and fear. But then Challis could hear thumping sounds in the background, tearing wood, a snarl: '*Get your fucking arse out here, right now.*'

And the line went dead, and Challis dumbly pointed the way for Greener, up onto the on-ramp, up the hill to an exit that looped down and under the freeway. His heart was beating hard.

Realising his phone was on, he broke the connection. It rang immediately. 'Inspector Challis? Rosebud cars are on the way.'

'Thank you.'

Challis pocketed the phone. It rang again; he checked the screen, saw it was McQuarrie calling and let it go to voicemail. They were on a paved street now, and then dirt side streets, the car bottoming out on potholes. He pointed again, and Greener pulled into Ellen's driveway, right up to the rear bumper of the green Hyundai. The sun was breaking through, the wind dropping, sprinklers ticking on a nearby lawn. They got out, Challis glancing across at the house where the marijuana growers lived.

A curtain twitched, and he imagined a hurried mobile phone call.

He said to Greener, 'Go around the back. If they come out, try to stop them, but no heroics. We'll find them again, the stupid fucks.'

'Got it.'

Challis climbed onto the deck and looked through the glass. In the dimness there was chaos, almost too much to take in, but then his crime scene management priorities kicked in, a habit so ingrained he'd never shake it: preserve life, preserve the crime scene, secure evidence, identify the victim or victims, identify the suspect or suspects.

Chairs upended, plates broken, the coffee table leaning on a broken leg. One of the boys was strapped to a fallen chair, the girl still upright, hands bound behind her back, legs bare under black knickers, T-shirt torn from neck to hem, spilling her breasts. The second boy was in another upright chair, bleeding from the mouth and nose. A strange stillness, as if it were all over. But then Challis shifted his gaze, attracted by movement. A man in greasy jeans and a sleeveless black T-shirt had a mobile phone to his ear, shouting, beckoning to the other man, who was similarly dressed and struggling with Larrayne Destry. They'd seen Challis, a shadow against the glass, and began to pantomime doubt, confusion, belligerence, and fury.

He slid open the glass door and saw the men vanish toward the rear of Ellen's house and heard the squeak of the back door, screams of '*Drop it, copper*' and '*I'll do you, you fucking dog.*'

Larrayne was bent over, gasping. Challis put an arm around her shoulder, bent his head to her cheek. 'You okay?'

She bucked immediately, striking him with her fists, then was holding on for dear life, crying hard. After a moment, he disentangled himself. 'Help your friends, okay? I'll be right back.'

'Please!'

'I have a man in trouble,' he said, communicating reluctance and urgency.

She heaved a wobbly sigh. 'Sorry. I'm okay, honest.'

Challis hurtled out of the room, through the kitchen, and into the backyard. He found Greener standing alone on the strip of dust beneath Ellen's rotary clothesline holding a handkerchief to a bloodied lip.

'Sir.'

Challis dropped an arm across his shoulders. 'Thought you were a goner.'

For a brief moment, Greener relaxed against the contact, then muttered that he was okay and moved away. 'I considered shooting them, but think of the paperwork.'

'Exactly.'

Shrieks and bellows were coming from the next house. Heavy bikes firing up.

Sirens in the distance.

'Not the Hollywood ending I was after,' Greener said.

'True,' said Challis, who'd never known real life to be anything other than messy, with a little bravery and common sense thrown in if you were lucky. 'Thanks for your help.'

'A pleasure,' said Greener, bending to tug at his trousers, which were torn and bloody at the knee.

'I guess we need to buy you a new uniform.'

Greener looked at him. 'That would be good, sir,' he said slowly, 'but I couldn't, in good conscience, put a strain on the police budget.'

Challis laughed. He called for an ambulance and re-entered Ellen's house just as four uniforms were pouring in. He sent one pair to the neighbouring house, telling them to call Rosebud CIU and issue a description of the attackers, then helped the other pair to free and tend to Larrayne's friends.

And as he was murmuring encouragement, cutting duct tape,

dabbing the blood from shallow cuts, he was looking for hidden truths, revealed in a glance, a mannerism, a flicker of emotion.

It came quickly. As soon as he'd ungagged the other girl, Nikki, she launched herself at her boyfriend, scoring his cheek with her nails, 'You arsehole. You stupid, stupid—'

'I'm sorry. Really, really sorry.'

'It was you?' said Larrayne. Before Challis could stop her, she whacked him, too.

He sulked. 'Yeah, well, it was Mark's idea.'

Larrayne, her face appalled, swung around on the tall, sweet, skinny boy, who didn't look so sweet now. 'How could you be so stupid?'

He shrugged, mopped at his torn ear. 'Yeah, well.'

'I want him arrested,' Larrayne said.

Challis glanced at one of the Rosebud officers, giving the nod, then he took Larrayne's arm and ushered her out of the house, to where the sun warmed the old decking furniture. She wrapped herself in the dressing gown and shivered. 'Thanks for coming,' she said, her voice small.

'Want me to call your dad?'

In fact, why hadn't Larrayne called him? Alan Destry was a policeman, after all.

'*No*. No, please don't. You know him, he'll overreact.'

'We can't keep it a secret.'

'I'll tell him later, when it's over—otherwise he'll come barging in and start bashing people up.'

She was probably right. Alan Destry had a temper. 'We need to tell your mum, though.'

Larrayne Destry was in the grip of doubts and frustrations. Her fists clenched. 'No, please, you can't.'

'Why not?'

'She'll want to fly straight home. I'm okay.' Then she slumped. 'I feel such a fool.'

Challis touched a thick, white, rumpled sleeve. 'You did nothing wrong. The boys stole the marijuana, not you.'

His words brought no comfort. 'What happens now?'

'Is there someone I can call, other than your father? A friend?'

'They're all up in the city.' She thought about it. 'Dad's girlfriend.'

Larrayne made the call. She was saying, 'No, I'm okay to drive,' when his mobile rang.

Jeannie Schiff, saying: 'We have a crashed car, abandoned on Coolart Road, dead woman in the boot. Naked, beaten, bound, strangled, probably raped.'

Chapter 24

Earlier that day, John Tankard's team were breathalysing motorists at the Tuerong Junction end of Balnarring Road, then on a stretch of the Nepean between Mornington and Mount Martha. Finally, in the early afternoon, they set up on Coolart Road. Two pursuit cars—they went like the clappers of hell—two powerful BMW bikes, and four constables and a sergeant. The hotshots got to do anything remotely interesting, like on-the-spot roadworthy checks, running numberplates through the on-board computers, processing the drunks. Meanwhile Tank was given the crap jobs. Setting up a stopping lane and waving cars into it, standing in the middle of the road with his fancy gear on. Hot gear, too. Temperatures in the high twenties, low thirties all week.

Not much action today—a guy taking his kids to school had registered .059—but Tank knew the Peninsula would be full of thank-God-it's-Friday booze hounds as the afternoon deepened. He waved another anonymous car into the stopping lane, another anonymous male driver at the wheel. Maybe this loser was the shotgun bandit. . . . Tank peered in as the guy slowed and stopped alongside the officer doing the breath test. Nah. Vague resemblance at best. Besides, there was a pregnant woman in the passenger seat, a toddler in the back, strapped into a capsule. Unless the bandit travelled with his family. God, Tank was bored.

'Mind on the job, Constable.'

'Yes, Sarge.'

The sun was early-afternoon high, the air still, birds squabbling in the roadside trees. A magpie was getting on Tank's nerves. It looked fully grown but hopped around squawking uselessly. Putting the pressure on mum and dad for another fucking worm.

A smell of horse shit wafting across from the adjacent paddock. A chainsaw in the distance.

And up in the wide blue yonder, ibis wheeled silently, and a few game, ragtag little birds were telling an eagle to shove off.

John Tankard sneezed explosively: there was a slasher working on the spring grasses along a nearby fence line. All in all, he felt that he'd pretty much exhausted his appreciation of nature this past week.

An hour or two later, the sergeant ordered them to shift location again, over near the freeway this time, the 80 km/h stretch near Humphries Road. It was Tank's job to stow the equipment and bring one of the cars, so he was the last to leave and was alone there on Coolart Road when a white Holden came barrelling over a rise, spotted him and snaked to a screaming halt. Tank read it. Drunk driving, drugs, or stolen goods.

Thank the Lord, action at last.

Cranking the motor, Tank planted his foot, accelerating up the slope to intercept the Holden even as it reversed into a driveway, turned tail, and shot back over the rise.

Just then, he sneezed again. His window was open; grass dust and pollen swirled around his solid head. He gasped, his eyes watered, the sneezes were galloping away from him.

By the time he'd recovered and could see dimly through his scratchy eyes, the Holden was far in the distance. He radioed it in, pressing hard on the accelerator, and sneezed again, his hand jerking the wheel, his body pitching about in his seat. He brought the car to a stop on the verge of the road, snuffled into a handkerchief, dragged a forearm sleeve across his eyes. He was still on the hilly part of Coolart Road and couldn't see the Holden.

When he'd recovered, Tank planted his foot again, swivelling his head left and right at the next couple of intersections: Waterloo far off in one direction, Merricks North the other, no white Holden.

He found it a minute later, buckled against a fancy stone gateway, as if the driver had intended to duck inside and hide, hoping the police would keep to Coolart Road and eventually assume he'd disappeared. Only he'd been going too fast, fucking moron, and he'd crashed.

Tank pulled in close behind, blocking the Holden against the stone pillar. He ran the rego number—the car had been reported stolen—called in his location, then got out, approaching the rear of the car with his baton in his left hand, his right hand ready to draw his service revolver.

No one in the rear seat, no one in the front.

He straightened his back, peering around at the lightly timbered paddocks on either side of the road. A man on foot could lose himself in open country pretty quickly—unless he'd decided to steal a farm vehicle or get himself a hostage. Tank glanced uneasily up the driveway to a farmhouse that was scarcely visible beyond a row of cypress and other trees. He pictured a man menacing a woman alone in her kitchen, a child playing outside, a teenage girl just home from school. . . .

Just as he was about to step between the stone pillars and down the driveway, the other members of his team arrived, full of noise and testosterone. Tank, it soon transpired, was to stay with the wrecked car while the heroes searched the grounds and woodland.

'Wait here for backup. Let them know where we are.'

'But it was me who chased him, Sarge.'

'Whereupon he crashed into a stone wall,' the sergeant said, 'endangering the lives of everyone around him. You know the drill on high-speed pursuits, don't you, Tank?'

'So what's the point of having a pursuit car with all the fancy shit on it?'

'Just stay with the car, all right? Check the registration. Search the glovebox. Make yourself useful.'

John Tankard made himself useful to the extent of finding a dead woman in the boot of the car.

Chapter 25

Challis arrived to find Tankard directing a long line of traffic past the car and the crumpled gatepost. Coolart Road on a Friday afternoon was always a nightmare of school buses, private cars, farm vehicles, delivery vans, 4WDs; of school kids, parents, tradespeople, city workers getting an early start on the weekend. Right now, they were content to be rubberneckers, in no hurry to arrive anywhere.

The first thing Challis did was order the traffic unit to set up a detour at Hodgins Road. Presently the flow of vehicles ebbed, then ceased. The departure of the unit's cars and motorbikes also eased congestion at the crash site, leaving only Challis's CIU car, an ambulance to convey the body, the pathologist's BMW, and a vehicle belonging to the crime scene unit.

Then he joined Schiff and Murphy at the rear of the crashed Holden. Today the sex crimes sergeant looked like a cross between a slinky schoolteacher and a certain young criminal lawyer famous for her front-page cleavage, client list, and corner-cutting. Schiff wore black leggings under a short red skirt, black top with a dramatic scooped neck, hair in a corkscrew at the back of her head. And different glasses, he noticed: rimless lenses, silvery titanium frames. Meanwhile Murph was dressed in thin cotton cargo pants, white running shoes, a fawn cardigan over a vivid white T-shirt. She shot him a grin, her body taut, almost quivering with energy, as if all she wanted to do was run, climb, swim, or knock heads in. The old Murph back again, after weeks of the doldrums?

He stood with the women, looking over the bowed back of the pathologist, Freya Berg. First impressions: a bloodied face, bruising, the slackness of death. A closer look. The victim was aged in her early twenties, plump, all tension gone from her trunk and limbs. Bruised thighs and neck, a bitten nipple, stubbled pubic hair. Her nose, squashed to one side, was caked with blood.

He backed away.

'Not getting any easier, Hal?' Dr. Berg said.

The pathologist had registered his presence without looking at him. 'Nope.'

'I hear you've been ruffling feathers.'

'Some other dude,' Challis said.

'That's what I thought,' Berg said, continuing to palpate the flesh and work the limbs. 'If you three fine police officers could just give me another five minutes. . . .'

Schiff said, 'Raped, punched, and strangled?'

'Five minutes,' repeated the pathologist, inserting a thermometer into the victim's rectum.

'Leave the doc to do her job,' Challis said, motioning Murphy and Schiff away from the car.

In the meantime, they speculated: terse, muttered, a mix of observation and guesswork perfected during similar cases over the years.

'Same guy who snatched Chloe Holst?'

'Could be. It's been a few days, time for him to feel the urge.'

'And this time things went too far.'

'Or he took them too far.'

'See the lividity?'

'She's been there for a while.'

The minutes passed. Challis and the women walked around to the front of the car, where Scobie Sutton was scrawling in a notebook. 'Anything?'

Sutton pointed his pen in the direction of the house at the end of the driveway. 'I spoke to the householder. She was in one of the front rooms, vacuuming curtains she said, and saw a man run a short distance toward the house then trip over that stone border and fall into the bushes. Then he got up again and ducked back through the trees toward the road.'

'Police uniform?'

Scobie shook his head. 'I really grilled her on that. He was too far away for her to get an impression of his face, but he was definitely wearing jeans and a T-shirt.'

Challis thought about it. The guy changed his clothing, or he had an accomplice, or he had nothing to do with the abduction and rape of Chloe Holst. Then he stopped thinking about it. Save it for the briefing. 'Anything on the car?'

Sutton flipped back a page. 'Reported stolen yesterday from the car park behind the TAFE College in Frankston. I spoke to the owner: Mary Mackenzie, college librarian, sixty years old.'

'Husband? Son, nephew. . . .'

'Widow. One daughter, lives in Perth.'

'Prints?'

'Plenty. Probably not his,' Sutton said. He nodded in the direction of the pathologist. 'The crime scene people haven't done inside the boot yet.'

'You were first on scene apart from Tank and the RBT boys?'

'Yes.'

'She was dead when you arrived?'

A spasm crossed Sutton's face, and Challis was reminded again why Scobie had never been a good detective. Okay with a paper trail or CCTV footage but bewildered by ambiguities, feelings, humankind's capacity for cruelty or indifference. 'Yes,' he said, voice cracking a little.

'It's okay, Scobe,' Pam Murphy said, shooting Challis a go-easy-on-him look. 'We'll get the details from Dr. Berg.'

But Sutton couldn't shake his distress. 'Someone used her as a punching bag, sir. I just can't imagine the kind of rage involved.'

'I know,' Challis said.

'And there is bruising around her, you know, her. . . .'

The words made pictures in Sutton's head, defiling and defeating him. Challis touched his forearm. 'Thanks, Scobie, that's all I need for now.'

Leaving Sutton and the others, he wandered away along the gravel verge of Coolart Road, between the tarred surface and the fence line, where the roadside grass was thick and browning, no longer scrappily nourished by spring rains but growing combustible, waiting for one of summertime's discarded cigarettes. The paddock grass inside the fence had been shorn for hay and baled in the form of huge, blue polythene-wrapped cylinders that squatted on the broad hillside like futuristic dwellings. This effect was enhanced by the presence of uniformed constables walking through and around them, heading upslope to a distant stand of trees, where a police helicopter chopped at the air. Challis watched. There was no sudden urgency, so he returned to the others.

Freya Berg approached them with her vivid smile. 'Preliminary findings. The neck is locked, the stomach on the way, but there's still some movement in the extremities. The blood is not fully clotted yet, so indications are she's been dead between six and eight hours. The boot of a car is a sealed environment, but I still think six to eight hours. If this were midsummer or midwinter, I'd probably revise the time.'

Schiff said, 'The lividity. . . .'

'All down one side. She was placed in the boot soon after death.'

'Anything else?'

Dr. Berg gave the sex crimes detective a tight smile and went on with her briefing. 'There are indications that she struggled with someone before death. Before her wrists and ankles were taped together, in fact. Petechial haemorrhaging indicates that she was strangled, but I'll know for sure when I get her to the lab. Blood and bruising around the genital area, broken nose, I'd say our hero was expressing a lot of rage.'

Challis said, 'Thanks, Freya.'

'How's Ellen?'

Challis was aware of Murphy and Schiff watching him. 'Fine. Overseas study tour.'

'I'd heard. You should join her.'

'I wish,' Challis said.

His mobile phone sounded in his pocket. He checked the screen, saw McQuarrie's name, and knew he couldn't keep avoiding the man. He answered, and McQuarrie said, 'What possessed you, Inspector, walking out on—'

Challis overrode him. 'A home invasion and then a murder, that's what possessed me.'

Silence, and he found himself adding, 'Doing my job, in fact,' guessing he was driving another nail into the lid of his coffin.

Chapter 26

Grace had decided to keep the rarest and costliest items from the Lascar collection for herself. The rest she traded to Steve Finch for $4,500, putting up with his usual shit, gazing into her eyes while trailing his knuckles over her breasts. The gaze she gave him was flat, wintry, and he shrugged indifferently, saying, 'Can't blame a bloke for trying.'

She could, but didn't. She left him there with his weak, moist dreams and continued north, crossing the West Gate Bridge, the windsocks limp today, and then via Kings Way to Dandenong Road. At Springvale Road she headed down to the bay and followed the Nepean to Frankston. When she reached the town's southern edge, a part of her was tempted to drive all the way down the Peninsula, hop onto the ferry, go home, and sleep. This was the part of her that was tired of the running, tired of the let-down that always followed the high of breaking in, scooping up, getting out. This part of her was loose, not ordered.

But order won. It always did. She needed to stash her takings before she did anything else.

And so she turned at the Coolstore on Eramosa Road and zigzagged her way to Waterloo. Kept her eyes peeled for the unmarked blue Commodore. Kept 5 km/h under the posted speed limits. The $4,500 was in a money belt around her waist, the Lascar stamps between the pages of the Golf's service book, the coins in the engine bay, inside a bolt-on canister that at a casual glance was part of the electrics.

By 4 P.M. Grace had stowed it all in her safe-deposit box and was heading back across the Peninsula, taking Coolart Road this time. And, as the Golf topped a rise and dipped into a hollow again, she saw a mess of red and blue flashing lights in the distance. Up and down another hill, the lights resolving themselves into half a dozen cop cars and stalled traffic. She slowed the Golf, turned on her indicators, headed into a side road named Goddard. The surface was chopped up, powdery, and wound between open paddocks, vines, untidy gumtrees, and commercial chicken farms, all of it coated in fine, clogging dust. Tense at the thought of her dust trail and the idle curiosity of the cops on Coolart Road, she was saved by an arrow on a gumtree.

She braked. The arrow was part of an ornate sign that said LINDISFARNE, OPEN GARDEN SCHEME, ALL WELCOME and indicated a dense cypress hedge broken by a massive open entranceway, a pair of solid wooden gates attached to curving concrete supports. On one support was a painted board that read LINDISFARNE and W. & L. NIEKIRK. No sign of the house itself, only the hedge and a hint of driveway. She scanned the road ahead of her: empty. Opposite Lindisfarne was an open farmyard with a droughty lawn in the foreground and a background sprawl of house, garden shrubbery and sheds. A trampoline lay tipped on its side, and in a broad area adjacent to the house she saw a reedy dam and a grove of fruit trees.

Unable to think of a good reason for driving into the farmyard, Grace turned left, through the gap in the Lindisfarne hedge line, and followed the gravel driveway beyond the cypress barrier. On the other side was a park-like stretch of lawn, silvery gums, garden beds, and a modern-looking house.

And a woman dead-heading roses. She straightened her back, knuckling a wisp of hair from her cheek. 'May I help you?'

'I saw the "open garden" sign,' Grace said.

'I'm so sorry, that was last weekend,' the woman said.

She was a collection of incongruities. Thorn-scratched fore-arms; limp blonde hair pasted damply to her temples; gold and precious stones glinting on her fingers and earlobes and around her throat; a face you might see seated in a box at the opera, nose tilted to detect odours; a horsy, tennis-playing body; an educated voice. She wore stained Levis torn at the knees, a fraying straw hat, and a grease smudge on the smile line next to her mouth.

She pushed back the hat. 'I've been meaning to take that sign down all week.'

Grace looked around now and said, a little wistfully, 'That's a shame. Such a beautiful garden. Have you been part of the scheme for long?'

'A few years,' the woman said. She removed a wrinkled glove and offered Grace a limp hand. 'Mara Niekirk.'

'Jenny Anderson,' said Grace. 'The grounds are looking gor-geous. Such a lot of work. You must be so proud.'

'Oh, you know,' the woman said with a laugh. She swiped the perspiration from her brow. 'Look, you might as well have a wander, now that you're here. Just ignore the occasional rake or wheelbarrow.'

'I don't want to impose,' Grace said.

'Oh, it's no bother. I only wish I could show you around, but I must finish trimming these roses. We all leave for Sydney tomor-row.'

'Holiday?' asked Grace lightly, looking around at the lawns and native plants, the curving driveway, and the cypress hedge. She noticed that neither the road, nor the farmhouse opposite, were visible from where she stood.

'Part holiday, part business,' the woman said. 'But a week is better than nothing.'

Grace smiled and continued scanning the grounds of Lindisfarne, this time paying more attention to the perimeter of the rambling public display area: garden sheds, clumps of shadow, coiled hoses, and a broad, creeper-choked wire-netting structure. The Niekirk woman had said 'we all leave.' More than two people.

Just then, movement in the wire netting. A gap, getting wider. Some kind of narrow gate, Grace realised, as a young woman raced out with a small child, both of them shrieking and elated as they slammed the gate behind them. 'My daughter and her nanny,' explained Mara Niekirk. 'They've been feeding the canaries.'

Grace smiled and began to stroll. She didn't give a shit about plants, gardens, or nature, went through life without seeing them, but she was super-alert right now, all of her senses hard at work. The air was scented, small birds snapped around the bottlebrush heads, bees hummed nearby. There was order in the disordered paths and borders. A small wooden shed wore bright green paint, and a tiny cactus grew inside an old boot beside a garden tap, as if to tell visitors not to take the garden too seriously.

Emerging from a long rose arbour, Grace found herself hard against a wall of the house. It was high, full of glass and darkly stained posts and beams. A steeply pitched roof, the apex at least eight metres above her head. Vaguely Tyrolean, but light and airy.

She moved along the wall. Now she could see that the house was in three, disproportionate sections, joined by glassed-in walkways. As with the cactus in the boot, the building resisted categorisation, as if the architect had taken direction from too many people. Grace continued to explore, ignoring the garden at her back, intent on what she could see through the glass. A lot of black leather upholstery, terracotta tiles, white rugs and cushions, a doll and plastic blocks on the tiles, crap art on the walls.

Not all of it was crap.

A small religious icon, hanging on a wall inside one of the walkways, jolted Grace to the core. She strolled once around the house, wanting a way in, hiding the tension that was building inside her.

Messer: the alarm system was a Messer.

Out of nowhere came a sharp pain and a snapping sensation on the crown of her head. Grace dropped into a crouch, ready to run or fight and saw a magpie climb out of its dive and bank as if to come in again. She hurried to her car, waving her arms about, turning on her heel from time to time in readiness for the hidden threats.

Chapter 27

The break-in at the Clare Valley house was reported to police on Thursday afternoon by a lawn-mowing contractor who'd spotted a smashed alarm box on one wall and a pane of glass leaning against another.

Now, Friday morning, Clare detectives were poking around, and when an AFP inspector named Towne arrived, Detective Constable Burke was given the task of liaison.

'Like I told you, nothing much to see.'

Towne nodded, offered a huge smile that had nothing in it, and continued prowling, hands behind his back, peering at the ground. He was young for an inspector. Burke, trailing the man, was guessing university fast-track and all that crap. Being a federal task force hotshot was the second mark against him. The third was the guy's appearance, effortlessly classy.

Burke saw Towne stop, crouch, stand, and move on again. He sighed, tugging at his collar, feeling uncoordinated, his suit a rotten fit.

The show pony stopped again. He peered, straightened, said, '*Ah-hah!*' half mockingly.

'What?'

Towne pointed down at the soil between a pair of stubby rose bushes. The roses were giddily perfumed bees droned and Burke sneezed.

'Gesundheit,' Towne said.

Burke trumpeted into a handkerchief. 'Footprints, so what? We took casts.'

'Size elevens?'

'Yeah.'

Towne nodded—he was a nodder—and moved on, glancing at the house now, veranda, windows, and eaves. 'Like I showed you,' Burke said, 'he used a glasscutter on the study window.'

'Yes. But why didn't the alarm sound?'

'It probably did, but he smashed it. We found a croquet mallet tossed under a bush. There are no neighbours anyway.'

'Not wired to the security company or local cop shop?'

'No.'

'The blessed ignorance of some people,' said Towne, shaking his head.

Burke had had enough. 'So what brings a man like you to our humble B and E?'

Towne ignored him, par for the course. Burke felt like smacking the guy over the ear hole. In his long experience, hotshots like Towne liked to keep you offside. Tell you everything was on a need-to-know basis—and of course someone like you didn't need to know.

Towne walked on. Then he stopped and said, 'I'll need to see the logs for the three days prior to this incident.'

Incident. It was a fucking burglary that had tied up four officers for two days. 'Looking for what, exactly?'

A car passed by on the dirt road, its suspension rattling. Then dust was pouring across the lawn toward them, Burke amused to see the AFP guy brush futilely as it settled onto the fine cloth of his suit.

'Burglary logs,' Towne said at last, blinking. 'Break-ins, high-end and domestic, anywhere in the Clare Valley.'

'You think he was active here for a few days?'

'She,' said Towne. 'It's what she does sometimes.'

'A female suspect?' said Burke, using the language of official reports. 'Wearing size eleven shoes?'

But Towne was walking down the driveway, toward the road. Burke scurried a little to keep up.

'Do you play golf, Sergeant?' said Towne, tossing the words over his shoulder.

'What?'

'It's good for all-round fitness.'

Burke's loathing grew. He joined the federal policeman at the road's edge. 'What are you looking for?'

'Trying to get a feel for her, that's all,' Towne said.

The wanky, outer reaches of police work, thought Burke. 'Do we have a name? Description? MO?'

Towne closed and opened his eyes and suddenly looked deeply fatigued, vulnerable, hair poorly combed. He looked almost human for a moment. But it vanished.

'She's youngish and presumably very fit, given the kinds of stunts she pulls. Good at throwing us off the scent.'

'The shoe prints,' said Burke with dawning comprehension. 'She shoves her shoes into larger shoes.'

'Exactly.'

'What else?'

Towne exhibited one of his abrupt mood shifts, spinning around and returning to the house. 'Highly mobile.'

Burke hurried after him. 'She gets around?'

'One month she'll hit a gated community on the Gold Coast, the next a few houses on the Swan River, the next some heritage houses in Battery Point, and so on. Every state, so far, except Victoria.'

Burke brooded on that. 'Could mean that's where she lives.'

It was clear from Andrew Towne's body language exactly what he thought of this observation. A hick observation. Made by a hick.

But then the federal policeman went very still, looking at Burke with a smoky, hellish darkness in his eyes. 'What did you just say?'

Chapter 28

By Saturday morning the station's main briefing room was cluttered, the air poisonous. Additional desks, phones, and computers had been scrounged from downstairs, detectives and collators from other police districts on the Peninsula. But it had been a big Friday night for some of these men and women. Breath was sour, alcohol leeched from their pores, eyes were grainy and bloodshot.

Challis cranked open the windows and said, 'This is Sergeant Schiff of sex crimes. She's here because we had an abduction and rape, and now we have a murder that might have started out as an abduction and rape.'

He watched as sets of eyes flickered over Schiff. She cast a last glance at her phone and stood, facing them down, before positioning herself at a commanding spot in the room. An attractive woman, Challis thought. Slim, vivid, and implacable, wearing a clinging skirt today, glossy hair not pinned up but swinging about her shoulders. Very attractive, in fact: intelligent, wry, competent, with an air of mischief under it all. He thought she'd irritate some of the women and arouse a mix of desire, hostility, and rivalry in some of the men.

He inclined his head slightly, signalling that the floor was hers. She positioned herself between the wall map and portable display board, swishing a pointer. 'The first victim,' she said.

With a flick of her slender wrist she tapped a head-and-shoulders photograph. 'Chloe Holst, twenty years old, worked part-time at the Chicory Kiln restaurant here—' she tapped the map '—and abducted here—' another tap '—when a man dressed in a Victoria Police uniform, and carrying police ID, stopped her car. He got into her car, and forced her to drive around at knife-point. She was sexually assaulted several times in the hours that followed and finally dropped at this nature reserve.'

This time Schiff slapped the wall map. It swung as if caught in a gale.

'Forensics?' a voice called.

Challis shook his head. 'Nothing much. According to Miss Holst, her attacker used a condom, and when he was finished with her he washed her down and combed out her hair.'

'The second victim,' announced Schiff, into the pause that followed. 'Delia Rice, twenty-six years old, from—' she hesitated over the word '—Moo-roo-duc.'

'Moorooduc,' half-a-dozen voices said fluently, some helpful, others with a faint sneer. There was little that Challis could do about the sneers. Jeannie Schiff would be watched and assessed over the next few days. If she passed, the eye-rolling would cease.

'From Moorooduc,' Schiff said. 'Recently divorced and back living with her parents—who reported her missing yesterday afternoon, about the time her body was discovered in the boot of a crashed and abandoned Holden sedan found *here*.'

The map swayed again. 'Now, similarities between the two cases. Both were found naked, with bruising around the neck and on the stomach, thighs and genital area. Signs of forced intercourse, with condom lubricant found in the vagina, anus and throat. Both women were washed in a bleach solution and it's likely that Delia Rice's hair was combed out, just as the first victim's was.'

'Pubes, too?' said Neil Staines, a Frankston detective. He was young, a smirker.

Schiff said, 'Since you find the genitalia of even a dead woman arousing, perhaps you're not the right person for the job.'

There was a stunned silence, then laughter, but Staines's two colleagues hooted, as if to say that Jeannie Schiff was being overly sensitive, couldn't take a joke. One of them muttered, 'Pre-menstrual.'

Schiff indicated both men, and Staines, with the pointer. 'You, you and you, you're off the case. Frankly, you're a dead weight and a disgrace to the force.'

They gaped, looking around for support and finding none. 'Yeah, well, good luck,' Staines said, climbing out of his chair in his lazy, fatalistic way.

As he sauntered out, Schiff whacked his backside with the pointer. He was shocked. 'You hit me.'

'You bet.'

'I'm reporting you.'

'Go right ahead.'

Challis looked on with amusement and faint alarm. If this became an administrative headache, he wanted no part of it, not on top of everything else. And he wondered if he could afford to lose three investigators, even bad ones.

When the three had gone, Schiff said, 'Yes, I will get into trouble for that. But that doesn't matter. What matters is catching a rapist and a killer.'

There was a ripple of intensity in her voice and body.

'To recap: there are similarities between the two cases. But Delia Rice died as a result of the attack on her, and we don't know if she was abducted or went willingly with her attacker, and if she *was* abducted, we don't know if he'd posed as a police officer. The man seen running away from the scene was not wearing a uniform. Now, how do we read this? One, it wasn't our man but a random hitchhiker who for some reason strayed onto the driveway of the house around the time the accident occurred, and I doubt very much that that is the case. Two, he was an accomplice of the main offender. Three, the cases are not related; this is a different offender. Four, he changed into ordinary clothes before dumping the body, fearing the uniform would be noticed.'

Challis stirred. 'Our man is forensically aware, by the way. He'll have burnt the clothes.'

With grim authority, Schiff said, 'But not the uniform. He needs it. It's his main tool. It's not something he can buy off the rack at K-Mart.'

'But what if we're dealing with an actual policeman?' Scobie Sutton said.

'Then we keep an open mind. Now, another difference. The first victim was driven around in her own car, attacked in her own car, dumped from her own car, which was returned to the abduction site. We have nothing like that in the case of Delia Rice. She'd encountered financial difficulties after her divorce and sold her car.'

'So where was she abducted?' asked a Mornington detective. 'How did she get there?'

Schiff looked to Challis, who said, 'Miss Rice was driven to the Frankston station by her father on Thursday afternoon. She was to take a train to the city and stay overnight with friends. They'd made dinner reservations and had tickets to a Missy Higgins concert. She didn't arrive.'

Schiff stepped in again, saying, 'The friends didn't think anything of it when she didn't show. Thought she'd changed her mind. It all came out yesterday morning when Delia's mother phoned, wanting to speak to her. After that the parents dithered a bit, rang around all of her friends, spoke to the ex-husband—who lives in Sydney, incidentally, we can rule him out—and finally called us. By which time Delia had been dead for several hours.'

She glanced at Challis. He said, 'Returning to the car business: Chloe Holst states that she was stopped by a man driving a late model white Falcon. She could be excused for thinking it was an unmarked police car. We doubt he was driving his own car. Scobie?'

Scobie Sutton felt the strain of the collective gaze. He coughed, tapped files and folders into neat piles. 'We looked at the theft of white, late-model Falcons, Holdens, and other family-sized cars going back four weeks. Forty-one in Victoria, five on the Peninsula. Most were found quickly, probably stolen by joy riders. Four were torched, two damaged. As for the others, I expect they've been through a chop shop.'

'If it's the same man,' Challis said, 'he used the same tactic. Delia Rice was found in the boot of a white sedan, a Holden this time, stolen from the car park behind the TAFE College in Frankston.'

Schiff gave a bright, hard smile. 'Which raises the issue of time. Chloe Holst was snatched at night, Delia Rice we're not sure of. But we do know that it was daylight when her killer was driving around looking for somewhere to dump her. What does that tell us?'

Pam Murphy lifted a hand. 'Her attacker is unemployed, or he works irregular hours.'

'Very good. And so we come to the fun part of the proceedings, divvying up the work load.' She pointed, moving swiftly from person to person. 'You, get hold of the CCTV coverage in and around the TAFE college. You, Frankston station, ditto—and nearby streets and shops, in case Delia decided to take a later train. You, drive to the city, talk to the friends. You, track down her Peninsula friends. You, another word with the ex-husband. Constable Murphy, you're with me.'

Challis watched, trying to read the shifts in Pam Murphy's face and demeanour to tell him if she needed a break from the high-powered sergeant. He saw Pam Murphy giving Schiff a little punch to the shoulder as if to say, 'Loved the way you sorted out that prick from Frankston.'

Chapter 29

No *Home Digest* or *Décor* this time. Grace had pictures in her head.

She dressed down that Saturday morning—a broad-brimmed green cotton hat, cheaply elaborate sunglasses, shapeless T-shirt and outmoded cargo pants—and drove to Geelong, where she bought time at an Internet café. She needed to find out more about the Niekirks without leaving the search record on her own gear. The disguise was for the CCTV cameras.

First she Googled 'Warren Niekirk,' assuming he was the main player, but quickly learned that he'd been no more than a vaguely competent real estate salesman who'd had the brains, or luck, to marry into the Krasnov family, prominent Sydney art dealers. Under their patronage he'd become a vaguely competent second-hand dealer, specialising in vintage and veteran motorcars and aircraft.

So Grace concentrated on Mara Niekirk. According to the official Krasnov website, Marianna was the daughter of Peter (born Pyotr) Krasnov and granddaughter of the late Theodor (Feodor) Krasnov, the man behind Cossacks, a successful gallery and art dealership on Sydney's North Shore. It was all froth and bubbles, so she searched other sites, finding whispers and

murmurs of Krasnov dodginess. Fake and stolen art, forged catalogues and provenance, and artist rip-offs.

Grace returned to the Krasnov website and a moment later
was reading something that made her scalp prickle. Mara's
grandfather came from a White Russian family in the city of Harbin, on the wild and sparsely settled Manchurian steppes. That
explained why she'd been so riveted by the icon she'd seen hanging inside the Niekirk's glassed-in walkway.

She closed her eyes. She hadn't journeyed through life with
much of a past to anchor her, only a couple of names— 'Harbin',
'Nina'—lurking in her consciousness, and one old photograph.

The photograph, currently stashed in her safe-deposit box,
showed an old man and an old woman posed against a white-
washed interior wall, a hint of sturdy peasantry in their squat
shapes, their shapeless coats, the old woman's headscarf. And,
hanging behind the old man's shoulder, was the Niekirks' icon.
Inked on the back of the photograph were the words: *Nadezhda
and Pavel, Harbin, 1938.*

Who were Nadezhda and Pavel to her?

What was Mara Niekirk doing with their icon?

If it was the same icon.

The town of Harbin linked them, so Grace Googled it.

Harbin had started life as a collection of tents erected by Russian railway engineers in the late nineteenth century. It remained
a railway outpost for thirty years and then, almost overnight,
became home to tens of thousands of White Russians who had
fled from the Red Army after the 1917 revolution. By World War
II, Harbin was a bustling regional city of some grace and culture: opera and ballet companies, a symphony orchestra, a con-
servatorium, a technical college, many fine Russian Orthodox
churches, Churin's department store, and exclusive schools in
the old St Petersburg style. But if Harbin's White Russian refu-
gees were preserving pre-revolutionary Russian life and culture

in Harbin, they were also waiting for anti-monarchist and anti-Christian Soviet Russia to fail. When that happened, they would return. 'We are temporarily deprived of our Motherland,' one man wrote, 'but the battle for the true Russia has not ceased, merely taken on new forms.'

Grace glanced around the Internet café. A couple of backpackers, one or two poor-looking students, some elderly men and women. No one was interested in her. They were reading their emails, looking for aristocrats or convicts in their family trees. She returned to the history of the Krasnovs.

Mara's grandfather Theodor was born in 1920, the son of a White Russian colonel who had escaped from Vladivostok in 1919 and married a young woman named Tatiana, a true *Harbintsy*, born and raised on the outpost, the daughter of an engineer on the Chinese Eastern Railway. The family had servants, wealth, influence. They prospered even during the Great Depression of the 1930s and the Japanese occupation of the early 1940s.

Wealth, thought Grace. Influence. How did they get it? How did they keep it? They even survived the Red Army liberation of Harbin in 1945, the year Mara's father was born, although according to the website they were passionate anti-Reds. There were plenty of stories of treachery in Harbin. Some White Russians collaborated with the Japanese, others spied on and harassed anyone with Soviet citizenship or sympathies, and a handful robbed and kidnapped wealthy Jews and even made their way west to help the Waffen SS fight the Red Army. But at the war's end the Krasnovs slipped through the net and by 1949 were living in Shanghai.

So who did they pay off? Where did the money come from? Grace pictured the old couple in her photograph; nothing to their names but a few treasures from the motherland, some jewels, an icon. An old couple like that might fall into debt to a family like the Krasnovs.

What was the true story of the Krasnovs in Manchuria? She Googled a range of words and phrases but found only references to the family website and the North Shore gallery.

And the sugar-coated story of how, in the emigration wave of the 1950s, with time running out for the White Russians in China and most headed for Europe, Canada, and the United States, the Krasnovs chose Australia. Theodor, by then in his early thirties, thrived as an art and antiques dealer—using valuables stolen from fellow Russians, guessed Grace—and set up the gallery, Cossacks. When he died his son, Peter, built on his success.

Not only that: Peter's daughter, Mara, true to the traditions of her family, had branched out to establish a successful art and antiques business on the beautiful Mornington Peninsula in Victoria.

Blah, blah, blah.

It was almost 1 P.M. Grace paid for another half hour and gave herself a crash course in icons. Strange tingles went through her as she searched, ghost memories, trace emotions from her childhood, echoing the punch to the heart she'd felt yesterday, when she'd peered through Mara Niekirk's glass wall.

First she tried to date the icon. More modern than the Kiev and Novgorod schools of the thirteenth century; smaller, too. Grace thought the icon hanging in the Niekirks' walkway, like the one depicted in her heirloom photograph, was about 20 cm by 30 cm. Most of the icons she found pictured and described on the Internet were three or four times that size, but the later ones seemed to get smaller. She found a Simon Ushkarov from 1676, *The Archangel Michael Trampling the Devil Underfoot,* that was 23 cm by 20.5 cm.

Subject matter: usually the Virgin or the Madonna and child. Painted on wood, the halo in gold leaf, sometimes the face and background, too. Considered to be the Gospel in paint. *Praises to the Mother of God,* they were titled. *The Softening of Cruel Hearts.*

Then Grace found *O All-Hymned Mother*, created in the late 1700s in the Old Believers' workshop in Holui village in the Volga River region of central Russia. It showed mother and child posing in vivid colours, a rich play in the folds of drapery, tender melancholy in the Virgin's face. Decorated with gold leaf and a thin film of tempera, it glowed on Grace's screen as if lit from within.

Not her icon, but pretty close; possibly from the same village.

'Oh, that's so beautiful.'

Grace turned carefully. An elderly woman was looking over her shoulder.

'Don't mind me, I'm just a busybody. You must be an art student.'

'Yes,' Grace said, and she reached, very carefully, for the mouse and closed down the site, sighing. 'And I've got an essay to write.'

Chapter 30

On Sunday morning, Pam Murphy propped herself on one elbow and said, 'I could teach you how to surf. I've got a spare wetsuit.'

One of the many appealing things about Jeannie Schiff was her laugh. Raucous, appreciative, all-conquering, it started deep inside her and set up a tremble in her breasts and stomach.

Pam punched her. 'What's so funny?'

Stabbing a forefinger into her own breastbone, Jeannie said, 'Me? Salt water, flies, sand sticking where it's not meant to stick? I don't think so. The great outdoors, fresh air, sunshine? Not this cute little body.'

Pam stroked that cute little body with her free hand, watching the flesh give and restore itself under her touch. She stroked where sand was not meant to stick. Jeannie closed her eyes, moist and warm and ready to go again.

Pam leaned over and, with the tip of her tongue, picked a croissant flake from a nipple. 'I could eat you up,' she said, and immediately felt stupid.

'As I recall,' Jeannie said, 'you already did that.'

Odd, thought Pam, how sleeping with a woman hadn't been the momentous, earth shattering event she'd thought it would be. It was simply nice, greedy, appreciative sex with someone who happened to be a woman. No big deal. Flesh on flesh. Good sex, thoughtful, skilled, slightly different mechanically. But the feelings stayed the same. Why was that?

'Or a walk,' she said. 'Bushranger Bay. Greens Bush.'

Jeannie Schiff stretched like a cat. 'Honey, I don't do the outdoors.'

Pam flopped back on her pillow. 'Our first disagreement. It's all downhill from now on.'

They seemed to click on many levels, including a sense of what was funny or absurd, but this time the sergeant from sex crimes didn't laugh. Leaning on one elbow, stroking Pam's inner thigh absently as if searching for the right words, Jeannie Schiff said, 'I live with someone.'

'I know, you told me.'

'Just making sure.'

'It's all right, Jeannie, honestly.'

'Fun, right? We're having fun.'

'Fun,' Pam said.

She smiled, and they kissed, and Jeannie went to pee, loud enough for Pam to hear through the open en-suite door. Jeannie Schiff wasn't a man, certainly wasn't mannish, with her softness, her curviness, her clothes. But somehow she wasn't any different.

Pam thought about it. She'd slept with maybe ten men—be honest, she knew exactly how many—but didn't think she was very good at relationships. She was frank, upfront, what-you-see-is-what-you-get. Not good at subtleties and games.

Not keen to be hurt again.

Was she setting herself up for that? Would sleeping with a woman mean there was more at stake?

She couldn't see it, frankly. Pam Murphy was honest, open. Perhaps too trusting, but she was good at examining herself. She didn't feel a scrap of guilt or shame or childish daring. She didn't feel unmoored. No momentous shifting inside her head. She'd just had a few nights of great sex and companionship, that's all. No big deal. And no false promises.

Jeannie re-entered the room, shaking water from her hands, a glint of mischief as she came bounding in and dived across the bed, her flesh flexing nicely here and there. They had the rest of the day together, and they had maybe a handful of other times before the case was closed, and she went back to her architect in the city.

Pam blinked, zoning out a little as a brain zap passed through her, but it was almost like a familiar companion, and all she wanted to think about was kissing and touching. So they made love, and then they cuddled, and then Jeannie Schiff had to go and spoil it a little.

'It's okay, you know.'

'What is?'

'I know you're not gay. I can always tell when someone isn't. It's okay just to have a bit of fun, you know.'

Well, screw you. Pam sat up and gave her lover a slap on the butt. 'Stay as long as you like. I'm going for a walk on the beach.'

A FEW KILOMETRES TO the east, Scobie Sutton was faintly irritable. 'Well, what's it entail?'

Roslyn Sutton stuck her jaw out, bottom lip pouting. 'You don't want me to do it.'

'I didn't say that. It sounds like a big commitment, that's all.'

His daughter put her little fists to her chest beseechingly. 'It would be so much fun.'

Sutton was setting the table for lunch—cheese, tomatoes, bread, butter, olives, lettuce, tahini, sliced beef from last night's roast—and Roslyn was hovering with a fistful of knives and forks. His grumpiness increasing, he slammed a plate onto the place mat in front of his wife, no response in her mute, helpless face.

Beth should have been spending the day out, as she did every Sunday, but this time her mother and sister were coming here.

He took a deep breath, looked at Roslyn, and said, 'I can see it would be fun, but there are things to consider. How many performances?'

'Four.'

'When?'

'Two weekends in November.'

'How late are the rehearsals?'

'Sundays between one and five, and Fridays between seven and ten.'

Scobie knew he'd capitulate. It wasn't as if his daughter wasn't a terrific singer and dancer.

'What about netball?' he asked glumly.

'I won't do it this term.'

'What about your homework?'

That bottom lip again. 'I'll fit it in. Plenty of kids do this every year, Dad.'

'It's a lot of driving around for me. What if I'm working a big case—like now?'

'You never let me do anything!'

Sutton made a mental list: lifesaving, netball, sleepovers, birthday parties, dancing classes. . . . 'Ros, within reason, I have never denied you anything.'

There had been a time when he'd have said '*We* have never denied you anything.' A time when the burden had been shared. He snatched the knives and forks from Roslyn's sulky hands and dropped them in place around the table. The running around would leave him ragged with tiredness. Resentment would grow corrosively. Right at that moment, he hated his wife.

'Please, Dad.'

Scobie drew in a breath. And just at that point a quiet voice said, 'Let her do it if she wants.'

Father and daughter stopped what they were doing.

'Mum?'

'I can drive you around. I don't mind,' Beth Sutton said. She glanced at Scobie, a little steel in it. 'No need to stare at me like that.'

CHALLIS WAS TRYING TO unwind. Uncertainty was an ever-present condition of his life, and he was beginning to hate it. He wanted Ellen Destry close; he wanted to be able to speak his mind in public and generate debate, not opprobrium. He wanted simple pleasures, in fact, like seeing his house in full daylight occasionally. The place was always draped in long morning shadows when he left for work and was a humped shape in starlight when he got back. And so he spent the first part of that Sunday morning with a newspaper, toast and coffee at his kitchen window, watching shadows wind back from his yard. Eight A.M. Nine A.M. Ten. Sunlight of great clarity, silently foraging ducks, a great beckoning stillness. He pulled on his old Rockports and walked up the hill, passing the orchard, the stockbroker's weekender cottage, the farm dogs that saw him as a new threat each time he approached their boundary. Then down the laneway beyond the brow of the hill.

A second coffee on his return, and then the sunlight beckoned again. He needed to be out in it, mowing, weeding.

Then it was mid-afternoon, and he decided to wash his car, which wore a patina of dust once more. He fetched the keys and got in, intending to drive around to the garden hose in the back yard.

Nothing. Not even enough juice to turn the starter motor over.

Challis was trying again when a car turned in from the dirt road that ran past his house. He got out, poised and wary. He didn't get many visitors—an occasional neighbour, lost tourist, or someone looking to buy a hobby farm—and always, at the back of his mind, was the expectation that an enemy would come for him one day, someone he'd put away. Perhaps a posse of Ethical Standards officers, keen to stitch him up for embarrassing the government. He glanced around quickly. A shovel that he'd forgotten to put back in the garden shed, tree cover on the next property, a tangle of peppermint gums, bracken, and pittosporums.

A grey Mazda. It pulled up behind the Triumph, and the driver and his female passenger got out, the driver lifting a hand to him. 'Hal.'

'Alan.'

Challis didn't relax, not fully. Ellen's ex-husband was a big man. Relations between them had always been awkward.

'Hope we're not interrupting anything.'

'Just pottering,' Challis said.

'I don't think you've met Sue Wells, my significant other.'

When Ellen had heard about the girlfriend, she'd said sourly, 'I bet she's young, no brains, boobs out to here,' but Challis saw a short, round, greying woman aged in her forties, wearing faded baggy jeans and a tired smile.

He shook her hand. 'We spoke on the phone. How's Larrayne holding up?'

'Sleeps a lot,' Wells said. 'A bit teary sometimes, other times angry, but basically she's fine.'

Alan Destry shifted on his solid feet. 'That's why we're here, Hal. It was great what you did. I can't thank you enough.'

Challis rolled his shoulders, looking for an escape. 'Coffee?'

'Just had afternoon tea in Flinders. Need to get back before the weekend traffic gets too busy.'

Challis felt a fugitive regret for the leisure time that had been lost to him over the years and envy for the early stages of love, when there is only promise, not heartache, in the air. He missed Ellen.

As if reading his mind, Alan Destry said, 'Heard from Ells?'

'Most days.'

'Good, good.' Destry toed the ground uncomfortably, then glanced at Challis. 'Read what you said in the paper.'

Challis was silent, gave a short nod.

'Took guts.'

'Fat lot of good it's done me, or the rank and file in general.'

Destry had run out of steam. 'Well, we won't keep you.'

'Actually,' Challis said, 'would you have a set of jumper leads in your car? Flat battery.'

Alan Destry was more comfortable with dead batteries than live emotions. 'Gis a look.'

With Challis behind the wheel, ready to turn the key, Destry raised the bonnet.

'Rats.'

Challis got out. 'Your leads won't fit?'

'No, *rats*. Furry animals with sharp teeth.'

Challis peered in. Holes in the radiator hoses, exposed wiring, and rat droppings, flecks of chewed rubber and insulation scattered on and around the engine.

He saw it as a sign. When the others had gone, he washed, polished and photographed his creaky old car, fired up the Internet, and posted it for sale.

Finally it was evening, and he could log on and talk to Ellen, who was in Glasgow. Her tiny image on the screen was a tonic as he outlined his day. 'So in the end I went over and fetched your car.'

'Good.'

'Thought I'd buy an old MG this time.'

'Like hell. Describe the view from your window,' Ellen said. 'Describe it exactly. I want to see it in my mind's eye.'

Challis told her about the play of failing light and deepening shadows on the stretch of lawn and trees between his house and the road, surprising himself. 'After years of report writing, I didn't think I could be so poetic.'

'Oh I miss that, I miss you. . . .'

'It's only been a few days,' he said.

'I know.'

'How's the sex crimes business where you are?'

'Same crimes, same criminals,' she said. 'Probably more sex slavery and human trafficking. Same police culture.'

Meaning that most police officers were male, and many believed at least partly that the victims of sexual assault brought it upon themselves in some way. The conversation drifted on to other things, Challis watching his liquidambar—what Ellen called his star tree—merge with the greater darkness all around it. A car crawled past at the end of his driveway, headlights probing the pines, bracken, blackberry canes, and pittosporums lining the road. He knew it was a local car. Newcomers went faster, somehow failing to take into account that the road was narrow, the dirt and gravel surface treacherous, the bends blind.

He said, 'Thought I might do a bit more work to your house during the week, if I can find the time.'

Fix the home invasion damage, in fact. There was an awkward silence, and Ellen said, 'Look—'

'Larrayne's been staying there,' he said, in an attempt to tease out what Ellen had or hadn't been told.

'So I understand. Look, Hal, you don't have to fix my house up, though I am grateful, honestly.'

'Honestly.' One of those tricky words.

Chapter 31

On Monday morning Jeannie Schiff tossed Pam Murphy the keys to the silver Holden and said, 'You drive.'

Great, a city trip in peak hour. One of these days, Murphy thought, we'll have autopsy facilities here on the Peninsula.

They were barely north of the town, stuck behind a Woodleigh school bus, when Schiff said, 'We're not going to have a problem today, are we?'

Pam darted her a glance: She didn't want to plough into the rear of the bus. 'Problem?'

'You and me. Sulks, the silent treatment.'

Pam burned. Sure, she knew she was being a little guarded, but she wasn't sulking. 'No, Sarge.'

'There's no need to use my rank, not when we're alone. We have been intimate, after all.' Heavy quotation marks around 'intimate.' Pam said nothing. She felt nothing, really. Her feelings weren't hurt, she wasn't in love, she didn't feel betrayed. . . .

Felt a little used, though. Maybe. She had gone into this with her eyes open, after all.

And so what if Jeannie hadn't wanted to walk on the beach yesterday?

The school bus slowed, pulled onto the verge, where a

couple of teenagers slouched, waiting, bags at their feet. They climbed onto the bus as if dazed, and Pam took the opportunity to spurt past. Now she was behind a line of cars. She glanced at the dash clock: 8 A.M. The autopsy was slated for 10 A.M.

Then she felt Jeannie Schiff's pretty right hand on her leg.

CHALLIS DROVE ELLEN DESTRY'S Corolla to work and found Scobie Sutton waiting in his office, standing tensely in a funereal suit coat and pants, the jacket flapping around him.

'Scobie.'

'Morning, boss.'

Challis waited. Sutton said tensely, 'I was wondering if you've seen this.'

A press release from police headquarters. Challis liked to kid that he had a special gift: He could tell if any printed or electronic document was worth reading merely by scanning the title, subtitle, and first line. Emails had a short life in his inbox. The contents of his pigeonhole had been transformed into a million egg cartons. 'New crime scene unit,' he said. 'What about it?'

'You suggested I should shift sideways.'

Challis paused. He shrugged off his jacket, pegged it, and sat behind his desk. 'Sit,' he said, staring through the window as Sutton folded his bones again. 'You'd need training.'

'Yes.'

The role of the new unit was to collect crime scene information in the first instance—fingerprints, fibres, DNA, photographs, and video recordings—and pass it on to the relevant division for analysis. The results would then be passed to CIU detectives, like Challis and his team, for action. Challis had mixed feelings about the new system. It would free CIU and uniformed police to concentrate on targeted operations, bringing increased speed and efficiency. But he *liked* standing in the middle of a crime scene, feeling his way into the who, what, and why.

'You'll work out of Frankston.'

'I don't mind. It's only a twenty minute drive for me.'

Challis made a decision. The work—collecting evidence for someone else to analyse—would suit Scobie. Less need for intuitive leaps. Less call for speculating about the needs, moods, impulses, and motives that drove other human beings.

'I can put in a good word if you like.'

Sutton blinked as if to say, Whoa, not so fast, then ventured to say, 'If you could, boss, that would be great.'

Challis stood, grabbed his jacket again. 'No problem. Meanwhile we need another word with Delia Rice's parents. Something's not quite right about the timeline.'

SCHIFF SQUEEZED PAM'S LEG in a way that was chummy yet undershot with desire. 'It was good, you and me. But not. . . .'

'I know,' Pam said very distinctly, hands fixed on the steering wheel. 'Not going anywhere. I know that. I wanted to have some fun, that's all, same as you.'

As if she'd not heard a word, Schiff said, 'I could sense a kind of reserve in you, as if you liked it OK, but it wasn't really your thing. I think, deep down, you prefer men.'

I prefer to do without the bullshit, Pam thought.

A final squeeze and Schiff removed her hand. 'No regrets, okay? Put it down to experience.'

Fine. Pam could insist until the cows came home that she didn't have regrets, wouldn't have them, but Schiff had a kind of worldly, older-woman thing going. She wasn't listening.

Well, I do have one regret, Pam thought. I regret that Sergeant Jeannie Schiff is as big an arsehole as some of the men I've encountered. Live and learn.

'Where was he going with Delia Rice's body?' she said. 'He'd have known he couldn't dump her in the reserve, so he must have been looking for another location. Wonder how well he knows the Peninsula?'

'What?' said Schiff, busy on the keypad of her phone. 'Look, save it for a briefing.'

DELIA RICE'S PARENTS LIVED in a low pale brick 1970s house set on three hectares of muddy yard near the Moorooduc primary school. Bill Rice was an all-purpose landscaping and excavation contractor, so the yard was crammed with tip trucks, bobcats, backhoes, excavators, and dozers. Challis and Sutton were shown into a dark, chilly sitting room and, moments later, learned that a crucial piece of their briefing information was incorrect.

'Let's get this straight, Mr. Rice,' Challis said. 'You didn't drive her to the Frankston station?'

'No. Like I said, I *was* going to take her there, but in the end I had a dentist's appointment.'

Challis kept his voice mild and even. 'So she didn't catch a train, didn't go to the city?'

'She did, but from *Somerville*,' Rice said, as if explaining to a dummy. 'Where my dentist is.'

Challis nodded in understanding. Somerville was on a small branch line that served the southeastern Peninsula towns: city-bound passengers changed at Frankston.

'I had a three-thirty appointment,' Bill Rice explained, 'and the plan was Delia would sit in the waiting room till I was finished, only the dentist was running late, so she said she'd catch the Somerville train.'

He was ravaged with grief, eyes raw, wispy hair limp and uncombed, grey stubble on his cheeks, jaw, and neck. Erin Rice said nothing but sat beside her husband, holding one of his huge, sausage-fingered hands in her plump lap. She was combed and tidy, but more stunned than her husband.

Challis thought through the cock-up. Between the Rices' initial missing persons' statement and the homicide investigation, a key first impression had gone unchecked. Bill Rice had told someone what the *intended* plan was, and by the time it reached Challis's team, it had become fact.

'You don't know for certain that she caught any train?' he said gently.

In a small voice, Rice said, 'I assumed she did. I mean, what else did she do?'

DR. BERG BEGAN THE autopsy at ten o'clock, Murphy and Schiff watching from the raised viewing bay, Berg's voice crackling from the wall-mounted speakers as she worked. The autopsy suite was large, square, and brightly lit by skylights and neon tubes. The floor and two walls were of small, gleaming tiles, with banks of refrigerated stainless steel drawers set into the other walls. The pathologist worked at one of the long, broad zinc tables, the surface cleansed by a constant stream of cold water that ran from the slightly elevated top end to a chrome drainage pipe at the bottom.

'Rigor begins in the face and jaw,' she said, as if talking to students or thinking aloud, 'followed by the upper limbs and finally the hips and legs.' She glanced up at the figures watching her. 'Unfortunately rigor and lividity occur at unpredictable rates. This poor woman died violently, meaning adrenaline, which is an accelerating factor. She was kept in a sealed environment for some hours, the boot of a car. The temperature within would have been fairly stable but gradually increasing if the car was in direct sunlight for any length of time. Meanwhile, the body was protected from insect activity, weather extremes, and other variables.'

She began to manipulate the body, first the feet, then each leg, lifting and bending, watching the knees. She proceeded to the abdomen, pressing down, and finally grasped and rotated the head a few centimetres left and right.

'Rigor has come and gone. I have no reason to reconsider my opinion yesterday, that the victim had been dead for six to eight hours when found.'

CHALLIS SIPPED HIS COFFEE. He hadn't asked for it, but it had been delivered, white, watery, and tepid. His knees were squashed between the sofa and a coffee table as solid as a brick wall.

'How did she intend to get to the station from the dentist? Taxi?'

'She walked. It's not far—five minutes?'

'She had a specific train in mind? She had a timetable?'

Rice blinked. 'Don't know. She doesn't usually take a local train.'

'What would Delia do,' said Challis carefully, 'if she were faced with a long wait?'

'What do you mean?'

'It's a limited service on that line, only a few trains each day.'

Erin Rice removed her husband's hand, placed it on his bulky knee, and they all eyed it briefly, a disembodied hand. 'Delia was always impatient,' she murmured. 'Impatient to marry that man, impatient to get to the city.'

Impatient.

Challis put his cup down and started the motions that would get himself and Sutton out of the house with the least disruption, pain, and haste. 'Thank you both for helping us clear that up. It will help us pinpoint Delia's movements.'

He didn't say *final* movements. He couldn't say it would bring her back. He couldn't promise it would identify her killer. Bill and Erin Rice were crying again anyway. They weren't thinking about blame or justice just yet.

◆ ◆ ◆

THE PATHOLOGIST LIFTED HER head and called, 'Lights.'

The room darkened. She ran a UV light over the body slowly, quartering the pale, slack flesh. 'Lights,' she called again.

The room brightened. 'No semen present on the surface of the body.'

'Get on with it,' Schiff muttered. 'Vagina, mouth, anus.'

'No fibres,' Berg said presently, 'nothing under the nails, nothing caught in the hair—apart from trace elements from the car itself.'

Schiff muttered, shook her glossy head, and restlessly checked her phone for messages.

More time passed. 'No semen present in the mouth, vagina, or anus,' Berg said.

And later: 'It is entirely possible that we'll find trace elements of a different order in the victim's eyes, nasal passages, and ear canals, telling us where she'd been before being forced into the car. Needless to say, analysis will take time.'

'Needless to say,' said Schiff.

She was standing very close to Pam. Pam moved away.

BEFORE STARTING THE CAR, Challis made a phone call. He asked a question, said thanks, pocketed the phone.

'There was a train through Somerville at eleven past three,' he said, 'but Delia Rice was still in her father's car then, on the way to the dentist. The next was at ten to five.'

Sutton said nothing. It was as if he hadn't listened or didn't know what to do with the information, so Challis started the car and pulled away from the kerb. There was silence as they passed a stretch of sodden grassland, a Christmas tree farm and one of the Coolart Road roundabouts. Injecting some sharpness into his voice, Challis said, 'You heard the mother: Delia was impatient by nature.'

Scobie Sutton came out of his fog. 'Right. . . .'

'Think about it. When she realised she'd have to wait for an hour and a half, she decided to hitchhike. Got herself rescued by a nice policeman.'

'And her father so close,' said Sutton tragically.

Challis tuned him out, checked his watch. Too soon to call Murph at the morgue.

QUIETNESS SETTLED AS BERG began to cut into the body. Pam watched with a clammy dread. The only sounds were the faint hum of the ceiling lights, murmured voices in distant corridors, fabric scraping against fabric as Jeannie Schiff grew increasingly restless. Finally the pathologist said, 'Major petechial haemor-rhaging . . . bloody froth caked around the mouth . . . damage to the hyoid. . . .'

She looked up at the detectives. 'Death was due to manual asphyxia.'

'Well, we all knew that,' Schiff said, striding for the door.

Chapter 32

At two o'clock that Monday afternoon, Steve Finch was absorbed in slotting more RAM into an old desktop PC when the air cooled and shifted. Or he'd imagined it. What he wasn't imagining was the man standing on the other side of the workbench that doubled as his counter and desk. He jumped, trying to hide the response. 'Didn't hear you come in.'

The man said nothing, and Finch thought, *cop*. He read him quickly: slight build, well dressed, aquiline nose, eyes twinkling with cold intelligence. The kind of cop, Finch thought, who catches criminals because he thinks like one.

'What can I do for you?'

'The name is Towne,' the man said, flashing ID.

Finch glimpsed the name, a logo, and some of the words before it was folded into a pocket again. 'Federal? What would the federal police want with me?'

'I'm told you're the go-to guy if someone wants to fence a stolen painting,' the man said.

Finch screwed his face into a scoffing dismissal. 'I don't know who you've been talking to, pal, but—'

Towne dug into another pocket and now held a small pistol. He wasn't listening to Finch but gazing as if amused up and down the nearby shelves. With a grunt of satisfaction, he shoved the barrel into a rack of army greatcoats and fired. The coats were excellent sound suppressors. Finch gaped and bent to protect his groin. Then he straightened, trying to present a smaller target to the mad policeman.

'You can't do that.'

'I just did.'

'I'll never sell them now.'

'Oh, I don't know, genuine army wear, complete with bullet hole,' said Towne.

Finch's commercial instincts clicked into gear. 'But still. . . .'

Towne pocketed the pistol and leaned over the counter in a matey fashion. 'Let's start again: I have it on good authority, namely the art and antiques squad, that you are the only show in town when it comes to fencing high-end paintings and other collectibles, like coins and stamps.'

Obscurely flattered, Finch said, 'I'm not confirming or denying.'

The pistol came out again, and Finch backed away. 'No. Jesus. Put the gun away.'

Towne didn't.

'All right, okay, what do you want?'

'You can start by telling me if you deal with this woman.'

A photograph of Suze, looking younger and a bit feral but still heart-stopping. Finch cast glances around his shop as if searching the dim recesses of his memory. He took in the front door, the CLOSED sign turned out to the world. 'Er, might do.'

Towne fired through the greatcoats again and said, 'Think what you can charge for a coat with *two* bullet holes in it. I don't want "might" or "maybe" answers, Steve.'

Finch slumped. 'Her name's Susan. Don't know her last name.'

'How do I find her?'

'She always contacts me.'

'She contacts you out of the blue and says I've got this genuine Brett Whiteley I stole yesterday.'

'Look, she doesn't usually flog art. It's mostly cameras, coin collections, jewellery, watches. . . . Nothing large or bulky. It has to be stuff she can hide.'

'You don't have a phone number.'

'No.'

'Address?'

Finch shook his head, desperately aware that he had little information to offer the trigger-happy cop. 'Like I said, she comes in and shows me her stuff.'

'I thought you said she contacts you.'

'Not always. Not in advance. She turns up with some gear, and I give her some cash, and if it's a rare item and I need to do a bit of homework, find a buyer, set a fair price, that kind of thing, then she'll contact me again a couple of days later and. . . .'

'You're babbling,' Towne said.

Finch shut his mouth with a click.

'I need to find her, Steven.' An air of finality, brooking no argument.

Finch was frustrated. 'Look, she never works locally. In this state, I mean. Always interstate.'

'Anything at all? How she made contact with you in the first place, what car she drives, who her friends are. . . .'

'I don't know anything. For a junkie, she's super cautious.'

Towne frowned. 'She's a junkie?'

'Yeah. Got an expensive habit to feed.'

'Who's her dealer?'

'How would I know?'

Towne wasn't satisfied. 'A super thief, super cautious. And she's a junkie?'

'Well, I mean, I *think* she's one,' Finch said. His eyes lit up. 'She's got a kid, little girl. I've seen photos.'

Towne seemed rocked by the news. He recovered and said, 'See, you *do* know things about her.'

'It's all coming back to me. She's worried the heroin's making her a bad parent so her sister's raising the daughter.'

'Sister? Where does this sister live?'

Finch muttered, as if talking to himself, 'Maybe if I blew up a still from the security video. . . .'

'Hello? Steven? Pay attention.'

Finch gestured hastily at the cluttered shelf above and behind him. 'Hidden camera.'

'Video or digital,' demanded Towne, rapping out the words.

'I'm fully digitised, permanent storage on hard drive.'

'So?'

'The other day she showed me some photos of her daughter and her parents.'

'Parents,' said Towne flatly, as if hearing more fresh information.

'They're old,' Finch said.

'Maybe she lives with them.'

Finch shook his head, keen to keep the air full of helpful information. 'Old folks home somewhere.'

'Where?'

'With a bit of tweaking I should be able to get good close-ups, you know, background detail. That help you?'

'Do it.'

'What, now?'

'You've just shut up shop for the day,' Towne said.

Finch complied, thinking, Good luck, Suze. You won't last long, with this guy after you.

Chapter 33

Day passed into night.

In Waterloo, Tina Knorr worked the four-to-midnight shift, coming off duty as the clocks edged into Tuesday. She didn't change out of her uniform, just grabbed her bag from her locker, said hi to the nurses coming on duty and walked out to her car, keys swinging from her forefinger. The staff car park was a broad lake of moonlit asphalt, shadowy at the far end, where she'd been obliged to slot her Barina, every other spot taken when she'd come on duty.

But now there were scarcely any cars left there, and none near the Barina, apart from a big white car. Cop car, must be, because a uniformed policeman got out of it as she approached. She saw him edge across to the Barina's driver's door, his back to her, and her mind raced. Roadworthy check? Damage? Someone hiding in the back seat?

'Anything wrong?'

He was an odd shape, or the uniform a bad fit, the shirt curiously tight in places, the pants too short, too wide in the hips, the cap too small. Without turning he said, 'We've had reports of a prowler, miss.'

Welcome to the world of public hospitals in Victoria, Tina

thought: bad lighting, no security cameras, doctors who think they're God, and now prowlers. A better than fifty percent chance of dying from a staph infection. 'Near my car?'

'Just checking. But I can't see nothin' so you can get in your car now, no worries.'

A rough, uneducated voice. It didn't seem quite right to Tina somehow, but by now she was almost beside him. And then a few things clicked into place, not that she was able to make sense of them: some kind of black knitted cloth in his left hand, flesh-coloured latex gloves, face averted. . . .

And she knew him. 'Darren?'

He jerked and swore, and she took a step back from him, drawing her thin, grey, ward-rounds cardigan around herself, seeking security in the stillness and emptiness of the night. Another step, and then it was too late, he'd grabbed her, a knife blade to her stomach.

'Please, Darren.'

His eyes were jumping out of their sockets and the smell of him: a kind of chemical rottenness. Terrific. He was probably ripped on something that made him violent and unpredictable, and she'd just let him know he'd been recognised. She could almost tick off the emotions about to rollercoaster inside his head: vulnerability, invincibility, bewilderment, rage, paranoia. Why had she said his name? He'd be totally panicked now.

Maybe she could humanise the situation. 'Darren?'

'Shut up. Let me think.' He thought for about a second. Then, 'Get in the fucking car.'

She never locked it. Who'd steal a Barina, especially one with 298,000 km on the clock, sun faded and streaked with birdshit? She made to go around to the passenger side, but he shrieked at her, 'Did I tell you to do that? Did I?'

'Sorry, Darren.'

She got behind the wheel, and he came in right on her tail, crowding her. Oh, so she *was* supposed to get into the passenger seat after all, but by sliding across from the driver's side of the car. Except in a Barina you don't exactly slide. She bumped her head on the rearview mirror, scraped a shin on the gearstick, tore her tights, put her back out.

'Keys.'

They were still swinging from her ring finger, and he tore them from her. In an instant of blinding pain, her finger went out of joint. She moaned, head sinking to her knees, the world swimming around her.

'Good, you got the right idea, keep your fucking head down.'

He ground the starter motor and found reverse. Then he searched for first gear, and the gearbox made its wretched grind and howl. 'You have to start in second,' Tina said. And, apologetically, 'Needs a new gearbox.'

'Did I tell you to fucking speak? Keep your head down.'

The car protested, and then they were bumping out onto the street. She made a mental map of the turns and stops in the minutes that followed. He was heading north and eventually would come to a roundabout and need to choose Dandenong or Somerville. Unless he took the road out to the wasteland of unloved paddocks leading to the shire rubbish tip.

Out to where he'd dumped Chloe Holst.

She said, 'Darren, that first girl, her name was Chloe, I bet you didn't know that I helped nurse her?'

She said it with her head to the side, neck craning to look up at him, hoping the words might strike home somehow.

Reality check. Did she really think she could get through to a guy like Darren Muschamp? He was more likely to stick her with the knife than show remorse. He didn't look like he'd even heard her. His mouth was open—concentration? Stupidity? Blocked sinuses? His eyes were jumpy.

She tried again. 'I mean, what a coincidence, eh? Or was it deliberate, snatching me from the place that treated her?'

She was genuinely curious. Her answer was a punch to the head with his knife hand, pebbly knuckles scraping painfully across her ear.

'Darren, please, I feel carsick.'

His knees jiggled, as if he didn't know what to do with the information.

'Can I sit up?'

She sat up. He didn't stop her. Without meaning to, she began to cry, and soon couldn't stop the tears.

'*Shut up,*' he screamed.

'I can't.'

'I can't stand it! Shut the fuck up!'

She wept, and he punched her ineffectually, his attention veering from her to the road and back again. By now they were heading north toward Dandenong. Or the ranges or even as far as New South Wales or Queensland. . . .

'Darren, please, you might accidentally stab me.'

He turned his rage on her. 'How the fuck do you know my name? I don't know *you.*'

'You're Mandy's cousin, right?'

He didn't reply.

Tina said, 'Mandy and me went to Cranbourne High together. You remember. We met at her twenty-first.' She sighed, sat back, her head resting on the padded support, said softly, 'That was a great party.'

It had the effect of mollifying him. 'You were the chick did the pole dance routine with a broomstick.'

Another chick, actually, and as twenty-first birthday parties go, it had been fairly dull. 'You've got a good memory,' she said warmly.

Get him talking. Take his mind off the knife and her vulnerable stomach. He took his knife hand off the wheel, stuck the blade tip between his teeth and made a flicking motion. She closed her eyes.

He made an unaccountable stop soon after that, pulling into a recessed farm gateway, darkness all around them, a wispy moon above. Took out a mobile phone and pressed speed dial.

'Hi, it's me, you got any gear?'

Oh, great, he was chasing. Tina edged her hand toward the door handle—and the knife tip was at her throat a millisecond later.

He was able to do that and simultaneously explode into the mouthpiece of his phone: 'I fucking do not . . . I fucking paid you . . . I did so . . . mate, you can't do this to me.'

Then silence as he jerked the phone away from his ear and stared at it in astonishment. 'The prick hung up on me.'

'Please, Darren, let me go home.'

He turned to her, still astonished, as if wondering who she was and what he was doing with her in the middle of nowhere. Then his face cleared, and the animal cunning was there again. 'You got any gear on you?'

'Me? No.'

'Gis your fucken bag.'

He grabbed it, rested it between the seats, and started rummaging. Her tampons flew into the footwell, a packet of tissues, electricity bill—please, God, don't let him check the address—and her hairbrush. Now the wallet, which he hunted through, pocketing the $45 that had to last her until payday on Friday, tipping the coins from the little zippered compartment into his palm, shoving them into the pocket along with the paper money.

How much stuff would her $45 buy him? He wouldn't be fussy, probably. Dope, ice, whatever was going.

He got out his phone again and pressed buttons and stared, aghast, as it beeped. 'Low battery? I don't believe it.' He swung his head close to hers, and the stench was stupefying. 'Gis your phone.'

It was in the cardigan pocket. 'I don't have it on me, I dropped it in the toilet this morning.'

'Fuck, fuck, fuck.'

They sat there, and she understood that he would want to cure his misery with her pretty soon, in the only way he knew how, so she said, in a conversational voice, 'Mandy told me you were her favourite of all her cousins.'

He muttered. What, she didn't know.

'She said you'd had a hard life.'

Mandy hadn't said anything of the kind about her loser cousin, but he acknowledged it with a nod, saying, 'That's one way of putting it.'

'Is that Mandy's uniform, Darren? She told me she was going to join the police when I saw her at Christmas.'

Fill the air with comforting nonsense, Tina, she told herself. Remind him he was human.

Another mutter, but his knee was bobbing again. 'What do you need, Darren? I could get something from the drugs cabinet at work.'

Get him back to town where there were lights and people instead of this blanketing night.

'What I want,' he said, 'is for you to shut the fuck up.'

'Sure, sorry.'

He was looking at her breasts, and she didn't want that. 'Remember you have to start off in second gear, plenty of revs.'

'Put the back of your seat down.'

'Pardon?'

'You know, recline it.'

'Darren, you don't. . . .'

The knife nicked her neck, quick as a flash, and first came the wetness, then the stinging pain.

'*Do it.*'

'Okay, okay.'

On her back now, knees locked together, arms rigidly at her sides. He tugged at the edge of her skirt, which she'd trapped under her thighs. 'What have we here?' he said roguishly as he pushed the hem up to her waist. She shuddered as fear and coldness crept through her.

'Darren, don't, what would Mandy say?'

She was expecting him to explode. Instead, he seemed fascinated by her crotch. He poked at her mound experimentally through the miserable cotton. 'I want to see your sweet cunty.'

She'd never heard it called that before. 'I'm embarrassed.'

'Don't be,' he said gallantly. 'I bet you're beautiful down there.'

Amazing. Suddenly he thinks we're on a date? 'Please, Darren.'

'Do you shave? Tell me you shave.' His voice was wobbly with it.

'Darren, I feel . . . it's my period.'

He recoiled as if he'd touched something unclean. The stickiness and the smell and the staining. She could see it all in his face. What sort of experience did a man like him have, come to that?

'Can't stay here,' he muttered.

He jerked her skirt down and shot off down the road, managing the second gear start perfectly. He's taking me somewhere to finish me off, she thought.

But all he did was drive and talk to himself. Up to Dandenong they went, over to Berwick, back down through Cranbourne, across to Frankston, and he didn't shut up once through the long hours. It was winding-down-from-a-high talk and made little sense to her. She would have signalled to other drivers, or pedestrians, if there'd been any or if he'd drawn close enough to them or if he hadn't deliberately kept to back roads and slow lanes, away from civilisation.

The night unfolded, a criss-crossing of the Peninsula, Tina feeling sleepy and acidic, until, in the queer light of dawn, they found themselves on the freeway, heading south. At this hour it was a broad, empty ribbon striping the hillside folds, with very little traffic. Then, somewhere inland of Mount Martha Cove, they spotted a highway patrol car in the act of pulling over a hotted-up Subaru. 'Losers!' shouted Darren, full of glee, and Tina Knorr reached across and heaved on the Barina's cracked steering wheel. The little car tipped gamely on two wheels, then recovered and ploughed toward the police car until the chequer-board pattern painted along the flank was all that Tina could see.

Chapter 34

During the passing of the days, Grace had walked the beach at Breamlea and argued with herself. The tides and the wind raced, dog walkers nodded hello, gulls slid through the layers of salty air, and Grace argued that she should never break her cardinal rule. Don't rob the Niekirks, she told herself. Too close to home.

In counterargument she pointed out that a one-off robbery would be okay since she wasn't known in Victoria, and the local cops had no MO to compare. Besides, the house behind the cypress hedge was tucked out of sight, the security could be bypassed, and her VineTrust safe-deposit box was close by. And it was clear, according to Google Earth, that plenty of escape routes were open to her. And the clincher? It was personal. In robbing the Niekirks, she'd be righting an old wrong.

And then Grace would finish her walk, return home, and log in to online poker and lose money.

By Tuesday, she was running out of time. A week's holiday in Sydney, Mara Niekirk had said. What if they came home early?

So after breakfast she caught a bus to Geelong and hired an eight-year-old Camry from WreckRent, 95,000 km on the clock but V6 power and the gearbox still tight. Fitting it with false plates, she caught the Queenscliff ferry and was on the Peninsula by noon, wearing a charcoal grey pencil skirt and plain white blouse.

The Niekirks' alarm system was a Messer. Grace headed up the freeway to Mornington, a new industrial estate where there was a Messer agency in a security installation firm. Using a clipped, professional woman's voice, she said, 'My mother has a Messer system in her house, and I was thinking I might get one installed, but I couldn't make head or tail of her owner's manual.'

The salesman drank her in. She knew he would. He actually rubbed his hands together. 'We have a good deal on Messer at the moment.'

'Yes, but that's no good to me if I can't understand the technology. Can you explain it?'

'Sure can,' the salesman said.

He dug out a few catalogues, called in an installer, and together they told her how the system worked. Grace nodded in all of the right places, but with an overlay of doubt. They tried harder. Her doubts receded. Another doubt, another reassurance. . . .

Finally she reached a decision, blessing them with a smile. And when she offered to pay a deposit of $100, any reservations they had flew right out the window.

'All righty. Address?'

Grace was a mite embarrassed. 'I've bid on two townhouses on the Esplanade,' she said, 'I won't hear until the weekend which one's mine. When I find out, I'll call with the address and arrange access for you.'

That was fine with them, and she drove out of the industrial estate and up to Frankston. When she failed to contact them again, they wouldn't follow up very strenuously: after all, they were $100 ahead on the deal.

From Frankston she headed northeast to Dandenong, buying a can of insulation foam in a hardware store. Then out to a chain motel on the Princes Highway in Berwick. The remainder of the afternoon stretched ahead. She ate sparingly but kept hydrated and filled in the hours with a walk, junk TV, and a booklet of Sudoku puzzles. She wondered how many more times she'd find herself in a nondescript motel room like this one. It seemed to her that rooms like this had become a big part of her life, a living-from-day-to-day life, with one sad, simple goal, to stay one step ahead of Ian Galt.

Once upon a time she'd dismissed the aims and achievements of ordinary people. It wasn't that she'd thought herself extraordinary. A family, a home, a job, holidays, a circle of friends, and someone to love and be loved by—they were extraordinary. They weren't the kinds of things she'd be allowed to have.

But now. . . .

She blamed the icon for unsettling her. The icon gave her hope, and she wasn't sure she wanted that.

By late evening she was scouting around in Lowther, a little town outside Waterloo and only three kilometres across country from the property known as Lindisfarne. She made a trial run, on foot, in the moonlight, then drove back to her anonymous motel.

Chapter 35

Pam Murphy leaned against the one-way glass and snatched a few minutes to read the *News-Pictorial*, the weekly hot off the press.

This time the paper had sought the viewpoint of senior police, who'd wheeled out an assistant commissioner to counter Challis's claims. 'I speak for the Commissioner, the Police Minister, and all Victoria Police members in stating that we take very seriously the fight against crime and. . . .'

And blah, blah, blah. Pam scanned through the article. Crime figures were only *apparently* on the increase. Crime *reporting* was improving, that's all. For example, domestic violence victims had become more confident about seeking police assistance. 'Other increases are trivial,' the assistant commissioner was quoted as saying. 'People fitting stolen number plates to their cars so they can drive off without paying for petrol, for example.'

That might be true, thought Murphy, but it doesn't address the issue of *resources*.

There was movement on the other side of the glass, and she folded the newspaper under her arm. Darren Muschamp was escorted into the interrogation room by a uniformed officer, who took up position in the corner. Then Sergeant Schiff and

Inspector Challis entered, sliding onto chairs opposite Muschamp, Schiff saying: 'So, Mr. Muschamp, three abductions and
rapes, one of which ended in murder.'

Muschamp was jiggling in his chair, occasionally sniffing then
wiping a sleeve across his nostrils, his gaze flicking into all corners of the room. 'Wasn't three. Wasn't even two. And I never
murdered no one.'

Schiff, sending off sparks of energy, said, 'Okay if I call you by
your first name, Darren?'

He shrugged.

'Are you feeling all right, Daz?'

He shrugged, not wanting to admit that he needed a fix.

'Because our doctor cleared you as fit to be interviewed.'

'Hit my head in the crash.'

Schiff narrowed her gaze. 'I don't see any serious damage.'

He had nothing to say to that.

'You've been offered a lawyer. I'm renewing that offer.'

'You got me, fair and square. I don't need a lawyer.'

'We do indeed have you fair and square. Abduction, assault
with intent to rape, sexual assault, and false imprisonment,
between the hours of midnight last night and six o'clock this
morning.'

'I can do the time.'

Pam knew a little of Muschamp's life story and had read his
criminal record. Grew up near Cranbourne, his mother a hair-
dresser, his father a taxi driver. Above average student, started at
RMIT but started taking drugs. Dropped out and returned to live
among his old high-school friends, many of them unemployed,
some of them with criminal histories. Soon he was stealing cars
and robbing houses to feed his drug habit. Arrested in 2008,
two years in jail for aggravated burglary. The victim, a twenty-six-
year-old woman who lived alone, had awoken one night to find
Muschamp stealing her plasma TV. He'd punched and kicked

her—but Pam was wondering now if he'd also assaulted her sexually, and for whatever reason she hadn't wanted to report it.
Maybe that's how he'd got his taste for rape? There was nothing
else in his file.

She watched Schiff lean back, twirling a pen in her slender
fingers. Gold glinted, and Pam could see, even in profile, the
dangerous, full-wattage certainty in Jeannie's face. A look she
wore during sex, too.

'Do the time, Darren? Life in prison?'

'Get real.'

He wasn't taking Schiff seriously. He was responding to her
presence but mostly watching Challis warily, as if waiting for a
proper cop to start asking the questions. Challis was yet to speak
or move, and Pam guessed he was stewing over the *News-Pictorial*
story. It probably seemed intimidating to Muschamp.

'Dazza,' said Jeannie Schiff in a matey voice, 'I've never been
more real.'

'Don't call me that.'

'Sorry, Darren, Mr. Muschamp. You attended a tertiary insti-
tution, after all, so you're a bright boy, deserving of my respect.
And being a bright boy, you're admitting the offences against
Tina Knorr, without benefit of a lawyer, hoping we'll leave it at
that and not charge you with anything more serious, like rape or
murder.'

'Because I didn't do no rape or murder.'

Schiff grinned. 'So, Daz, you like wearing women's clothing?'

Muschamp flushed, picked at a gouge in the table with a grimy
nail. 'A cop uniform is a cop uniform.'

'Your cousin Mandy's cop uniform, to be precise.'

Pam saw the tension in Inspector Challis's shoulders. He'd
given Scobie an earful at the morning briefing for not listing
women whose uniforms had been stolen.

'So what if I want to dress up as a cop?' retorted Muschamp.

'A bit more than that, Darren. You dressed as a police officer in order to give a false sense of security to women so that you could abduct and rape them.'

'*One* woman, last night. And I never even got my end in.'

Muschamp grinned as he said it, confident she'd rise to the bait, but Jeannie Schiff said mildly, 'Ms. Knorr feared for her life, and with good reason, given that you'd murdered your previous victim.'

'Nup. No way. Wasn't me.'

'And before that you abducted Chloe Holst and raped her several times over several hours.'

'Can't prove that either.'

'I think you'll find that we can. At one point you took Ms. Holst into a nature reserve northeast of Waterloo, correct?'

He shook his head. 'Not me.'

'But you know the area,' Schiff said. She glanced at her notes. 'You're a part-time delivery driver for Waterloo Rural Supplies, correct?'

'So?'

'A witness has you driving one of their trucks on a back road past the reserve about two weeks ago.'

Pam saw another shift in Challis's shoulders. He'd got lucky with a list of numberplates collected by an old man who lived near the reserve. Because the witness was a bit cracked in the head, he'd put the information to one side, almost forgetting it. But then he'd run the numbers and hit the jackpot.

Muschamp grinned again. 'I deliver all over the Peninsula.'

'Gives you the opportunity to scout around for body-dump sites.'

Muschamp said heatedly, 'I never stepped foot in that reserve place, whatever you call it, and you can't prove I did.'

He sat back, smirking confidently. In his mind he'd been super careful, leaving no evidence at the scene or on his victims.

Challis said mildly, 'We found several crime scene textbooks, forensic science textbooks, in your house.'

Muschamp shrugged, gazed critically at his fingernails. 'I like to read.'

'Darren,' Schiff said, 'I'm renewing my offer: You may have a lawyer present.'

'Can't afford it.'

'The system will provide one free of charge.'

'Last time it did that, I got some kid barely out of school. He never did nothing for me.'

'As you wish.'

'So get me bail and let me go.'

'You say you like to read. That's admirable, Darren. I've been to many houses where there's not a book in sight. I suppose you know quite a bit about trace evidence—from your reading?'

Edginess crept over Muschamp again, as if he were re-creating the crime scenes in his mind's eye, looking for evidence he might have left behind.

Schiff continued to push. 'What do you know about the human voice, Darren? Think it's possible Chloe Holst would recognise your voice?'

Muschamp processed that slyly. 'This is the chick worked at the Chicory Kiln, right?' He sat back, folded his arms. 'Well, I've eaten there a few times, so maybe she *would* recognise my voice, but so what?'

Unfazed, Schiff said, 'Let's look at the pattern.' She ticked her fingers: 'The use of a police uniform to gain authority over the victim. The abduction, the sexual assault, the use of a stolen car that resembles an unmarked police vehicle. I could go on.'

'Wouldn't want to stop you. It's a free country.'

'But what happened with Delia Rice, Darren?'

'Nothing happened—not involving me, anyway.'

'Did you mean to kill her? You didn't, did you, it was an accident.'

'Didn't kill her, never met her, wasn't there.'

'It was an accident. Let's call it manslaughter, not murder. You'll do a few years, fewer than ten, be out on good behaviour before you know it.'

'Didn't murder no one, didn't manslaughter no one.'

'You didn't intend to kill her. Accident, right? You put your hands around her neck in the throes of passion and accidentally throttled her.'

He had his arms folded. 'Nup.'

'Or she was crying, is that it, Darren? You hate it when they cry, don't you? It makes you feel kind of bad inside. You just wanted her to stop.'

'When you find the guy, why not ask him?'

'You were seen stumbling away from the scene, Darren. We have a witness. A man matching your description.'

'What, tall, good-looking guy?'

'See, what I think happened is, you suddenly had this body on your hands, and you panicked. Didn't know what to do. Shoved her in the boot of the stolen car and just drove around for a few hours, wondering where to dump her, trying to work it out.'

Muschamp stared stonily at the table, and Pam Murphy sensed that he was reliving exactly that scenario.

'You'd been playing with her—for want of a better word— all night, and then she died, and now it's daylight, people all around, and you can't keep her at your place, and you can't take her to the nature reserve, can't go back there, so you simply drive around and around. Maybe hoping to find a deserted back road—except the Peninsula is pretty closely settled, there's always someone driving along the back roads. Right, Dazza?'

'If you say so.'

'Of course, you couldn't risk driving around wearing a police uniform, not with a body on board. So you changed into a pair of jeans and a T-shirt.' She paused. 'I hope you burned them afterward, Darren.'

He gave her a level smile, and Pam knew that's what he'd done. The thought that they wouldn't get him on the murder depressed her.

'I'm finished talking,' he said, and in a fair approximation of anguish added, 'Look, I wasn't myself last night. I've been depressed, you know, my judgement's shot, maybe I'm suicidal, all these mitigating circumstances, and I think maybe a lawyer can help me now.'

Schiff faltered then. Challis didn't see it, but Pam did. A short acquaintance, only a few days, but she knew what it meant when Jeannie pursed her lips and examined the ends of her hair. It meant doubt, and Pam wanted to say, 'Keep pushing him.'

Unaccountably, then, she pictured Chloe Holst sitting on her hospital bed, sneezing. Why had she recalled that? Sympathy for the victim? No, it was something else. . . .

It came to her in a rush. She walked down the corridor, scrolling through the numbers stores on her mobile phone. Craig, her favourite lab tech.

'It's Spud,' she announced. He called her that. 'I wonder if I could run an idea past you. . . .'

Chapter 36

Ian Galt had been trying since Monday to make sense of the CCTV images he'd scared out of Steve Finch. Anita had a child. Was it his? And elderly parents? Back when he'd known her, she'd had no apparent history at all.

But meanwhile he'd had to fly back to Sydney, word coming through on the grapevine about a body fished out of the harbour. He watched the investigation for a couple of days, standing well behind the scenes, the murdered man on the periphery of his old life.

And now it was Wednesday morning, and he was back in Melbourne to begin the hunt.

He started at the childcare centre in Hurstbridge. Huddled under gumtrees on a minor road leading into the town, it looked threadbare, understaffed, and underfunded. Meaning it was probably operated by a millionaire type peculiar to Australia, discredited, overextended, and obscurely attracted to childcare centres and nursing homes. First flashing his fake Federal Police ID, he showed the administrator a still from Steven Finch's security camera, a toddler and a young woman standing side by side outside the front gate of the centre. A photograph of a photograph, in fact, with a messy blur in the bottom right that was the woman's hand in the act of displaying the photo to Finch.

The administrator, round and motherly, would only concede that the photograph had been taken in front of the centre.

'But the kid did attend?' he asked.

'I'm sorry, Inspector Towne, I'm not at liberty to say.'

'Is she still here?'

'Perhaps if you tell me what this is about?'

Galt cast around for a story that might tug at the heartstrings and involve the Australian Federal Police. 'We fear that an attempt might be made by a family member to kidnap her.'

'Really.'

Sensing that he was on thin ground, Galt said, 'This is a routine inquiry. We have not been able to track down all members of her extended family and—'

'This child did attend here, yes, but has since moved on.'

'You mean she's attending primary school now?'

There was a long pause. 'No, I don't mean that.'

'Look, this is a preliminary inquiry,' Galt said. 'We were alerted anonymously that the child might be at risk.'

Another silence that lasted for a few centuries. 'The family moved back to England, that's all I know.'

'Back to England?'

'Both parents took her.'

The sun had passed the midpoint of the sky, and the light, filtered by the dense tree canopy, fell to the ground in a pattern of interlocking circles. But Galt was in no mood for spring or beauty of any kind. 'Madam, are you sure you can't tell me more about this child?' He tapped the photo. 'Or her mother?'

'The thing is, that isn't her mother. I don't know who that is.'

'They're standing next to each other.'

'And so are other children, and if I'm not mistaken, the photo has been cropped, that's the arm and shoulder of another parent.'

The woman was correct, of course. Galt kicked himself. He said, 'So a stranger insinuates herself into a group of parents and children.'

'She could be anybody. An aunt. A friend.'

Or a red herring, Galt thought.

Chapter 37

E very small community has its eyesores.

Lowther was a pretty collection of houses, but here and there on the outer edges rundown dwellings stood on largish blocks, the kinds of places defined by unexplained traffic night and day. Car bodies and truck chassis melded with unmown grass, and newish cars, utilities, and 4WDs crammed the driveways, the parched lawns, the kerb outside.

Inside, through the dope haze, the décor would be beer-can pyramids and pizza boxes, the detritus of the residents and assorted uncles, cousins, girlfriends, neighbours, temporary pub mates, and hangers-on. Long periods of stunned calm would be punctuated by flaring violence around who swiped the last beer.

On Tuesday night Grace had picked out one such house on the outskirts of Lowther, and now, 10:30 on Wednesday evening, she parked the rented Camry outside it, squeezed between a hotted-up Holden panel van and a rustbucket Kombi. No one would look twice at the Camry; it could belong to anyone on that street.

She got out, carrying a nylon duffle bag. Inside it were two similar bags folded to the size of paperbacks, spare clothes in a waterproof compartment, a bottle of drinking water, and the tools for this job: screwdriver, Swiss Army knife, wire cutters, a chisel, nail pullers, torch, duct tape, prepaid mobile phone, digital camera, a thin steel pry bar, and the spray can of insulation foam. No size eleven shoes this time. She didn't want the cops to link this break-in to any of her others.

It was a three-kilometre walk across country to Lindisfarne. First she skirted the little town, then climbed a fence and passed through wooded areas and across vineyards to Coolart Road. The vines hemmed her in, high on either side. The white netting that draped them was rendered a ghastly silver by the moonlight. Good cover, though.

She crossed Coolart Road, climbed through the fence on the other side and walked parallel to Goddard Road. When she reached the farmhouse opposite Lindisfarne's cypress hedge, she stopped for a while, watching and listening. When she was satisfied, she crossed to the hedge and got down on her hands and knees to force a way through to the other side.

ABOUT ONE HUNDRED METRES farther down Goddard Road, Audrey Tremaine slapped at a mosquito. The compensating twitch of her buttocks on the camping stool almost tipped her into the bracken. She lathered herself in Rid again and continued to fume.

Only one car since 10 P.M. It had raised a plume of dust, dust in her eyes and tiny grit missiles stinging her cheek. But sufficient moonlight for her to recognise the car and the husband and wife schoolteachers from the mud brick house farther along the road. They hadn't stopped to spraypaint a slogan on her new gate, and she'd have been most surprised if they had.

She continued to watch. Third night in a row. It wasn't as if anyone else was willing to mount guard—not the shire's environment protection officer, the police, or her don't-want-to-get-involved neighbours.

'Leave it, Audrey,' they'd said, in the weary tones they used with her now, complete with a bit of eye-rolling if they thought she wasn't looking and even when they knew she was.

'It's not right!' she'd said, fists clenched.

'Yes, but what can you do?' A shrug in the voice.

'Catch them red-handed.'

'How? Wait behind a bush all night, being eaten alive by mosquitoes?'

'If necessary,' Audrey said stoutly.

'Then what? Chase after them and make a citizens' arrest?'

Audrey had thought about that. 'Write down their numberplate, plus time, date, and location. Collect empty spray cans so the police can take fingerprints.'

Like that's going to happen, their looks said. But it wasn't just the desecration of property that got to Audrey. It was the vicious boredom of the young people responsible. What made them like that? It was the puzzle element as much as the outrage that drove Audrey Tremaine, aged seventy-one, retired bookkeeper and owner of the lavender farm with a brand-new set of gateposts a short distance farther along Goddard Road.

She'd set up surveillance on the bend halfway between her farm and the cypress hedge at the front of the Niekirks' big house. Perched on a camping stool among the bracken and roadside gums, she could see for long distances in each direction. Well set up, too: flask of coffee, pocketful of muesli bars, torch, notebook and pen, mobile phone. She was plugged into Radio National and had all night at her disposal. The only danger she could envisage was being conked on the head by a spray can.

The light was tricky, the shadows fluid. Audrey blinked: One shadow had detached from the others. It crossed the road and ducked into the cypresses.

FIRST GRACE WATCHED THE house from inside the hedge—but without focussing, as if she were daydreaming. The focussing would come next: Right now a wide-eyed stare was the best way to detect movements in the foreground and at the periphery of her vision.

All was still. No dogs, sentries, or insomniacs. Thirty minutes passed. At 11:30 P.M. a light came on in an upstairs room and ten minutes later in a downstairs room. She waited; eventually both went out, one some time after the other. She ignored the lights for now and eyed the house and grounds, restricting her focus to one narrow field of vision and then the next, from left to right. Tennis court, shrubs, bushes, an overturned wheelbarrow, then the veranda, doors, and windows of the house itself, and finally more shrubbery and a garden shed.

Nothing. Only the lights, on the same cycle as last night, the ground floor light switching off and on at ten-minute intervals, the other at fifteen. The Niekirks were still in Sydney.

All the while, she listened. She heard a couple of cars far away on Coolart Road, here and there a wind eddy in the trees, night creatures restless in the undergrowth. She windmilled her arms at one point, heart in her mouth, as a silent death dealer swooped at her head.

Some kind of bird. An owl, probably. She was probably a hindrance in its hunting field.

Time to move. Grace approached the house, keeping off the driveway and gravel paths, the crunch and rattle that might wake a light sleeper. On the veranda she paused to listen, then made her way to the front door, which was fitted with a fanlight and glass side panels. A faint gleam leaked out from somewhere inside the house. This light wasn't on a timer. She took the mobile phone from a buttoned pocket of her jacket and dialled the Niekirks' number. A moment later, a telephone chirped softly within the dim reaches of the house. After eight rings the answering machine cut in. Grace repeated the process several times, watching the glass around the door. There was no sudden increase in the light intensity, no angry householder turning on a bedroom or hallway light as he or she stumbled to silence the bell.

She continued to wait and listen. If she'd breached an infrared beam outside the house, stepped on a pressure pad, made an unwelcome sound, then there should have been a police car or security patrol by now, flashing lights, a caterwauling alarm sounding under the eaves. Not for the first time, Grace reflected that people like the Niekirks had a misplaced faith in their seclusion.

Finally she walked around the veranda to the Messer alarm box. She now knew that in the event of a break-in, a power cut or the box being tampered with, the alarm would sound at both the house and Messer HQ.

'What if someone found a way to freeze the little switch thingies inside the box?' Grace had asked the installation tech, wrinkling her brow prettily.

The guy scoffed. 'How? Can't happen.'

Grace moved a small, paint-chipped wooden bench into position, stepped onto it carefully, distributing her weight, and sprayed insulation foam into the heat and moisture vents of the alarm box. She waited, still watching and listening. She was sure that she could hear the foam expanding and solidifying, ultimately paralysing the relay switches and circuits.

DEFINITELY SOMETHING. AUDREY CHEWED on it for a while. Fox? Too big for a fox. Someone's dog? People were careless about their pets. Bought huge Dobermans and what have you, too lazy to feed, train or exercise them, let them roam free.

But the bent-over shape had been wrong for a dog.

She hadn't heard or seen a vehicle.

Perhaps someone from the farmhouse, sneaking across the road for some shenanigans with one or both of the Niekirks?

But the Niekirks were in Sydney, as Audrey knew full well.

Standoffish, more money than sense, and seemed to think she didn't mind being asked to feed their blessed canaries whenever they went away.

Audrey chewed on the matter for ages. Would she be able to hear the hiss of a spraycan from here? Eventually she rose from the camping stool and walked toward the heavy gates set in the cypress hedge. Her shoes made a shocking racket on the gravel.

GRACE MOVED THROUGH THE house, testing the shadows, a routine as familiar to her as breathing. Satisfied that she was alone, she switched on her torch, all but a square centimetre of the lens blocked with insulation tape, and made a more thorough search. Her main aim was to steal the icon on the wall of the glassed-in walkway, but if the Niekirks had that, they probably had other treasures.

First photographing the icon where it hung, she removed it, secured it in bubble wrap and placed it in one of the bags. Then she made a quick pass of the main rooms. Given that the Niekirks dealt in art, Grace didn't think much of their taste. The living areas groaned with overdone oils of beaches and bushland and western desert and dot paintings of no significance or originality; she suspected the Howard Arkley near the piano was a fake. Not a single one was worth stealing. Yet in an office filing cabinet she found catalogues and provenance papers for paintings by Brett Whiteley, Sydney Nolan, Grace Cossington Smith, and Robert Dickerson. She photographed every one, then took a closer look at the house.

The nursery was two spaces in an open plan arrangement, one a small child's bedroom—a short, narrow bed under a mobile of moons and stars, cute wallpaper, and a handful of stuffed toys—and, through an archway, a more chaotic space where the babysitter slept, overlooked by a huge teddy bear on a mantelpiece and posters from a vampire movie. Grace had no memories of her own early years, and none that she cared to recall from her later ones.

There were three other bedrooms. One, sterile and stale, was probably for guests. A second, neat and masculine, was the husband's. The third, untidy, indulgent, stinking of perfume, was Mara Niekirk's.

And here she struck gold.

IT TOOK THE POLICE long enough to answer Audrey's call. What if she were being raped or murdered? She said as much to the fat man driving the patrol car.

'The Peninsula's a big area to cover,' he said. Tankard, his name was. A younger constable sat in the passenger seat.

Audrey told them what she'd seen, a mysterious figure crossing the road and ducking through the hedge. The flicker of what might have been a torch inside the house itself.

'No worries, we'll check it out,' the fat constable said, his tone barely civil.

IT WASN'T THE KIND of house, nor were the Niekirks the kind of people, to boast a tiny Paul Klee. Grace couldn't figure it out. But it hung above the wife's bed and clearly mattered. After photographing it *in situ*, she removed it for closer inspection. Signed and dated 1932, titled *Felsen in der Blumenbeet*, it showed pastelly grey-blue shapes choked by exuberant blue, yellow, red, and green shapes: cones, triangles, crosses, rhomboids, all skewed in shape. It was similar in size to the icon, about 25 cm by 30 cm. She hardly dared fall in love with it, but it was stunning. She wrapped it, tucked it into her bag.

But the icon was personal, and the painting might be hard to shift, so she went looking for iPods, laptops. . . . And had barely re-entered the main living areas when she saw a flicker of lights outside. At once she ran down the hallway, out through the door.

She was heading back through the shadowy garden beds when a spotlight lit her up.

'Oi.' The policeman's voice was hesitant, as if he didn't quite believe his eyes. 'Excuse me.'

Grace swivelled neatly and ducked into the shadows.

Now he believed it. 'Stop! Police!'

One glimpse was enough, a patrol car and two constables, one standing beside his open door, training the spotlight, the other peering straight at her. Grace slipped deeper into the dark region between the house and the road. The spotlight tracked her, throwing up shadows and flares of light in her path. Then she heard a door slam, the gunning of a motor, a spray of gravel. Headlights swept over her spine, and now feet were thudding. They've split up, Grace thought, the car to cut her off at the road, the guy on foot to box her in.

She reached the hedge and crawled into a hollow, scratched by twigs and stubby little branches. Crouching now, she watched the play of the lights. The police car tore onto the road, fishtailed, overcorrected; finally the tyres gripped, and it came toward her purposefully, keeping to the centre of the road, lights on high beam. If she darted out of the hedge now, she'd be spotted. The other cop was still behind her, jerking his torch beam at the base of the hedge. He did it badly, rapid sweeps betraying excitement or nerves. But he'd spot her sooner or later, pin her with his probing light.

The patrol car drew adjacent. It idled a while, then began to creep past. The driver was trying to steer, watch, and manipulate the spotlight. His swivel-necking was inefficient and too regular. Timing it carefully, Grace darted across the road and slithered into the ditch on the other side. A rough-edged stone smacked her knee bone. Mosquitoes whined. She recovered and, at a half crouch, crept along the ditch, keeping pace with the car.

Soon she reached one of the culverts: concrete drain pipe,

heaped sand and storm wrack, water-flattened dead grass. Careful not to trample the grass or leave footprints in the sand and grit, she parted the stalks at the entrance to the pipe, releasing stale air, musty-smelling rather than damp. The gap yawned, too small for her body but not her tools or the paintings. She opened the camera and pocketed the memory card, then stowed the camera in a waterproof bag with the icon and the Klee. She shoved the bag deep inside the drain, kept the pocketknife and change of clothing.

Meanwhile the police had called in backup. She could hear a siren, see headlights. As she slipped into the grounds of the farmhouse opposite the cypress hedge, a second patrol car arrived, followed by a divisional van. About six cops, she thought, scouting around for the best cover. The closest was a trampoline that had been tipped onto its side. After that, garden beds and the house, sheds to one side. If she could reach the fruit trees and the dam she. . . .

A shout. She'd been spotted.

Grace darted behind the trampoline. It was rectangular, black mesh mounted to thick galvanised legs and frame. In daytime it would offer no concealment at all. Grace was relying on the confounding shadows it would throw if a torch swept over it at night.

As she crouched there, a farmhouse porch light came on, the front door opened, and a man and a woman stepped out. They wore pyjamas, and the man, clutching at his drooping waistband, said, 'What's going on?'

'And you are?' said one of the cops, a heavy man, bristling with belligerence.

'We live here. What's going on? Who are you?'

'My name is Constable Tankard, and I'd like you to step back inside please,' the cop said.

'But what's going on?'

'An intruder. Have you seen anyone running past here any-time in the last few minutes?'

'We've been asleep.'

'Please, both of you, go back inside. This person could be dangerous.'

'Dangerous?'

'Please, go inside, lock all your doors and windows.'

'But what if he's in there?'

Grace heard rather than sensed the frustration and watched the man named Tankard approach the house. He banged heavily past the occupants, into the house. Then he came out again. 'All clear.'

'You sure?' said the husband.

Tankard ignored the couple. He began to shout and eventually some order settled on the milling uniforms. Grace heard them call reassurances to each other as they began to split up. She started to back away.

An elderly woman came wheezing in from the road by torch-light. A constable who'd been left with the cars shouted, 'Police. Stop right there.'

The old woman jumped. Her torch jerked, the light finding the trampoline. Grace ran.

'Oi!'

Grace zigzagged, darting feints left and right, into the lee of a pump shed, then a garden shed, a fowl house, a farm ute, a thicket of oleander bushes. She reached the fruit trees and then the dam as the police converged on the officer who had spotted her. Still carrying her dry clothing, she slipped into the water and submerged herself among the reeds at the water's edge. She waited.

Before long, her teeth rattled, her limbs shook, iciness reaching deep into her core. She felt for the pocketknife and clamped the plastic handle between her jaws and continued to shake.

The police were shouting, five men and one woman. They were excited, jumpy. One remained standing near the trampoline, the others split up to circle the dam. Grace peeked: They were keeping hard to the edge, shining their torches into the tangled reeds. Scooping mud from beneath her, she pasted it over the paleness of her face and hands. Now she was a black shape among a mess of shapes—indistinguishable, surely. It was Grace's experience that humans possess a kind of sixth sense, a residue of instinct for one other's proximity, and so she averted her gaze and emptied herself of thoughts, or personality. She was nothing, a featureless blob of matter. She didn't gasp or move when a heavy black shoe stood on her leg, squelching it deeper into the muddy reed bed. The torchlight fingered the reeds, and then the pressure let up, and the man moved a short distance away, to step into the mud again and poke around with his torchlight.

'Waste of time,' said the woman cop, sometime later.

'Yeah.'

Grace stayed where she was through the long hours. It was possible that the police had packed it in and gone home, equally possible that they'd left a couple of officers to watch for her.

At dawn on Thursday there was stirring in the farmhouse. A woman's voice called, 'You two must be miserable, how about a cooked breakfast?'

'Coffee would be good,' the man named Tankard said.

'Yeah, coffee.'

'Don't be silly, you need more than that,' the woman said.

'Catch the guy?' her husband asked.

'He's long gone,' Tankard said, disgust and resignation in his voice.

Grace waited. The woman brought coffee, toast, eggs, and bacon to the sentry cops, and now the air was filled with cheery commiserations and bragging. Grace slithered out of the dam. She crawled on her belly and through a fence into a paddock of unmown spring grass. Still she crawled. Later, the vines. Here she got to her feet. She ran.

The running warmed and loosened her, even as the water sloshed in her shoes and the wet clothing chafed her skin. After three kilometres she came to the township, and, crouching behind a line of bushes, watched her car for several minutes. Nothing, and no action at the house, only a kind of poleaxed stillness that said no one would rise before noon.

Checking that she was unobserved, Grace stripped off her wet clothes. She used the shirt and knickers to wipe off the bulk of the mud, then washed the rest away with her drinking water. Then she dressed in the clothes from the waterproof bag—underwear, a white satin blouse, tailored black pants and strappy sandals, finally finger combing her short hair. There was still mud in the roots of her hair, her fingernails, even her ears, but at a distance she'd pass for a brisk young woman off to her office job. She got into the Camry and drove away.

Thursday was rubbish collection day in Waterloo, bins waiting outside every front gate. Grace dumped the soiled clothes into a side street bin. Then she drove to the motel in Berwick, checked out, checked in to another in Dandenong. Here she showered and slept fitfully, still shivering a little, a residual chill from the muddy water in which she'd spent the night.

Late afternoon she bought a small digital camera powered by AAA batteries and replaced its memory card with the one she'd pocketed after the break-in at the Niekirks'. She scrolled through her photographs. They were sharp and clear.

She collapsed on the thin bed cover and stared at the marks on the ceiling. The icon was a part of her heart and her bones, and now she was falling in love with the Klee. Otherwise she'd walk away this minute, leave them both to rot in the culvert.

Unless there was a flash flood, they'd be safe until the morning.

Chapter 38

In Waterloo, Challis was pouring coffee and thinking about his date with Ellen on Skype last night. He'd logged on, and there was her left breast watching him. The left, not the right. To his mind, both were perfect, but she considered the left better than the right. Then she'd had a fit of the giggles and covered up, and they'd tried to talk sensibly. Sensibly with desire palpable in the air. He grinned and thought he'd better get working.

First the overnight log.

The usual bar fights, car thefts, and break-ins—but one of the latter, on Goddard Road, Constable John Tankard attending, had occurred at the home of Mara and Warren Niekirk. According to Tankard: *Intruder spotted leaving the house carrying a bag.*

Given that he'd met Mara Niekirk, Challis was mildly curious. There was no answer when he called their home and business numbers. Meanwhile, Tank would be off-duty and asleep, so he called the witness who had reported the intruder.

Audrey Tremaine's voice was elderly, but clear and forceful. 'Young, old, man, woman—it was too dark, Inspector.'

'I'm surprised that Mr. and Mrs. Niekirk didn't report it.'

'Been in Sydney all week. I called them last night, and they said they'd catch the first flight back this morning.'

Challis rang off, ordered a crime scene van to attend, then went looking for Pam Murphy. 'Feel like checking out a break-in?'

'I don't know—after a serial rapist the excitement might be too much for me.'

'You'll manage.'

They clattered downstairs to the main corridor, encountering the usual crush of civilian collators, support staff and uniformed police, some idling at the water fountain or reading FOR SALE notices, others banging in and out of doors with equipment or paperwork.

'I expect we'll be taking your car, boss?'

The rat story had got around. 'Very funny,' Challis said, making for the front desk to sign out the CIU car. He made his habitual scan of the people in the foyer. No familiar faces this morning, just honest citizens wanting a statutory declaration signed or reporting a missing wallet. Still managing to look shifty, a meta-morphosis that afflicts everybody who walks into a police station, Challis thought.

He collected the key, joined Murphy in the car park. 'You drive.'

She got behind the wheel, he into the passenger seat, watching as she jotted time and date in the logbook, set the trip metre to zero, adjusted the rear-view mirror, turned the ignition key. Then they were on the open road, and she was flicking through the traffic without surging or braking, eyes everywhere at once. Her competence was palpable; he could see it in the way her driver training flowed through her body to the car and the road, taking in the world of potential hazards that slipped past her window. If he had a squad of Pam Murphys, his clear-up rate would double.

'Boss?'

'Yes?'

'Are they going to sack you?'

'Probably not,' he said slowly, as if giving it some thought. 'I take it you've seen yesterday's paper?'

'Yes.'

It seemed clear to Challis that Jack Porteous and the *News-Pictorial* were playing one side against the other. Porteous had quoted Challis last week, to see what the reaction would be. This week he'd quoted senior police bureaucrats. He hadn't sought a reaction from Challis, just gone ahead and printed Force Command's weasel words. 'Statistics show that in fact . . . blah, blah, blah.' 'Changing times and changing priorities mean that policing methods must keep pace and blah, blah, blah.' And an acknowledgement that the pressures of the job did in fact put a strain on the work and domestic lives of certain police, such that they might develop a false perspective. . . Meaning, Challis thought, that one certain detective inspector was having a meltdown.

'They're trying to discredit me,' he'd said to Ellen last night.

'And they'll follow that with ostracism,' she said. 'That's how it works.'

He said to Pam Murphy now, 'Look, I embarrassed them, so they're huffing and puffing a bit. It's not as if I went on national television. It's not as if the Melbourne dailies are interested. It's local. But they still need to respond.'

'They still need to reprimand you?'

Challis slumped in his seat. 'Somehow or other, they will do that, yes. Wait and see, Murph, wait and see.'

'If they drive you out, can I have your office?'

'That's what I like about you, Pamela, one hundred and ten percent support.'

'But seriously, what can they do?'

'Who knows?'

'Demote you?'

'Maybe.'

'Put you back in uniform and send you to the outback?'

'Wouldn't have a clue.'

Pam Murphy wriggled behind the wheel, getting comfortable. 'Think I'm getting the hang of formal crime-fighting language. "Who knows?" "Maybe." "Wouldn't have a clue." If I learn to use these expressions correctly, will it make me a better detective?'

Challis punched her lightly on the upper arm. 'No one likes a smartarse.' He paused. 'I understand that you asked the lab to check Muschamp's uniform for pollen traces.'

'Yes,' she said tensely.

'Sergeant Schiff was concerned about running over budget.'

'So you're not going to authorise it, is that what you're saying? Sir?'

'Settle down, Constable. It was a good call, I signed off on it.'

Murphy subsided. 'Sorry, it's just that she got a bit pissed off with me, said pollen is pollen, it might indicate he was at one of the crime scenes but not that he did anything.'

'Murph, it was a good call. That's how cases are built, one plank at a time. Or grain.'

She nodded. The car rode with the sun behind it. 'So, tell me, why are we investigating a break-in?'

'The Niekirks cropped up in another case recently.'

Challis told Murphy about the Bristol Beaufighter, its question-able provenance and seizure by the government. She laughed. 'Who'd call an old plane "whispering death"? They all sound like lawnmowers.'

'I've noticed this about you, Constable Murphy: You have absolutely no regard for heritage values.'

'That's right. So these people, the Niekirks, would have a house full of expensive art and antiques?'

'I guess so.'

'I'd better add that to my list of crime-fighting terms: "I guess so."'

'Next left,' said Challis. 'Look for a sign saying "Lindisfarne."'

Pam Murphy made the turn onto Goddard Road, hand over hand on the steering wheel, her upper body leaning with the motion, and in that brief moment Challis saw her collar gape, saw a fading love bite. Who? The car shuddered on dust corrugations and pebbles pinged inside the wheel arches. Then the sign and a pair of massive gateposts.

Pam turned in, through to a big house on the other side of a cypress hedge. Eyeing it, Challis said, 'You might call it ugly.'

'But pretentious.'

'. . . And yet so much worse inside.'

A crime scene van was parked on the driveway, two young men beside it, wearing bulky blue oversuits and white overshoes, aluminium equipment cases in their gloved hands. Confronting them was a man dressed in a short woollen coat over black trousers and leather shoes, while, closer to the house, a young woman whom Challis recognised as the nanny was unbuckling a child from the rear seat of a big BMW. Standing back, watching the confrontation, was Mara Niekirk, carrying a purse and an open-topped bag. Soft toys, disposable nappies, the edge of a blanket.

Challis and Murphy approached, Challis calling, 'Is there a problem?'

The man swung around. Tall, fair, late forties, handsome in a blockish, retired-footballer way. A bony nose, sleepless eyes, a crooked front tooth. 'Who the hell are you?'

Challis gave his name, Murphy's name, and shot out his hand. 'You must be Mr. Niekirk. We're sorry to hear about the break-in.'

The anger evaporated, but Niekirk was tense. 'Not much of a break-in. Intruder, that's all. No need for this lot—' he gestured at the crime scene officers '—to trample over everything.'

Sometimes it helped to play one person off against another.

'Hello, Mrs. Niekirk.' Challis smiled past the man's shoulder. 'I'm sorry we have to meet in unfortunate circumstances again.'

A tight smile. 'Except that last time you didn't tell me you were a policeman.'

Challis made an apologetic gesture. 'I was there strictly as a civilian.'

Warren Niekirk was frowning, a step behind the conversation. 'You two know each other?'

His wife explained, and he turned to Challis with an expression of frustration. 'I bought that plane fair and square and—'

Challis didn't want to get into it. 'I'm sorry, both of you, but I'm afraid we do need to investigate. A report was made, and the police were called to your house, and someone was seen exiting through the front door, carrying a bag of some kind. We'll dust for prints, have a quick look around, and be out of your hair in no time.'

'I've looked,' Warren Niekirk said. 'Nothing was stolen or broken.'

Mara Niekirk gave her husband a complicated glance, then turned to Challis and said, 'We have no objections.'

'We'll be quick. Perhaps you could both walk us through the house first, show us to where you keep your valuables.'

Then the nanny was standing there hand-in-hand with the child, looking on avidly. Mara Niekirk, her face and voice tight, said, 'Tayla, please, she's been cooped up in a plane. Why don't you take her over there to play for a while.'

'Sorry, Mrs. Niekirk, of course.'

The nanny wheeled around and trotted with the child toward a distant swing set.

'Hasn't the sense she was born with,' Mara Niekirk said apologetically.

'Uh-huh,' said Challis. 'Shall we go inside?'

'If you think it will do any good.'

They entered the house. Challis found himself walking through a series of sterile rooms. It was as if the decorators had looked at a set of plans and phoned in some suggestions. Not even the presence of a child had softened the place. He could feel the hand of absolute control at work, admonishing, whisking away crumbs, allocating chores.

Meanwhile, the Niekirks were looking about keenly: at walls and shelves, into drawers and cabinets.

'Nothing's missing.'

'No damage anywhere.'

Then the bedrooms, and Challis realised that husband and wife slept apart. 'You had something hanging on that wall,' he said, in Mara Niekirk's bedroom.

An empty hook. 'Oh, that? We're always hanging and rehanging things. I don't like static decorations, do you? I'm still wondering what to hang there.'

Then they were back on the veranda. 'What about small items? Jewellery, iPods?'

'As far as I can tell, nothing was taken,' Mara Niekirk said.

'Even so, my officers will need to dust for prints.'

The last straw for Warren Niekirk. 'Is that really necessary? Whoever it was would have worn gloves, and they were disturbed before they could take anything.'

Ignoring him, Challis said, 'The back door is down this way, I believe?'

He led the way around the veranda, glancing at windows and doors, glancing up, leaving eddies of frustration in his wake. Reaching the alarm box, he asked, 'Does this bench belong here?'

With an air of reluctance, Mara Niekirk said, 'Well spotted. It used to be over there.' She pointed to a spot further along the veranda.

'Dust it,' Challis told the crime scene technicians. 'Dust the alarm box, the front door, and the most likely interior surfaces.'

'Oh for God's sake,' Warren Niekirk said. 'That'll take hours.'

Chapter 39

It did take hours. When the Niekirks were alone again and Tayla was somewhere in the house, doing whatever it was that nannies did, Mara Niekirk slapped her husband's face. 'Are you out of your tiny mind?'

He screwed up his handsome features in concentration, but the question defeated him. 'What do you mean?'

'Mister Lord of the Manor, antagonising the cops. Do you want them to suspect us of something?'

'But you said yourself the Arkley might be a fake,' said Warren, sulky and aggrieved, 'and that inspector guy noticed straight off the Klee was missing. What, do you *want* them poking their noses in?'

Mara closed her eyes, rocking with pain. The Klee. A twenty-first birthday present from Grandfather Krasnov and her most treasured possession. She knuckled away the tears and fed the rage. 'Wouldn't *normal* people want the police to investigate if they'd been burgled? Moron.'

They were in the kitchen, the coffee pot bubbling. Mara had been dying for coffee all morning, but no way was she going to make any while the cops were present, obliging her to offer them some. She especially hated the young detective, Murphy. She had that lithe, sporty look Warren liked. I bet she wears a jogging bra and white Bonds, thought Mara. I bet she drinks after-work beers with her male colleagues, and she calls them 'mate.'

'Something happened here,' she continued. 'There was a break-in. Witnesses, a formal report. The police *have* to investigate; it's what they do. And what *we* do is play the role of victims. But no, you have to antagonise them.'

A gorgeous fuckwit, her husband. It always felt good giving him a tongue-lashing, and God knows she'd done it often enough over the years. Mara's eyes filled with tears again, pain and rage. Late morning, and she wondered if coffee was going to do the trick. What she needed was a stiff drink.

Thinking about it further, she saw one central reason why the police had made a big deal of the break-in: Warren and his damn plane. He'd tried to play the big-shot wheeler-dealer, and where had it got them? Unwelcome attention not only from the Federal Government but now also a local police inspector. Of course the man was going to prick up his ears when he heard the name Niekirk again. Otherwise the break-in wouldn't have attracted much police attention at all.

She scowled at her husband. Be careful what you wish for, she told herself, for the millionth time. She'd wished, five years earlier, for a good-looking hunk to hang on her arm, and that's exactly what she'd got—but God, the brains of a gnat.

She paused. What had Warren wished for, back when he was courting her? Her family connections, a whiff of the arts? He should have stuck to real estate and sleeping with teenage girls. He had absolutely no eye for quality, only for what was cheap and commonplace. Teaching him the finer points of painting, music, gastronomy, and dress sense was an uphill battle, and the garden she'd slaved to create, destined to be a talking point, visited by tourists, photographed for the glossy magazines . . . did he know the name of a single plant?

'Sorry, Mar,' he said now, reading her face.

'So you should be.'

That fucking plane. Well, the man who'd sold it to them was feeding the sharks off Sydney Heads now. *Whispering death* indeed—he hadn't seen or heard a thing, before she conked him on the head.

'Tell me, Warren, here and now, are there any more cock-ups on the horizon? Any more little surprises for me? Any more messes for me to clean up?'

He flushed. She realised he was standing close to a block of sharp knives and moderated her tone and manner. 'You can tell me, sweetheart. Forewarned is forearmed.'

'Didn't you notice? We lost more than the Klee.'

She was genuinely puzzled. 'Like what?'

'That icon in the walkway.'

She had to think for a moment. She had found it in her grandfather's effects. Just an old relic, religious nonsense, worm-riddled timber, worth maybe a few hundred dollars, not the kind of thing that interested her one way or the other, but Warren had fallen in love with it. He said it was haunting, beautiful, peaceful—wank words like that.

So she'd hung it where she'd rarely have to see it. 'No loss.'

A squeaky little voice came from the doorway: 'Excuse me, Mrs. Niekirk.'

'Oh, what?' she snarled.

Tayla blanched. 'Excuse me, but I can't find Natalia's inhaler, I think we left it in Sydney.'

'*We?*'

'*I.* I did. She's wheezing quite badly.'

Dripping acid, Mara said, 'Well, why don't you hunt out the prescription, and get into the car, and drive out onto the road, and point the car toward Waterloo, and go into the chemist, and get a new one? Think you can do that?'

'Yes, Mrs. Niekirk.'

Tayla seemed to evaporate from the doorway rather than scuttle or even walk away. Warren watched her go, and Mara wanted to wipe the look off his face. 'Put your eyes back in your head and your dick back in your pants,' she said.

The look he shot her was a mix of guilt and triumph. Yes, she'd caught him ogling the nanny again, but why? Because Mara didn't satisfy him and never had.

A fly on the wall could watch all this and wonder how I got pregnant, Mara thought, with almost a pang.

Speaking of ogling the nanny. . . .

'Is the teddy bear cam working?'

He gave her a cruel, concupiscent look. 'Why? Want to look at Tayla getting her gear off?'

'I want to look at our burglar, you fool.'

His face cleared. Pennies dropped. 'Oh, right.'

Horror stories from other married couples had persuaded them to install a teddy bear spy camera in the nursery. How do you know your nanny isn't a drug addict? What if she's got a temper and takes it out on the baby? What if she sneaks her boyfriend in to have sex while your baby smothers to death? Hence a pinhole lens concealed as one of the teddy bear's bead eyes, a digital feed recorded on a hard drive.

The camera worked beautifully—but two things had become apparent to Mara: Every nanny they hired was blameless, and her husband liked to watch them undressing on his laptop. Not that Mara minded too much; it kept him occupied. And now it might prove useful in other ways.

She glanced out of the kitchen window. Tayla was bundling Natalia into the car. 'We've got maybe forty minutes.'

'I'm on it.'

About the only thing he was.

◆ ◆ ◆

FIVE MINUTES LATER, MARA was jabbing her forefinger at Warren's laptop screen. 'Freeze it there.'

Their thief was a young woman dressed in black. They'd watched her scouting around the nursery quickly, offering no clear image of her face, but then, for a brief second, she'd gazed straight at the teddy bear. '*She was here,*' said Mara, outraged. 'I recognise her. She rolled up one day last week, wanting to look at the garden. It crossed my mind at the time she might be a cop.' Warren was peering at the image, eyes a little glazed, probably hoping the burglar would start undressing for him. 'Wakey, wakey.'

He jumped. 'What?'

'Can you clean the image up, print out a head-and-shoulders shot?'

'No problem,' said Warren, the go-to man when you wanted something practical done.

Mara chewed her lip. 'How did she find us? Who knew about the Klee? Was it stolen to order?'

'And the icon.'

'Forget the icon. It's got nothing to do with anything. The Klee is another matter. We need to put the word out.'

'Where?'

'Where do you think? Not that many places you can move high-end art in these parts.'

Chapter 40

Friday, the light of pre-dawn, Grace waking with a hammering heart.

In her dream, Galt's little posse of bent coppers had entered her room, surrounded her bed and stared down at her, faceless, remorseless, vigilant.

She scrubbed her face with her hands, swung her feet to the floor, and crossed to the window. The motel parking lot was cold and still, the street lights casting a miserable wash over the empty road.

She ran the shower. If Galt came for her—and he would come, she knew him—wouldn't he come alone? She'd always thought of him as a loner, even as he'd kept the gang close to him. Secretive men, economical; the type attracted to police work because it allowed them to bully and connive. The type that became, if not policemen, criminals. Dictators, union thugs, CEOs. . . . Vigorous men, brawny, cunning, cynical, contemptuous. Heavy drinkers. Divorced, usually. Not well educated but quick and intelligent. The policemen you sometimes saw on the news, towering over their lawyers as they walked free down courthouse steps.

She'd spent a lot of time with such men. Under their gaze, the flat eyes that said they knew things and nothing impressed them.

And Grace was nothing, women were nothing. In the face of that coldness, she'd often found herself hugging and kissing Galt as if to thumb her nose at them.

Galt was like them, and he was different from them. A hard, suspicious, sideways-looking man. Clever. A killer, she'd thought, from the first time she met him.

She was seventeen years old, living in a Glebe squat. One day she'd lifted $5,000 cash, a string of Broome pearls and a Bulgari watch from a Darling Harbour apartment, unaware that it belonged to a call girl who was paying Galt for client referrals and protection. Galt had started hunting Grace the moment he got the phone call. By late afternoon, he'd found her fence. By nightfall, he'd found her.

She'd just burgled some houses in Vaucluse. She had three diamond rings, a drawstring bag of Krugerrands, and a couple of grand in cash in her little daypack and was tossing the pack onto her grungy mattress when he jumped her. The beating was long, clinical, remorseless. He left her face intact but her breasts, ribs, stomach, and back were a mess. No more slipping through windows for a while.

A killer. A killer with a wife and three children of whom he never spoke.

And compelling. When she'd fled and he'd found her again, a part of her was ready to yield. 'Don't hit me,' she'd said.

'I don't want to hit you,' he'd said, 'I've come to give you my card.'

Work number, private number, and before long she'd called those numbers. Arrested for loitering at the rear of a Paddington terrace house, she was back on the street within an hour.

She should have kept clear; she should have done the time. But he offered a kind of job security. He had contacts in insurance, in burglar-alarm companies. He told her who to rob, and when; where the alarms and cameras were located; who, if anyone, would be home; and probable police response times and how to evade patrols and roadblocks. He told her what the police were trained to see and expect. All the time he was extending her natural abilities, teaching her to think, anticipate, take pains, assess risks, and hone her body: weight training, aerobics, distance running. Finally, Galt taught her how to pass through life without a trace—no name, no history, no lever that might tip her out into the open.

'You need me,' he'd say. 'You're the queen of cat burglars, but without me you'd be in jail now. I took you off the street, I protect you, I pay your rent. You like the Harbour view, right, Neet? That cute little Audi? Without me you'd have nothing.'

And one day he cocked his head at her and added, 'Without me you'd *be* nothing. I was doing some digging: You're practically invisible, Anita, no past to speak of. Who are you?'

Well, she'd barely known that herself. The only past she had, apart from the orphanage, the foster homes, were the Harbin photograph and a couple of ghost names in her subconscious.

And now, she thought, towelling her hair, I have Galt.

GRACE WAS AT GODDARD Road before dawn. Any later, there'd be farmers getting an early start on the day, the newspaper delivery guy, shire workers, local residents walking the dog.

Driving the WreckRent Camry, she steered by her side lights to the Niekirks' driveway entrance, raising only a little dust. Nothing there to indicate that the property had been a crime scene. Reaching the culvert, she pulled over, motor running, and got out. She stretched the kinks in her spine, checking both ways for the gleam of approaching headlights. Only stillness and the murkiness of another predawn, as the sun waxed and the moon waned.

She darted into the ditch, her fingers masking the lens of a tiny torch, and found the waterproof sack. Ten seconds later, she was behind the wheel again, driving straight ahead to Balnarring

Road, which she took to Frankston-Flinders Road, turning left and looping up through Waterloo and finally back to her motel.

Here she showered, changed into jeans and a T-shirt and found a café for breakfast. Then she checked out, returned to Waterloo, and entered the VineTrust bank. The sooner she had *Felsen in der Blumenbeet* stowed away in her, safe-deposit box, the better.

Not the icon. It was a part of her, and she took it home.

STEVEN FINCH KNEW HE'D been a little sloppy, allowing the Fed to surprise him like that. So he was alert that Friday, watching his security monitors, and saw Mara and Warren Niekirk park their BMW, get out, look both ways along the street, and enter the shop—Mara the witch wearing a spring dress, fair hair loose around her shoulders, legs bare. Not that Finch was fooled; he grew tense, in fact. As for the Ken-doll husband, he just trailed behind Mara looking stupid.

'Mara. Warren.'

'Steven Finch, Esquire,' said Mara breezily, and his insides curdled a little more.

His mind flashed back through their recent encounters. He'd once offered them a dicey Dickerson, not knowing it was a fake. No money had changed hands, and they'd accepted that he'd acted in good faith and continued to do business with him. But Mara's wrath had been pretty impressive.

'Everything okay?' he asked, matching her breeziness.

He wished he could say, oh by the way, he happened to have a Nolan for them, a Blackman, even a Central Australian dot painting, anything to ease the tension. But it wasn't as if he bought and sold art works every day.

'No, Steven, everything is not okay.'

Mara was wearing dark glasses. Finch wished she'd take them off. Something was wrong, but without seeing her eyes he couldn't gauge how wrong. 'Sorry to hear it,' he said inadequately.

Mara slapped a photograph onto the counter. A4 size, a little grainy, but clearly Suze, face on, all in black, doing what she did best, he was guessing. He glanced expressionlessly at the photo, tilted his head this way and that, looked up with a questioning look.

'Who is it? Is it your place?' he asked. Thinking, Suze, what the fuck have you done?

'It is indeed our place, and we thought you might know who this person is,' Mara said, tapping with a hooked fingernail.

The goods for sale on Finch's shop floor seemed closer suddenly, darker. 'Sorry, never seen her before.'

Mara stood back from the counter and regarded him with a scary smile. 'We have done business in the past, Steven. Correct?'

His mouth was dry. 'Correct.'

'Paintings, drawings?'

'Yes.'

'We've never asked you where these items come from, and you have never asked us what we've done with them, correct?'

'That's how it works,' Finch agreed.

'So you probably think our walls are dripping with art works.'

Finch didn't like where this was going. 'I've never thought about it.'

And that was no lie, but tell her that.

'Really, Steve? Never wondered idly what treasures we might have at home? Thought to yourself, I hope their security is adequate for all those valuable paintings they have hanging on their walls.'

Deciding not to be bullied, Finch said, 'Mara, spit it out.'

'This . . . *person*,' said Mara Niekirk, 'broke into my home on Wednesday night and stole two items from me. Both had sentimental value, but one also had a very high dollar value.'

'Oh. Sorry.'

'You don't know her?'

'Sorry, no.'

'But you do know people like her? They bring you things: TV sets, iPods, cameras, the odd Albert Tucker painting?'

'Yes, but—'

Warren Niekirk, looking left out, spoke up. 'Look Steve old son, all we're asking is, if this chick comes into the shop wanting to sell you a Russian icon or a little Klee painting, let us know, all right? We'll take it from there.'

His wife's dark glasses flashed, but he forged on. 'We want both items back, no questions asked, okay, Steve?'

'Sure,' said Finch, thinking that Mara had something other than no-questions-asked in mind. 'But I can't think why she'd come to me.'

I can't think why she robbed a house in her own back yard, he thought. He also thought he'd better act quickly if he was going to make any money out of the situation. Get to Suze before anyone else did.

'Can I keep this?' he asked, lifting the photograph from the counter top.

It was the kind of thing an honest man might say.

Chapter 41

The bullet, when it came, was disguised as an email from Human Resources.

It has come to our attention, etcetera. Three months' long-service leave, to be taken forthwith, etcetera.

Late Friday afternoon, and Challis checked the calendar. The bastards were giving him less than a fortnight to clear his desk.

He propped his feet on the open bottom drawer and swivelled in his chair. The chair screeched for want of lubrication, but he didn't hear it. The view from his window, the books on his shelves, the photographs on his desk.

The photographs. His sister and niece in outback South Australia—it was time he saw them again. And there was Ellen Destry with a wide grin that tugged at his heart and made him feel shy. More photos on a pinboard beside the window, a record of his history with his old aeroplane: the Dragon in bits, and on the back of a truck for the journey down from Queensland, and being offloaded in Tyabb, and having a new tailplane fitted, a hole repaired. Finally, sitting on the tarmac, a strangely beautiful insect.

He'd put out feelers to museums and collectors. Now it was a waiting game.

There was another photograph in the room: his dead wife, face down on the top shelf, gathering dust. Guilt was a strange thing; he'd never been quite ready to throw her out.

Meanwhile, he had work to do. Calling an impromptu briefing a short time later, he leaned against the whiteboard while Murphy and Sutton took their positions at the long table. 'I don't like coincidences,' he said.

He was in shirtsleeves, the long room holding the day's accumulated heat. As he peeled his shoulder from the whiteboard, it came away imprinted with blue marker, a reversal of a question mark scrawled there. Craning his head to examine it, plucking at the cotton, he said, 'I guess that will teach me.'

'New police insignia, boss,' Scobie Sutton suggested.

Challis blinked. It was rare for Sutton to make a quip about anything.

'Our new slogan,' Pam Murphy said. '"CIU: We get things the wrong way around."'

It was the time of the day for weary humour, and grinning tiredly, Challis slumped at the head of the table. 'Coincidences,' he repeated, and explained, for Scobie Sutton's benefit, about his two encounters with the Niekirks.

'You think they're bent?'

'I honestly don't know. On the surface, they seem to be the victims of two quite different crimes: cheated by a man who sold them an iffy aeroplane and broken into by a burglar who didn't steal anything.'

'But?'

In answer, Challis dialled a number on his mobile phone. 'John? Come on up.'

They waited. John Tankard edged into the room, gazing about. 'Wow, is this where the action is?'

'Thank you, Tank.' Challis sighed. 'The Niekirks' intruder.'

'What about him? Her?'

Challis paused. 'Her?'

Tankard screwed up his pouchy face in concentration. 'It's just, you know, a feeling I had. Could've been a bloke, could've been a woman. Something about the—what do you call it—body language.'

'You didn't mention this in your report.'

'Wasn't sure, to be honest.'

Challis didn't pursue it. 'But this *person* was holding something?'

'Kind of a gym bag.'

'Full? Empty?'

'I had the feeling it was full.'

'How long between the call to triple zero and your arrival at the scene?'

'Dunno. Twenty minutes? Half an hour? We were busy.'

'Thanks, John.'

Tankard went out, looking short-changed, trying to catch Pam Murphy's eye.

'So,' said Challis, 'we have an intruder on the premises for up to thirty minutes, seen leaving with a bag that appeared to have certain items in it. Tools? Stolen goods? We don't know. The Niekirks claim nothing was stolen, but something about all this bothers me. Don't be proactive, just continue working your usual cases, but keep your eyes and ears open, maybe you'll hear something about other break-ins or about the Niekirks.'

'Boss.'

Scobie Sutton got to his feet first, then hesitated. 'Something on your mind?' said Challis.

In a rush, Sutton said, 'Are either of you doing anything on Sunday afternoon?'

Challis and Murphy went very still, and their minds raced. 'I have a buyer lined up for my car,' Challis said. 'Why?'

'Roslyn's school concert, if you're interested. The tickets are cheap.'

'Sorry, Scobe.'

'I'm having lunch with my parents,' Pam said.

'Oh well, next time,' Sutton said, and he left the room.

Watching him leave, they exchanged small, guilty smiles. Sutton had talked about every stage of his daughter's progress over the years, inviting everyone to share in it.

'Are you really selling your car on Sunday?'

'I am, in fact. Are you really going to see your parents?'

'I am now.'

Challis grinned, gathering his papers together, and saw a sudden alteration in Pam Murphy. Her eyes lost focus, she gave a tiny, involuntary body spasm. Realising he'd seen her do it before, he said, 'Are you okay?'

Her eyes spilled a couple of tears.

'Hey, hey,' he said, moving toward her but stopping short.

'I did something stupid.'

'We all do that.'

She blinked at him, a look of fury on her face, but directed inwards, and he remembered the love bite and guessed that she'd entangled herself with the wrong person. Who, though? He was only human; he'd like to know.

'Want to talk about it?'

She didn't hesitate or prevaricate. 'Nope.'

So they went their separate ways. Challis thought, Lost opportunity, and so did Murphy.

'I'D RATHER DISCUSS YOUR breasts.'

'Not going to happen,' Ellen said in her no-nonsense way. 'McQuarrie's *forcing* you to take long-service leave?'

'Yes.'

A pause and she said, 'Starting when?'

'End of next week.'

'The alternatives?'

'They sack me, demote me, send me to a station way out in the Mallee somewhere.'

'Put your thinking cap on,' Ellen Destry said.

Chapter 42

On Saturday Ian Galt drove out through Gippsland to Lakes Entrance and the Autumn Years Retirement Village.

The little town and the coastal waters were vivid in the sunlight, and another man might have drawn an appreciative breath after his long drive and admired the gumtree leaves, variously dun-coloured, olive-toned and silvery, the municipal flowerbeds splashed yellow, red, and blue. Another man might have stopped for coffee, sat at a sidewalk café to sip and watch the locals buying the Saturday papers, the women in their springtime dresses, but Galt had no interest at all in the beauty of his surroundings.

He found the retirement village along a leafy side road behind the main street. The lakeside charm was absent here, away from the tourist beat. The houses were pale brick scabs from the 1970s, mute and disappointed, as if ashamed of the men who'd designed them. The admin building and cottages of the retirement village were in keeping with the neighbouring houses. Everything was pink and grey inside the foyer, and the air was stale, redolent of industrial solvents and urine.

This time he kept his Andrew Towne ID in his pocket, unable to think of a good reason for a federal policeman to pay a formal visit to a retirement home in a small coastal town. During the long drive from Melbourne, he'd settled on an honest-citizen story, and with his teeth bared in a smile, eyes crinkled, he explained to the receptionist that he'd been overseas for twenty years, returning recently because his last surviving relative, his aunt, had died. 'The thing is, among her effects there was this photo.'

An elderly couple standing with a young woman outside Autumn Years. 'That's my half sister,' he said, tapping the image. 'We lost contact a long time ago, and I don't know how to find her and thought maybe the old people standing with her could help me, whoever they are.'

The receptionist was delighted to help, but had bad news: Mr. Ingles had died. 'But Mrs. Ingles is still here, bless her.'

Galt glanced down the corridor, at the rows of doors, old men and women inside them, pissing their beds. 'Well, that is good news.'

'Mind sharp as a tack, too.'

To Galt's relief, he was shown to a cottage in the grounds. The receptionist knocked on a glossy red door. The woman who answered was frail, stooped over a walking stick, but recognisably the woman in the photograph. Her gaze spent very little time on the receptionist and even less on the spring sunshine, but fixed hard on Galt.

What are you staring at, you old bag? he thought.

The receptionist said, 'Eileen, this young man has come a long way to see you, isn't that exciting? He needs help finding his sister.'

Eileen's face seemed to say, I'm not a child. 'Is that so?'

Sensing that the ruse was going to unravel, Galt said, very quickly, 'Thank you, I can take it from here,' and when the receptionist was gone, said, 'I'm trying to get hold of your daughter, Mrs. Ingles. This is Susan, I believe?'

Eileen Ingles regarded him for so long that Galt wanted to snatch away her walking stick and beat her with it. 'Mrs. Ingles?'

'I don't have a daughter.'

Galt shook the photograph under the old bag's face. 'Explain this.'

'That is certainly me, and that is my late husband, but who the young woman is I couldn't tell you.'

'So why the hell is she in the photo with you?'

'Don't you get narky with me. As I recall, she simply materialised one day, claiming she was writing an article on regional facilities for the aged, and wanted her photograph taken with us. If I remember correctly, she said her name was Grace.'

Galt curled his lip. 'If you remember correctly.'

Mrs. Ingles cocked her head. 'There's grace,' she said, 'and there is the absence of grace.'

Galt didn't say 'break a hip,' but he thought it.

Chapter 43

O n Saturday, Grace nailed a hook to her sitting room wall, positioned the icon, and stepped back and tried to flow into it, as if
it might tell her something about herself. Deep peace, she thought,
losing herself in the gold-leaf virgin and baby. Healing light.

But she didn't have the patience for too much of that. She
scrolled through her Niekirk photographs again. Perhaps the
little Klee painting might tell her something about the Niekirks
that would fill in the gaps.

She drove to Torquay, found an Internet café, and logged in
to a couple of stolen artworks sites: Art Loss, on which galleries
and individuals listed stolen and lost works of art, and Trace It,
which aimed to trap thieves offering stolen paintings to auction
houses and dealers.

She ruminated as she searched. There'd been enough dodgy
invoices and other documents in the Niekirks' study to indicate
they were crooked, so what was the story with the Klee? Stolen,
presumably. From a collector? A gallery? Here? Europe or America? She knew that small galleries were notoriously under-pro-
tected. Even if they could afford first-rate security systems, they
couldn't afford the staff to monitor them. Or they switched their
systems on only at night. Meanwhile, art thieves were often well

organised. They stole to order, or had buyers in mind, and were able to forge impressive pedigrees—provenance papers, sales and auction records, catalogue entries.

She froze.

She'd found the Klee.

Felsen in der Blumenbeet, stolen from a gallery in the Swiss town of Liestal, in 1995.

How had it found its way to Australia? Where had it been since 1995? Had the Niekirks commissioned the theft? Did Mara drool over it in private every night? Maybe the Niekirks were intermediaries. Or the Klee was a means to an end—collateral in a loan, for example, or finance for a drug deal. Or a ransom was being sought from the gallery or the insurance company. But so many years later? And would the Niekirks risk auctioning the painting in Australia? If it came with convincing papers, would anyone check? Maybe they had a Japanese collector in mind. Grace had sometimes sold small paintings and art deco jewellery to collectors in Japan, where it was possible to claim legal title to stolen works after only two years of possession.

It was pointless to speculate. The beautiful little Klee was hers now.

In a safe-deposit box on the other side of Port Phillip Bay.

Perhaps she could ransom it back to the Niekirks?

No. It was beautiful. She wanted it.

Out of curiosity, she Googled 'theft of Russian icons' and learned that customs officers at Sheremetyevo Airport seize 6,000 icons each year—maybe only a tenth of those being smuggled out of Russia in suitcases, diplomatic bags, and general cargo. The Russian Mafia was involved, too. In the upheavals of the 1980s and 1990s it wasn't only nuclear arms that were stolen but also icons and paintings from the country's galleries.

But Grace knew that her icon had been stolen four or five decades earlier than that, from her family in Harbin.

Before returning to Breamlea, she checked her email.

One message. Steve Finch.

'*You hit the wrong people Wed night. Got you on camera. Flashing your pic around. No cops involved yet, but not nice people. Give us a call, urgent.*'

She closed down immediately, left the café, and walked along the beach, gnawing at the inside of her cheek. She needed to think about Finch and the Niekirks, but Galt was there in her head.

One day he'd got a phone call. She was with him on the sofa with the Harbour view, and he had one hand inside her pants—lovely slender fingers, really, for such a cruel man—and her head was resting against his, so she heard quite clearly the voice in his ear saying: 'Woof, woof.'

Meaning dog, meaning the dogs of the police force, the Ethical Standards officers, were sniffing around.

Galt had said 'Fuck,' shoved her aside and simply walked out of the flat.

She'd tried to imagine what he'd do, where he'd go. They'd been after him before, he told her one night, both of them slick from lovemaking. 'There was this sergeant, looking at me funny for a few weeks.'

'What did you do?'

'Put a bullet in his letterbox.'

The message plain: *This has your name on it.*

'What happened?'

'He transferred to a station in the bush, that's what happened.'

'To you, I mean.'

A raised eyebrow. 'Nothing.'

But this time something had happened. The dogs had come for her a few days later, threatening serious jail time in order to get at him. Sweetening the deal with the offer of witness protection. Instead, she'd protected herself.

Her aloneness had been her chief advantage. No friends, family or work colleagues to tug at her heart, no one who might unwittingly or deliberately feed information to the wrong people. No habits, gym routine, favourite pub, or hobby magazine subscription that might give her away. And rather than become someone with a definable character and lifestyle, she'd become a flibbertigibbet, a young woman who seemed to change her looks, job and car every few months. The fact that there wasn't a job didn't matter, it was all about appearances. She gave people a box to put her in. She didn't do anything to attract the law—well, apart from being a career thief. No speeding tickets, no drunk driving, no arguments with noisy neighbours. When the Breamlea house was burgled in her absence last year, she hadn't reported it, not wanting a police investigation, a fingerprint search. And she'd told herself that she could walk away in an instant. If she were in bed and heard a noise, she wouldn't think, 'It's a burglar,' she'd think, 'It's the man who has come to kill me.'

She hadn't counted on a threat from another direction.

Grace returned to the main street and found a public phone. She didn't give Finch a chance to talk. 'You know who it is. There's a payphone in the 7-Eleven around the corner from where you live. I'll call you on it in five.'

'How do you know the number of—'

She cut him off. She counted down the minutes, called the 7-Eleven payphone, and demanded: 'What exactly did they say?'

'Hello to you, too.'

'*Steve.*'

'Okay, okay. Look, I've done a bit of business with them over the years, so they know I handle the odd *objet d'art*, and they came into the shop yesterday, showed me your picture.'

'They asked if you knew me?'

'Yes. I said no.'

'Then what did they say?'

'They said if you, or anyone else, came in wanting to offload a little Klee oil painting, I had to let them know, pronto.'

Grace chewed on that.

'You robbed the wrong people, Sue.'

'Let me think about this.'

But she didn't hang up.

'Tell you what, we can make a few dollars out of this,' Finch said.

'How?'

'I'll tell them you *did* make contact, and it was quick because you were nervous, and you told me you'd heard about me on the grapevine as someone who deals in art from time to time, and I asked did you have something in particular you wanted me to handle, and you showed me a picture, and it was a Paul Klee oil painting, and I said I might be able to shift it for you.' He paused. 'That's what I'll tell them.'

'In fewer words than that, I hope. Steve, get to the point.'

'Okay, so I tell them I can get the painting back for them, only you want ten grand. Five each, Suze.'

Five grand was five grand. If she didn't return the painting, they'd continue to hunt her down. Maybe even inform the police.

'I can't get at it until Monday.'

'You're doing the right thing, Suze,' Steve Finch said.

Chapter 44

Mara Niekirk was a good hater.

And she really hated Steven Finch.

Late Saturday afternoon: He'd driven down from William-stown all excited, saying, 'Guess what?'

Warren was somewhere in the house, her daughter and the nanny somewhere else in the house, so Mara was obliged to deal with the grubby little man. She wasn't in the mood for games, merely stared at him.

'That chick you showed me a picture of, she was in the shop this afternoon. Definitely her, and she definitely has the painting.'

'Really,' said Mara flatly.

'I know,' said Finch, shaking his head at the wonder of it. 'Couldn't believe it myself.'

'It's just as well we notified you,' Mara said.

'Exactly.'

Mara watched him wander around her sitting room as though he owned it, tilting a vase to read the maker's mark on the bottom, peering into her china cabinet, cocking his head at her Howard Arkley.

He pointed his chin at it. 'Original?'

'Yes,' said Mara, wondering what his game was. Had he bought the Klee from the thief? And she wasn't entirely convinced that he hadn't commissioned the theft in the first place.

Meanwhile the moron continued to examine her Arkley, his face dubious. 'Easy to fake, that airbrushed suburban house in a riot of fluorescent colours schtick.'

Mara recalled the Dickerson. 'You would know.'

'Now, now.'

Mara said, 'You want a finder's fee? Is that it?'

'The woman who stole it wants a fee. I'm happy to be the middleman.'

'Expecting that we'll be appropriately grateful.'

Finch shrugged, still looking at the Arkley painting. 'Opportunity knocks, and all that.'

Mara watched him from her fat round armchair. If she sat there long enough, addressing his scrawny back, maybe it would dawn on him what a rude bastard he was. 'Leaving aside the money for the moment, what if we said we'd changed our minds, didn't want the painting returned? What then?'

Finch swung around on her with a sharkish smile. 'You'd just give it up? A beautiful painting like that? Maybe worth millions?'

And, without invitation, he was sprawling in the chair opposite, his bony knees too close. Mara's skin crawled. Somewhere in the depths of the house, delighted laughter broke out, and she glanced at the diamond encrusted Cartier on her wrist: Natalia's bath time. She also heard the deeper note of adult laughter. *Two* adults, Warren and the tart who called herself a nanny.

'I have things to do. Get to the point, then get out.'

A flash of something nasty in Finch's face. 'It's not all about you, Mara. There are other people who might be interested.'

'How much?'

Finch shifted on the expensive fabric of her armchair. 'Twenty thousand,' he said. 'I managed to beat her down from fifty.'

'That was big of you,' Mara said.

The seconds ticked by, and she watched him expressionlessly. Emanated a chill, perhaps, but that was normal. Shadows were gathering beyond the window, populating her garden with lump-ish shapes. A young woman perhaps known to this awful man had stood out there one afternoon and chatted about the beauty of the landscape, the headiness of the perfumed air, blah, blah, blah. And then had come back and robbed her.

Playing for time, she said, 'It *is* a beautiful painting.'

The relief was palpable. 'It is, it really is.'

It was as if he needed to act now, before his luck slipped away. 'Twenty thousand?' she asked.

He leaned forward until their knees touched, and she wanted to gag. 'Look on it as goodwill money, Mara.'

'You get the money *only* when we get the painting.'

Steven Finch held his arms wide. 'Not a problem. I can get it to you after work on Monday.'

LATE EVENING, MARA SOUGHT out the nanny. 'We'll be gone tomorrow and Monday.'

Feeling super responsible, she added: 'I don't want Natalia to wake up in the morning and wonder where we are.'

Tayla, reading in bed after an exhausting day, blinked at Mara, who was a forbidding shape backlit by the hallway light. 'But tomorrow's my day off. '

'All right, all right,' Mara snarled. 'Triple pay. Satisfied?'

'I mean, what about Natalia?'

'What about her?'

Tayla tried and failed to find a common moral, ethical, and commonsensical ground with her boss. 'She was looking forward to Mummy and Daddy taking her to the pirate ship playground tomorrow.'

'*She'll . . . have . . . you,*' said Mara, and Tayla recognised the warning signs: rapidly blinking eyes, heightened colour, and clenched jaw and fists.

She thought hard about the triple pay, and swallowed. 'I guess I could take her.'

'What a good idea,' said Mara, hugely bored already, heading back down the hallway to her husband's room. 'Aren't you ready yet?'

'Almost.'

But he wasn't, and she told him what she'd thought about that for a while. That had him shoving clothing and toiletries into an overnight bag, until, at long last, Mara was able to drive the Mercedes van out onto Goddard Road.

'I didn't say goodbye to Natalia.'

'I said it for you,' Mara said, wondering why on earth he wanted to say goodbye to a sleeping child. What was the point?

They set off in the moonlight. After a while she relaxed and, with almost sleepy nonchalance and sensual grace, steered the big van up through Frankston and on to Eastlink. What they were about to do, use Finch to find the woman who'd robbed them, gave her a peculiarly sexual tug deep inside. She fondled the bulge in Warren's trousers for a while, until he gasped and folded over his lap and said, 'Thank you.'

'You're welcome.'

The road unwound all the way up to the tunnel and across to the city's northern exits and finally into downtown Melbourne and out the other side to Williamstown.

Chapter 45

Only one person had responded to Challis's advertisements, a man in Albury named Hopgood. He'd emailed Challis to expect him late on Sunday morning, and now it was 11:30 and Challis was reading the *Sunday Age* at his kitchen table, waiting for a knock on his door. Would long-service leave be like this, a lot of sitting around, waiting?

When the knock came, he found a grey haired man on the veranda, a restored Mk II Jaguar in the driveway—British Racing Green, wire wheels, a lovely car.

'Coffee?'

'Mate, I'm in a bit of a hurry.'

So Challis took him around to the rear of the house, and the first thing Hopgood said was an incredulous 'Twenty-five grand?'

'There's one in Canberra going for thirty-five,' said Challis mildly.

'Bud, I've seen that car. Overpriced, and in a lot better nick than this one.'

Challis glanced at the sky. Warmish, a slight threat of rain by nightfall, and when it came it would bucket down. Typical spring weather, in fact, and he wanted the sale to go through before it rained. It had to go through, didn't it? The guy had driven a long distance to be here and owned an outfit named Brands Hatch Classic Cars.

He gave Hopgood a quick once-over. About sixty, wiry, weather-beaten, inclined to be impatient and self-important. Challis saw a man who bullied his male employees, fondled the female, and over-charged his clients.

His mind drifted. It often occurred to him that crime and criminals were closely bound up in motor vehicles. Transport, getaway, an expression of personality, a weapon, a tomb. A pay-off. Cars could be tied to everything he'd ever investigated, yet were taken for granted. They deserved their own science.

'Rust, bottom of both doors.'

Challis knew that. You could see it with the naked eye, and he'd said as much in the ads.

'Yes.'

Hopgood took a fridge magnet from his pocket and, with a no-flies-on-me air, tested every square inch of the car. It seemed to cringe under so much scrutiny: 'Sorry, getting old, got a few flaws. . . .'

Then the guy was poking around in the engine bay. 'New hoses.'

And new spark plug leads, thought Challis, new coil leads, new everything that had been chewed by the rats. 'Yes.'

After that, Hopgood took the car for a test run. He was gone for twenty minutes, and when he returned he stood in Challis's driveway with his hands on his hips and fired a summary:

'She's burning oil, so she'll need a new set of rings. Rides the bumps rough, so new suspension. I'll need to replace the wind-screen and offside turning light, both import items. Goodish tyres. Seat fabric's OK but stretched. New soft top needed, get one of these made up in Sydney. Bloke does a lot of work for me.'

So, are you making me an offer? thought Challis. He glanced at his watch and said nothing. He'd told Hopgood that another buyer was coming, which was an outright lie.

'Fifteen grand.'

'Twenty-two fifty,' Challis replied.

'Come on, you must be joking. Sixteen.'

'Twenty.'

'Don't arse me about. Look, I'll give you eighteen.'

'Sorry,' said Challis with his heart in his mouth, 'twenty.' And after the restoration you'll sell for thirty, thirty-five.

'Eighteen. Take it or leave it.'

Challis sighed and said he'd take it. Hopgood fished a thousand dollars in hundreds from his wallet and promised the rest when he picked up the car. 'I'll come back with a flatbed truck this evening.'

'Sure.'

And Hopgood left, the Jag purring down Challis's driveway. Just before reaching the gate it braked suddenly for a sickly-green Hyundai, which sped in from the road, saw Hopgood, and swerved onto the grass. A moment later, the Jaguar slid unfussily out onto the road, and Larrayne Destry jerked back onto the driveway and in erratic surges toward Challis.

She got out, looking jittery yet annoyed. 'Who was that? He gave me this really strange look, kind of smug.'

'He thought you'd come to buy my car,' Challis said, explaining what had happened. 'You should have come a few minutes earlier; he might have offered more money.'

Larrayne looked doubtfully at the Triumph. 'If you say so.'

Challis laughed. 'I'm glad to get rid of the thing, frankly.' He toed the gravel with the tip of his shoe. 'Everything all right?'

'Fine.'

'The boyfriend?'

'Dumped. Kind of.'

Challis nodded. The boyfriend hadn't seemed too bad, just an idiot. 'Have you heard from your mother?'

'She emails me like every day.'

Challis, too. A phone call, a text message, or a Skype conversation every two or three days.

Larrayne Destry blurted, 'I was wrong about you.'

Challis opened and closed his mouth warily.

'I mean, I didn't like what was happening with Mum and Dad, and I took it out on you.'

He shrugged. 'Oh, well.'

She said fiercely, as though she were a fierce small child, 'You're not my father.'

'I know that.' Challis didn't even want to be her friend, really. Just civilised, that's all.

'Are you the real deal? As far as Mum is concerned?'

'I'll try to be.'

'You're supposed to reassure me.'

'I'm supposed to be truthful,' he told her. 'Your mother and I, we're getting to know each other. No pressure, a lot of kindness, a reasonable amount of companionship.'

Larrayne Destry chewed her bottom lip, looking for loopholes in what he'd said. After a while she shrugged. 'Okay.'

Pam Murphy arrived at her parents' house in Kew with a roast chicken, supermarket coleslaw, and a head of broccoli—three minutes in the steamer for the broccoli. Make that five, she thought, thinking of their elderly teeth. If she were not so helpless in the kitchen she might have offered to cook everything from scratch, but this was easier, and she didn't want to burden her mother. She didn't want a fuss, that's what it boiled down to. Or an *unnecessary* fuss. There was going to be some fuss, no matter what she did.

The fuss started the moment she walked in the back door, the mild astonishment that greeted her.

'Weren't you expecting me?'

When they realised that they had been, her father cocked his head at her. 'You're a bit later than usual.'

There was no usual time, her visits had become rare and sporadic, but she said, 'Had to stop for petrol.'

Her father looked at her cunningly. 'They always put the price up on Sundays. It's best to fill up on Tuesdays.'

'I'll try to remember that.'

'Car running well?'

'Fine,' she told him.

Since she'd got into trouble with the repayments a couple of years ago and borrowed the money from him, it was as if he owned the damn thing.

'I hope you're servicing it regularly, sweetheart. Every five thousand kilometres no matter what the book says.'

Pam said nothing, hoping a smile would suffice, and after a while her father harrumphed a little, and they went through to the sitting room. Rain clouds were gathering above Melbourne, but it was still warm outside and boiling inside. 'Let me open a window. Or at least turn the heating down.'

That caused more fuss, and she mentally smacked her forehead. They were old, and they felt the cold.

She'd barely sat on the sofa to catch up, when her father said, 'Let's eat.'

Another mistake: the time was 1 P.M., and her parents always ate lunch at 12:30 P.M. 'I'll serve up,' she told him. 'Back in a minute.'

Pam glanced at the sideboard and mantelpiece as she left the room. Both surfaces were crammed with photographs of her brothers: graduating, receiving awards, basking in the love of their wives and children. As far as Pam knew, the one photograph marking her achievements, the police academy passing out parade, was collecting fly spots on the side table of the spare bedroom.

She found her mother in the kitchen, boiling the broccoli to death. Giving the frail shoulders a quick hug, she spooned the coleslaw into a shallow bowl and cut up the chicken, her mind drifting. Should she have poured her heart out to Challis over a drink after the Friday briefing, explained exactly what she'd meant by saying she'd done something stupid? He didn't strike her as the kind of man to flounder in embarrassment if a woman friend said she'd slept with another woman. He was straight, but not that straight. So why her reticence? Because it was private, she told herself. Because he's not my friend. Because I've always had to solve things myself.

And the reasons for that stem from my childhood in this house.

They were eating within fifteen minutes of her arrival. She'd brought a couple of Peninsula wines along, a Merricks Creek Pinot and the Elan Gamay, her father opening the Pinot with a flourish. 'Let's save the Gamay for summer.'

Then they told her all about her brothers, their wives and children, their university positions. They asked nothing about her life and work. She didn't mind, not really, the story of her life. The boys, and her father, were the brains of the outfit. She was just a girl. Good athlete, topped her class at the police academy, promising young detective, etcetera, etcetera, but her parents didn't begin to know how to talk to her about any of those things.

'It would be nice if one of these days you brought someone with you,' her mother said.

For a brief second, Pam imagined Jeannie Schiff in the fourth chair at the table.

The image didn't hold.

MEANWHILE SCOBIE AND BETH Sutton had settled themselves onto stiff metal chairs with vinyl seats in the hall of their daughter's school. Located in paddocks inland of Dromana, it offered views to the sea in one direction and vines and hills in the other. A longish bus ride for Roslyn, and Waterloo Secondary College was closer, but a policeman didn't send his kids to school in the town he served in. Scobie didn't want the psycho sons or daughters of someone he'd arrested taking it out on Roslyn, a kicking behind the toilet block, a shafting in a dim corner of the library.

He glanced at his wife. As usual, Beth was subdued, a bit foggy in the head, but seemed generally more engaged with the world and their daughter than she had been earlier in the year. Back then it would have been impossible to get her to accompany him to something like today's school musicale.

He'd paid a gold coin for a copy of the programme and searched it for Roslyn's name. There it was, correctly spelt. He ran his gaze down the other names, noting that his daughter went to school with a Jarryd, a Jarrod, a Jared, and a Jarrold. Oh, wait: and a Jhared.

First up was a Year Seven four-piece, who didn't quite mangle the obligatory 'Smoke on the Water.' There's more talent in a high school than a primary, he decided. The afternoon progressed. A sweet alto solo of 'Danny Boy'. A six-piece woodwind version of 'Scarborough Fair.' And an incredibly funny extract from 'Tubular Bells,' the final section where different instruments are introduced in turn, one overlaying the other, until the final, rousing explosion of the tubular bells—except that the boy who announced each instrument really camped it up, and the instruments didn't quite match. 'Glockenspiel,' he said solemnly, but what you got was a piano accordion, and when he cried 'Tubular bells!' Roslyn came out shaking a wind chime.

Scobie thought his face would split from grinning.

The final act was an all-school orchestra and choir version of 'Bohemian Rhapsody,' and what made the day perfect for Scobie Sutton was Beth giving him a sly nudge and asking, 'In what way is a drum solo like a sneeze?'

Scobie eyed her carefully. She was making a joke? 'Don't know.'

'You know it's about to happen, and there's not a damn thing you can do about it.'

He wanted to laugh and cry, wanted to celebrate the return of his wife, even as a tiny corner of his mind wondered if she'd entered some final stage that, like a sneeze, couldn't be halted.

Chapter 46

By 3 P.M. on Monday, Grace was back on the ferry, wearing one of her going-to-the-bank outfits, a slim-line black skirt, charcoal tights, cream silk shirt, bright-red waisted jacket. The glasses with the purple rims, hair in a French coil, and carrying a cheap red leather satchel on a shoulder strap, large enough to hold the Paul Klee painting and everything else. Flat shoes; she never wore heels. You can't run in heels.

Leaving the Golf near the Rosebud police station, she rented a Commodore, and by 4:30 P.M. was parked behind the K-Mart in Waterloo. The Safeway car park was closer to the VineTrust, but a corner of her mind said: Don't park too close to the bank.

Then she was in the foyer. Monday, close to closing time, so she was expecting a busy, distracting atmosphere, but the bank was quiet, two tellers finalising the day's figures, the financial planner closing the venetian blinds, and one customer, a young guy in painter's overalls, paint dotting his boots and the toolbox at his feet.

Suddenly Rowan Ely was crossing the grey carpet, wearing his I'm-so-glad-you-bank-with-us and I-wish-I-could-peel-your-clothes-off smile. 'Mrs. Grace! Always a pleasure.'

'Mr. Ely.'

'I've told you so many times, it's Rowan. Now, what can we do for you today?'

Grace had thought about this. She'd had a similar encounter with the manager on Friday, when she'd stowed the Klee in her safe-deposit box. Today it was her intention to clean out the box, never to return. She'd be missed eventually; Ely and his staff would scratch their heads over her—but that would be later, maybe weeks later, when it didn't matter. Arousing their curiosity *today* was a different matter. So she said she wondered if they could sit in his office and discuss some of the VineTrust's business banking opportunities.

'Certainly. Follow me.'

Grace followed. Behind her the housepainter was saying, '. . . open a business account for, you know, me painting business.'

The words faded to nothing as Ely shut his door. Grace sat erect on the chair facing Ely's desk. She was never coquettish. She never flirted or signalled, consciously or unconsciously, but men always responded to her as if she did these things. Rowan Ely beamed at her as if his assistance to this beautiful woman had been special, and especially noted by her. It gave him a peculiar glow.

They talked for a while. He showed her brochures, swung his computer monitor around to show graphs full of brightly coloured lines. They settled on one of his 'products,' and then he was escorting her out to the foyer, chatting away, saying she should come earlier next time, they were about to close, and if she came earlier they could have a cup of tea and a chat, even a proper drink, his eyes on her chest the whole time.

That's why she noticed the shotgun before he did.

She shifted her gaze to the man holding it and recalled that the housepainter had been wearing dark glasses, a black beanie, and a bristly moustache earlier, when she'd entered the bank.

The beanie was over his face now, but the point was, she'd stuffed up. After all, she was the hiding-in-plain-sight expert and should have been able to tell when someone else was doing it. Instead, like an idiot, she'd been concerned for the bank's carpet, hoping the guy didn't have paint on the bottoms of his boots. And now he was waving some kind of sawn-off shotgun in her face.

Chapter 47

It was Joy, the senior teller, who'd activated the silent alarm. The gunman had ordered her to step back from her window, but then he was distracted by the sudden emergence of Mr. Ely and Mrs. Grace from the manager's office, so she'd darted forward, pressed the red button, darted back again.

But Challis didn't learn this until many hours later. Right now all he knew was an alarm had sounded at the police station, a handful of Waterloo uniforms under Jeff Greener had responded, and he and Murphy had a siege on their hands.

The first thing he did was try the bank's back door. Locked. He went around to the High Street entrance. Also locked. Then someone on the inside opened the venetian blind briefly. He saw a huddle of people in the middle of the main room, controlled by a man wearing a balaclava and pointing a shotgun. The blind was closed again.

So he phoned the bank. Rowan Ely answered, sounding frightened, and Challis said, 'Rowan, I need to talk to him.'

He heard muffled sounds, as though Ely was holding the phone to his chest, then the manager was back, his voice crackling in Challis's ear: 'He says you don't call him, he calls you,' and the connection was cut.

This was the heart-in-the-mouth stage, adrenaline fuelled, a sense of sand running out, and Challis's chest tightened. He turned to Pam Murphy and ordered the closure of High Street and its side streets and alleyways for two hundred metres in each direction. 'Nobody allowed in, and shopkeepers and shoppers to be screened before being allowed out.'

'Boss.'

Then he made a number of phone calls. First, the Force Response Unit; second, a hostage negotiator; third, reinforcements from other Peninsula stations; fourth, the superintendent.

'Just in case you feel tempted to complain to the press about resources, Inspector,' said McQuarrie, 'how about I put a bomb under Force Response and the negotiators?'

'I've already contacted them, sir,' said Challis.

Wondering if he'd redeem himself today, he pocketed his phone and walked into the middle of High Street with a megaphone. There was movement in the bank's front window again, a hooked finger twitching the blind slats. Then the gap disappeared, the blind trembling briefly behind the glass.

He raised the megaphone to his mouth.

A small window, set high in the wall above the ATM, blew out.

Glass and shotgun pellets flew over his head. He jolted in fear and retreated to the police line.

'Boss?' Pam said, grabbing at his arm. 'You all right?'

'Back to the drawing board,' Challis said shakily. He glanced around, his gaze alighting on Café Laconic. 'Command post,' he said, and strode across to negotiate with the owner.

Then nothing. Late afternoon edged into evening. The Force Response Unit arrived, a dozen men and one officer, armed with assault rifles and dressed like extras in an American cop film. And acting like it, too: They were rarely called upon to do anything but take part in training exercises, and now here was the real thing. Their eyes gleamed, and their forefingers twitched.

The commander was a man named Loeb, sculpted out of a blond hardwood. 'We can use that busted window,' he said. 'Toss in a teargas canister, stun grenade, the guy's disorientated, my guys rush in and take him down.'

'He has a shotgun, determination, and an itchy trigger finger,' Challis said. 'We wait for the hostage negotiator.'

'I say we consider—'

Challis shook his head. 'We give the hostage negotiator a chance, you know the drill.'

'It's getting dark.'

'I can see that.'

'Could take hours for the negotiator to get here.'

'Could do,' agreed Challis.

He was saved by the Café Laconic staff, who brought out trays of coffee and sandwiches. Challis gulped his latté. Strong, as he liked it.

His mobile phone rang. He answered, listened, pocketed the phone again. 'The negotiator's about ninety minutes away.'

'Jesus.'

Challis shrugged. He was in charge, and as far as he could see, that meant saying 'no' to everything. He didn't tell the FRU officer that the hostage negotiator had only just touched down at Melbourne airport. Her name was York, and she'd been attending at a hostage situation in Shepparton. A fruit grower, burdened by debts and claiming that a Mafia standover man was bleeding him dry, had shot the family dog and threatened to shoot his family.

In the end, he'd shot himself.

I can't see that happening here, Challis thought. Meanwhile it was his job to tell the gunman that a hostage negotiator was on the way. He swallowed a few times and walked out into the intersection again. 'I need to speak to you,' he called, hunching to present a smaller target.

Nothing.

Challis turned around on the spot, a quick reconnaissance of the intersection and nearby streets. The town seemed to be filling rapidly, an avid crowd of locals and strangers forming behind the barriers, possibly drawn to Waterloo by the TV images. Plenty of media, Challis noted: reporters, cameramen, the Channel 7 helicopter, four or five women holding microphones to their flawless mouths. They were all hungry and, like the crowd—and indeed the police—would be swapping guesses, black humour, and misinformation.

He wasn't fired upon. He walked back to the command post.

Then Jack Porteous was blocking his way into Café Laconic. 'Quick update, Inspector?'

'How did you get though the cordon?'

'Is it true you were fired on from inside the bank? Are the police properly resourced for a siege situation?'

Challis nodded to Greener, who came forward from the shadows. 'Senior Constable Greener will escort you back behind the line.'

Then more stasis.

Movement, when it came, was quick and clean. The main door of the bank opened and three figures appeared. Challis recognised the senior teller, just as she lurched forward as if shoved in the back, stumbled, fell to her hands and knees in the street. Now he could see that another woman was behind her. Young, dark-haired, attractive, scared. Scared because a powerful forearm was choking her windpipe and a shotgun was tucked into the hinge of her jaw. Of the gunman, all Challis could see was the forearm and a black woollen head.

And just as quickly they were gone, disappearing inside the bank, and Challis and Murphy were scuttling across the road to help the teller. Her knees were scraped. 'It's all right, you're safe now,' Pam said, and Joy staggered, almost a dead weight, as the detectives guided her into the café.

'I say we go in,' said the FRU officer, hovering over them.

'And to hell with collateral damage, right?' said Pam, elbowing him aside.

'My boys are trained. . . .'

They ignored him, Challis asking, 'You up for a few questions, Joy?'

She smiled shakily. 'A stiff drink would help.'

Challis glanced at the café proprietor, who nodded and reached for a brandy bottle and a glass. When it had been delivered, and the teller had swallowed a couple of mouthfuls, Challis began:

'First things first: we need to know who's in there.'

'Apart from the holdup man?'

'Yes.'

'Mrs. Grace, Mr. Ely, Erin, and Maddie.'

'Who was the woman in the doorway with you?'

'Mrs. Grace. Susan Grace. She has a safe-deposit box with us.'

'Erin and Maddie are staff members?'

'Yes. Erin's our financial planner. Maddie's just a trainee, only been with us a month, poor thing.' Another gulp of the brandy. 'Sorry, I'm all shaken up.'

She was a slight woman with a cap of red-blonde hair, and she began to cry. Pam hugged her, giving Challis a look that he couldn't decipher. He frowned, raised an eyebrow, but she turned to the teller and said, 'Joy, about the customer, Susan Grace—are you sure that's her name?'

'Yes.'

Challis cocked his head at Murphy. The question hadn't been frivolous. 'Do you know her from somewhere, Murph?'

'There was an incident a couple of weeks ago,' Pam said, going on to describe it, a woman with a foreign accent being accosted in the street.

'You're sure it's the same woman?'

'Positive.'

'She'd been to the bank?'

'I think so.'

Joy was swinging her gaze from one to the other. 'Mrs. Grace isn't foreign.'

This was a side track they didn't have time for, so to cut it short, Challis said, 'Is she local, this Mrs. Grace?'

'Oh yes.'

'Did she give you the impression of knowing the man with the shotgun?'

'Good God, no.'

He turned to Murphy. 'You made a note of the time, date, description, car rego?'

'Of course.'

'Follow it up later.'

'Boss.'

He turned to the teller. 'Have you seen the gunman before?'

'Never.'

'Can you describe him?'

'Not very well. He's wearing a beanie and sunglasses and has a moustache. Average height.'

'Is there a reason why he let you go, Joy? Does he intend to let the others go soon?'

'No. He was very clear. He wants blankets and clothesline twine.'

'What?'

'Four or five blankets, huge ones,' the teller said.

Chapter 48

Mara and Warren had been shadowing Steven Finch since Saturday night, hoping he'd meet with the bitch who'd robbed them, but all he did was move between his house and his business.

Now it was early Monday evening, and they were parked half a block from Finch's house, watching it through the side mirrors of the Mercedes van, the air ripe around them. Nothing was happening, so Mara said, 'To hell with this,' and fished out her phone.

'Steven? I thought we had a deal?'

His voice croaked, betraying fear. Fear was good. 'I was about to call you, honest.'

'And tell me what, precisely?'

'It's not my fault. How was I to know this would happen?'

Mara shook her head as if to clear it but wasn't about to admit she had no idea what he was talking about. 'Indeed.'

And soon she'd teased it out of him: It was all over the TV, a bank siege in Waterloo, and one of the hostages was the woman who had stolen the Klee. 'I mean,' Finch said shakily, 'what if she's arrested? She'll spill to the cops.'

'It's definitely her?'

'Turn on your TV. They keep running the same footage.'

Mara weighed it all up. 'This is what you do, Steve: grab anything incriminating in your house, then do the same at the shop, and disappear for a few years.'

She terminated the call and immediately started Safari on the iPhone. She found a news report, and indeed, there was the woman who'd robbed them.

She turned to her husband. 'Let's do it. He'll be coming out his front door pretty soon.'

'Do what?'

Mara ignored him, climbed into the rear of the van. Finch's house was as heavily secured as his shop, but from tailing him she knew that he was vulnerable for a short period as he walked between his front door and the driver's side door of his car. An Audi coupe; mind you, funded in part by Niekirk money, parked in the street because the houses were renovated workers' cottages a hundred years old, no garages or carports.

Everything was going swimmingly for Mara now, after days of twiddling her thumbs. She opened the van's rear door a crack, saw that she had a clear line of sight to the junk dealer's front step, and removed her Steyr rifle from its slipcase.

When Mara was a teen, she'd spent school holidays on Grandfather Krasnov's farm in New England, and the old émigré had taught her how to fire a rifle fitted with a telescopic sight. Tin cans, usually, plus the occasional watermelon—just like the assassin in *The Day of the Jackal*, Mara enjoying the satisfying, pulpy explosion as the bullet hit. Sometimes kangaroos, foxes, and rabbits, and, once, a neighbour's stray sheep dog—a spectacular shot, 500 metres at least.

She stretched out on the camping mattress, propped the rifle on a small tripod, sighted the German lenses, and waited, unseen, the van's fittings and metal skin ideal for deadening sound. Was that a shot? people would say. They wouldn't be sure.

She wiggled about until she was comfortable, and after that was absolutely still, breathing shallowly, feeling nothing, not even anticipation. She didn't even register the jitteriness that was her husband.

Finch stepped out of his front door and for a moment remonstrated with someone within the house, then the door was slammed and he presented himself to Mara, there was no other way to describe it. He stood there for a couple of seconds too long, carrying a black holdall, a panicky look on his face as he scanned the street, his gaze passing over the van. Mara placed the cross hairs on the centre of his chest and breathed out in one long, slow, exhalation and squeezed the trigger.

'You must squeeze, never pull,' Grandfather Krasnov had taught her, and Mara, packing the rifle away now, folding the tripod, shutting the rear door, telling Warren to drive away slowly, realised anew that there had never been a man in her life like the Krasnov patriarch.

'Another loose end cleaned up,' she told her husband as he drove in his nervy way out of Williamstown and back to the Peninsula. 'Now it's time we all took a long overseas holiday.'

Chapter 49

The blankets and clothesline were delivered to the bank and time passed.

McQuarrie called. 'Well, inspector?'

'Wait and see, sir.'

'Can't you go in?'

'Still waiting for the hostage negotiator.'

'I don't want any loss of life, Hal.'

'Nor do I, sir.' So I'm 'Hal' now? And you want me to send the marines in *and* avoid loss of life? He paused. 'Got to go, the negotiator's here.'

Senior Constable York was a forthright, large-boned woman, reminding Challis of the rural women he often encountered on the Peninsula, who worked with horses and married cheerful, open men. He outlined the situation quickly, and she said, 'Huh. You'd expect something concrete by now. Deadlines, demands, a lot of panicky to and fro. . . .'

Challis shrugged. 'Well, this guy hasn't said a word.'

'Okay, let's get squared away,' York said.

She'd arrived with a special van fitted with digital recorders, phones, camera monitors, a TV set, scrap paper, pens, and a whiteboard and markers. There was also a small, soundproofed inner compartment fitted with a chair, a monitor, and a tele-phone. 'The throne room,' she grinned, 'so I can talk to him without distraction.' She gestured at the white board. 'And this is for intel.'

Challis grunted. There was no intel, only supposition. 'For what it's worth, I think we're dealing with a holdup man who's been robbing banks along the coast south of Sydney and more recently in Gippsland. Those robberies were quick and smooth, in and out, no hostage situations.'

'And he's said nothing,' said York flatly, bending to a keyboard and watching one of the monitors.

'Not directly. *In*directly he's asked for blankets and clothesline.'

York shook her head. 'Don't like the sound of that. What if he's planning a murder-suicide and doesn't want to see the faces of his victims when he shoots them?'

'Could be some kind of shield.'

'Either way, I've got to get him talking,' York said.

Challis gave her phone numbers for Ely and the bank, and she shut herself inside the small compartment. After a while, she came out again, shaking her head. 'When they talk, I'm on firm ground.'

Challis nodded. He couldn't help her.

'Normally,' she said, 'I walk into a situation that's volatile, not calm, and it's my job to talk the hostage-taker down, even if it takes hours. And it's surprising what you can learn in that time. You know, personal information—he's upset or depressed because he's been sacked from his job or his wife's got a lover or he's stopped taking his pills—and environmental.'

'Environmental?'

'Like he's got a gun, or the room's too hot, or one of the hostages is pregnant, stuff like that.' York shook her head. 'But *this* guy. . . .'

Challis began to tune her out. York was thinking about the hostage-taker in an immediate sense; he was thinking about the man's long-term intentions. He wasn't dealing with a nutter but a planner. The man had found himself trapped, but knew to wait for the cloak of darkness. And he'd asked for blankets and twine because he was a planner, not some volatile schizophrenic or speed freak.

Challis reached forward and turned on the van's TV set, channel surfing for a while. The siege was receiving extensive air time, viewer interest teased by constant replays of the gunman on the steps of the bank, shielded by the woman known as Mrs. Grace. It had everything: a gun, a masked man, a beautiful victim, a heavily-armed cordon of police.

He muted the sound track and stared out at the car park between the rear of the bank and the Safeway supermarket. Almost all of the cars were gone now, part of the evacuation plan, but some drivers had still to be located. Meanwhile, according to a numberplate check, all but two of the cars were local: a white Nissan, which had been reported stolen in Gippsland four days earlier, and a burgundy Commodore, rented in Rosebud earlier that day. He'd wanted to play it safe and place a tracking device on both cars, but owing to budget cuts, only one tracker was available, so he'd selected the stolen Nissan, figuring it was the gunman's.

Challis shivered: the waiting, the stillness, the underside of the evening sky lit queerly by the street and parking lot lights. He turned back to York, who was tilted back in her swivel chair, frowning at her monitors. 'I mean, ideally,' she said, 'you guide the dialogue until the guy talks his own way out, and along the way you get him to release some or all of the hostages. . . . This guy, zilch.' She reached for one of her phones. 'I'll try again.'

Challis stepped out of her booth, sealing her in, and watched her make the calls, knowing the gunman wouldn't answer. Presently she came out again, gesturing in frustration. 'I don't like it,' she said. 'What have we got here? Suicide by cop, except he's going to shoot his hostages first?'

Challis shook his head. 'This guy's given no indication he's suicidal. He's too collected. He's got a plan.'

'Yeah, well, maybe,' York said. She chewed on her bottom lip. She didn't want a breakout, she wanted to be able to say she'd sweet-talked a nutcase into giving himself up.

In silence they watched the bank. Ten P.M. and the onlookers were beginning to drift away. The force response officer ambled over from Café Laconic, and his clutch of body-armoured and visored men and said, 'What gives? My boys are getting antsy.'

'Antsy?' said York. 'You mean they're not well trained?'

Challis laughed. The FRU man's face tightened. 'They put a media hound like *you* in charge?' he scowled, sauntering back to his team.

'It's important to let them flex their egos,' York said.

'Guys like Loeb?'

York shook her head. 'Sorry, I mean your average hostage-taker. You let them think they have the upper hand, when ultimately it's the negotiator who holds all the cards, the negotiator who denies and delays gratification.'

'Uh-huh.'

'A personal relationship, that's the first step.'

Blankets, Challis was thinking. Cord to bind them together into one big invisibility cloak.

The image took hold in his head, as York continued to explain the intricacies of her job. 'In the end, you learn to recognise the signs, what we call a surrender ritual, a handing over to the nego—'

'They're coming out,' Challis said.

An apparition emerged from the bank. It resembled a lumpy tent or a knobbly creature with a rounded back and many legs. The range made it difficult to see clearly but he was betting the holdup man was under there, together with bank staff and Mrs. Grace. The creature moved on mincing, shuffling legs across the car park. No way can we take a shot, he thought, glancing at the armed response team, shaking his head at them.

They all watched as the huddled figures passed the Nissan and paused at the burgundy Commodore. Damn, thought Challis. Wrong car. Then the cloak shifted shape as if it were a sack full of kittens, and one by one, the gunman and the hostages slipped into the front and rear of the car. He couldn't tell who had got behind the wheel; the cloak still covered them.

Then a passenger door opened as the car began to creep away. A young woman tumbled out, falling to her knees. The car stopped again, fifty metres away.

Challis waited a moment, expecting a trap, then ran, trailed by Pam Murphy. With one eye on the Commodore, he helped the woman to her feet. 'You're Maddie?'

She gulped and hiccoughed. 'Yes.'

'It's okay, you're safe now.'

She shook her head violently. 'He told me to give you a message. He'll release the others as soon as he feels safe. But if he sees anyone follow him, he'll shoot to kill. No cars, no helicopters, that's what he said.'

The Commodore crept a short distance, stopped again. Challis's mind raced with counter plans. He held up a hand, took out his phone, waved it at the car. He got his answer: the car accelerated toward the dark edge of the night.

IAN GALT WAS IN a city motel, at the end of a fruitless day, propped against the headboard of a lumpy bed, unwinding before the TV set bolted to the wall. Days of wearing out good shoe leather, he thought, and what happens? I find her on the evening news. In a place where I can't get at her.

The best he could hope for now was that the man with the shotgun would blow her pretty little head off.

And he thought: what was she doing in that bank?

Chapter 50

'I guess I wasn't making much sense last night,' said Rowan Ely in the Waterloo police station the next morning.

Last night he'd wandered dazed and disorientated onto the South Gippsland Highway, near a drainage channel beyond the township of Tooradin, where a truck driver stopped to pick him up, calling the police and an ambulance. Now Ely looked pale and doughy in his banker's suit, his hands scratched, his forehead bruised where he'd been clubbed by the shotgun.

'It wasn't a night for making sense,' Challis replied, thinking that the bandit had in fact made plenty of sense.

Eight thirty A.M., and because forensics officers were still poking around in the bank, Challis was conducting this interview at the station. The victim suite, because it was kitted out like a family den—albeit the den of a family without taste or character—but better than an interrogation room.

'He freed Maddie in the car park. Who was next?'

'Erin, then me,' Ely said. 'Mrs. Grace was still with him, the last I saw of them.'

Challis tapped the front page of the *Age*, the upper fold filled with a now-famous photograph of the gunman on the steps of the bank, his forearm around a woman's throat. 'Just to be clear: Is that Mrs. Grace?'

'Yes.'

'When you were released, what direction did they take? Still heading east?'

'Yes.'

Challis plotted the route mentally. Did the gunman intend to head deeper into Gippsland—where he'd already come from, robbing two banks along the way—and then up the coast, or would he head inland, north into the alpine country and up into regional New South Wales? Or had it been a bluff, he'd connected with the M1 and doubled back to lose himself in Melbourne?

'How are the others?' Ely asked.

'Fine. Like you, a bit shaken and scared, but fine.'

'They'll need counselling,' Ely said. 'I hope they realise they're not needed at work today.'

Challis didn't bother to reply. 'Tell me more about Mrs. Grace.'

'Such as?'

'Anything.'

Ely stared into the distance, a curious loosening around his eyes and mouth. Love, desire? 'A businesswoman,' he said, 'well-off, always very friendly and polite. Private. Lovely woman,' he concluded, uttering a little cough.

'Is there a Mr. Grace?'

'I understood she was divorced.'

'Her accent: German? Danish?'

Ely shook his head. 'What accent?'

'She was accosted in the street two weeks ago by a man who claimed to know her. One of my officers intervened and heard her speak with a strong European accent.'

'Different person. Had to be.'

Challis grunted. 'Did you get a sense that Mrs. Grace knew the gunman?'

'Good grief no.'

'Nothing about her manner, her voice, things she said or did? Nothing that hinted of a previous connection?'

The pinkness of health and outrage had returned to Ely's face. 'I saw nothing to suggest that.'

'Okay, then what kind of interaction *did* they have—apart from this?' Challis said, tapping the front page photograph again.

Ely narrowed his pouchy eyes. 'Are you suggesting Stockholm syndrome? She started to sympathise with him?'

Challis knew there hadn't been time for Stockholm syndrome to develop. He said, 'Did she resist? Was she scared? Did she talk to him, try to get him to let you all go or give himself up? Did she try to keep him calm, give him suggestions of any kind?'

But Ely seemed to swell mulishly, as if his image of his favourite client were being sullied, so Challis held up his hands placatingly. 'I'm sure she was only interested in saving lives, avoiding bloodshed.'

Ely gave him a suspicious frown and said stiffly, 'I didn't see or hear anything untoward.'

'She's the only one unaccounted for.'

'One hostage is easier to manage than several,' Ely retorted.

'True.'

'Or he's killed her,' Ely said, his features cracking a little.

'Or she's wandering along a back road somewhere.'

Both men visualised it. The little room was stuffy, the generic framed prints no longer comforting, the armchairs too soft. Outside, in the corridor, life went on, police officers and civilian staff elbowing past each other with reports and car keys in their hands.

'Why that car?' said Challis.

Ely shuffled about to get comfortable. 'He asked which of us had driven to work. The girls were smart, they lied, said their husbands had driven them. I said I walked as usual—which is true. So he asked Mrs. Grace where she was parked.'

'He was agitated when he asked it?'

'Quite calm, actually.'

'So you could see his face all this time?'

'No, he kept the balaclava on.'

'So he *sounded* calm.'

'Yes. And his body language.'

'Do you think Mrs. Grace was trying to calm him down by offering her car?'

Ely said stoutly, 'I think it was a brave thing to do. For all we knew, he'd go off the rails and start shooting us if he thought there wasn't a way out. She wanted an end to it. She offered her car so he'd leave.'

'What can you tell me about his height, build, voice?'

Ely eyed Challis. 'Your overall build.'

Challis was tall, a little stooped sometimes, medium build. He said, 'How much cash did he get away with?'

'Being as it was a Monday, not a lot. Ten thousand?'

There was a knock, and Pam Murphy stuck her head around the door. 'Forensics have finished inside the bank, and we've found the car.'

Challis smiled at Ely. 'It's all yours.'

Ely was staring at Murphy's retreating figure. 'I wanted to ask her if Mrs. Grace was in the car.'

Meaning: Mrs. Grace's dead body.

EIGHT FORTY-FIVE A.M. NOW, and they made a rapid trip north and east of Waterloo, Murphy driving the CIU car, Scobie Sutton in the passenger seat, Challis lounging in the rear, where he could think and dream.

Koo-Wee-Rup was a pretty town between the South Gippsland

Highway and the broad fast ribbon that was the M1 motorway, many kilometres to the north. Flat farming country scored, to the northeast of the town, by deep drainage channels. That's where the Commodore had been spotted, on a track beside a drain one hundred metres in from the road. A woman delivering her children to an isolated school bus stop had called it in, worried it might be another rural suicide. As the CIU car passed the bus stop, Challis could see her point: a lonely spot, swept by ever-present winds, speaking of lost hopes and chances.

The local policeman had created a broad perimeter around the car, using wooden stakes and crime scene tape. Challis got out, stretched his back, noting the wind, the sun warmth, and the water birds wheeling over his head, above the empty stretches of land.

'A good place to dump a body,' Pam Murphy said.

The local constable hadn't seen a body, but Challis shared Murphy's concern. He thought of the water running high in the drain, he thought of the closed boot of the Commodore. Yet he stood with the others outside the tape and scanned the scene for a while, noting these details: Both front doors were open; he could see the keys in the ignition; a cup of takeaway coffee sat on the roof above the driver's door. He didn't know what any of that meant except that since the cup hadn't blown away, there was coffee still in it, and he thought: DNA.

He pulled on latex gloves. 'Let's look inside the boot, but don't touch anything else until the crime scene people get here.'

No body in the boot, but there was a small suitcase. Challis opened it: women's underwear, two T-shirts, jeans, a plain skirt, tights, a travel pack of toiletries.

No handbag, but Scobie Sutton, wandering fifty metres along the drain, called out: 'Over here.'

Challis joined him. The grass was damp, the air laden with moist earth smells and the murmur of water rolling by. Below them, at the edge of the stream, was a red satchel.

'I recognise it from the news footage,' Sutton said.

Challis scrambled down the bank, clasping tussocks of grass to save him from falling, and grabbed the bag by the broken strap. Then, braced on the acutely angled slope, he poked at the contents with a pen from his pocket. 'No purse or wallet.'

He clambered to safety, leaving the bag for the forensics team, and returned with Sutton to the car. Pam Murphy was peering at the soil beside the passenger side door.

'Blood here.'

Challis peered, confirmed it, and took both of his officers back behind the tape.

'Okay, Scobie, how do you read it?'

Sutton considered the sky gloomily. 'More questions than answers,' he said at last.

'Such as?'

'Has he got the time for a leisurely cup of coffee? Where did he buy it? If the woman was with him, what was she doing in the meantime? Dead in the boot? Alive and in cahoots with him? Bound and gagged in the back seat? If she's dead, where's her body?' He stared gloomily at the channel. 'In there?'

Pam Murphy said, 'Maybe it's *his* blood. Maybe *she* put *him* in the channel.'

'Then where is she?'

'We'd better check stolen car reports.'

'Or we have a third person involved, an accomplice with a car.'

'Or we have another hostage situation in some out-of-the-way farmhouse,' Pam said, gesturing at the flat empty world all around them.

Challis smiled tiredly. 'We need DNA from the blood and the cup, see if they match. We need prints from the car and the shoulder bag. We need a search of the drain.'

'I'll see if the bank has a clearer image of her face,' Murphy said.

Just then her phone rang. She covered one ear against the wind and turned away. Challis heard the fragments of her conversation:

'She give you an address?

'. . . Cash? I thought you'd require a credit card? . . . You're sure about the name? Not Grace or Anita or any variation? Have you been watching the news? . . . The hostage—is it the woman who rented the Commodore from you?'

Then she listened for a while before pocketing the phone and rejoining the men. 'That was the car rental firm in Rosebud. It seems they rented the Commodore to a woman calling herself Nina. Signature illegible, yesterday morning, payment in cash, not credit card. It also seems that they forgot to take down her driver's licence details. But they're pretty sure it was the woman we know as Mrs. Grace. I suggest we show her photo around all the motels in and around Rosebud.'

Challis nodded, thinking through the stages. The wind blew; the clouds were wispy streaks high above their heads. A white van appeared in the landscape, small and far away. Forensics, he guessed, and said to the others, as if coming out of a trance:

'We need to open her safe-deposit box.'

Chapter 51

They raced back to Waterloo, Challis sprawled across the rear seats again, working his phone this time, first arranging a warrant to open the safe-deposit box and then calling the bank and asking to speak to Ely.

Joy answered. 'He's with a federal policeman, Mr. Challis.'

Federal? Given that the shotgun bandit had been operating in two states, and possibly three, perhaps the AFP was involved, but no one had informed Challis. And did he want to work with one of the more inept and morally bankrupt of Australia's police forces? He didn't have time to think more about it and said, 'Shouldn't you be at home watching daytime TV or selling your story to Channel Nine?'

She laughed. 'Roadworks outside my house, and I only watch the ABC. I'm better off at work.'

'Fair enough. Look can you do me a favour?'

'Personal loan? Second mortgage?'

'Being held hostage clearly agrees with you,' Challis said. 'Could you look up Mrs. Grace's records, please?'

Joy said automatically, 'I'm not sure that I have the authority—'

Challis was no longer inclined to be breezy. 'Joy, the woman's still missing. Many questions still need answers. I fear for her life. If she's dead, we'll need to inform her family. She might be lying injured somewhere. She might even be at home, recovering. We need to send someone to her house immediately.'

'Just a moment.'

Challis heard fingers fly over a keyboard, then a more regular *click click click.*

'Susan Grace, Peninsula Fine Arts, 35 Rigby Cutting Road, Red Hill. That's her home and her work address.'

Challis knew the area. Ellen had bought him a book of day-and-half-day walks in Victoria, and together they'd tried some of the Peninsula walks. He knew Rigby Cutting Road as an access track from Arthurs Seat Road to a small segment of the state park. There were no galleries along it, no buildings at all.

She'd named an area that was local but unlikely to be known to many of the locals, such as bank tellers. 'Did your statements ever come back marked "Return to Sender?"'

'There were no statements. She rented a box from us, that's all. Paid for five years in advance and asked that all correspondence be emailed because she often travelled overseas.'

'What ID did she show you?'

More keyboard tapping. 'Driver's licence, passport, credit card, voter registration.'

None of that meant anything. Challis said, 'Please advise Mr. Ely that I'll be there late morning with a warrant to search her safe-deposit box,' Challis said, and closed the connection.

He leaned into the gap between the front seats. 'Murph, tell me again about the encounter you had with the Grace woman.'

Pam turned her head to him slightly but held her gaze to the road. 'High Street, not far from the bank, a man raising his voice to a woman who had her back to him. I saw him grab her by the arm and spin her around, but she gave every appearance of not knowing him. That seemed to piss him off. He called her Anita. Her accent was vaguely foreign but a bit all over the place.' She paused. 'She looked different that day. Different hair, different clothing, but the same woman.'

'And the man?'

Pam snaked a hand into the inside pocket of her jacket and fished around for her notebook. 'It's all in there.'

Challis found her notes, a Friday in early September, the name 'Corso' and New South Wales numberplates. He took out his phone again and called the station with the details. 'Contact police and motor vehicles in New South Wales for anything you can get on him: addresses, phone numbers, criminal record. If he has a record, a list of known associates.'

Pam Murphy's phone was in the dashboard cradle. It rang, and she removed it, held it to her ear without looking away from the unwinding road. Challis watched and listened as she said, 'Okay,' 'Yeah,' and 'Thanks. Email the results, I'm coming back to the station now.'

She rehoused the phone. 'That was the lab. They've found something that ties Darren Muschamp to the Rice murder.'

'You want to re-interview him?'

'Yes.'

'This morning?'

'Boss, I'd love to be there when you open the box, but I need to see this through.'

Challis could see the tension in her.

A SHORT TIME LATER, he was standing inside the VineTrust Bank, saying, 'Christ Almighty, Rowan, please tell me you didn't leave him alone with the box.'

Ely shifted about awkwardly. 'It was federal police business, Hal. I had no choice.'

'Did he take anything away with him?'

'He asked to use the photocopier.'

'I hope he was wearing gloves.'

'He was.'

'And he didn't show you a warrant?'

Rowan Ely said, 'He was a very forceful individual, Hal, and I'm still a bit, you know, dazed.'

'What name did he give?'

'Towne. Inspector Towne. I don't know his first name.'

Challis rubbed his temples with the tips of his fingers. 'He showed ID?'

Ely drew himself up. 'Give me credit. Naturally I asked him to show me ID. It looked real to me. He had the manner, the language, if you know what I mean.'

'I hope to Christ he didn't remove anything that might lead us to your client.'

Ely said, 'He told me he was going to see *you*. I thought you knew all about it.'

You've only just thought it, Challis said to himself. 'I assume you have him on camera.'

Ely swallowed. 'He took the tapes, said he needed to watch the robbery and siege unfold.'

Chapter 52

When she arrived at the Frankston remand centre, Pam Murphy was obliged to cool her heels for a while, before Jeannie Schiff arrived late morning in a blaze of demands:

'What's this about pollen? An exact science is it, pollen? I hope you—'

They were interrupted by the arrival of two guards and Darren Muschamp and his lawyer, a short, soft-looking man. One of the guards unlocked the interview room door. The air inside was faintly layered in dust and forlornness, but that was all Pam noticed before Jeannie Schiff turned on both recorders and said:

'Present are Sergeant Jeannie Schiff, Sex Crimes Unit, Detective Constable Pam Murphy, Waterloo Crimes Investigation Unit, and. . . ?'

Muschamp's lawyer leaned toward the tape machine and said, 'Jason Ikin.'

Pam zoned out briefly. She wondered how many Jasons she'd met over the years. Hundreds. Thousands. They were all in their thirties and forties now, most of them balding, unheroic, and soft around the middle. Encounter a homophobe or a racist footballer, and more often than not he was a Jason. Jasons were still wearing their hair in mullets or ponytails long after those fashions had died. They were vacantly cheerful, narrow and viciously dumb. In fact—

The others were staring at her oddly. Had she uttered something aloud? Meanwhile, a cross little frown was twisting Jeannie Schiff's fine eyebrows. 'Constable? I understand you have further questions for Mr. Muschamp?'

The timing was bad. Pam suffered a brain zap just then, just for a millisecond.

'Constable!'

Pam said quickly, 'Darren, in those forensic science textbooks we found at your house, did you happen to read the sections on insect activity, airborne contaminants and so forth?'

He gave her a look that said: What are you on about?

'If you had read those sections you might have considered burning the uniform after what you did to Ms. Holst. But of course you couldn't do that, you needed the uniform, you couldn't just go to the supermarket and buy another one.'

'Oh, good,' Ikin said, settling back in his chair. 'A meandering mystery story. Take your time.'

'Pollen,' Pam said.

Schiff glanced at her irritably. Ikin said, 'What about it? Are you saying my client left pollen on someone?'

'Wouldn't have a clue. Did you, Darren?'

'Pollen?' said Muschamp.

'Microscopic pores released by certain plants at certain times of the year.'

Muschamp was warier today. Either he'd got his hands on some pharmaceuticals over in the lockup or his body responded well when his system was clean. But he stank. Pam began to breathe shallowly. 'I assume you have shower privileges in the lockup, Mr. Muschamp?'

Ikin said, 'I fail to see—'

'You're provided with soap, shampoo, toothbrush, and paste?'

The flush and the eye glint were danger signs. Muschamp half rose in his chair. 'I have a condition, okay?'

Pam said, 'One of your victims described her attacker as having the most god-awful odour.'

Ikin said, 'And that's proof my client attacked her? I hope the police can do better at trial—if matters get that far.'

Pam glanced at the clock: almost noon. Would Challis have opened the box yet? She wanted to be there. She also wanted to be here. She said, 'Getting back to the pollen.'

The lawyer was watching her carefully, his mind hunting. 'As I understand it, pollen is carried on the wind. Spring on the Peninsula is always windy. Multi-directional winds, too.'

Pam knew that. Back tracking, she said, 'Now, you washed your cousin's police uniform to rid it of DNA evidence each time you abducted and raped someone. You were very careful, but I should inform you that we found microscopic spores caught in the weave of the fabric, tying you to the nature reserve.'

'So? My cousin's a cop, she would of worn that uniform all over the joint. All kinds of stuff would of got on it.'

'But did her duties ever take her to the nature reserve where you dumped Chloe Holst? No. We checked.'

Ikin said, 'Are you saying the vegetation there is unique? I hardly think so. I bet I can find any number of university botanists prepared to say, under oath, that the reserve's trees, grasses, weeds, fungi, you name it, can be found in any uncleared land on the Peninsula that you care to nominate.'

The Jason-ness had disappeared. Inside the pudgy boy was a steelier man. Pam tried to formulate a comeback as Jeannie Schiff shot her a look that said, I hope you know where you're going with this.

Pam said, 'DNA can be extracted from plants. We can match spore DNA on your client's clothing with the DNA of an individual plant, a plant at the roadside clearing where Ms. Holst was pulled out of the car by her hair and kicked in the ribs by your client and told to keep her mouth shut.'

She ignored Jeannie Schiff's appraising look and concentrated on Muschamp. He was agitated, looking to Ikin for salvation.

Ikin complied. 'My client drives all over the Peninsula in his day job. He stopped at the reserve to relieve himself one day.'

'Good try. Wearing his stolen police uniform?'

'Yeah,' Muschamp said. 'Sometimes I wore the pants when my jeans were in the wash.'

Pam sensed Ikin smiling at her from the other side of the chipped plastic table and knew the direction his courtroom cross-examination would take. At that moment, she suffered a tiny zoning out that she found almost comforting and found herself gazing at the ceiling.

'Constable!'

Jeannie Schiff's face was forbidding, the beautiful features concentrated in a scowl.

Pam blinked and said, 'Tell me, Darren, have you ever visited 2012 Coolart Road?'

'Me? Dunno. I been all over the place.'

'Have you ever made a delivery to 2012 Coolart Road?'

'Pardon me, Constable Murphy, but what or where is 2012 Coolart Road?'

'It's a big house with a stone gateway, situated near Hunts Road.'

'And?'

'It's where we found the body of Delia Rice concealed in the boot of a car driven by your client.'

'Do you have evidence that my client was driving the car?'

'No.'

'Was it his car?'

'No.'

'Then I fail to see—'

'He was seen running from the scene.'

'A foolproof identification was made by an eyewitness, I take it? She or he will pick my client out from a line-up or photo array?'

Ikin was enjoying himself.

'Your client was wearing a distinctive T-shirt that day.'

'Distinctive in what way?'

'On the back were the immortal words, "If you can read this, the bitch has fallen off".'

She was lying, and Schiff knew it, giving her impatient side-long glances. The search team had found such a T-shirt in Muschamp's bedroom, but it had nothing to do with the case. He would have burnt every scrap of clothing he wore that day. She wanted to see him relax, that's all, before she slipped the knife in.

'You found pollen on this T-shirt, is that what you're saying?'

'Still to be tested.'

Muschamp was grinning at her, Schiff frowning.

Ikin said, 'As we have established, my client's job takes him all over the Peninsula. He might well have made a delivery to that house or one nearby, a delivery on a windy day.'

'Yeah. I remember now, I stopped for a leak near there about two months ago.'

'Urinate in public a lot, do you, Darren? For the record, the only time you were in the vicinity of that house was two months ago?'

'Yeah.'

Pam referred to her notes. 'There is an unusual combination of pollen producing plants at that address.'

Ikin said nothing. Muschamp remained cocky.

'*Echium plantagineum*, commonly known as Paterson's Curse. *Sumex acetosella*, or sorrel, and Golden Cypress and Silver Birch. All growing close to each other, and all releasing pollen at this time of the year—precisely at this time of the year,' Pam said, 'not two months ago.'

Ikin looked worried, but Muschamp grinned. 'So, I got the date wrong.'

Pam said, 'Unfortunately we didn't find that combination of pollen on any of your clothing, Darren.'

'In other words, you got nothing.'

'But we did find it on *other* items, and each one links uniquely to you.'

He paled. 'Like what?'

'You like to clean the wax out of your ears with a cotton bud, right, Darren?'

He knew. He looked sick. Ikin glanced at the ceiling. Schiff was shooting her looks that said, Did you search his place again without telling me?

'The lab tested cotton buds and tissues found at your flat, Darren, and found not only traces of pollen from the four plants I just mentioned—pollen spores in a unique combination, and linked by DNA to trees growing at 2012 Coolart Road—but also *your* DNA, and yours alone. Not some friend who dropped by to visit you, in other words. How do you account for that?'

Pam wasn't expecting a confession, but got one. It came suddenly, Muschamp's eyes filling with tears, his mouth releasing a howl of frustration: 'All the stupid bitch had to do was shut up.' He looked at the women opposite him and the lawyer beside him. 'She just went on and on. . . .'

Chapter 53

Denise Rodda was tired.

The crime scene officer had printed the whole bank with her colleagues from the forensic unit, and now the local CIU inspector wanted her to print the contents of a safe-deposit box.

She'd already printed the exterior, emailed the prints to the Fingerprint Branch in Seaford to be compared to those of the bank's staff, wasn't that enough? 'Sir,' she pointed out, 'I've been here half the night already.'

'Won't take long,' he said.

And then the man smiled, a transformative smile, the air of fatigue and prohibition vanishing from his face. A thin face, she noticed, a little too sharp-edged for her taste, but warm and quite attractive when he smiled. Overworked and underpaid, she thought. Like the rest of us.

Except the rest of us don't have the guts to complain to the media about being overworked and underpaid.

So she returned his smile, said, 'Just as well I adore my job,' and watched as the manager opened the box.

Challis watched, too. It was a sizeable box, deep, broad, long. 'Heavy,' Rowan Ely had said, as he'd slid it out of the wall. Utilitarian grey metal. Challis glanced at the battery of similar boxes and wondered what secrets and wealth they contained.

'Voilà!' Ely said.

Challis stepped forward and peered in. Immediately under the lid was a flat object wrapped in white tissue paper. With one gloved hand, he folded back the paper to reveal a small painting. Splashes of vivid colour, random shapes. On closer examination the shapes resolved into rocks, and he recognised the signature.

'Paul Klee.'

Ely said dubiously, 'Who?'

'European artist of the first half of past century. If this is an original it's very valuable.'

Challis lifted out the painting and turned to Rodda. 'I need you to print this, please.'

He returned to the box. The next item was a small aquatint signed 'Sydney Long' with a Hobart gallery label on the back. He made a mental note to contact the gallery and see who had bought it.

Under the Long were many smaller items: gold coins, individually wrapped in a small drawstring chamois bag; a matchbox containing a 1930 penny wrapped in tissue paper, another an old gold coin dated 1620; a small gold ingot; rare stamps and banknotes in individual plastic sleeves; a paperback history of the Kelly gang; and three sets of ID: passports, licences, credit cards, Medicare cards. Lying on the bottom were an old photograph, a tiny digital camera, and a memory card encased in clear plastic.

Challis placed each item on the table, Rodda testing them one by one, and examined the sets of ID. The same face appeared in each, the woman known to Rowan Ely and his staff as Mrs. Grace. Are you still alive? he wondered. Her face was young but her gaze old, as if she'd seen and felt a lot in her short life.

'Quite a collection of keepsakes,' Ely said.

Challis nodded absently. He didn't think he was looking at keepsakes but at stolen goods. He peered at the photograph. It was small, washed out, reminding him of the family snaps he'd seen as a child, long-dead aunts and grandparents caught awkwardly by Kodak box cameras. A room in a cottage, a white-washed wall, a man and a woman in the bulky, stiffly formal clothing of an earlier era. Stolid-looking people, barely smiling. A respectable peasant couple, maybe. Slavic appearance. He was pretty sure the setting wasn't Australia.

Then he peered more closely, straightened his back. An icon. Valuable? Also stolen? But the photo seemed to be a family keep-sake. Would it help him find the woman known as Mrs. Grace?

Rodda's phone rang. She turned away from the table, phone to one ear, hand to the other, as though the little room was full of discordant sounds. 'Yep. Uh-huh. Thanks. Did you get the batch I just sent? Yeah, chop chop. Bye.'

She finished the call and said, 'The prints on the outside of the box belong to bank staff only.'

The federal cop had worn gloves. 'And this stuff?' Challis asked, gesturing at the items arranged across the surface of the table.

'So far all I've been able to lift are two partials, one on the memory card case, the other on the battery of the camera. I've asked the lab to put a rush on them, but there could be more partials that aren't so evident. You want a thorough job, I'll need to take everything to the lab.'

Challis nodded. 'Do what you can for now,' he said, knowing that even if they found Mrs. Grace's prints, it meant nothing if they weren't on record.

Ely pointed at the memory card. 'We should plug it in and see what she's been photographing.'

'Soon enough,' Challis said.

Some time later, Rodda's phone rang again and she took the

call. And then she was casting him a complicated look, handing him the phone.

'Challis.'

'Sir,' a voice said, 'those two partials: they're both in the system, both flagged.'

Chapter 54

Almost noon now.

As Mara Niekirk fed another set of forged provenance papers and fake catalogues through the shredder, a shape passed the window: Tayla, chasing Natalia around the bonfire, bouncy and smiling in a way that inflamed her. The unwarranted happiness, the baby talk, the bovine simplicity, and the perfect teeth, hair, nose, breasts, and legs. Mara despised the nanny and often let it show; why not? Tayla was too dumb to recognise the sarcasm.

Stupid cow.

Mara contemplated a perfect world, one in which she had no husband—or the one she had was the brains of the outfit, a man like her father or her grandfather. Or, she had an attractive lover, one who made her feel desired. One who found *her* arousing, not some spy-cam image.

What is it with voyeurs? Mara wondered. What happens when they encounter actual flesh and blood? Does it all just vanish? Mara was exhausted from picking up after her husband's screw-ups.

'Get a move on.'

'Stop rushing me,' he said.

He was flipping through paperwork going back years. Did she trust him to find everything that needed the shredder or the match? 'Here, swap places.'

And she was right not to trust him. Within a minute of taking over from him she'd found an unmounted Charles Blackman drawing that was in fact a fake, together with the 'receipt' that proved they'd bought it from an Adelaide gallery.

She glanced across at the portable TV she'd mounted on the desk. The noon news update, the face of their burglar flashing across the screen again. *Have you seen. . .? Police are concerned for the welfare of. . .* And according to the *Herald Sun*, the bitch had rented a safe-deposit box at the bank. That's what had tipped the balance for Mara. She was betting the Klee, with her prints all over it, was in that box. If she's found alive, Mara thought, she'll want to bargain her way out of trouble. 'I can give you a crooked art dealer.' And, alive or dead, if she's rented a safe-deposit box, the police will want to search it.

Mara grunted. The house in Vanuatu was looking pretty good right now. She glanced across at her husband, intending to suggest they get an earlier flight, but the idiot was watching Tayla through the window. Showing more flesh than clothing, as usual. Mara was incandescent. 'Keep your filthy mind on the job.'

'I am.'

She stewed. It made sense for the nanny to accompany them to Port Vila, but, good God almighty, could she stand it?

'I've a good mind to sack the bitch.'

Warren drew himself up and said, with great dignity, that a young child shouldn't be uprooted and plonked down somewhere new without some consistency—in this case, Tayla.

'What crap,' Mara said and scowled out at the nanny, still dancing with their daughter. She shook her head. Did the little cow even know what was fuelling the bonfire? 'Genuine' Nolans and Boyds and Chippendales, that's what.

Meanwhile the shredder was shaking itself apart. Jammed probably, not that Warren had noticed. Mara closed her eyes briefly, drawing strength. The first thing to do in Vanuatu was disappear Warren and the nanny, preferably at sea, and then hire some native woman to raise the child.

And later start again somewhere new. Thailand? Bali? No, Europe. A chance to get out of this primitive corner of the globe.

'Warren? The shredder?'

He jerked. 'Right, sorry.'

The wind changed direction. Smoke licked at the open window and drifted into the room. Her husband, too dumb to find his way out of a paper bag, failed to notice. 'Shut the window,' Mara said, barely able to squeeze the words out.

A voice behind her said, 'Excuse me, Mrs. Niekirk.'

'What now?' shrieked Mara.

Tayla and Natalia had somehow disappeared from the garden and materialised at the door to the study. With a cute little squirm, a cute ash smudge on her cheek, the nanny said, 'Talia got smoke in her eyes, didn't you, gorgeous? She wants her mummy.'

Natalia flung up her arms. Mara backed away. 'Can't you see we're in the middle of something?'

'Sorry, Mrs. Niekirk.'

'And her name is Natalia, not Talia, not Nat, not—'

'Mummeee. . . .'

Mara turned a raptorial glint on to her daughter. 'I have told you, darling, many, many times, that I cannot abide being called "mummy."'

'*Mama.*'

'Well?'

The child lost courage, and Tayla stepped in with her air of practicality and capability. 'A quick cuddle should do the trick, Mrs. Niekirk, and we'll be out of your hair.'

Mara eyed the nanny. 'What's that you're wearing? I can practically see that stupid butterfly tattoo.'

A tattoo that Warren adored, the way it flexed inside the young woman's groin, centimetres from her pubic hair, every time he replayed the footage of her undressing.

Tayla went very still. 'I'm sorry, what did you say?'

Whoops, thought Mara, not really caring.

Chapter 55

An early afternoon briefing, Challis too wired to sit, or prop up a wall. He paced the room, waiting for the other detectives to assemble. Scobie Sutton had wheeled in the AV unit. Pam Murphy was already seated. She looked lit with achievement and energy, no longer curiously lost and perplexed, and he raised an eyebrow at her inquiringly.

'Result?'

'He confessed.'

'Fantastic. Terrific job.'

'When he heard about the pollen evidence, he just gave it up.'

Challis smiled at her. 'You trusted your instincts. They're good instincts.'

She stretched like a cat under his gaze. Meanwhile Sutton had slipped a DVD into the machine and pressed the play button. The main stretch of High Street appeared on the screen.

Challis took over, pointing a remote at the AV unit.

'This,' he said, 'is footage from the closed circuit TV system operated by Nerds-R-Us.'

An electronics store two doors south of the bank, one of its gimmicks was a hidden camera monitoring everyone who passed by the main window. Challis pressed the pause button, catching a pedestrian in mid-stride. Slight build, close-cropped hair, narrow features, well dressed—almost dapper.

'That man,' Challis said, 'entered the VineTrust bank this morning waving a warrant to search the safe-deposit box of the woman we know as Mrs. Grace. He showed AFP identification in the name of Andrew Towne and was granted access to the box. Neither the warrant nor the ID was challenged by the VineTrust manager.'

'Who is he?' Pam asked.

'We don't know, but he left a partial print on a memory card for a digital camera.'

'Not wearing gloves?'

'He was, but I think he removed them because they hampered his movements. The card was in a tiny plastic case, which he'd have found difficult to open. He wiped the case but not the card.'

'The partial matches someone in the system?'

Challis nodded. 'Red flagged, so I doubt his real name is Towne, and I doubt he's a federal policeman.'

He pressed another button, and the famous photograph of Mrs. Grace filled the screen, her features clear despite the arm around her throat, the gun to her head.

'This is the woman known to the bank staff as Mrs. Grace. We believe she's a professional thief. We found three sets of ID in her safe-deposit box and valuable coins, stamps, and paintings. We need to track down who owns these items and who this woman is. It's probable that she operates Australia-wide, so Scobie, I want you to confer with the various squads around the country, looking at high-end burglaries, especially where a woman was thought to be involved.'

'Boss.'

'And compile a list of anyone known to fence stolen artwork.'

'Boss.'

'Meanwhile, does the second flagged print belong to Mrs.

Grace? We don't know, so Pam, I want you to spend the afternoon following up both sets of prints. Who do they belong to? Why are they flagged? Are they connected? How do they connect to this Corso character?' He paused. 'The guy walking past the electronics window: not Corso, by any chance?'

Pam gave him a deadpan look. 'What we trained detectives call a long shot, boss.'

'My specialty,' Challis said.

He inserted a CD into the machine. The screen flickered, then a washed-out image appeared, two vases on a little table. Other images unfurled slowly as Challis set the machine to slide-show. 'Scobie, these photos were stored on the memory card in the safe-deposit box. I imagine they're a record of the houses that this woman has robbed and may help you track down the owners of the various items in the box.'

'Boss.'

'Meanwhile we don't know where our mystery fed is. Did he take anything from the box? Does he know where the woman is? How did he know to come here?'

Pam sprawled in her chair and said, 'Saw her on TV?'

'Could be. Anyhow, I want you to find out who he is.'

She nodded gloomily. 'What's the betting I get stonewalled?'

'Do your best. I'll be out of the station for most of the afternoon, showing the icon and the paintings around the Monash Fine Arts department.'

'Some people get the good jobs,' Murphy said.

'Some people,' said Challis airily, 'are bosses, others are drones.'

Chapter 56

G race had to run now.

But first she had to go home. Retrieve the icon, then run. Home.

She caught herself. The word aroused complicated feelings of achievement and loss, impermanence and security. She'd attached it to too many houses over the years. An orphanage and several foster homes, every one of them run by strangers; some cruel, none warm. They'd been where she lived, and so she'd used the word home.

But the Breamlea home she'd bought fair and square—admittedly from the proceeds of crime, but she alone had selected it. She alone had decorated, managed, and lived in it.

Yet the moment she drove her Golf onto the ferry at Sorrento, that Tuesday afternoon, she knew that the Breamlea house was just that, a house, a shell, like all the others back along the short, tumultuous years of her life. All she'd have when she left Breamlea, ninety minutes from now, would be the Golf, a pocketful of cash, and the icon. Not the lovely little Klee painting. Not her fake ID, her coins, her stamps, her photos of the houses she'd intended to burgle again.

She queued to buy coffee on board, and there was her face,

front page of the *Age* and the *Herald-Sun*, heaped beside the cash register. Grace went cold, and her skin prickled.

The man behind the counter saw the direction of her gaze and performed a kind of flirting, comical double-take. 'Gorgeous, if I didn't know different, I'd say that was you.'

Managing a light laugh, Grace said doubtfully, 'You think I look like her?'

Together they examined the photograph of the woman held hostage by a man with a shotgun. 'Yeah, a bit.'

'I guess so,' Grace said, knowing better than to deny it vehemently. She could feel the gunman's meaty forearm at her throat, almost smell him. And her jaw ached, bruised by the twin barrels. 'Poor woman,' she said. 'Must have been scary.'

'I'll say,' the man said. He shook his head. 'And it's not going to end good, is it?'

'No.'

'No.'

Grace bought coffee and a copy of the *Age* and, trembling a little, took them to a table under a starboard window. She felt scrutinised, trapped, no way out of this steel box until it reached its destination. Galt would see the photograph. He would come.

In fact, she thought bitterly, I've been living in a fool's paradise for two years; I've been living on borrowed time.

Think how easily he'd found her that first day.

Grace forced herself to sip her coffee and read her newspaper. She lingered over a sidebar story on the front page, about the senior cop at the siege. His name was Challis. Apparently highly regarded, currently in hot water for speaking out publicly against a lack of police resources, incurring the wrath of force command and the police minister. He looked hunted to Grace, a man casting repressive, vigilant looks at the probing cameras on High Street last night.

On page two was a grainy snap of the escape to the car head-lined GUNMAN OUTWITS POLICE.

No, *I* did, thought Grace. The blanket idea was mine.

She turned the pages.

Steve Finch was at the bottom of page three. Gunned down outside his home; known to police; no apparent motive.

Grace stared out at the choppy waters of the bay. The Niekirks? Looked like. Thieves *and* murderers.

She climbed the stairs to the upper deck and stood where she'd not be heard over the booming of the exhausts. Taking her iPhone from her bum bag, she looked up the phone number for CIU in Waterloo.

'Inspector Challis's phone, Constable Sutton speaking.'

'I'd like to speak to the inspector, please.'

'I'm sorry, he's out. Can I take a message?'

'Could I have his mobile number?'

A pause. Sutton said, 'I'm afraid not. What's this about?'

'I have information that will interest him.'

'About what?'

'What happened at the bank.'

'You can tell me.'

'Could I have his email address? I want to send him some photos.'

'I'm sorry, I'm not prepared to do that. Why don't you—'

She cut the connection and sat for a while. What she wanted to do was tell the sad-faced policeman named Challis about the gunman, the contents of her safe-deposit box, the connection between Steve Finch and the Niekirks. She wanted to email him her photos of the Klee and the icon *in situ*, the closeups of the Niekirks' dodgy invoices, deeds, and provenance papers. . . .

It could wait. Right now they were calling drivers to their cars. She headed down to the Golf and waited for the ferry to dock and unload.

Finally to Breamlea. Slowing at the outskirts, she crawled along the little main street, eyeing the houses in a mental good-bye. The place probably wouldn't have remained a haven anyway. Lifestyle writers had discovered it, and that always brought doom.

She stepped inside her front door and into the sitting room, and Ian Galt said, 'Hello, Neet.'

Chapter 57

Pam Murphy had been eating lunch at her desk when Scobie Sutton took the call meant for Challis.

A miserable-looking salad from the canteen. A canteen meal because she couldn't afford to lunch at Café Laconic very often, and the High Street deli was now a Youth Initiative drop-in centre, serving cheap food prepared and sold by kids she'd arrested, questioned, or reprimanded.

Scobie had been eating at his desk, too, a sandwich from a plastic lunchbox. That's all he ever ate, sandwiches lovingly prepared by his wife—except for that period when the wife had a meltdown. The sandwiches resembled the wife—small, neat, bland—and Scobie pecked and nibbled neatly, blandly, patting his rubbery lips with a paper serviette after every bite.

As for Challis: Who knew what Challis was eating, or where? She glanced at her watch: 1 P.M. He was meeting the Monash academic at 2 P.M., so maybe he would snatch a meal at a uni caf. Why was she thinking about any of this? Going off the antidepressants had brought her some uncomfortable symptoms but also a crazy kind of clarity about random things, irrelevant to life and police work.

She watched Scobie as he took the call in Challis's office,

listened to his stiff proprieties, watched him return to his desk.

'What was that about?'

'Crank call.'

'What kind?'

'A female wanting to speak to the inspector. I said he was out. She said could I give her his mobile number? No. Could I give her his email address, she wanted to send him some photos? No.'

'What kind of photos?'

Scobie shrugged, his skinny arms emerging from the sleeves of his white shirt. 'She said it had to do with the siege at the bank.'

'Scobie!'

'A crank call, Pam.'

'How can you be sure? What if it's the woman we're looking for?'

'Face it, she's dead. The woman on the phone just wanted some attention, you know how it is.'

'If she calls again, give her the email address. We know she takes photos, and these could be important.'

'Suit yourself,' Scobie Sutton said, and he ate his sandwich and continued to search the database for high-end burglaries.

Then Pam's phone rang, an AFP inspector returning her call—through the switchboard, checking that she was who she'd claimed to be. He had some news.

'We don't have an Inspector Towne working for us.'

'How about the man in the CCTV footage? Do you recognise him?'

'No.'

'Maybe our witness misheard the name and the rank. The man we're keen to speak to claims to be attached to a task force, something to do with investigating an international operation.'

There was the kind of silence that says, Did you not hear what I just said?

'Okay,' Pam said finally, 'so it seems we have a man running around impersonating a federal police officer.'

'Then you'd better catch him,' the AFP man said.

She'd also sent information on Corso, Mrs. Grace, and Towne to the New South Wales police, with a request for identities behind the two flagged fingerprints. Until someone responded, she could do little but go to the tearoom and prime Challis's espresso machine. Short black, double shot.

Thirty minutes later, the phone rang. It was a sergeant in the New South Wales major crimes unit. 'What's your interest in Bob Corso?'

She told him about the incident on High Street.

'Is he still in your neck of the woods?' the sergeant asked.

'Don't think so,' Pam said. 'He was on a road trip with his family when I saw him.'

The sergeant grunted. 'That accords with our intel. He went off the radar a few weeks ago. Basically, the guy's a standover merchant, bodyguard, and bouncer at a few strip clubs in the Cross, loving husband and father the rest of the time.'

'He called the woman he accosted "Anita." Do you know her?'

'I'm looking at a picture of her even as we speak,' the sergeant said, 'front page of the *Australian*.'

'So you know who she is.'

'Anita Sandow—or that was the name she was using, there's no independent record of anyone, anywhere, with that name—and to answer your next question, one of the partials you found belongs to her.'

'But why was she red-flagged?'

'A long story. The short version is she was offered witness protection by the New South Wales police.' He paused. 'Then she disappeared.'

'Went feral, you mean. She's been breaking into houses all over the country, as far as we know.'

'Yeah, well, we thought she was dead, but it seems she was up to her old tricks.'

'I'm sorry, sir, but you're not giving me much information here.'

'I'm wondering how much to tell you. Who's your boss?'

'Inspector Challis,' said Pam distinctly, 'and he's busy, and he asked me to track down who left those prints in the bank.'

A long pause. So Pam said, 'Did you get a chance to look at the video clip?'

'I did,' the sergeant said, his voice freighted with meaning.

'And?'

Another long pause. It was almost 2 P.M., and Murphy felt wired from the coffee and from an investigation that now seemed to be teasing at the edges of something nasty and dark.

'Sergeant?' she prompted. 'I take it he left the other finger-print, and his name isn't Towne?'

The major crimes officer made up his mind. 'His name is Ian Galt. Ex-New South Wales police sergeant, arrested and charged with corruption late last year.'

'Let me guess: the charges didn't stick.'

'I'm embarrassed to say.'

'What did he do?'

'Let's start with what he's doing now.'

'Okay.'

'I think he's probably on a mission to kill Sandow. She was a registered informant, and Galt was her handler and sometime boyfriend.'

'She informed on him,' Pam guessed. 'You turned her, you promised her witness protection—she got spooked before it went to trial.'

The sergeant didn't contradict her. 'It all started when Galt arrested her. She was a cat burglar, very good at it, too. Worked alone, but on the fringes of a few organised networks, so she was useful. Had access to information he could use—money laundering, movement of stolen goods, break-ins, stuff like that.'

'She was never charged?'

'Correct. And after that, he owned her. He'd supply the intel—security patrol routines, where the cameras were, the roadblocks—and she'd go on a spree, break into four or five North Shore houses in one night. He'd give her a cut.'

'Galt was already dirty?'

The sergeant's voice took on a tone of disgust. 'Galt and his mates had their own thing going long before Anita appeared on the scene. Kickbacks from dealers and brothel owners. You name it. They'd lose evidence, stand up in court and give character references to scumbags. And they had an arrangement with bent officers in Victoria and Queensland. One of your guys—cop in a suburban station or one of the squads, like the armed robbers—would send through word about a payroll, say, and Galt and his mates would make a fast trip over the border, grab the payroll, head home again. The bent locals'd run interference for them. Meanwhile it didn't occur to the *good* guys to look for an interstate crew.'

'What happened? Galt got careless? Greedy?'

'They all did. And once we got onto the phone-taps, bank accounts checks, whatever. . . . The upshot was, Galt and the others were arrested, and the girlfriend was offered a deal: Go to jail, or give evidence against them and go into witness protection. Apparently Galt used her as a punching bag sometimes.'

'But he spooked her, so she ran.'

'Took the money, too, what we heard. Meanwhile he got himself a good lawyer, and it turned out our case was a bit leaky. . . .'

'Now he wants revenge.'

'Wants it *badly*,' the NSW officer said.

Pam thanked him and was hanging up when a probationer appeared at the entrance to the open-plan CIU office. 'Excuse me, there's a woman downstairs, got a little girl with her, and she needs to speak to someone in CIU.'

'What about?'

'People called Newkirk? Some name like that.'

Pam glanced at her watch. Two fifteen P.M., and she needed to contact the New South Wales ethical standards department for more on the man named Galt. But a call like that took patience, tact, and determination; she'd do it later when she had a free half hour. She followed the probationer downstairs and stuck her head around the door of the victim suite.

Tayla, the nanny, was holding Natalia on her knee. 'They lied to you.' She said. 'Stuff *was* stolen.'

Chapter 58

At that moment, Galt was trying a let's-talk-this-over approach. 'Actually, I don't think I ever knew your real identity, Neet. According to the title deeds for this place—and that was foolish, by the way, storing them in your bank—you're going by the name Susan Grace, but—'

Grace dived through the sitting room window.

She hadn't tested this as a means of escape, but she had planned it and spent money on it, knowing that someone like Galt would come for her one day. Hence, shatter-proof glass on all the windows, secured by beading designed to pop out of the frame when pressure was exerted.

Like now. 'Jesus, Neet,' Galt said, as Grace's body described a tidy parabola through to the lawn on the other side. In the three or four seconds it took for him to cross the room and fire her own Glock at her through the empty window frame, she was feinting left and right into a thicket of garden trees and bushes.

From there she scuttled around to the back wall where the land sloped down, leaving a gap under the house. A useful space, somewhere to store timber offcuts, a chewed-up surf board, her extension ladder. And her backup gun, which was a Beretta. Grace located the concrete stump that supported the laundry floor, slid her hand in, felt around for the shallow wooden box she'd nailed there, retrieved the little pistol.

She worked a shell into the firing chamber then extended her arm, sighting along it: the left-hand corner of the house, then the right, then the garden trees, and finally the back door, trying to anticipate what Galt would do.

He was here to kill her, of course—but he could have done that without chewing her ear off, so he was also here for his money.

Except it wasn't his. He and his mates had put her to work, but she had succeeded beyond their expectations. By rights, the money was hers. Not that any of it was left. She'd spent the lot: this house, her car, the guns, the fake IDs, the clothes, the travel. . . .

The online poker.

Grace exploded away from the wall, ducking and weaving to the neighbour's fence, clearing it at a run as the next bullet buried itself in the soft pine beside her, missing her thigh by a whisper. A Tuesday afternoon in spring, nobody around, a wind rising from the sea beyond the dunes.

Grace ran along the far side of the neighbour's house, an old-style dwelling on stilts, and darted across the street. A sizzling sensation, a tiny shock wave, as a bullet singed the air beside her ear. Grace whimpered, ducked, sidestepped down into a ditch.

Was Galt shooting to wing her? He'd won pistol-shooting awards. She'd seen the trophies in his Bondi flat, seen the loving way he handled his guns, and almost been jealous.

Grace doubled back along the drainage channel, toward the caravan park, which was screened from the road by scraggly trees.

She stopped for a while, listening, wondering what Galt would do. He was generally quite direct. She'd asked him once what he wanted, and he'd said, 'Simple. I want money, I want you.'

Grace swiped at the perspiration beading her face. Then she jumped, hearing his voice nearby, calling, 'Anita! I just want to talk!'

She didn't move. Scarcely let herself breathe.

'No hard feelings, Neet!'

Sure.

Grace climbed out of the channel and crouched in dense shrubbery to glance both ways along the road. She jerked back: Galt stood on the far side, scanning the undergrowth as if aware she'd come out sooner or later, a half-amused expression on his lean face.

How had he known she was here in Victoria? Mates all over the country, she supposed. Keeping their eyes and ears open. He probably knew her MO by now, knew about the Hobart job, the Clare job, all the others.

She saw him tip back his head again. 'You probably think I want to pop you, don't you, Neet? Look, I just want to talk, okay?'

Grace slithered back into the ditch, his amused face in her head. 'Pop you.' They had their own language, Galt and his gang. 'Chow practice' was an all-day, all-night drinking session, 'paying for shoe leather' was petty pilfering, to recoup what they'd spent on petrol and phone calls.

They'd been untouched for so long that they thought they could get away with everything but, in the meantime, had got greedy and careless. All that money coming in, but for Galt it was never enough. Then the market crashed, and he got serious; 'I need you, Neet,' he'd say, drunk after a big session. And then, his lean mouth twisting, 'If I can't be with you, no one can.'

And he'd say: 'Who are you, Anita?'

The road into Breamlea was deserted, and Grace, prone on the grass in a thicket of stunted trees, sprang up and darted across. Another sharp noise as the bullet scorched across her shoulder blade. The pain came moments later, then the blood, trickling down to her waistband.

She scuttled back.

'Anita!' he yelled.

He didn't seem to care who saw or heard him. The shadows were closing in, a time for men and women to return from their office jobs in Geelong and Queenscliff. Time to drive up, park, empty the letterbox, walk the dog, drag out the garbage bin for tomorrow morning's collection. See a stranger with a gun walking down the crown of the road like a character in a Western.

Well, he had a gun and a badge; who would challenge him? And the real law was thirty minutes away. Grace knew he wouldn't give up. He'd kill her. She'd turned on him, transgressed some precious, insane code.

Grace retreated farther. Here, between the road and a creek, the soil was marshy. Shallow pools dotted miserably with stunted plants and miasmic with mosquitoes. She was in the open, and if Galt came parting the branches, he'd spot her immediately.

So Grace sloshed back the way she'd come, welcoming the shadows but wishing she had a pond to hide in. A treacherous marsh, that's all she had here. She scrambled up to the tree line again, thinking she could be living in happy, witness-protected anonymity instead of fleeing a madman in the mud.

No. Who was she kidding? Galt would have found her somehow; he'd have found a way to get hold of her file. It had made sense to run—run with all of the Galt money and valuables she could scrape together—and create her own new identity.

She would never have tolerated witness protection anyway, even if they could have guaranteed her safety. She needed this; she *needed* to steal. To climb, bend, flex, balance, and coordinate; to visualise spaces, the arrangement of objects, traps, and escape routes. She couldn't have given any of that up.

And now she'd made a stupid mistake and allowed Galt to find her.

As Grace darted across the road again, heading for the houses huddled where the dunes shielded them from the swamping sea, a man shouted at Galt, 'I'm armed, and I've called the police.'

Grace hugged the grass, her shoulder blade on fire, her clothing wet with blood.

'Fuck you,' Galt said, barely interested, his gaze on Grace and a flat smile showing.

He was standing in the middle of the road again, taking aim, and didn't care at all about citizens who cried out in fearful, wavering voices that they were armed, citizens who were badly frightened but trying to be brave, who simply wanted the bad guy to go away and not come back. Didn't care at all, and Grace huddled to make herself smaller on the ground.

'I mean it,' the voice wobbled. 'I have a shotgun.'

When the shot didn't come, Grace lifted her head. Galt had turned away from her. He'd been challenged, and it irritated him. He stood and faced the man who'd made the challenge and said, 'Really, really mean it?'

'Leave us in peace,' the man said, and Grace recognised him, Kim . . . Tim? An engineering lecturer who lived most of the week in Melbourne but had evidently decided to stay on for a few days. A duck shooter, she recalled, seeing him kitted out for a trip to the wetlands one day.

She stood. 'Get back,' she urged him, 'go inside. He'll hurt you.'

'Damn right,' Galt said, grinning at the lecturer, grinning at her.

Grace didn't know how to fire a gun; she'd never tried it. But there was a sudden calmness, a needle-like appreciation of sound, light, colour, and texture as she lifted and aimed her little pistol.

She fired as Tim fired.

Chapter 59

Romona Ludowyk told Challis that she was a jack of all trades. 'Curator of the University's permanent collection, but also chief conservator if any item we own or buy is damaged in any way. And sometimes,' she said, 'I even lecture.'

She smiled. They were on an upper floor of the Arts Faculty building at Monash University's Clayton campus. The unlovely outer suburbs complemented the unlovely university buildings and stretched as far as Challis could see, through the window behind Ludowyk. The sun beat against the glass, and the room was stuffy. The wind howled around the building, too, shaking it minutely.

'You get used to it,' the academic said with a smile, seeing his body register the movement.

She was short, slight as a bird, her greying dark hair in a roll at the back of her head. Half-lenses perched on the end of her nose, and she glanced down through them now, at the Paul Klee and the little Sydney Long aquatint resting side by side on a long bench.

She tugged at a powerful light on a counter-balanced arm, positioning it above the art works. The air around her was scented with oils and cleaning agents, and the available surfaces were littered with cloths, brushes, bottled chemicals. Challis had also noted plenty of books, a couple of grubby computers, a colour laser printer, lab coats on wall hooks, packets of latex gloves, a large contraption that he supposed might be a dehumidifier.

Ludowyk screwed a jeweller's lens into her eye socket, leaned over, and began to examine the Klee and the Long more closely, angling them to the light, peering at the frames and backing. She straightened, removing the lens. 'We'd need to run chemical tests to be sure, but I'm confident that both are genuine.'

A knock on the door and a young man entered, as ravaged as a crack addict, dressed in torn jeans and a T-shirt. He said immediately, 'Any chance of an extension on the essay, Romona?'

She waved her hand at him. 'Friday at the latest.'

'You're a doll,' he said and disappeared.

Ludowyk eyed Challis with amusement. 'The dope-head look is an affectation. I doubt he takes anything stronger than aspirin. Clever, too.'

'You like teaching?'

Another smile. 'Frankly, I'd rather work with the art than those who profess to study it.'

Challis wondered where he stood. He'd rather work with the evidence than the people who left it? 'I'm glad you're not teaching this afternoon.'

She snorted. 'Not that universities teach any more. Revenue farming mostly.'

Challis nodded. 'I can see a day when the police force is less about solving crimes than running workshops.'

Ludowyk bent her head over the Klee again and murmured, 'This was stolen.'

'You can tell by looking?'

She straightened her back. 'See here in the corner, flecks of . . . at a guess, watercolour paint.'

'Meaning?'

'I'll check the stolen art register in a moment, but my guess is this was stolen from a regional gallery somewhere in Europe. Little or no security. The thief snatched it off the wall and walked out with it and smuggled it out of the country by posing as a tourist on a painting holiday. He or she painted an inept watercolour over the Klee and concealed it among an armful of other inept watercolours.'

'It's not Nazi loot?'

'I doubt it. A bit too modern for Nazi tastes. Anyway they went in for wholesale removal from galleries and private homes, looting by the truckload. They didn't need to conceal individual items with a layer of watercolour paint. But let's check.'

She went to one of the computers and logged on to a site that asked for a password. Challis watched briefly as she flashed through the links, then he idled around the room for a while, flipping through the pages of the art histories on the shelves. Five minutes later, Ludowyk pushed her chair away from the computer and said, 'Eureka.'

Challis read the account. The little painting had disappeared from a regional gallery in Switzerland in 1995. 'Pity it doesn't say who stole it and brought it to Australia.'

'That's assuming it's the same person,' Ludowyk said. She opened her arms as if to encompass all possibilities. 'The thief might never have been to Australia. The painting might have passed through many hands. Was it stolen with the Sydney Long?'

'We don't know,' Challis said. 'They were stored with coins and stamps, but—'

Ludowyk smiled. 'But if your thief stole from a thief, then you'll hit a brick wall.'

Challis felt weary to be reminded of it. 'True.'

'We know the Klee is stolen, but there's no indication online that the Long is. Someone might have bought both items in good faith, or the Klee knowing it was stolen and the other knowing it was legit. . . . There are many variables.'

'Great.'

'If you do find someone who admits to being the legitimate owner, check if they also own drawings and paintings by local artists such as Whiteley, Dickerson, Nolan, and Blackman. Artists with a big, undocumented output. Fakes are turning up all the time. Some are recognised in time and quietly destroyed; others disappear after the alarm is raised, only to be offered for sale again years and years later.' She paused. 'Indigenous art, too. As much as twenty percent of it is fake.'

Challis closed his eyes. 'I'm just a humble regional plodder.'

'I'll bet.'

Challis decided that he liked Ludowyk; he liked the practical, chemical smell of her room. It must be a good job, he thought, to work with your hands, recreating, solving puzzles. 'Let's say someone acquired the Klee knowing it was stolen. . . . What's your reading of that person? What makes him or her tick?'

Ludowyk cocked her head at him. 'I'm not a profiler.'

'Yeah, but—'

'Okay. We might be looking at a collector who couldn't afford to pay the market price. Or an art lover who liked to gloat over the painting in private. Or a crook who intended to wait a few years then put it up for auction with false provenance papers.'

'But it was stolen in 1995.'

Another who-knows gesture. 'Inspector, you don't know where it's been all these years. It might have financed several drug deals in the meantime or been used as collateral for loans. Anything.'

Challis heaved his shoulders and said, 'I'd like you to look at this photograph.'

He tapped the icon on the wall between the old couple. 'Is that valuable?'

'Nowhere near the value of the Klee. A family keepsake?'

'Could be.'

'It looks old, certainly. But icons were not produced to make an individual artistic statement in the way that the Klee probably was. There was no ego involved. A master artist and a handful of apprentices in some little Russian village would have made dozens of these to the glory of God.'

Challis stared gloomily at the man and the woman. Were they long-lost relatives of the woman who called herself Mrs. Grace?

'The place and date are significant,' Ludowyk said, reading the back of the photograph. 'After the 1917 revolution, thousands of White Russians fled to Harbin, joining an already established population. Then in the late 1940s and early 1950s, many of them were allowed to settle in Australia. Very traditional and patriotic, some of them. The church, Mother Russia. This icon mattered to someone.'

Challis knew all that. He'd typed 'Harbin' into Google before making the drive up to Monash.

'I have an officer checking burglaries here and interstate.'

'A big job.'

'Oh, yes.'

'Want me to contact the gallery in Switzerland? I imagine they'll want their Klee returned.'

'Thank you—but tell them it could take a while.'

CHALLIS WAS BACK AT CIU by 4:30 P.M. that Tuesday. Murphy wasn't there. Scobie Sutton was.

He unfolded his gangly legs as Challis walked in, got to his feet, and said, 'Sir, a ton of phone calls have come in, plus I have some odd bits and pieces to tell you.'

'Okay.'

'First, that list of fences you asked for, those specialising in coins and stamps and art.'

A pause; Sutton simply stopped talking. He often did this, waiting for encouragement to continue.

'And?'

'One of them was shot dead outside his house last night.' Sutton glanced at the sheet of paper in his hands. 'Steve Finch, second-hand dealer in Williamstown. His shop was torched fifteen minutes later.'

Challis stored the information. There wasn't much else he could do with it yet. 'What else?'

'Pam had a few calls in to the AFP and the New South Wales police.' Another pause.

'Scobie. . . .'

'Oh, okay, well, the man calling himself Towne is not employed by the federal police. His name is Ian Galt, and he was state police, recently acquitted on corruption charges but sacked anyway.'

'Do they know why he's poking around down here?'

'Pam had to go out; I didn't get the full gist of it.'

'Where did she go?'

'Note on her desk,' Sutton said. He walked around Challis to fetch it. 'Says she's doing a follow up with those Niekirk people.'

Challis didn't know what that meant, and he was mildly annoyed. There were more pressing cases she could be working on. 'If she comes back or calls in, tell her I need to see her.'

'Sir. Oh, and some woman called you.'

'Who?' said Challis.

Then his office phone rang, and he turned away from Sutton to take the call. 'Challis.'

A young, uninflected voice said, 'The blankets over the head, that was my idea.'

Challis missed a beat, the slightest beat, then nudged the door shut. 'I thought it might have been.'

'Don't try to trace this. It will only waste time and resources and get you nowhere anyway.'

'Okay.'

'I need your email address.'

'And what *I* need is to know the current location of the guy with the shotgun.'

'I let him go.'

Challis laughed. 'You let him go.'

'He thought he was in control. He wasn't. I got him out of the bank and told him to run. I don't know where he is. But he's not clever, just lucky.'

'You staged the scene by the drain, the abandoned car?'

'Did it mess with your head? Your email address, please.'

Challis complied, nudging the mouse to awaken his computer. He logged on to his email and said, 'What are you sending me?'

'Photos, if you can be patient.'

'What's your real name?'

'Today? Today I'm Nina.'

'Right. Russian?'

It was her turn to hesitate. 'You've been doing some home-work.'

'A little. Care to tell me—'

'Shut up. Sending now.'

Challis waited. Then a number of images arrived in his inbox: the icon and the Klee, photographed *in situ*, and close-ups of several documents. 'It seems you're keen on home interiors,' he said. 'We found a camera card loaded with snaps.'

'I like to keep records,' Nina said.

Challis was about to deliver another wry observation when his attention was caught. He peered at the icon and the painting again. 'I know this house.'

'It was broken into recently.'

'The occupants claimed nothing was taken.'

'Well, they would say that.'

'Would they? Why? How did you know they owned the icon?'

'I didn't know. Chance encounter, and that's the honest truth. The thing is it's not theirs. Mara Niekirk's family took it from my family.'

Challis chewed on that. 'You possess an old photograph that depicts a similar icon and you call that proof?'

'Why don't you do some digging into Mara's family, hotshot? The apple doesn't fall far from the tree, as you'll discover when you examine the other stuff I sent you.'

Challis shrugged, clicking on the documents one by one, adjusting the zoom until the text filled the screen. 'Invoices, receipts, catalogue entries. . . . So what?'

'First, I think you'll find they're not kosher. The Niekirks have been faking histories for years.'

Challis couldn't see much point in playing the policeman in this situation but went through the motions anyhow. 'I need you to go on record as saying that you found, photographed, and—'

'You need me to get killed, you mean.'

'What?'

'I've just sent you a copy of an email sent to me by a man named Steve Finch. He was trying to get the Klee painting back on the Niekirks' behalf.'

Challis went cold. 'Someone shot him last night.'

'Exactly.'

Challis got to his feet, thinking of Pam Murphy. Going around the desk, he opened his door and signalled wildly to Scobie Sutton, miming hands on a steering wheel, meanwhile saying, 'By the way, a man named Galt is looking for you.'

'Was,' the woman named Nina said.

Chapter 60

Pam Murphy climbed into her car, musing on the statement made by the nanny.

Why, if the Niekirks knew they'd been robbed, had they persisted in claiming it was a failed break-in?

'I'm invisible to them,' Tayla said. 'They don't know I'm there.'

Meaning she'd overheard them talk about a missing icon and a missing painting.

And now they were *burning* paintings?

Seeking answers, Murphy drove to the house on Goddard Road.

And when she reached the entrance, she braked. The words IF YOU THINK THIS IS TASTEFUL had been spray painted on one gate support. TAKE A GANDER AT OUR HOUSE ON THE OTHER. She laughed, released the brake, let her Subaru roll through the gap.

And braked again. She was nose to nose with the flat white face of a Mercedes van, Warren Niekirk at the wheel. They stared at each other for a few long seconds, and Murphy saw, even through both sets of glass, a flicker of panic, a search for a way out.

She decided not to reverse but slid the gear lever into park and switched off. She wanted answers. She had no intention of coming back later, at the Niekirks' convenience.

As she stepped away from her Subaru, she saw a BMW sedan rock to a halt behind the van, heard a door slam, and then Mara Niekirk was advancing on her, furious, erect, nose tilted like a woman born to rule, the driveway gravel complaining under her feet.

They're *both* going somewhere? Separately? 'Hello, Mrs. Niekirk.'

'Are you going to leave your car there like that? We have a business to run.'

At 5 P.M., when most people are heading *for* home, not away? 'A couple of quick questions.'

'Did you see what they did to my gate?'

They, the great unwashed, the faceless, the nameless. *My* gate, not *our* gate. 'Shall I report it for you, Mrs. Niekirk?'

'What's the point? You people. . . .'

My people what?

And here was Warren, leaving the van and joining his wife, getting some courage and stature from that simple act. 'Is there a problem?'

'No problem,' Pam said. 'As I told your wife, I—'

With his newfound determination, Warren cut her off. 'Have you found the woman who broke into our house?'

Woman? thought Pam. How did they know it was a woman? On her guard now, wondering what was in the van, she said, 'Sometimes when people are burgled, they discover they're missing certain items days afterward. Weeks.'

'Nothing was taken,' Mara said.

She was angular, powerful, her mouth a slash across the tight flesh of her face, her body a vibrating spring inside tapered black pants and a grey cotton top. Hair scraped back from her forehead, no makeup. One scary woman, Pam thought.

To see what would happen, she said, 'Perhaps I could talk to the nanny. Is she up at the house with your daughter? Maybe she's missing something, an iPod or a camera.'

'Nothing was taken,' snarled Mara. 'Now, get out of the way, please.'

Behind Pam a ute rattled by, a yapping dog on the back. She hoped it might turn into the farm opposite the Niekirk's, hoped there would be a witness when everything went wrong, but it merely slowed for the corrugations in the road and faded away into the distance. The shadows lengthened around her.

'I understand you had a Russian icon hanging in the glassed-in walkway.'

Warren turned a wondering look upon his wife and almost slapped his forehead in a pantomime of forgetfulness. 'You know, she's right? Mara, we did, remember that little thing?'

He turned to Pam, shone his salesman's beam on her. 'You know how it is, you put a trinket on a wall or a shelf and forget you had it?'

'Trinket,' Murphy said flatly.

'Look,' Warren said, 'it's just a piece of tourist junk, a keep-sake. We won't be lodging a claim or anything.'

He flashed her a good-guy smile, probably in exactly the way he closed all his deals.

But Mara wasn't in the business of making a sale. Her eyes narrowed at Pam. 'Tayla told you.'

'Tayla?'

Venom now. 'The ungrateful little slut came running to you after all we've done for her. Where is she, by the way?'

'Shouldn't you be wondering where your daughter is?'

Mara's dark eyes shifted, and Pam felt a kind of dread. She backed away, feeling for the Subaru with her left hand, intending to put the driver's door between herself and the witch. Swing behind the wheel, slam and lock the door, call for backup.

She was hit by a brain zap. It was like all of the others, the world yawing, her gaze briefly unfocussed, her body frozen, her jaw rictal. And when she recovered, Mara Niekirk had the hard barrel of a little handgun in her ribs.

'They sent you out here alone?'

'If I'm not back by—'

'If you're not back,' Mara scoffed. She turned to Warren. 'Get some rope.'

'What?'

'You heard me,' Mara said, prodding Murphy toward the rear of the van. 'Tie her arms and legs.'

'But she's a policeman. Woman.'

Mara slapped her husband's face. 'Rope.'

Warren blinked and hurried away.

'Are you running out?' Pam asked, curious.

Ignoring her, Mara continued to prod with the little gun until they were invisible from the road. Warren had opened the van's rear door. Stacked canvases, some hideous rugs and a couple of antique chairs and chests. 'Tie her up, throw her in.'

'Mara.'

'Do it.'

'Okay, okay.'

Mara's husband relieved Pam of her handcuffs and manacled her wrists, then used too much rope and tape on her arms and legs. He said, apologetically, 'We'll put you where they'll find you quickly.'

By his voice and manner, he didn't believe a word of it. Nor did Murphy.

Chapter 61

Early evening now, the sunlight no longer striping the Peninsula but retreating from the horizon, a yellow fireball at the end of the tunnel of dying gumtrees along Goddard Road. Challis was forced to squint as he drove, the visor down, a headache threatening, and he almost missed the Niekirks' driveway.

'There!' Sutton shouted, his finger stabbing the side window of the car.

Challis made the turn, intent only on speeding to the house, but Sutton pointed at the defaced gateposts and groaned, 'Not another one.'

Challis didn't care about the gateposts; he hadn't cared about any of them. He swung the CIU car along the blind driveway to the ugly house at the end.

It looked shut up.

'Think they've done a runner, sir?'

Challis stared at him. 'We're not here to speculate. How about you check the grounds.'

'Sorry, boss,' Sutton said, and disappeared.

Challis turned to the garage. Two of the three bays were empty, and it was a kind of permanent emptiness, unrelieved by the presence of a boat and trailer in the third bay. He'd checked with the Department of Motor Vehicles before leaving the station: The Niekirks owned a Mercedes van and a BMW four-wheel drive.

He swept his gaze at the gravel and where the gravel merged with the lawns and garden beds, but who knew what kind of tracks Pam's Subaru might stamp there? He sniffed the air: smoke.

He walked to the glossy front door and rapped it with his knuckles. Was astonished when it opened on the nanny and the child and wasn't sure where to start. 'Is Constable Murphy here?'

'No.'

'Has she been?'

The nanny screwed up her face in thought. 'Don't know. Maybe.'

'She didn't give you a lift after you'd been to see her?'

'No.'

'Have you been here long?'

'About a year. I—'

'When did you get back after visiting Constable Murphy?'

'A couple of minutes ago.'

'Do you own a car? I didn't see one outside.'

'We took a taxi,' Tayla said. 'Mr. and Mrs. Niekirk have an account,' she added proudly.

Behind her the house resounded hollowly. Challis could see a hall stand and a rug inside a distant doorway, but there were gaps where other items had been and any vestiges of love and comfort had been stripped away.

'Was anyone home when you got here?'

Tayla shook her head.

Challis contemplated the Niekirks' daughter. Natalia stood like a lost child on the echoing floorboards, an almost sentimental pose; she looked like a painting in a community art show.

'When did you last see Mr. or Mrs. Niekirk?'

'Earlier this afternoon.'

'Before you visited the police station?'

'Yes.'

'Did they know you were going to Waterloo?'

'No.'

'They didn't see you leave?'

'They had something to do at the shop, so I waited till they'd left.'

'What exactly did you tell Constable Murphy?'

Tayla's face twisted in concentration. 'I told her this, like, little religious painting was stolen.'

'An icon.'

'Whatever. She seemed interested.'

'Did she say she was coming here?'

'I had to take Tasha to the toilet.'

It was going to be one of those conversations. 'Do you know where Mr. and Mrs. Niekirk are?'

'I think they came home and went out again. Both the cars are gone.'

Tayla glanced uneasily at Natalia, who seemed to take fright at Challis and sprinted back into the emptiness of the other rooms. The nanny, torn, said, 'I don't know what's going on,' and stumbled after her charge.

Challis followed and found them in the vast sitting room, where the massive items of furniture remained and the walls were flat and empty. 'I'm worried about Constable Murphy.'

The statement was difficult for Tayla to get her head around. 'I don't know what I'm supposed to do.'

'Did something happen this afternoon, Tayla?'

In a rush, the nanny said, 'They were like burning all this nice stuff, paintings and that, plus Mrs. Niekirk was really mean to me.' She blushed. 'Plus I think she's a peeping tom.'

So you got your own back, Challis thought. He reflected that it was a variation on the tail light phenomenon. Every year a

criminal genius would pull some undetectable murder or robbery, only to be stopped for a vehicle check or failure to wear
a seatbelt, whereupon the cops would find the concealed body
in the boot. Mara Niekirk had been dealing in stolen art with
impunity for years, only to be let down by her own cruel mouth.

Scobie Sutton came in from one of the rear or side doors, calling, 'Hello!'

'In here.'

He appeared in the doorway, and Challis asked, 'Find the car?'

'What car?'

Challis said heavily, 'Pam's Subaru.' If Scobie Sutton did
become a crime scene investigator, he'd tear the arse out of iden-
tifying, cataloguing, and collecting what was there, and never
give a second's thought to what wasn't.

'No car, boss. Signs of a bonfire.'

Challis nodded. Three vehicles unaccounted for. Three drivers—unless one of them had come back for the third vehicle?

He said, 'The Niekirks have an antique shop in Tyabb and a
shed at the airstrip. Call for backup and have a poke around.'

'You're staying here?'

'Yes. And I want you to put out a general alert for Pam's car
and the Niekirks' van and car.'

'I don't like it, boss. What if they come back, you know—' he
shielded his mouth with his hand '—for their daughter?'

'I'll deal with that if and when it happens.'

Scobie Sutton left in the CIU car, and Challis glanced at his
watch. Six o'clock. The roads of the Peninsula would be choked
with wage earners, heading straight into the westering sun, some
at speed, some running into trees or the car in front of them. A
busy time for the uniforms, and no money in the budget to back
up a CIU inspector who'd found himself alone with no one to
watch his back. But he called anyway, the duty sergeant confirming his fears. 'Can't send you anyone for the next hour, Hal, sorry.'

So he'd wait. He pocketed his phone, smiled at the nanny. 'I'll be back in a moment.'

She nodded incuriously, and he wandered down to the cypress hedge lining Goddard Road. He found the Subaru wedged in a dark, overgrown corner. He wandered back to the house.

The nanny and the child hadn't moved. 'Let's go to the kitchen.'

A marginally nicer place to be, stools around an island bench, a huge window looking out onto the sloping lawns, coppery pots on wormy black hooks above the sinks and stovetops. And food, if the child got restive. Fruit in a bowl, ice cream in the freezer.

'You told Constable Murphy that an icon was stolen when the house was broken into.'

'Yes.'

'Anything else?'

'I heard them arguing about a painting.'

'Did a man named Steve Finch ever come to the house?'

Tayla frowned prettily. 'Sometimes they spoke to a Steve on the phone. Who is he?'

Challis ignored the question and searched for the right way to ask his next. In the end, he simply put words in the nanny's mouth. 'Did your employers ever have business dealings, or visitors, or phone calls or mail or courier deliveries that struck you as odd? Valuable items in the house one day, gone the next? Conversations that you walked in on? Paperwork you might have seen on a desk or a table?'

'I'm here to look after Natalia, that's all.'

'Guns,' said Challis gently. 'Rifles. Is there a gun cabinet anywhere?'

Tayla gaped at him, badly frightened. 'Guns?'

Challis probed and tweaked as the minutes passed and got nowhere. His phone rang. Sutton.

'I'm out at the airfield, boss.'

Challis waited, and Sutton waited.

'I'm not getting any younger, Scobie.'

'The shop was empty, and so's the shed on the airfield here.'

'The van? The BMW?'

'No sign.'

'Did you question anyone? Mechanics, pilots?'

'Everyone's gone home, boss.'

'Okay, come back here, eyes peeled.'

'Boss.'

Suddenly Natalia was standing beside Challis's knee. Her bewilderment had fled, and she seemed to want comfort. Without thinking he hoisted her onto his lap, thinking how heavy she was, for someone so slight and small-boned. Then she began to talk and didn't stop.

Tayla deciphered. 'She's talking about her favourite movie.'

Challis heard an engine revving outside, and to his ears it wasn't Sutton in the CIU car. 'Stand back from the window,' he said, lifting Natalia to the floor. 'Better still, take Natalia somewhere safe. Is there a room. . . ?'

Tayla didn't answer. She whimpered and gathered Natalia and clattered away with her. Challis walked through to the front room and peered around a window edge. A Mercedes van stood at a slewed angle in the driveway, driver's door open, and then a horn protested, loud and prolonged. A head jerked up from the steering wheel and the horn stopped.

Warren Niekirk stepped out. He was bleeding, one shoulder useless and blood dripping from his fingers. Challis watched as he went to the rear doors of the van. Time passed, and he reappeared, unsteady on his feet, lurching toward the house, falling to his knees as he tried to step over a garden rock.

Then he was in the house, stumbling down the hallway to the kitchen, while out on the driveway the van stood empty.

Challis followed in time to see Niekirk cross the kitchen floor like a drunk man and reach his good hand to the block of knives while the bloodied hand dripped.

'I don't think you want to do that,' Challis said, clamping his fingers around a trembling forearm.

Niekirk rocked where he stood, blinked. 'I can't untie her.'

'Who can't you untie?'

'The policewoman.'

Challis removed the knife from Niekirk's fingers. 'Constable Murphy?'

'She's in the van,' replied Niekirk.

'Alive?'

'I told Mara I couldn't do it. She just turned around and shot me.'

'Did she also shoot Constable Murphy?'

'Almost. I said, "Mara, you can't shoot a cop," and she shot me and drove away.'

Then Niekirk fainted, a dead weight dropping to the floor. Challis turned him onto his side, called triple zero, and went out to the van. He supposed he did everything swiftly, but it was like trudging over heavy sand.

He paused at the door to the van. Looked inside. 'Murph,' he said, with a kind of giddy relief, 'unless you're tied up at the moment, maybe you could help me search the house?'

'With respect, sir, get stuffed.'

Chapter 62

On his last day, Detective Inspector Hal Challis set about clearing his heaped in tray of files, memos, and correspondence. Start at the bottom and work your way to the top, one of his old sergeants had told him. His mobile was switched off. He hoped his desk phone wouldn't ring.

He stared mulishly at the paperwork. It seemed to him that police duties at inspector level consisted more of admin than catching thieves and murderers. But clearing the decks like this would be a distraction from glancing at his watch all the time. His flight left at midnight. He'd work through the day, endure the little wake—celebration?—his colleagues would throw for him, be at the airport by ten o'clock. He flipped over the tray of correspondence and started on the top sheet of the upside-down pile. A memo regarding the car park at the rear of the station: Police members were reminded that space was at a premium and the parking bays narrow, so please position your vehicle carefully between the painted lines, thus avoiding damage to other vehicles. Why the fuck had he kept it? But he did swivel around in his chair and look through the window at the car park and his new car, a 2003 BMW 318i with only 47,000 km on the clock. It had cost $18,999 and had cruise control. Not all BMWs of that era did, apparently.

Ellen, after he'd told her: 'I'll say it again: Do I want to be with a man who drives a BMW?'

'Heated seats.'

'Well, in that case.'

It was parked snugly between Pam Murphy's Subaru and someone's Kia.

He binned the memo.

Next were email printouts, outdated, their subjects resolved, so in the bin they went. Crime scene reports, which he filed with the relevant case notes, witness statements, officer-attending reports, other bumf.

An old memo from Superintendent McQuarrie regarding the spraycan vigilante. The tone was peevish, indicating that pressure had been applied by the kinds of people he golfed with. The kinds of people who put up huge, defaceable gateposts outside their Peninsula pads, in fact. Challis emailed a reply:

Re: offensive graffiti

Dear Supt McQuarrie,

I am pleased to report that a man has been arrested in connection with this crime.

Yours sincerely,

H. Challis (Inspector)

ONE MAN, BUT CHALLIS suspected that three or four men and women were involved. John Tankard had made the arrest, a young architecture student found loitering outside a Main Ridge property in possession of a spraycan—but not in the act of defacing its gateposts, and he had airtight alibis for the previous incidents. So, a gang was at work, and the guy would skate, probably. Challis pictured them: young, mobile, educated, and angry. Good luck to them.

He raced through the paperwork, binning most of it. A letter approving Detective Constable Scobie Sutton's transfer to a new crime scene unit based in Frankston. Scobie had been told of the appointment but hadn't seen the official notification, so Challis made a copy and placed it in an envelope on his desk.

He was nearing the more recent correspondence now and found a letter unrelated to his police work. Postmarked Darwin, it was from the Pioneer Aircraft Museum.

'I am writing to advise you,' it began:

> that our archivist has examined various government and commercial archives and concurs with your belief that your Dragon Rapide did in fact play a significant role in outback mail delivery, geological survey work, and minerals exploration in the 1930s.
>
> For that reason, we are delighted to accept your kind donation of the aeroplane for our permanent collection. As you know, we are a not-for-profit institution, reliant on the goodwill of the public, and rarely in a position to make outright purchases, but I am pleased to inform you that your donation has been approved under the Commonwealth Government's Cultural Gifts Program, entitling you to claim a tax deduction. It is common to apportion twenty percent of the total allowed per year for five financial years.

THEY'D ALREADY SENT AN expert to examine the Dragon, run the motors, take it for a short flight. And now it was in pieces again, on the back of a truck somewhere, inching up the red centre of the continent.

Then newspaper clippings from the *Age*: the arrest of Mara Niekirk attempting to flee Sydney Harbour in a yacht, and the shotgun death of a disgraced ex-NSW policeman in the sleepy coastal town of Breamlea. According to witnesses, the shooter, a local man unknown to the dead man, had acted in self-defence. Meanwhile police were looking for a young woman who had fled the scene.

Good luck with that, thought Challis.

Next was a print-out of the Human Resources email ordering him to take long-service leave. It didn't say 'Don't hurry back,' but Challis was reading it that way.

Finally, two reports that had been niggling at him since landing in his pigeonhole on Monday. They were the DNA results from the coffee cup and the blood found on the ground beside the abandoned Commodore. There was no way of knowing who'd been drinking the coffee. Certainly not the shotgun bandit. Challis was betting that the woman now calling herself Nina had swiped a stranger's half-finished coffee from a takeaway joint after escaping from the VineTrust bank.

The blood DNA, that was quite different. Challis didn't know how Nina had shed the blood drops, but he was betting it was deliberate, perhaps a razor nick to a finger pad, and intended to confuse the police. What she didn't know—or did she?—was that the blood contained sufficient DNA markers to suggest a familial connection to the victims of a vicious unsolved triple homicide dating back to 1990. The victims were Piotr Saranin, his wife Grace, and their nineteen-year-old daughter, Nina. Saranin, the son of White Russian parents, was born in Shanghai, China, in 1948 and had come to Australia as a toddler in 1950. His parents died in a car accident when he was seventeen, by which time he was an apprentice electrician and engaged to Grace Owens, born in Sydney, 1951. They married in February 1970; Nina was born in December 1970.

All three were shot dead in a house in Sydney's west in May 1990, shot in the back of the head, execution style, with a 9 mm pistol. Given that neither Saranin nor his wife and daughter had a criminal record or known criminal associates, police were baffled. Saranin belonged to a social club for White Russian émigrés, but efforts to find leads in that direction had failed.

The thing was that a three-year-old girl had been found in a back room of the house. When it was discovered that her father was unknown, and no close or extended family existed for Owens or Saranin, she was placed into foster care.

That three-year-old grew up, Challis thought. She bounced around in the system; she learned and honed certain skills; and one day a crooked policeman found her.

And through it all she kept a keepsake, an old photograph.

But who had murdered her mother and grandparents? Challis was betting it had something to do with the icon. He knew a lot about the Krasnov family now. Mara's arrest had generated a great deal of publicity; people had come forward with information and accusations. A nasty piece of work, the old patriarch from a brutal dynasty. And the granddaughter had learnt her ways at his knee. The likely scenario, he thought, was that the Saranins had lost the icon to the Krasnovs back in Harbin, a grievance that lingered and festered and was passed down through the generations. Then one day maybe Piotr Saranin heard something, saw something, picked up a rumour around Sydney's White Russian émigré community. He'd approached the Krasnovs, and it got him killed.

Challis heard Pam Murphy in his doorway. 'Just scribble your signature on everything, boss. It could be my promotion, a salary upgrade, approval to study policing on the Riviera. . . .'

Challis rocked back in his chair, gave it a squeaky swivel. 'Or an invitation to address the kindergarten kids at St Joseph's. . . .'

'Bring it on,' Murphy said, looking clear-eyed and ready for a challenge. Rubbing her wrists unconsciously, where Warren Niekirk had ratcheted the handcuffs tight.

'How did it go?'

He'd sent her west of Melbourne to bring back a prisoner. The shotgun bandit hadn't left the state but gone to ground in the goldfields country, where he'd held up a lottery agency in sub-urban Ballarat and been stopped for failing to wear a seatbelt. Nina had been telling the truth. She hadn't left him lying dead in a drain-age channel. Just another one of her smokescreens.

Murphy snorted. 'He asked me where the siege chick was. He wanted to thank her, maybe she could get him out.'

When the phone rang, Challis stared at it. If he answered, would it jinx his flight plans? Challis on Skype that evening: 'Sorry, Ellen, something came up.'

It was the front desk. 'Inspector, someone from the DPP is here. He needs all the evidence for the Niekirk committal hear-ing on Monday.'

'It's in the safe.'

'We looked. It's incomplete.'

At once Challis felt a prickling along his arms and over his scalp. He stood, feeling electric and alert. 'I'll be right down.'

He rounded his desk and jerked his head at Pam Murphy. 'Come with me.'

They clattered down the stairs. The evidence safe was no more than a large locked cupboard inside a storeroom located along a side corridor between interview rooms. A cupboard, but securely locked. You'd need to know the key code. It was used to store evi-dence from ongoing cases: dusty packets of cocaine and heroin, pill presses, bundles of cash, knives, pistols, shotguns, knuckle-dusters, the occasional samurai sword—and the loot from Nina's safe-deposit box.

And that loot was incomplete. The Sydney Long was there, the coins and stamps, but not the Klee, not the photograph.

Challis stared at Pam Murphy, and she at him, and somehow the knowledge passed from one to the other. It would have hap-pened in the deepest hours of the night, a young woman arriv-ing at the front desk, looking like a lawyer, waving a convincing subpoena. Convincing manner, too. Whoever she was.